THE RUSSIAN

A LANCE SPECTOR THRILLER
BOOK 2

SAUL HERZOG

AUTHORCONTACT

1

On a frigid morning in 1965, the sun shone weakly over the Soviet city of Volgograd. A thin fog hung on the frozen river, making a drab, gray city drabber and grayer.

In every direction, the buildings spread in a monotonous grid few places in the world could rival. The Soviet State was addicted to concrete, and nowhere was it on show more than here. The streets were treeless, devoid of vegetation of any kind. On the far bank of the river, many buildings had yet to be repaired, and their windowless walls stretched toward the sky like shipwrecked hulls.

Twenty years of reconstruction hadn't been enough to erase the scars of the most destructive battle in human history. This was the place where Hitler and Stalin had crashed up against each other. It was the place fascism wrote its epitaph, a raging lament etched on the graves of countless dead.

Stalin knew how to hold a city. He forbade all mention of evacuation, of retreat, of surrender. Even the city's women, its children and elderly, were ordered to stand and fight. If they fled, if they even spoke of escape, they were summarily shot. Children as young as four were executed for cowardice.

Precious few survived the siege. The bombings. The snipers. The hunger. The cold.

At the battle's outset, four hundred thousand people were squeezed along a stretch of the Volga's west bank three miles wide. Six months later, fewer than one in ten still lived. In their place were two million corpses and the smoldering hulks of six thousand tanks, three thousand aircraft, and fifteen thousand broken artillery pieces.

And rubble. Endless rubble.

It was still being cleared, corpses still being found. The passage of twenty years could not erase so much death.

In 1965, it was four years since Nikita Khrushchev had renamed the city. Volgograd, city on the Volga. Before that— Stalingrad.

It had once been a Tatar fortress, then a tsarist garrison, and later still, a Cossack cavalry base. A stone church to Saint John the Baptist was erected in 1608. Slaves were captured there by Kuban raiders in the eighteenth century, and again by the Nazis in the twentieth.

By 1965, the slaves were gone. The priests were gone. The Cossacks and Tatars and Kubans were gone. And a new caste had quietly taken their place.

The orphans. Parentless, abandoned, disabled, unwanted. They were a scourge. A plague. There were thousands of them, and each passing year only brought more.

The government knew where they came from. All those munitions, toxins, chemicals. Bulldozing couldn't fix that. Couldn't fix the water.

And the people had been savaged—first by the White Army, then the Red, then Hitler. They had seen how easy it was to silence the laws of God. To rewrite the laws of man. To forget the stories of their ancestors. They learned how gentleness could be erased. How motherhood could be forgotten.

A team of three nurses in white polyester dresses and the distinctive red neckerchiefs of the Communist Young Pioneers stood on the steps of a squat concrete building. They smoked cigarettes and rubbed their arms for warmth. Beside them was a wooden wheelbarrow.

From a distance, they looked like a welcoming committee, ready to care for the new arrivals. The curves beneath their uniforms were feminine, youthful. The oldest of them was eighteen, the youngest, fifteen.

But a closer look revealed worrying signs.

They didn't smile. They didn't speak. They sucked their cigarettes absently, their eyes flat and still, staring into the distance as if watching an approaching storm. Their uniforms were stained, the insides of the collars brown with sweat. Their fingernails were dirty.

These girls were a breed apart. They were people who'd been, from the earliest moments of their lives, treated with cruelty. They'd been whipped for bed-wetting. They'd been beaten unconscious for stealing food. They'd been abused in all the ways a girl in the custody of the state might be abused.

All knew what it was like to wake up in a hospital bed and not know how she got there. A broken limb. Blood between the legs. A concussion so severe she would suffer migraines for the rest of her life.

They'd been powerless, they'd suffered, and now that they were the ones in uniforms, they were going to inflict that same suffering.

On the wheelbarrow was a small stack of neatly folded burlap sacks about the size of pillowcases. The sacks bore the stenciled logo of the state coffee importer and the words, 'Five Kilos Net Weight'.

In front of them, stretching away from the building toward the feeble sun, was a new concrete street, straight as a politburo draftsman's ruler. It had smooth, wide sidewalks and metal posts that would soon hold electric streetlights. To the right was a new children's hospital, and to the left, inauspiciously, a crematorium. The neighborhood was new, laid out in advance with intersections that led nowhere and traffic lights yet to be wired up.

The girls watched the approach of a vehicle, a new transport van, freshly delivered from the Ulyanovsk Automobile Plant. It emerged from the gate of the children's hospital, turned left, and entered the grounds of their own building. It was a journey of a hundred yards. And every one of the girls knew that a hundred yards could well make the difference between heaven—or at least a life with some semblance of normalcy—and utter hell.

The van was more gray than blue, and the driver wore his hat so low it hid his eyes.

He pulled up in front of the nurses and cranked the handbrake. The van rose on its suspension when he stepped out. Without acknowledging them, he went to the back and opened the door. A sound like the mewling of kittens filled the air. He stepped aside, and as the girls began their work, he turned his back on them and lit a cigarette.

He couldn't watch.

The girls moved efficiently, stubbing out their cigarettes and wheeling the cart into position. They unfolded the burlap sacks and peered into the van. Its seats had been removed and replaced with wooden crates, lined with layers of cotton swaddling from the hospital. In the crates, wrapped in more swaddling, were newborn babies. A batch of seven.

The van was very warm. The heater was on full blast, and the controls had been removed. The driver couldn't turn it down. He couldn't open the windows. It had been learned the hard way how susceptible these newborns were to winter air.

A hundred yards away, in the hospital's Department of Defectology, these babies had been officially classified by the Soviet State as unsalvageable. One had a cleft lip. One was anemic. One was cross-eyed. Three had fetal alcohol syndrome.

"Look at this one," a girl said, pulling one of the crates across the floor and picking up a boy by the ankles.

The other girls burst out laughing.

He was enormous, fully twice the size of the others. On his head was a thin tuft of white hair. His eyes were the palest blue, almost white, and growing from his gums were sharp white little protrusions.

"Is he a child or an animal?" the girl shrieked.

"He's an albino," an older girl said.

He wriggled and belted his feeble cries into the cold air.

"Put him down before he bites you."

"He can't be a newborn."

The older girl checked the tag on his ankle. "Born in the night. The mother died."

"I'm not surprised," the girl said, holding him up like a carp pulled from a lake.

"He has teeth," the older girl said. Then added, "Disgusting."

They put him in one of the burlap sacks, pulling the drawstrings around his neck so that his four limbs were enclosed and only his head stuck out.

Packing them like this was less work than changing diapers, and the babies might be kept that way for days, even weeks, at a time. The girls called them shit bags.

They loaded all seven into the cart and wheeled them into the building.

If the orphanage records were accurate, only one would live long enough to be discharged. He would be eight years old by then, already the size of a grown man, with fists like hams and eyes so pale they appeared blood-red in the sun.

When the girls were gone, the driver stubbed out his cigarette and turned back to the van. The springs creaked as he got into his seat. He tried to open the window before remembering it was locked, then looked around to make sure no one was watching.

When he was satisfied he was alone, he looked to the sky and crossed himself.

2

P*resent Day*
  Genadi Surkov woke with a start. The beeper next to his bed was going off like an alarm clock, its red light blinking urgently. He picked it up and pressed the plastic button on its side, illuminating the small digital screen.

He rubbed his eyes.

It was a code seven. One target. Three asterisks, indicating a level-three threat. The most dangerous.

He got up and flipped open his laptop. The target's name was Tatyana Aleksandrova. A Russian female with GRU training. He lingered on the picture. She was very attractive. Just his type, with dark hair and eyes that smoldered like coals in a fire.

It was a shame they wanted her dead.

There was an address to a small hotel in Kapotnya, an industrial district southeast of the city. It was poor and contained one of the largest oil processing plants in the country. Genadi knew it well. He knew it was not a bad place for picking up women.

Targets inside Moscow weren't unheard of. There was a time when they'd been common. Those had been easy years for men like Genadi. The president had still been consolidating power and paid good money to get rid of any number of fat, unsuspecting politicians. Genadi would show up for a job, and maybe there would be a lone private security guard, sometimes just a dog.

This was different. A poor neighborhood. A cheap hotel. GRU training. This had 'defection' written all over it. And that meant danger. The target was on the run. She'd be on edge. On the lookout.

Genadi looked at his watch. It was just after two. He took a cold shower and dressed in a pair of black civilian pants and a crew neck. He tied a cloth handkerchief around his neck that could be used as a mask if necessary.

He lived in Kubinka, twenty miles west of the city, in the Special Purpose Center, a secret military facility for Spetsnaz elite units. It was surrounded by a high concrete wall topped with barbed wire. He used to live in the barracks, but since being made a special operative, he had his own apartment in the officers' block. It was on the top floor, which had seemed like a perk until he learned the elevator didn't work.

He put on his boots, a pair of black leather gloves, and a leather jacket, and grabbed his wallet and cell phone before leaving the apartment. His car was parked outside, an old BMW M3 coupé, and he fired up the engine and put the heat on full to melt the ice on the windshield. Then he got back out of the car and walked across the lot to the armory.

Inside, he had access to a vast array of weapons, everything generally available to Spetsnaz GRU units, as well as a few custom items that had been developed for one-off missions. He showed his credentials and picked up a large canvas bag from the supply desk.

The first thing he grabbed was a PSS silent pistol, a Soviet-era gun with a sealed cartridge system that had been specifically designed for KGB assassinations. It was an ugly little gun with a six-round detachable box and an effective firing range of just eighty feet. He had the newer model, which used the custom SP-16 cartridge that at least packed somewhat of a punch. When the gun fired, the piston sealed the cartridge neck, preventing noise and smoke from escaping the barrel. He wasn't fond of it, but put two in the bag, along with ammo.

As a backup, he took the far more reliable Glock 17. He also grabbed a Vityaz-SN, the standard-issue submachine gun for all branches of the Russian military. It was a lot louder than the PSS but wouldn't be traceable back to the GRU.

He looked at a GM-94 pump-action grenade launcher but decided against it. The target was level three, which meant he was cleared to use any weaponry he deemed necessary, but a grenade launcher in the city would attract too much attention. If his bosses wanted to put on a show, they'd have called in the regular troops, not an assassin.

He did grab an AK-105 carbine, as well as a Ratnik ballistic vest. The heavy metal plates had already been removed, which was against protocol, but it made the armor about ten pounds lighter.

As he pulled his car out of the compound, he tuned the radio to an AM sports station and let his mind wander. He lit a cigarette as he got on the highway. Twenty minutes later, he was taking the Kapotnya exit.

Even at night, the place was ugly, with the enormous cooling towers of the Tets-22 power plant rising above the interchange. As he entered the district, an oil pipeline crossed overhead before running alongside the road.

By the time he reached the hotel, it was almost three. He pulled up outside and saw that a strip club on the ground floor was still open. It was later than local bylaws permitted, but it didn't look like the kind of place that cared.

He had the two fully loaded silenced pistols in holsters beneath his jacket, and he slid the Glock into the waistband of his pants. The larger guns remained in the canvas bag on the backseat of the car.

He walked up to the club. "Still open?" he said to the bouncer.

"Not really," the bouncer said.

"I just need a drink."

The bouncer shrugged, and Genadi walked past him. Inside, the place was deserted. No dancers, no customers, no bartender.

He walked through the club, through some doors, to the hotel lobby. A half-asleep man sat slumped in a chair at the reception. Genadi walked past him to the stairs.

He went to the second floor, turned on the corridor lights, found the room he was looking for, and listened. There were twelve rooms on the floor, and not a sound was coming from any of them. It looked like a straightforward job.

He drew one of the silenced pistols and stepped closer to the door. Listened again. Nothing.

He looked at the door and made sure it would open on the first attempt.

Then he raised his leg and brought it down hard. The wood of the latch split, and the door flew open.

He stepped into the room. The light from the corridor was just enough for him to make out the bed. He extended the pistol and fired six shots. Even in the dim light, he saw the dark stain of blood seep through the covers.

3

Lance Spector sat in the corner of the bar by the window and watched the snow. It came down the street, gusting off the river in flurries, whipping around vehicles as they made their way slowly in the evening traffic. The few pedestrians, buffeted by the wind, held tightly to their coats.

"What can I get you tonight?" the bartender said in Russian.

Lance looked at her. She was a solid woman, accustomed to labor. He pegged her at about fifty. "Same as last night," he said.

"You don't want something a little stronger?"

He shook his head.

She nodded and left. When she came back, she had a pot of coffee and a white mug. She left the pot on the table and went back to the bar.

She and Lance were the only two people in there. He'd been coming every night, and every night was the same. He sat by the window sipping coffee. She sat on a stool at the bar and watched soap operas on a small TV with the sound off and subtitles on. The place was quiet, which suited him, and the woman didn't bother him.

"You can turn on the sound," he said.

"What's that?"

"The sound. You can turn it up."

"The boss doesn't like that."

"He's not here," Lance said.

She lit a cigarette. Lance did the same. The microwave dinged, and she brought over a bowl of borscht.

"Thank you," he said.

Her skin was pale, freckled, and her hair was somewhere between brown and red. "You sure you don't want some vodka?" she said when she put down the bowl. "It's freezing outside."

"Do you have any bread?"

She left and brought back two thick slices of rye and a full bottle of vodka. "You come every night," she said to him.

He nodded, stubbing out his cigarette.

She picked up his pack and helped herself. He offered her a light.

"You're American," she said.

Lance nodded. There was no use denying it. He dipped some bread in the soup and put it in his mouth. "No sour cream tonight?"

"We ran out."

He nodded.

"We don't get many," she said.

"Many what?"

"Americans."

He looked at her. He'd looked at her a thousand times. He'd been trained to notice things and saw nothing now that he hadn't before. She arrived at the bar at four every afternoon and worked until it closed ten hours later. The work wasn't difficult, but she moved like she was tired. He thought she might have another job during the day. She chain-smoked. She wore knee-length skirts and practical shoes, and in the gap between her socks and skirt, he could see thick, blue veins on her calves. Her accent was a little west of Moscow—Obninsk maybe, home of the world's first nuclear power plant.

They were in the working-class neighborhood of Kapotnya, an industrial sprawl just off Moscow's main ring road with a large oil refinery, power plant, and colossal state factories that had all shut down in the years since the Soviet collapse. The streets were narrow and dingy with old-style streetlamps that cast an orange glow on the cobbled sidewalks.

"I don't think there are many foreigners in this area," he said.

She nodded. "We don't offer what they want."

"And what's that?"

She tapped her cigarette on the side of his ashtray. "You know," she said.

He looked away, glancing out the window. The traffic was light. A bus went by, laboring against the wind, its headlights revealing two fierce blizzards in front of them.

The woman went to the bar and returned with two shot glasses. "My cousin married an American," she said, taking the seat across the table from him. It was the first time she'd said more than a few words to him, the first time she'd joined him, and he didn't mind the company. She poured them each a few ounces of the vodka.

"Nice guy?" Lance said.

She made a face. "He was old."

Lance looked out the window again. His building was across the street, a nineteenth-century tenement with a door that opened onto the sidewalk and a staircase leading to eight units on four floors. His was on the third floor. The back overlooked a brick courtyard with a fire escape.

He'd seen the apartment advertised on a handwritten notice, posted on a bus stop not far from where they were. He'd called the landlord, arranged to meet in person, and paid in cash for three months.

He'd needed a place to lay low for a few weeks. He wanted to let the dust settle before leaving Moscow. It always paid to tie up loose ends. Often after a job, something would crawl out of the woodwork that you didn't want to let fester.

Lance had always been thorough, and even now, when he no longer considered himself an employee of the US government, he couldn't let that old discipline lapse.

But there was another reason he hadn't left the city. Tatyana. She'd refused to leave with him.

She said she had a contact, an informant she couldn't leave behind, at least not without seeing her one last time. Lance understood that. When an agent defected, it was a death sentence for those left behind. Warning them was the right thing. But only if you could do it safely.

"You're risking your life," he'd said.

Tatyana shook her head. "You wouldn't understand."

"Try me."

"I have to warn her. I can't abandon her."

"Her?" Lance said.

Tatyana shook her head. "Just a few days," she said. "Then we'll leave. I promise."

"The entire GRU is after you."

"I know that, but I can't hang this girl out to dry. I won't. She's…"

"She's what?"

"She's… special."

Lance dropped it. He needed the time anyway. His leg was healing, and a few more days would help.

He'd rented the apartment with the idea he and Tatyana would stay together, but she'd refused.

"They're after me," she said. "You'll be safer if I'm not around."

"My leg's fine," Lance said.

"It's not fine."

He eventually agreed to her renting a room at a nearby hotel. She'd been there three nights, and unknown to her, he made a habit of checking on her.

He looked at the bartender across the table. She was leaning forward like she was ready to pounce.

"You don't like older guys?" he said.

She held his eye and knocked back her shot. Her cigarette dangled precariously from her fingers, and she brought it to her mouth like Lauren Bacall trying to seduce Humphrey Bogart. "I prefer younger," she said.

4

Lance left the bar and walked the two blocks to Tatyana's hotel. It was a seedy place with a strip club on the ground floor, the smell of cigarette smoke in the air, and a few middle-aged, down-on-their-luck dancers shaking their tits around.

Tatyana knew Lance's apartment was close by. She'd chosen the hotel for that reason.

Lance was uncomfortable with the risk she was taking. She should have fled the city as soon as she killed Aralov. Moscow was no place for traitors. But she insisted on making contact with this one asset. It kept Lance up at night. He was sure she was accessing the GRU database. In her position, he'd do the same. There were records to delete, sources to protect. You didn't just walk away without cleaning house, without burning your files.

Not if you wanted your closest contacts to go on breathing. And not if you wanted a chance at surviving life on the outside.

You had to lay the groundwork for your escape. You had to keep your network intact. You had to be able to continue the fight. What Tatyana was doing was saving the lives of her network. But she was also putting herself at risk.

Every time she accessed the system, she created an opening that a GRU hacker—if they were lucky, if they were in the right place at the right time—could use to track her right back to her hotel room. No amount of IP masking would protect her if they found an access socket still open.

There was no doubt about it. Whatever she was up to was dangerous enough that she had refused to stay in the apartment with him. If she kept it up, they would find her. And when they found her, they'd send an assassin.

As he walked down the street, he kept an eye on the cars parked by the sidewalk. On his first night out, he'd memorized every license plate on the block. Every night since, he kept note of which cars were new. There were usually a few he didn't recognize, and tonight was no different.

He'd seen enough GRU assassinations to know what to watch for. They would come at night. Usually, they would send a lone gunman, but in Tatyana's case—because of her training —they might send a crew. The operation would be crude. They were inside Russia, which meant there was no risk of a diplomatic incident. There would be no attempt to disguise what had happened.

Tatyana was a traitor, and the Russian government was very clear about what happened to people like her. They wouldn't be subtle. The police and local press would find a body riddled with bullets and a hotel room splattered in blood.

He walked briskly, hurrying his pace.

It was a little after midnight when he reached the hotel. He tipped the night watchman, as he always did, and went up to the second floor. He walked quietly to Tatyana's door and listened.

What he heard was the unmistakable sound of two people

having sex. The headboard thudded rhythmically against the wall, and a man grunted and groaned like a glutton on the first bite. He prayed she hadn't been reckless enough to call someone she'd known in her prior life. That would be suicide. She knew better. But then, people made strange decisions when they were stressed and alone.

He shook his head. She wasn't like that. She was a smooth operator, all business. There was no one in her life, certainly no man. Lance would have known if there was.

This was someone new. Someone she'd only just met. One of the creeps from downstairs. A guy with a beer gut, bad breath, and a wife and kids.

He shook his head and kept walking. He'd already spent more time thinking about it than it warranted. He told himself it was the recklessness that bothered him, but he knew it wasn't just that.

He went back to the bar and lit a cigarette. A topless bartender asked him what he wanted. He ordered a beer. He didn't drink it, just held it in front of him and watched the dancers do their thing. One or two girls came to speak to him, but he wasn't feeling chatty.

No one stuck to the rules all the time. It wasn't possible. There really did come a point when slipping out for a drink, ordering room service, or letting a stranger into your bed was worth the risk. He knew of operatives—highly-trained, ruthless, killing machines—who were dead because they'd given in to the temptation of a pack of cigarettes or, in one case, the crossword section of the *New York Times*. Everyone slipped up eventually. Every person on the run went to a convenience store, or a restaurant, or a movie theater. That was why the GRU, the CIA, and every other spy agency spent so much time teaching their assassins one lesson.

Patience.

Nine times out of ten, it wasn't a question of who moved faster or hit harder. It was a question of who could wait longer.

Tatyana was on the run, still in Moscow while defecting to the American side, risking her life to protect an asset, and she still couldn't sit tight for three nights without going down to the hotel bar to pick up. That didn't make her a bad agent. It made her human.

Lance was self-aware enough to know he was human himself. What he felt now wasn't a cold, calculated, professional risk assessment. It was plain old jealousy. Nothing crazy. He and Tatyana weren't lovers. But he wondered what kind of man she'd brought up with her. Who'd made the cut? Who got to see the inside of her room?

She'd said staying in the apartment with him was too risky, but then she'd gone and done this. Maybe if she'd stayed with him, he'd be the one in bed with her right now. And maybe that was the real reason she was at the hotel.

One thing was clear. It didn't say much about his powers of seduction.

After thirty minutes, he went back upstairs and listened by the door again. He could hear them talking, their voices muffled. Tatyana and her man, her lover. He couldn't make out the words, but the tone told him it was relaxed, idle, meaningless.

He felt like a voyeur at the door and went down the corridor to the small alcove that served as a common area. It had an ice machine, a coffee machine, and a vending machine with a few snacks. He put some money in the coffee machine and waited for it to spit out a cappuccino in a small plastic cup. He took a sip and grimaced.

There was a chair in the alcove, and he sat on it, leaning back against the ice machine at an angle that gave him an oblique view down the corridor. He wanted to watch the man leave, but after an hour, it still hadn't happened, and Lance began nodding off.

He was tired. Sleeping had been difficult the first few nights in the apartment because of his leg.

He woke with a start to see someone kicking in Tatyana's door. His vision focused just in time to see a single man in black extend a gun in front of him and step into the room.

5

Tatyana stood naked in front of the bathroom mirror, examining the fine lines around her eyes, telling herself they weren't a sign of aging.

Life was cruel. She wasn't even thirty.

She'd been lying asleep next to some guy she'd picked up in the club downstairs. It was a seedy place, and he wasn't her type, but she'd needed the release.

She felt a chill and threw on a t-shirt hanging on the towel rack. She'd have liked to get rid of the man in her bed—she was done with him—but she supposed that would be unladylike. He also warmed the bed, which in this hotel was something not to be thrown out lightly.

She was about to go back to him when she heard movement in the corridor outside the room. She listened at the bathroom door, motionless, holding her breath. The bedroom door crashed open. The sound was followed by the six heavy thuds of suppressed bullets hitting flesh.

They'd found her.

She was unarmed, her gun was in the room beneath her

bed, and she had no idea who was out there. She heard the floorboards creak as someone entered the room, and her instincts took over.

She silently wrapped a towel around her fist and ran to the window. She punched out the thin pane of glass and leaped through it. She knew there was a deep snowbank beneath her window, and she hit it hard. She rolled and was on the ground in an instant, the snow searing her feet.

She was halfway across the parking lot when the gunfire started. A man at the bathroom window was shooting at her. He'd discarded the silenced PSS, and the cracks rang out loudly in the still night.

Tatyana was a trained professional, and she'd scouted her escape route in advance, but she'd been caught, quite literally, with her pants down.

The gunfire stopped, and she didn't have to look back to know she was being chased. From the lack of cover fire, she guessed the assassin was alone.

Across the parking lot was a ten-foot-high chain-link fence. She knew where it was loose against the support posts and could be pulled aside. She grabbed the fence and slid through, disappearing into the brush on the other side.

She didn't know how close behind her pursuer was. She couldn't hear him. She was unarmed, almost naked, and couldn't afford the luxury of looking over her shoulder to check.

The ground sloped down toward a railway track, and she slid down the hill, getting cut and scratched by the brush.

She ran along the track and leaped down the slope on the other side toward a six-foot cinder block wall covered in graffiti. She pulled herself to the top, and as she lowered herself to the other side, she turned and looked back up the slope. A well-built man was emerging from the brush back up the track. He stopped and pointed his gun at her.

"There's no use running," he called out.

She dropped behind the wall as two bullets hit the cinder block, sending chips of concrete flying.

She was on a narrow pathway through the brush. It went in both directions, but she knew she'd never outrun the man barefoot. Across the path was another fence, and she began climbing it.

Her feet were numb with cold. Her hands were beginning to shake. The initial burst of adrenaline was wearing off. As she struggled to the top of the fence, she knew she wouldn't make it over in time. The assassin would peer over the cinder block wall any second, and when he did, she'd be a sitting duck.

That knowledge made her panic. She lost her grip on the fence, and her foot slipped. Some loose wire cut a deep gash in her ankle.

She kept climbing, desperately pulling herself up the fence, and just as she swung her leg over the top, she heard the voice of the assassin behind her.

"Don't move," he said.

She froze. She could leap down the other side of the fence, but he'd simply pull the trigger the instant she moved. The chase was over.

No one escaped the clutches of the GRU. It was impossible. The organization put more effort into tracking down and killing its own defectors than it did pursuing foreign agents.

What had she been thinking? The moment she betrayed the agency, she'd signed her own death warrant.

Her mind grasped desperately for options.

She knew he was going to kill her. Whether she ran or not made no difference. He hadn't been sent to bring her back alive.

She turned to look at him. He wasn't a man she recognized. He'd pulled himself onto the wall and was sitting on it.

"Who sent you?" she said.

"You know who sent me."

"Who are you?"

"Does that make a difference?"

"I guess not," she said.

"My name is Genadi Surkov," he said.

He was scarcely twelve feet from her, and she could see his face clearly. He looked back at her, her body barely covered at all under the t-shirt. She was shaking so vigorously now that she felt she might lose her grip and fall from the fence.

"You're GRU, aren't you?" he said.

"Until a few days ago," she said.

"What happened a few days ago?"

"I killed my boss."

He nodded. "Igor Aralov? I heard about that."

"They're saying it was a robbery," Tatyana said.

"I knew it wasn't a robbery."

"Well, now you can say you killed the woman who killed Aralov."

Genadi nodded. "It's a shame I have to do it," he said. "You look so lovely in the moonlight."

"Just get it over with," Tatyana said. She shut her eyes, held her breath, and braced herself.

The bullet rang out with the clean, crisp snap of a breaking tree branch. She felt nothing. She waited. She knew what a bullet felt like, but nothing happened. All she felt was the icy numbness in her feet and hands and the bitter cold of the breeze.

She opened her eyes.

The assassin was on the ground. He'd fallen from the wall, and blood spurted from his right arm in steady gushes.

He writhed on the ground, and Tatyana looked around frantically to see who'd shot him. In the darkness beyond the wall, she saw no one.

Genadi was still on the ground, his gun three feet away from him. She looked at it, then back at him. He hadn't seen it yet, but if she moved for it, he would.

She leaped from the fence, falling into the heavy brush on the other side, and rolled down another twenty feet of slope. The ground was steep, and she lost control as she fell, crashing through leaves and branches until her head hit something hard, and everything went black.

6

Lance got to his feet and, ignoring the pain in his leg, ran to Tatyana's room, pulling his gun from inside his coat. He scanned the room for the intruder but didn't see him. What he did see was crimson blood seeping through the white sheets on Tatyana's bed.

He was too late.

Then he heard two shots from the bathroom and rushed toward it. The window was smashed, and the thin curtain blew in the breeze. Lance looked outside and saw a man chasing someone across the parking lot.

He leaped out the window onto the snowbank directly below. The shock of the landing hurt his already injured leg, and he had to limp across the lot, struggling to keep up.

He came to a high chainlink fence and climbed over it. There were two sets of footprints in the snow, and he picked up his pace, running through the brush blindly as he followed the footsteps.

He heard a man's voice up ahead and more gunshots. The ground began to slope downward, and he half ran, half crashed through the brush until it opened onto a railway track. Across the tracks, further down the slope, was a cinder block wall. The assassin was on top of it, a hundred feet away, pointing his gun at Tatyana on the other side.

They were talking to each other.

Lance didn't wait to hear what they were saying. He took a deep breath, held out his gun, steadied his hand, and pulled the trigger. His bullet hit the man on the shoulder and knocked him off the wall.

Lance stayed where he was and waited. Approaching the wall would expose him. He watched for about ten seconds, but nothing happened.

He would have waited longer, but he knew Tatyana was behind that wall.

He made his way cautiously along the track, approaching the spot where the man had been, and had to dive for cover when three shots came at him from behind the wall. He fired back, hitting the wall twice.

He waited another few seconds before inching forward, keeping as low as possible. He kept his sights on the wall, moving cautiously. If the assassin looked over, he'd have a clear line of sight. In the moonlight, Lance would make an easy target.

But the assassin didn't look over. Instead, he reached over and fired more covering shots without aiming. They hit the ground around Lance, and he rolled off the track into the shallow ditch between the track and the wall. He lay against the wall, knowing he had to get over it.

He waited a few seconds, then stood and pulled himself to the top. He could see the spot where he'd shot the assassin. The man wasn't there. Neither was Tatyana.

Lance listened, then climbed over the wall, proceeding cautiously. There was a trail of blood leading down a rutted path in the direction of the power plant. Lance was about to follow it when he saw a fainter trail of blood leading into the brush on the other side of the fence.

He called out, "Tatyana?"

She didn't answer. He climbed the fence and went down the slope into the brush. The ground leveled out, and he saw her lying on the ground, face-down in the snow.

7

Tatyana woke in a bright room, a ceiling fan spinning above her head. She didn't know where she was and reached under the pillow for her gun. There was none there.

She sat up and was about to make for the door when a man entered.

It was Lance.

"What happened?" she said.

"You're awake."

She looked at him, then around the room. "We're in the apartment," she said.

"Yes, we are."

"My things?"

"I went back to the hotel and cleared your room."

"What about my...." Her voice trailed off.

Lance looked at her, forcing her to say the word.

"My... friend."

"Your friend?"

She shook her head. "The man who was in my bed, Lance."

"Oh, *that* friend."

"Yes, that friend."

"He's dead."

She leaned back in the bed.

"I hope he was at least a good lay," Lance said.

"Shut up," she said.

"That was a risk you didn't have to take."

"I said, shut up."

Lance shrugged. There was a chair next to the bed, and he sat on it, stretching out his leg.

"How is it?" Tatyana said, indicating his leg.

"It's getting there."

"Did you kill my assassin?" she said.

"I shot him in the arm. He got away."

She nodded. "I know you told me to be careful," she said.

He looked at her. "I'm sure you were doing something important."

"I didn't realize they'd track me so quickly. I used every safeguard."

"And your people? Are they safe?"

"I deleted my source records, contact reports, anything that could be used to get to them," she said. "I don't know if I got everything in time, but I had to do it, Lance. Those people trusted me."

Lance nodded. She was grateful he wasn't fighting her on that.

"It's going to be hot around here," Lance said. "They'll send more guys. We can't go back to the hotel."

"I know," she said.

"And no more accessing the network."

"I'm done with that," she said. "I'm ready to leave the city."

"Good," Lance said. "We need to get you on a train as soon as possible."

"You're not coming with me?"

He didn't say anything.

"We should stay together," she said.

"Things aren't finished here," Lance said. "I know there's more coming. The Dead Hand was trying to start a war."

"We killed them," Tatyana said. "Davidov, Timokhin, Aralov. They're all dead."

"This isn't over," Lance said. "The Dead Hand goes straight to the president. If the Kremlin wants war, killing a few generals isn't going to stop it."

"Whatever they do next," Tatyana said, "is not your responsibility. You've done what you came to do."

Lance shook his head. "I'm not leaving yet. I can't."

She looked at him and tried to read what he was thinking. She'd thought he was done with the CIA, that he'd had enough of their dirty work. She couldn't imagine that had changed.

"All right," she said. She looked across the room to where her things had been stacked neatly on a desk. Papers, laptops, clothing.

"You done with the electronics?" Lance said.

She nodded.

"All right. I'm going to get rid of them. When I get back, we're going to the train station."

"Leningradsky Station?" Tatyana said.

"Too risky. They'll be expecting you to go west."

"I have to go to Leningradsky."

"Paveletskiy will be safer," Lance said. "You can go south to Astrakhan. You'll be on the Caspian there."

"And you have a boat waiting for me?"

"No, but you'll think of something."

Tatyana shook her head. "I know it's riskier, Lance, but I have to get to Leningradsky. There's something I need to do there."

"What do you need to do?"

"Leave someone a message."

"Your loose ends almost cost you your life last night."

"I know, Lance."

He shook his head.

"This person is more than just a contact," Tatyana said. "It's personal."

Lance looked at her.

She said nothing more.

He sighed and got up. He went to the desk and began packing the electronics. Two burner phones, two laptops, and a small plastic box that looked like someone had pried open an old Gameboy to expose the electronics. It contained a 580 megahertz processor, some flash storage, two ethernet ports, and was able to automatically redirect data over the Tor network.

"Did you make this?" Lance said, holding it up.

She nodded.

He looked at it a little closer. "Is this GRU hardware?"

"No," she said. "It's off-the-shelf stuff."

"Do you mind if I keep it?"

She shrugged.

He put it in his pocket and slung the bag over his shoulder. "All right," he said. "I'm going to get rid of all this. You take a shower and get ready. As soon as it gets dark, we're leaving."

She watched him go and then went through the things he'd salvaged from her hotel room. Her Browning handgun was there. It had been a gift from Lance a long time ago, and she brought it on every mission. If he'd left it behind, she'd have gone back to the hotel for it.

She packed it, along with three fake passports, a credit card and some cash, and whatever clothes and toiletries he'd gathered.

There was something else. Another item she'd have risked her life to go back for. She felt a flood of relief when she found it under the clothes. A small shoebox. She opened it and looked at the shoes inside. Her eyes glazed over as she looked at them.

Then she dressed and went into the kitchen.

She checked the refrigerator. It was empty. Lance wasn't much of a cook. There was some coffee, and she put water on the stove to boil. Then she looked around the rest of the apartment, snooping more than anything, seeing what she could learn about this American man who'd saved her life.

Most of the apartment was empty, untouched since he'd moved in.

He'd set himself up in the bedroom overlooking the street, and it seemed he spent most of his time there. There was a lamp next to the bed and a leather-bound book. It was a notebook, a diary. She picked it up. She was about to open it when she heard Lance returning. She put the diary down and hurried out of the room.

Lance opened the front door. "Looking for something?" he said.

"No, I was just...."

"Snooping."

"I need toothpaste."

"Right," he said.

The kettle on the stove began to whistle, and she used the distraction to escape. She went to the kitchen and prepared coffee. Lance followed a moment later with a tube of toothpaste.

"Thanks," she said, embarrassed, thinking how she'd never know what was in that diary.

"I bought some bread and cheese," he said, putting them on the counter.

"Oh," Tatyana said.

"I figured you'd be hungry."

She nodded. "I made coffee."

They went into the living room, which was sparsely decorated but had a sofa and a view of the street, and sipped coffee and ate the bread and cheese. Lance lit a cigarette, and she asked for one.

At dusk, they went down to the street and caught a cab.

"Where to?" the driver said.

"Leninsgradsky," Lance said.

Tatyana looked at him. "Thank you."

He nodded. "I just hope we don't regret it."

The evening traffic was heavy, and it took over an hour to get downtown. Neither spoke on the way, but when they arrived, Tatyana turned to Lance and said, "Are you sure you don't want to come with me?"

"I'll come in and make sure you get to the train," he said.

"But you don't want to get on it?"

He thought a second before saying, "I can't leave yet."

"Do you even know why you're staying?" she said.

He looked at her and was about to answer when the driver said, "Hey, I don't have all night."

They got out of the cab, and when Tatyana looked at Lance, it was clear the moment had passed. She followed him into the station, which was packed with people, all rushing in the evening commute.

Tatyana had insisted on this station for one reason—a storage locker on the lower level, where the commuter lines were serviced.

"The ticket office is this way," Lance said.

"I'm not buying a ticket," Tatyana said.

"What do you mean?"

"They'll be looking for me on the express trains."

"You're taking a suburban service?"

"I know how to get across Russia," she said. "I've lived here my whole life."

Lance shook his head.

"What?" she said.

He sighed. "Nothing."

They took the escalator down to the Khimki platform, and Tatyana pulled her scarf over her hair. On the platform, she sat on a bench and adjusted her makeup. She had a few tricks with an eyebrow pencil that could alter her appearance—not enough to confuse a human, but it would require a far broader search by facial recognition algorithms. The GRU would be scanning every public camera in the country, running a search for her face, and a few simple changes could buy her weeks of processing time.

"I'll get the ticket," Lance said.

Tatyana nodded. She watched him go to the kiosk, then got up and crossed the platform to a bank of coin-operated lockers. The last locker on the left was number fifty, and she opened it with a code. Inside was a notebook and pen, which she took and placed in her backpack. In their place, she put the shoebox she'd brought with her and a pack of matches.

She glanced around the platform. Nothing was out of the ordinary. She saw Lance at the kiosk, paying for her ticket. She took one last look at the contents of the locker, breathed deeply, and shut the door.

8

L arissa Chipovskaya only ever wanted to be a dancer. As a little girl, she'd dreamed of being *prima balle-rina* at the famed Bolshoi Theater. She pictured the crowds in London and Paris and New York giving her rapturous standing ovations. When she shut her eyes, she could almost smell the roses that would rain down on her, flung from the balconies of the world's most beautiful opera houses. She would stand in front of the mirror in her bedroom and imagine the sequined gowns, the diamond tiaras, the giant Swarovski crystal chandeliers that would bathe her in the light of a thousand bulbs.

Life, however, had other ideas, and she found that her stage was not to be at the opera house but in a gentleman's club in central Moscow. It was a club where, at that moment, an overweight Japanese businessman slipped American dollar bills into her thong.

"Shake it," he yelled, his Russian barely comprehensible. He was so drunk he could hardly stand, but he had money, so she shook it. The louder he yelled, the faster she went.

Like a dog doing tricks for a biscuit, she thought.

After her three-song set, she found him slumped over the bar, being rude to the waitress. She could smell the vodka from five feet away. She pulled up a stool and cleared her throat. "There you are," she said.

He turned and almost fell off his seat. She had to prop him up. "You almost made me forget where I was," he said in his heavy accent, nodding toward the pole she'd been spinning on.

"Thank you," she said.

"You're just like a tiger," he said, slurring the words.

She wasn't sure what he meant but took it as a compliment. "You like what you saw?" she said, trying to make eye contact. She always tried to look a man in the eye before locking herself in a room with him, but this man was so drunk she couldn't get a feel for him. He stared at her, blinking slowly, and then his gaze dropped to her chest.

"You really ought to get me in the champagne room," she said, taking his hand.

"The champagne room?"

She nodded toward a set of glass steps leading to the VIP area. "You're going to love it in there. I even know how to say 'daddy' in Japanese."

"Japanese?" he slurred. "I'm not Japanese."

"What are you?"

"I'm from China."

She leaned in and brushed her lips against his ear. "Then let me take you upstairs," she said, getting down from her stool. "I'll show you things they've never even heard of in China." She pressed her body against his and pulled him from his seat.

He followed her, stumbling so badly the bouncer had to help him with the steps.

Once in the private room, she got straight to work. She had to make as much money as possible before he passed out. There was a cordless credit card terminal, and she keyed in the five hundred dollar room fee, which went straight to the house, her three hundred dollar entertainment fee, and a two hundred dollar tip, which she split with the bouncer.

"Come on, baby," she cooed as he fumbled for his wallet. Only when the transaction cleared did she let him order a bottle of blue label Johnnie Walker from the waitress.

His money bought him an hour of dancing, during which he could get away with quite a lot, but not everything. Some of the girls offered extra services, but Larissa was not one of them. She was a dancer. On that point, she was adamant.

They could look. They could touch. She'd even sit in their lap and beg them to rescue her from her life of misery. "Take me home with you," she'd coo. They loved nothing more than to hear her beg.

But she was no whore.

Once she had them alone, it wasn't unusual for the men to lose control, to forget themselves, to do and say things they shouldn't. In such situations, it was surprisingly easy to get a man to divulge secrets he was sworn to protect. Secrets that should rightly have been taken to the grave. Secrets that would cost lives if they ever got into the wrong hands.

And Larissa gathered them up like the treasures they were. She collected them. They were the only reason she could still look at herself in the mirror without wanting to smash it.

The club was located just blocks from the Kremlin, halfway between the infamous Lubyanka, home of the FSB, and the gigantic Stalinist tower that housed the Russian Ministry of Foreign Affairs. It was a place powerful men gravitated to, drawn like flies to shit. They let down their guard there. They lost their money, blew their load, and most important of all, made mistakes.

Larissa hadn't expected much from this man. He wasn't her usual type. He gave out information too freely, told her he was from Beijing. He looked like a company man making the most of his overseas trip. His suit was well-tailored. His watch was

Patek Philippe. She watched him pour whiskey down his gullet and wondered how long it would take before he became incomprehensible. Then he said something she hadn't expected. He said he'd spent the day in Moscow's tallest building.

Her eyes widened.

She'd heard it called that before. He wasn't referring to one of the sleek new skyscrapers in Presnensky, where six of Europe's eight tallest buildings now stood. He wasn't referring to the fancy new hotels on the Garden Ring that soared above the neighboring blocks. She immediately knew he meant the nine-story, baroque Lubyanka building, the former home of the Cheka and the KGB—the place where Russian political dissidents had been taken and tortured for over a century. There was a dark joke from Stalin's time that it was Moscow's tallest building because Siberia, and the Gulag, could be seen from its basement.

Larissa, sitting on his lap, leaned in close and ran her lips along his neck. "Who did you meet there?" she whispered.

"I met a real-life polar bear," the man said.

"A polar bear?"

"They called him a polar bear. He's a freak of nature, big as a bear and white as snow."

"A big man?"

"Even his eyelashes are white," the man said. "It doesn't look right."

"And what did you discuss with this polar bear?" she said, biting the lobe of his ear.

His answer made her blood freeze.

Instinctively, she knew it wasn't a trick. Her heart pounded in her chest. This was what she'd been waiting two years to hear. Real, actionable intelligence.

The man was blackout drunk, and when he passed out a few minutes later, she slipped out of the room and made her way to the staff area. There, she locked herself in a bathroom stall and threw up.

"Rough night?" one of the other girls said to her when she came out.

"Something I ate," Larissa said.

The other girl shook her head. "Naughty girl."

Larissa nodded. She liked the other girls. They weren't catty. They looked out for each other.

Larissa got dressed and clocked out early.

Her boss caught her on the way out. "Where do you think you're going?"

"I'm not feeling well," she said, brushing past. "Probably my period." It had worked with her high school gym teacher, and it worked here.

Her beat-up Volkswagen was in the lot behind the club, and she got in and turned the ignition. It took a few tries, the Moscow winter was hard on old cars, but eventually, it fired up. She drove straight to the Leningradsky train station on Komsomolskaya Square. It was the middle of the night, and there was no traffic.

The station, all but deserted, was one of the biggest in the country. It served as the terminal for high-speed connections between Moscow and Saint Petersburg, a seven-hundred-kilometer trip the trains covered in just four hours. It was faster than flying. The station also served a number of commuter routes, and at the platform for one of these local services was a bank of coin-operated lockers.

Larissa went to the last locker on the platform and entered a four-digit code. The door clicked open. She expected to find a pen and notebook. For two years, that was how she'd been communicating with her contact in the GRU. Instead, there was only a black shoebox. An ornate logo was embossed in silver on the lid.

She glanced around the terminal nervously. It was deathly

quiet. She'd been warned only ever to access the locker when the station was busy. She suddenly wished she'd listened.

She reached into the locker and opened the shoebox carefully. There was blue crepe paper inside, and beneath that was a pair of baby blue Prada stilettos. She recognized them instantly and a knot of emotion caught in her throat. Her eyes filled with tears.

On top of the shoes was a cardboard matchbook, the kind given out at restaurants and bars, and when she saw it, she knew the worst had happened.

Tatyana was burned.

9

***

Larissa didn't know what to do. Tatyana had told her this day would come, the day she would no longer have a protector, but now that it was here, she felt unprepared.

She put the matchbook in her pocket and walked out of the station with the shoebox under her arm. Even though she'd brought her car, she walked right past it and got into one of the waiting cabs.

"Where to?" the driver said when she failed to say anything.

"I don't know," she said quietly.

"Lady," the driver said, "are you all right?"

"I'm fine."

"You look like you just saw a ghost."

She looked at his reflection in the mirror. "I'm sorry," she said, getting back out of the cab.

"You need some help?" he said, but she shut the door without answering.

Her heart pounded at a million miles an hour. For two years, her life had had a sense of order. She'd had a purpose. She'd known what she was supposed to do. It wasn't perfect, it was hard, but she knew that if she kept showing up to work, she'd be able to gather information. And she knew that if she kept going to the locker in the train station, she'd be able to write that information in the notebook for Tatyana.

She didn't know what Tatyana did with the information.

She didn't know if it changed anything.

But she felt she was a part of something. She was part of a resistance.

Now, with Tatyana gone, she felt alone. Alone and vulnerable.

She began walking toward the Garden Ring. The wind was bitingly cold, but it helped calm her. She needed to clear her mind. She lit a cigarette with a match from the matchbook and sucked on it like her life depended on it.

She'd only ever met Tatyana one time. It was on the street on her way home from work. That was two years ago.

Some men had been outside the club when she got off work, and they'd followed her as she walked toward the metro station. She didn't recognize them. They hadn't been inside the club. One wore a leather jacket and jeans, the other a gray coat. She still remembered their faces.

They seemed drunk, following her down the street, catcalling and whistling. She'd increased her pace. Walking to the metro was dangerous. Many of the girls took cabs, but Larissa refused to waste good money on that. She'd had a driver once who'd scared her, so she didn't feel like she was much safer either way. That night on the deserted street, with two men following her, she'd have given anything for a cab to pull up and let her in. But none came.

She could hear the men gaining on her but was afraid that if she started to run, they'd chase her down. She kept walking as briskly as she could, and when she rounded the corner of a small, private park, within sight of the Bolshoi where she'd once dreamed of dancing, she panicked and broke into an all-out run. Almost immediately, the men were on top of her. One grabbed the strap of her purse and yanked it, flinging her hard against the iron fence that enclosed the park.

She fell to the ground, and when she tried to get up, the other man put his boot on the back of her head and pushed her back down. They laughed.

Larissa looked at the concrete pavement in front of her face and took a deep breath. In that moment, her thinking became very clear. The contours of her life came into stark relief. She knew who she was, she knew what her country had become, and she understood that she had only two options. Either she fought tooth and nail, or she surrendered.

She clenched her fists, ready to claw out the eyes of the first man to lay hands on her, but neither of them did. They'd stopped laughing, and she turned to see why.

A slick BMW with blacked-out windows had pulled up to the curb on the street. An expensively dressed woman stepped out, and Larissa saw her draw a gun from a Gucci purse. She pointed it at the men. They raised their hands.

"We were just having some fun," one said.

"Get away from her, or I'll shoot your nuts off," the woman said.

They backed away, then turned and ran.

The woman came up to Larissa and helped her to her feet.

"My name is Tatyana," she'd said. "Let me take you home."

Larissa got into the car and gave her the address to her apartment. Neither spoke during the drive. Larissa clenched the handle on the door and stared at Tatyana's purse. It was black alligator skin, and the clasp was the jewel-encrusted head of a panther. She thought she'd never seen anything so beautiful.

They arrived at the building, and Tatyana double-parked in front of the door.

"Thank you," Larissa said, her hand on the door.

Tatyana put her hand on Larissa's. "Invite me up," she said.

Larissa was still staring at the purse, the sparkling panther. "You don't..." she said, searching for the words. "You don't want... *sex*, do you?"

Tatyana laughed. "I assure you, you're not my type."

Larissa was finding it hard to breathe. She was afraid she was going to burst into tears at any moment.

She got out of the car and took deep breaths of the cold night air. She pulled a pack of cigarettes from her purse, lit one, and began walking toward her building. She didn't look back but heard Tatyana follow.

Neither spoke in the elevator, although they looked at each other, sizing each other up like two schoolgirls on their first day.

Larissa saw Tatyana's face in the light for the first time and her breath caught in her throat. "You're..." she stammered, her voice trailing off.

"I'm what?" Tatyana said.

Larissa shook her head. How was this possible? She felt as if she was looking in a mirror.

The elevator stopped, and Larissa led the way to the door, although she sensed by now that Tatyana already knew the way. She dropped her keys while trying to unlock the door, and Tatyana put a hand on her shoulder. "Relax," she said.

They entered the apartment, and Larissa led the way to the small kitchen. It wasn't a fancy apartment, and Larissa remembered feeling embarrassed. She felt like Tatyana was used to more luxurious surroundings. Her cat came out of the bedroom and rubbed against Tatyana's legs.

"Sorry for the mess," Larissa said.

"It's nice," Tatyana said.

Larissa looked at her again, then looked away. She had to force herself not to stare. She filled the kettle and put it on the stove. "Tea?" she said, her hand shaking from nerves.

"You really should try to calm yourself," Tatyana said. "You're safe."

Larissa nodded. She looked into Tatyana's eyes.

"What is it?" Tatyana said.

Larissa shook her head. "We could be mistaken for sisters," she said.

Tatyana nodded, as if none of this surprised her. She sat down at the kitchen table and put her hands in front of her. "We do look alike," she said.

"Although I'd kill for a pair of shoes like that," Larissa said.

Tatyana smiled. Some of the tension lifted. Tatyana was wearing a pair of baby blue Prada pumps. She looked down at them and said, "I thought strippers made crazy money."

Larissa said, "How do you know where I work?"

"I'm on your side," Tatyana said again. "You're safe. I promise."

Larissa didn't know what to make of that. The kettle came to a boil, and she poured the hot water into the teapot. She held a teabag by the string and bobbed it up and down in the water.

"How do you know where I work?" she said again.

"Larissa," Tatyana said, "believe me when I say we're on the same side."

Larissa brought the teapot and two china cups to the table. "And what side is that?" she said. She was holding the pot of scalding tea just inches from Tatyana's face.

"Put that down," Tatyana said. "Please."

Larissa put the pot and cups on the table and said again, "What side?"

"The side that's tired of the way things are," Tatyana said, pouring the tea.

"I don't know what you're talking about," Larissa said.

"I'm talking about an Akula-class submarine that went down almost thirty years ago."

The blood drained from Larissa's face. "Who are you?" she said.

"I'm a friend."

"I think you should leave."

"Larissa, sit down."

"Get out."

Tatyana finished pouring the tea. "Do you take sugar?" she said.

"Get out of my apartment right now," Larissa said, her voice trembling with emotion.

Tatyana picked up her cup and took a sip. "I'm here to give you a chance to get even," she said.

Larissa stared at her.

"Please sit," Tatyana said.

Larissa sat down. Tatyana passed her a teacup. Larissa tried to pick it up, but her hands were trembling so badly that she spilled some of it.

"It's all right," Tatyana said, her voice as soft as if soothing a child.

"I don't understand what you're talking about," Larissa said.

Tatyana looked at her. "Don't you want to get even?"

Larissa let out a laugh. "There's no getting even in this world."

Tatyana nodded. "That's what I thought," she said. "My father was also on that submarine."

Larissa shook her head. She couldn't believe what she was hearing. "Who are you?" she said.

Tatyana reached into her pocket and pulled out an old photograph. It was black and white and very worn. It showed two men, both in the uniforms of the Akula-class nuclear submarine Larissa's father had died on.

Larissa took the photograph and looked at it closely. "That's my father," she said.

Tatyana nodded.

"Where did you get this?"

Tatyana reached out and put her hand on Larissa's. "The man next to your father," she said, "that's my father."

Larissa dropped the photograph onto the table.

"It's true," Tatyana said.

Larissa nodded. "Who are you?" she said again.

"I already told you. My name is Tatyana."

"Tatyana what?"

"Tatyana Aleksandrova."

10

Tatyana knew how to evade capture. She knew the methods of the GRU, and she knew how to counter them.

On the platform, there was a small kiosk selling clothing, and she had Lance go to it for her.

"I need something to wear," she told him.

He returned with a pair of John Lennon sunglasses, a scarf for her hair, and red lipstick that was a little darker than strictly tasteful. It wasn't exactly her style, but every item was chosen to trick the government's facial recognition system. That system was tied into police CCTV cameras across the country, and two of the most closely monitored areas were the train and bus stations. The trains themselves weren't yet equipped with cameras that could run the software.

She put on the glasses, and Lance grinned. "The sixties called," he said.

"What?" she said testily, pretending not to get it.

"Nothing," he said.

She thought of the Prada shoes she'd just left in the locker

and wished she could go back for them. What she wore now
was a humiliation.

"Come on, Yoko," Lance said. "You're going to miss your
train."

She glanced one final time at the locker. What she'd done
was a risk. It was a decision she knew would have consequences. Maybe for her, certainly for Larissa.

As well as the shoes, which she was sure Larissa would
remember, she left a matchbook from the hotel in Kapotnya.
She'd also set up a secure phone line in advance and rerouted it
to her cellphone. Before she shut the locker, and against all her
own rules and protocols, she wrote its number inside the
matchbook.

She couldn't leave Larissa alone. She wouldn't. She'd
brought her into this world, knowing she wasn't equipped for it.
She hadn't been trained. She wouldn't know what to do. She'd
panic, and then she'd make a mistake. A mistake that could cost
her life. Better to leave her with something, even if it was only a
number.

Carrying the phone was dangerous. Any networked electronic device was susceptible to tracking, but she'd taken what
precautions she could. She told herself if she didn't hear from
Larissa in the next week, she'd disconnect the number permanently and destroy the phone.

It went against her instinct for self-preservation, but as far
as she knew, Larissa was the only living family she had left. She
couldn't abandon her.

Lance walked her to the train, and the two of them looked at
each other before she boarded. It felt like one of those scenes
from an old war movie, except here, there was no soldier
wearing a handsome uniform, and the man who was there
wasn't in love. He had no tears in his eyes. He was doing a job,
nothing more. Also, this was the rush hour commuter service to
Khimki, and when she got on the train, she had to stand in the

aisle, so she couldn't have watched him from the window as the train pulled away.

She stood, pressed against a middle-aged man in a pinstripe suit, breathing into his armpit, and got off fifteen minutes later with the swarms of office workers.

On the platform, she inhaled deeply and looked around. She knew this station to be the last government building the German Wehrmacht ever captured on its march to Moscow. The bridge the train had just crossed marked the spot where the Red Army had held the line and ultimately turned the tide in the Battle for Moscow. She remembered being taught, as all Russian children were, that it was just nineteen miles from Stalin's office in the Kremlin. According to German myth, it was from the steel supports of that same bridge that soldiers of the fourth panzer army had been able to read the clock on the Kremlin's Spasskaya Tower.

Tatyana wasn't so sure of that. The city's skyline had changed in the intervening decades, but as she crossed the footbridge over Luzhskaya Street, she turned east and removed the ridiculous sunglasses Lance had given her. In the distance, not even the lights of the new skyscrapers in Presnensky could be seen.

She walked the short distance to a gas station on the main Moscow to Saint Petersburg highway and lit a cigarette. She was glad it was night. If the government cameras hadn't picked her up yet, they were unlikely to.

She went to the edge of the road and stood on the filthy snowbank, each passing car spraying freshly melted slush onto her shoes. She held out her hand, and in just a few minutes, one of the enormous westbound tractor-trailers was heaving and down-gearing to a halt.

She ran to it and climbed the step to the passenger door, holding herself up by the handle.

The driver opened the window. He had heavy stubble, a

large belly, and a cigarette dangling at the edge of his mouth, an inch and a half of ash still holding on precariously to the butt. "Where are you headed?" he said.

"Tver," she said, which was a city about a hundred miles northwest.

He motioned for her to get in, and she did. He offered her a cigarette, and she took it. He asked her a few questions—small talk, weather observations—but mostly, they drove in silence.

He didn't try anything, which was good for him. If he had, she'd have snapped his wrist.

At Tver, she got out at another gas station where she left the main highway and caught a ride southwest to Rzhev, a dreary town on the Volga where Russia had lost two million men to the Germans in the series of battles that became known as 'The Meat Grinder.'

Her driver was better looking than the one before, chattier, and smoked the same brand of cigarettes. In the darkness of the cab, it seemed he was a little more confident in his talents as a seducer than the first driver had been.

"You want to earn your way?" he said to her when they'd been sitting together about fifteen minutes.

"Why don't you keep your eyes on the road?" Tatyana said. "It'll be safer for both of us."

He returned his eyes to the road, but his hand, as if acting independently, crept across the center console and found its way onto her lap.

Tatyana sat motionless, looking at his hand as if it was a small, harmless animal. Then she turned and looked at the driver. "You're lucky you remind me of someone," she said.

"Oh yeah?" he said, his hand moving up her thigh. "Who's that?"

"An American. I was with him before I began this trip."

"Did you let him slip you a quickie before you left?"

Tatyana thought for a second, then said, "I didn't."

"Well," the driver said. "We could fix that. Pretend I'm him. I don't mind."

"That's a very generous offer," Tatyana said, reaching into her coat.

The driver began pulling the truck over to the side of the road as Tatyana drew the Browning pistol.

"How about you keep driving, and I don't shoot your nuts off?" she said, cocking the gun.

The driver took one look at it and pulled his hand back. They didn't speak again, and Tatyana forced him off his route so he could drop her at the train station in Rzhev.

The train line at Rzhev connected directly with Riga, but Tatyana knew it would be easier to cross the border into Belarus than try to get into the European Union directly. Security along the EU border had been upgraded multiple times. The Belarusian crossings remained completely neglected.

She bought a ticket as far as Pustoshka, about twenty miles shy of both the Latvian and Belarusian borders. Any closer, and she would have had to show the conductor her passport.

She spent the hour before her train arrived sitting on a bench, sipping watery coffee from a machine. She kept her gaze away from a camera over the platform, never looking in its direction. She was the only person on the platform for most of the hour, and she went back to the machine three times for more coffee.

By the time the train arrived, there was a pile of cigarette butts on the ground beneath the bench.

The train arrived from the east, and behind it, a thin sliver of dawn colored the sky.

She boarded. Her carriage was empty. She stretched her legs across several seats and watched the countryside drift by. By the time they pulled into the station at Pustoshka, it was late afternoon.

In Pustoshka, she walked from the station into the center of town and checked into a small inn. The town was provincial, a frontier outpost so far from the center of power that it didn't even have traffic lights at the intersections. She passed a police station and post office and avoided both. Her picture could have been faxed to either of them from Moscow, and in a town like this, new arrivals stood out.

She paid cash at the inn and ate in the dining room. It was a grand stone house with as many fireplaces as rooms, and after her time on the road, she was glad to be there. There were a few other guests, travelers on the Moscow-Riga highway, and they were different from travelers in less out-of-the-way places. These people weren't anonymous. They seemed to carry their stories with them. There was an old man in a handmade, old-style fur coat with a hunting rifle propped against the side of his chair. There was also a woman wrapped in layers of cloth that, somewhere around her bosom, concealed a small baby. She rocked and cooed as she spooned soup into its mouth.

Another man came in and sat close to Tatyana by the fire. "Beautiful country," he said. He was about fifty and wore wire-rimmed glasses that gave him a severe look.

Tatyana nodded but kept her eyes on the chicken cutlets on her plate. "It is," she said.

"Heart of the Motherland," the man said.

She nodded.

"Although the Germans had a garrison here for three years."

"The Germans had a lot of garrisons," she said.

He nodded.

She wanted to eat in peace. She was hungry and tired, but he seemed determined to keep her talking. "What brings you all the way out here?" he said.

"*All* the way?"

"I assume you're from Moscow."

"Yes," she said, looking at him more closely. "I'm going to Riga tomorrow for a job interview."

"What sort of job?"

"Director of an art gallery."

"Strange place to get off the train," he said.

"Hotels are cheaper on our side of the border," she said.

He nodded.

"What about you?" she said, wanting to move the conversation along. "What do you do?"

"I'm a teacher. Literature. I specialize in Pushkin. He spent a lot of time in this area."

"I didn't know."

"Yes, he did. I was at the Orekhovno Manor today. Have you visited it?"

"No," Tatyana said, spreading butter on her bread roll.

"Very nice museum there."

She nodded.

"Have you read his 'Ode to Liberty'?" the man said.

"In school," Tatyana said. "Not recently."

"'Tremble, O Tyrants of the Earth!'"

"Ah yes," Tatyana said, pretending it had jogged her memory. Then she added, "I like that he died fighting a duel for his wife."

"As a woman, I can see how that would attract you."

Tatyana looked up. "As a woman?"

"With your romantic notions," he said.

Tatyana nodded. "Ah yes," she said, getting up from her seat. She left some money on the table, and her server asked if she would like a nightcap.

"What have you got?" Tatyana said, sitting back down.

"Warm rum with honey."

Tatyana shrugged. "Why not?"

She stretched her legs in front of the fire and thought, this might be her last night in Russia for a very long time.

She was exhausted when she finally got to her room. She

locked the door and sat on the bed. She'd intended to bathe but fell asleep before getting to it.

She was woken a short while later by a knock on the door. Instinctively, she drew her gun. "Who is it?"

"Your friend from the dining room."

"My friend?"

"The Pushkin scholar."

"What do you want?"

"I wondered if you wanted company."

She got out of bed quietly and crept to the wall next to the door. She listened for any sound that might suggest he wasn't alone. She looked at the crack at the bottom of the door. The sliver of light was broken by only two feet.

"I'm a married woman," she said.

"Oh," the man said. "You weren't wearing a ring."

"Goodnight," she said.

11

L arissa crossed a large intersection and threw her cigarette on the ground.

It was the photo that had done it. Without that, without seeing her father's face, she didn't think she would have joined Tatyana's cause. Politics was one thing, and Larissa had as much reason as anyone to hate the Russian government, but family, that was the real force that moved her. That was what made her willing to risk her life.

She'd believed for a very long time that she was alone in the world, that all her family was dead. Tatyana made her believe that wasn't true.

She remembered the moment the realization had washed over her. She was sitting in the kitchen next to Tatyana, both of them looking at the photograph of the two sailors.

"They look like they were friends," Larissa said.

Tatyana nodded. "This was taken the day they set out on their final voyage."

"What is this?" Larissa said quietly. "What is this really about? Why are you here in my apartment?"

"I work for the GRU," Tatyana said.

Larissa felt the blood drain from her face. It took her a moment to catch her breath. "I hope you're not here to bring me into the fold."

Tatyana fixed her in her gaze, then, speaking in a level voice, said, "I'm here to recruit you."

"No," Larissa said, shaking her head. "You can't recruit me. Your bosses can all rot in hell, as far as I'm concerned."

"I agree with you," Tatyana said.

Larissa looked at her.

"I already told you, Larissa. We're on the same side, you and I."

Larissa shook her head. She looked more closely at Tatyana. It was true, what she'd said earlier. They really could be mistaken for sisters. "What age are you?" she said.

"Twenty-nine."

"I'm twenty-nine," Larissa said.

"I know. Our mothers were both pregnant when the sub went down."

Larissa felt a knot of emotion in her throat.

"Do you remember what your life was like as a child?" Tatyana said.

Larissa shrugged. "I remember it wasn't easy."

"There were problems with the authorities?"

Larissa looked at her. The way she said the words made her think Tatyana already knew the answer. It was a difficult thing for her to speak of. She'd spent her life building a wall around it. She'd learned it was dangerous. "The police came some-times," she said. "Especially in Saint Petersburg."

"That's why your mother brought you to Moscow, isn't it? To get away from the authorities?"

Larissa nodded.

"Your mother had rocked the boat," Tatyana said.

Larissa shrugged. "She'd done something they weren't happy about."

Tatyana nodded. "Mine did too."

Larissa shook her head at the memory. The police coming by the house when she was a child, scaring her, upsetting her mother. Her entire childhood, she'd lived under that cloud of fear.

"I found some files," Tatyana said. "Saint Petersburg police reports from the time of the submarine accident. Your mother and my mother were mixed up in something together."

"In what?"

"I'm not sure. I haven't been able to get to the bottom of it. The records were suppressed."

"You know something," Larissa said.

"I know the reports were sent to Moscow."

"But you haven't found them?"

"Not yet, but I will," Tatyana said. "And one thing's for sure. They weren't just fighting over their widow's pensions. This was something the authorities in Moscow took notice of."

Larissa sighed. She'd always known something like that had been going on. Her mother's calm exterior could only hide so much. She remembered the way her mother would grow tense every time she heard a police siren. Even after they moved to Moscow, that sense of dread followed them. It never left.

"The authorities always made such a big deal about how they took care of military widows," Larissa said. "But from what I saw, they treated my mother as if she was an enemy of the state."

"They knew how to hit where it hurt," Tatyana said.

Larissa looked at her. "What does that mean?"

"Ever wonder why your offer to attend Vaganova was withdrawn?"

Larissa looked up. The Vaganova Academy in Saint Petersburg was the most famous dance school in all of Russia. Since the 1700s, it had trained the most renowned dancers in the world. Larissa had attended her first lessons there when she was four years old. Every summer, her mother signed her up for intensive workshops and recitals. Never once did she complain about the enormous cost. After they moved to Moscow, Larissa begged her mother to take her back in the summer. At age ten, she began the formal application process, and when she was fourteen, she was accepted to the most prestigious program in the entire academy, the elite ballet workshop.

It was the happiest day of her life, the culmination of years of blood, sweat, and tears. All the work she'd put in, all the sacrifices her mother had made, were validated in a single sweep of the admission officer's pen. It was the first step in her journey to the stage of the Bolshoi.

And then, without a word of explanation, the offer was withdrawn.

Larissa spent the next ten years of her life trying to figure out why. She'd done everything right. She'd played by all the rules. At school, on the dance floor, in the local youth organization. She'd stared at the letter a thousand times, trying to read between the lines, to decipher meanings that weren't there.

Larissa Chipovskaya,

It is with regret that I rescind your offer to attend Vaganova Academy.

Thank you for your interest in our institution.

It was signed by the secretary of the office of administrative affairs, someone named Hilde Freindlich, a woman Larissa had never heard of before or since.

"That was connected to my father's death?" she said.

"I don't know everything," Tatyana said, "but I do know some paper-pusher in Moscow made a connection somewhere."

Larissa shook her head. "And that meant I couldn't attend the academy?"

Tatyana nodded. "Your mother died soon afterward, didn't she?"

Larissa looked down at the table. Her mother died from an overdose of sleeping pills not long after that. Larissa was the one who found the body, splayed on her bed, her clothing soiled, a copy of a Solzhenitsyn novella still in her hand. "She never recovered from the ordeal with the academy," she said.

Tatyana nodded. "They got to my mother too," she said.

"Who did?"

"The paper-pushers."

"How?"

"She got sick."

"With what?"

"Tuberculosis. It's curable, but they refused to approve the medication in my mother's case. She died when I was four."

"I'm sorry," Larissa said, and she meant it. Losing her own mother had been devastating, but to lose her at four years of age would have been unimaginable. She wondered how Tatyana had managed to survive at all.

"Larissa," Tatyana said, "do you know the lockers on the Khimki platform at Leningradsky Station?"

"You know I do," Larissa said. Larissa and her mother had gone to Leningradsky every time they traveled to Saint Petersburg for the dance recitals. She'd been there dozens of times.

Tatyana nodded. "Locker fifty," she said. "The code is 4422."

"The submarine's number."

"Yes."

"What's in the locker?"

"A pen and a notebook. If I have something to tell you," Tatyana said, "I'll write it in the notebook. If you have something to tell me, you do the same."

"What if I don't want to?"

"I won't force you."

Larissa nodded.

"But if you do, Larissa, you have to be careful. If anyone ever finds out about this, we'll both be dead."

Larissa thought about that for a minute, then said, "What do you want me to do?"

"You know the type of men that visit your club?"

"Yes, I do," Larissa said.

"You can find things out for me. Things I can use. To resist."

12

L arissa looked across the street, where the Moscow Hilton glowed like a lamp, spilling warm light onto the sidewalk.

A girl didn't end up in Larissa's line of work by accident. Certain things had to happen in her life.

Those things had happened to Larissa, and they'd changed her. They'd given her a sixth sense, an ability to read situations, to tell when people meant her harm, to smell the difference between the truth and a lie. It was that sensibility that had made her so valuable to Tatyana.

And she knew that Tatyana had been through similar things. Those wounds that had carved her so painfully into the person she was, she saw them in Tatyana too.

They truly were two of a kind.

She remembered how she'd felt with Tatyana that first night, sitting at her kitchen table. She'd felt like she was no longer alone.

"When was the first time you saw my photo?" she'd said.

Tatyana shrugged. "A few months ago."

"How did you find it?"

"I was looking for my mother's file."

"And that's when you found the connection?"

Tatyana nodded.

"What was the photo?"

"You were in a ballerina's outfit. A little girl. You couldn't have been more than six or seven."

"And you were taken by the resemblance?"

Tatyana smiled. "Yes, I was."

"Did you ever wonder why we looked so similar?"

Tatyana nodded. "Of course I did."

"Did you ever wonder if our mothers were more than just friends?"

"I wondered," Tatyana said, "if maybe they'd both been in love with the same man."

Larissa nodded. Her heart pounded. She'd never met her father. He'd died before she was born. All she had of him was a grainy, black-and-white photo of a man in a sailor's uniform. "Tell me what you found," she said.

Tatyana let out a short laugh.

"What's so funny?"

"There's no beating around the bush with you, is there?"

"This is important," Larissa said. "You don't need to be a detective to see there's a resemblance between us. That can't be a coincidence."

Tatyana nodded. "All right," she said. "I pulled up both our birth certificates."

"And?"

"Our mothers are our mothers," she said. "That much is clear."

"But our fathers?"

Tatyana smiled. "You're good at this."

"I have an instinct," Larissa said.

Tatyana held up the photograph. "My mother was married to this man," she said, pointing to the man she'd said was her father. Then she pointed to Larissa's father. "Your mother was married to this man."

"Being married doesn't make them fathers," Larissa said.

Tatyana shook her head. "No, it doesn't."

Larissa looked at Tatyana intently. The resemblance was just too clear to ignore. "We're half-sisters then?" she said.

Tatyana stared back at her for a long moment. Neither of them said a word.

Eventually, Tatyana let out a heavy sigh and looked away. "You know," she said, getting up from the table, "our jobs aren't so very different."

"I'll believe that when I've got a pair of shoes like those," Larissa said, nodding at Tatyana's feet.

Tatyana smiled. She put on her coat. "You can keep the photo," she said.

Larissa looked at her. "Are you sure?"

"It's safer with you."

Larissa nodded. "Do you have any idea which one's our father?"

Tatyana shook her head. "If I find our mothers' files, I'll know more."

Larissa nodded. "I have one last question," she said.

Tatyana looked at her. "Yes?"

"If our files were tainted, if we were under suspicion, how did you get into the GRU?"

"Good question," Tatyana said.

"And?"

"I haven't gotten to the bottom of that yet, either."

"Maybe someone made a mistake," Larissa said.

"They do make a lot of mistakes," Tatyana said, "but I don't think this was one of them."

"You think someone pulled strings for you?"

"I think someone must have made sure my file was clean."

"Why would someone do that?"

Tatyana shrugged. "Why do they do anything in the GRU? They had an interest in seeing me on the inside." She threw her purse over her shoulder and walked to the door.

Larissa watched the way she moved. Even the way they walked was similar. Tatyana stopped at the door and turned. "Eventually, this game will get us," she said. "It always does. There's only one way it ends."

"I'm all right with that," Larissa said.

"Are you sure?"

Larissa looked at her—her expensive clothes, her perfect hair, her gloved hand already on the handle of the door, ready to walk out and disappear.

"When did you know you wanted to fight back?" she said. "What was the moment you decided?"

"I'm not sure," Tatyana said.

Larissa shook her head. "Sure you are."

Tatyana sighed. "I remember when my mother died."

Larissa nodded.

"I was only four, but I was trapped in the apartment with her. Days passed before anyone came."

"Do you think it's possible to make a decision like that so young?" Larissa said.

"I don't know," Tatyana said, "but I know that was the beginning for me."

Larissa nodded.

"Whoever our parents were," Tatyana said, "they were fighting against something. When I find our father's file, I'll know what it was."

"I don't care if this fight ends up costing my life," Larissa said. "I'm ready."

Tatyana opened the door. She was about to leave and then stopped. "If I ever get burned," she said, "I'll put a matchbook in the locker. If you see that, don't wait, don't look for me—run."

"Run?"

Tatyana nodded. "Run for your life." She left, shutting the door behind her.

Larissa went to the window and watched her a few moments later cross the street and get into her car. That night was the first and last time she ever set eyes on her sister. Her half-sister. She'd thought she was alone in the world, and then Tatyana had walked into it, and everything changed.

And from that day on, Larissa fed information back to Tatyana with the diligence and courage of a true fighter. Whatever she heard, she went to the locker and wrote it in the notebook. It took her time to learn what was valuable. She made reports about foreigners, businessmen, Russian politicians, and gradually, Tatyana directed her toward what she needed most.

Most of it seemed trivial. She couldn't imagine how Tatyana would make use of any of it. But she always knew that eventually, something really big would come her way.

And when it did, she would be ready.

She hadn't figured on something happening to Tatyana first. She realized now that she'd always refused to allow herself to think of the possibility of Tatyana being harmed. It wasn't logical. Tatyana was playing an even more dangerous game than she was. They both knew something would happen to one of them eventually. Larissa had only ever allowed for the possibility that her turn would come first. The thought of being without Tatyana was worse than the idea of being caught by the GRU.

She stopped walking and took the matchbook from her pocket. The word '*Europa*' was written on it, and inside, written in pen, a Moscow phone number.

She knew what the matchbook meant. It meant 'run'.

But the phone number. Tatyana had never mentioned that.

She crossed the street to the hotel, and a doorman in a black coat and top hat opened the door for her.

The warmth of the lobby hit her. She took a deep breath

and looked around. There was a fancy bar, but it was closed. To her right was the check-in desk and concierge, and across the lobby were the elevators. Just before the elevators were some old-fashioned payphones, and Larissa walked over to them and inserted a coin. She dialed the number on the matchbook and waited.

A recorded voice told her to wait while her call was directed, and she heard the clicks and tones of an analog connection being made. The dial tone changed to a steady beep, like a line that had gone dead, and Larissa waited, holding her breath.

If this didn't work, she would be alone. She would have to flee the country and never look back. She would never know what had happened to Tatyana. She wouldn't even know if she was alive.

This was her last chance, the last thin thread connecting her to the only family she had in the world.

And then a voice answered.

13

Tatyana heard rustling by her bedroom door and walked over, opening it suddenly. The Pushkin scholar was standing there in his socks and briefs, the top few buttons of his shirt open.

"What do you think you're doing?" she said, taken aback.

"I... I don't know."

"Who are you?"

"I told you at dinner."

She looked at him. It didn't make sense that anyone could have followed her from Moscow. She'd been too careful. And besides, this wasn't how GRU assassins operated.

"I told you I'm a married woman," she said.

"I thought I might be able to help you prepare for your interview tomorrow."

"Really?" she said. It didn't serve her purpose in any way to kill someone unnecessarily, it would only draw unwanted attention, but this man was making the prospect difficult to resist.

"I know," the man said. "I shouldn't be here. I'm sorry."

"I'm going to close this door," Tatyana said, "and this better be the last time I set eyes on you."

He nodded.

"If I see you again, I'm going to cause trouble."

He seemed to have gotten the message.

She shut the door and went back to her bed. She was unsettled. The man bothered her. He was strange. Men like that were the reason women didn't travel alone. She went to the window and pulled back the curtain. The single bulb of a streetlamp lit the scene. There was a bar across the street, and a few people still seemed to be inside. Two decrepit taxis waited outside, the drivers smoking in their seats, engines running, talking to each other through their open windows.

Tatyana lit a cigarette. She sat by the window and watched a drunk stumble out of the bar and get into a taxi. In the morning, she would be leaving this country behind, maybe forever. It was her home, her Motherland, the land of her birth. She thought about the things she would miss. Small things. There weren't that many of them.

She was about to go back to bed when she heard a beep from her backpack. She froze, her cigarette an inch from her mouth.

When it beeped a second time, she stood up and grabbed the backpack. She found the phone and looked at the screen. There was an incoming call. She went to the door and confirmed that the man was gone. Then she went back to the window and looked outside. Everything was as it had been.

Her heart pounding, she answered the phone.

"Tatyana?" a worried voice said. It was Larissa. She was breathing rapidly. "Tatyana?" she gasped again, bursting into tears.

"Larissa, it's me."

"Oh, thank God."

"Are you all right?"

"I've got information," Larissa said, her voice trembling. She was speaking under her breath, and Tatyana immediately feared she was in danger.

"Where are you?"

"I'm in a hotel lobby. Close to the station."

"Are you all right? Are you safe?"

"Yes, I'm all right."

"Were there men at the train station?"

"No. No one. I was at work. I went to the train station to leave you a note, and I found the matchbook."

"I've been compromised, Larissa. You must never go back to the locker again. It's not safe."

"What happened?"

"You must never call me again. Do you hear me? Throw away the matchbook and forget you ever knew me. I'm burned."

"But Tatyana!"

"They're coming after me, Larissa. I've been found out. I've got to escape the country. You're on your own now, and you have to make sure no one ever connects you to me. You have to forget about me and never mention what we did to anyone."

"But I have information."

"Forget it, Larissa. Do you hear me? It's over. Forget all of it. Forget you ever met me."

"I can't, Tatyana. We're... blood."

"They'll kill you, Larissa. Do you hear me? For the sake of your life, burn this number and never contact me again."

"There's going to be an attack on the US embassy in Moscow," Larissa stammered.

Tatyana paused. She made to reply and stopped. She didn't know what to say.

"I was with a Chinese diplomat," Larissa said. "He was drunk. He said there's going to be an attack, and someone called the Polar Bear is behind it."

"The Polar Bear?"

"Yes. From the Lubyanka. He must be a Russian agent. He's a

large man. An albino. He wants to start a war with the Americans."

"Larissa, you can still walk away from all this."

"No. I told you I want to fight."

"We're burned, Larissa. It's over for us. Someone else will have to take up the fight."

"You can't just drop me like this," Larissa said. "You can't. You have no right. We're..."

"We're what?" Tatyana said.

"I thought we were family."

"If anyone ever hears you say that, they'll kill you."

"Don't do this, Tatyana. Don't just hang me out to dry. You can't."

Tatyana wanted to hang up, it was the only thing she could think of to keep Larissa safe, but something stopped her. It was the second time in as many days she was going against her instincts, breaking her own rules. "You'll have to fight without me," she said.

"I know."

"You're sure you can do that?"

"I've never been so sure of anything in my life."

Tatyana didn't know what to do. She felt something for Larissa she didn't feel for anyone else on earth. They *were* blood. They *were* family. They were sisters.

"This might cost you your life, Larissa."

"You'd do the same thing," Larissa said.

That much was true. Tatyana couldn't believe she was doing this, sending Larissa into the fray with no protection. "Larissa, what I'm about to tell you, don't write it down."

"I won't," Larissa said.

It terrified Tatyana. It risked the only person in the world she held dear. But she had to do it. "There's an apartment in Kapotnya," she said. "Remember this address." She gave Larissa the address of Lance's apartment, and her voice quivered with emotion when she thought of what might happen when Larissa went there.

"What's there?" Larissa said. "What will I find?"

"Do you speak English?"

"Yes," she said. "All dancers do."

"There's a man there," Tatyana said. "An American. Go to him."

"Can I trust him?"

"Give him my name. Tell him I sent you."

"He'll help me?"

"He'll be hard to speak to. He'll think you're GRU. The second you try to approach him, he might disappear."

"Disappear?"

"He might even kill you."

"What?"

"He's—how should I say this? *Unpredictable.*"

"What kind of man are you sending me to?"

"He's the only one who can help you. Go to him, but approach cautiously. Tell him what you heard, and tell him you need to get out of the country."

"Will you tell him I'm coming?"

"He's off the grid. I can't contact him."

"What if he doesn't help me, Tatyana? What if I scare him off, and he disappears?"

"I'm sorry, Larissa."

"What does that mean?"

"If he doesn't help you, you'll be on your own."

"Tatyana!" Larissa said, her voice cracking.

"I'm sorry," Tatyana said again.

"Give me his name, at least."

Tatyana paused.

"You have to give me his name."

"It's Lance Spector." Tatyana hung up the phone and held it

against her chest. Taking that call changed everything. She was exposed now. The phone was traceable.

She needed to move, and she needed to do it quickly.

She packed her things and slipped silently out of her room into the hallway. There was no one there. She went down the stairs, every step creaking torturously, and let herself out the front door.

She looked around the front of the building to make sure no one was there. The only sign of life was the bar. She crossed the street and approached the nearest taxi. The driver was an old man. The car was battered and rusty. A phone number was stenciled on the door.

The driver had his window open, and Tatyana said, "Can you give me a ride to Ustavnoye?"

He looked her up and down. "Now?" he said. He was used to driving drunks home after the bar closed. Ustavnoye was twenty miles away. "That's a bad road to be out on at night," he said.

"I can pay double," she said.

The man didn't seem to have any teeth, and he smacked his lips while he thought about it.

Tatyana counted out a thousand rubles—not a crazy amount, not enough to attract attention, but more than any cab ride in the area would cost.

"There's nothing out that way, you know," the driver said.

"I'm crossing the border."

He sighed. "It's such a treacherous road at night," he said again.

She counted out another thousand rubles and handed him the money.

He nodded to the seat next to him, and she got in. The drive took about thirty minutes, and he was right about it being a bad road. It was narrow and windy, but it had been kept clear by the plows, and apart from a few stretches where they almost got stuck, they made it to the village of Ustavnoye without incident.

Just before the border post, she told him to pull over. The place was quiet. There were a few farmhouses in the surrounding hills, but they were pitch black. She wondered if they had electricity. There were orchards on the slopes, the branches of the trees completely bare, and she could hear a dog barking. It wasn't snowing, but the temperature was below zero, and she wasn't dressed for it.

The old man turned and looked at her. "There's nothing here," he said. "I'll take you to the border post."

"No, this will do," she said, although she didn't open her door.

She knew the border post was about a mile ahead, a desolate little building with two guards sleeping on the job. The walk would be cold.

"You don't want to cross in the forest," the old man said. "Not at night."

He knew something was up. He thought she was going to sneak across. It wasn't unheard of. The border charged duties, and traders would avoid those if they could. For them, a walk in the woods was worth it.

"I'm not going to cross in the forest," she said.

He nodded. She certainly didn't look ready for a hike. He looked her over one last time—her fancy clothes, her impractical coat. "I can't leave you out here," he said.

"Yes, you can," she said. "I know the guards at this post. They're waiting for me."

"If that was true, you'd let me drive you all the way."

She looked at him blankly, saying nothing. He could make this as easy or as difficult as he wanted.

After a moment, he shook his head. "Please don't go through the forest. There are wolves out there. We find dead bodies every spring when the ground thaws."

"I assure you," Tatyana said, "the wolves in Moscow are worse."

He sighed. He knew she was up to something, but it was out of his hands. What he was waiting for now was more money to pay for his silence. Tatyana reached into her purse and pulled out her cigarettes. She lit one and opened the window.

This part was important. If she offered too much, she'd scare him. And if she offered too quickly, he'd want more.

"I'll give you fifty euros if you forget you brought me here."

"A hundred," the old man said.

"Seventy-five."

"A hundred."

She handed him the money and got out of the car.

"Good luck," he said to her.

"Drive carefully," she said.

She began walking the mile to the border crossing, and it wasn't long before she could see its lights. There wasn't much to the place—a small brick building for the Russian border guards and another a hundred yards on for the Belarusians. She approached the Russian guardhouse, smoking as she strode past a sign telling her she was exiting federation territory. She ducked under the vehicle barrier and stopped.

She listened. The place was entirely silent. The snow on the road was clean, unsullied by traffic. No one had used the crossing in hours.

The guards were asleep. They were always asleep. Most of them had full-time day jobs they never declared. A single desk lamp lit the interior of the office. She stood outside and waited for something to happen, for someone to say something, but no one did. There was a security camera above the traffic barrier, and she looked right at it. She wasn't worried about that now. She was tempted to blow it a kiss, one final act of defiance, but she merely flicked her cigarette butt at it.

A hundred yards ahead of her was the second barrier. Next to it was the Belarusian flag and a sign that informed arrivals of Belarusian national highway speed limits. They were the same as in Russia.

The Belarusian guardhouse was the same as the Russian one. Both were built hastily after the Soviet break up in 1991, and the administrators on both sides drew from the same standardized design they'd been given by the Buildings Bureau in Moscow decades earlier.

Between the two barriers was nothing but a patch of clean, white snow.

This was what it was like, she thought. This was what it meant to defect, to turn her back on the country of her birth, to betray the Motherland.

She walked toward the Belarusian barrier, and the only sound was the crunch of snow beneath her feet.

Long ago, she'd forced herself to memorize the terrain and configuration of every Russian border crossing. There were hundreds of them, stretching from Europe to China and North Korea. She'd always known she'd be crossing one of them under circumstances like these.

She knew that the first village on the Belarusian side was Gorbachevo, a tiny farming community about three kilometers to the west. She looked at the horizon. The sun would rise before she got there.

Traffic would pick up then.

In Gorbachevo, she would pay a local farmer to drive her to Rasony, the first town of any size, and from there, she'd catch a bus to the capital city, Minsk. The bus would stop at every little village along the way, taking over six hours to cover the two-hundred-mile journey.

She would be dropped off at Minsk's enormous railway station, a monument to the country's ruler that had taken over twenty years to construct and was now one of the largest passenger train stations in the world. At least in terms of raw square footage, it was. In terms of passengers, it barely registered.

She'd been there many times. She knew the GRU had access to its security cameras. She also knew they'd have someone waiting for her when she got there.

She couldn't worry about that now. One step at a time. She would slip through the station in the evening crowd, buy a ticket to Warsaw, and after another painfully slow journey that involved taking the train into a huge wooden warehouse at the Polish border, jacking up all the carriages, and re-gauging them so that they'd fit European tracks, she would be inside the European Union and NATO.

She'd breathe easy then. In Warsaw, she'd catch a high-speed connection to Berlin, and two hours later, she'd be in the German capital.

By then, she thought, she would have traveled, in reverse, the same journey the Wehrmacht made during Operation Barbarossa. It was a distance of eleven hundred miles and took the German war machine five months. By the time they were stopped at the bridge over the canal at Khimki station, millions of corpses lay in their tracks.

She didn't hate her country. She was proud of it. It was the Russians, not the British or the French or the Americans, who'd stopped Hitler. It was their sacrifice that saved the Allies. The West was used to thinking of the Soviets as an evil empire. She knew the truth was more complicated. Were it not for her country, the twentieth century may well have belonged to Hitler and not America.

She picked up her pace. She felt she was already there, in Europe, free, when a set of floodlights came on, lighting the snow on the ground so brightly she had to shield her eyes.

She stopped walking.

Before her, her shadow stretched out like it was the personification of all her hopes for the future.

Behind her, dogs were barking.

"Halt!" a voice yelled. "Halt, or I'll shoot!"

14

L ance arrived at the bar slightly earlier than usual, and there were a few other customers there.

"The usual?" the woman said.

He'd come the night before, after putting Tatyana on the train, and she'd brought a bottle of vodka to the table without his asking. They'd ended up working their way through it together.

He nodded and sat in his usual spot by the window.

She brought him his soup and coffee and then stood by the table looking at him. "How's your head?" she said.

He hadn't intended to drink, but when she'd opened the bottle, one shot quickly turned into more. It had been hard saying goodbye to Tatyana—harder than it should have been. "How's yours?" he said.

She laughed and went back to the bar. He watched her polish a glass. She looked up at him more than once.

She wasn't an attractive woman, but he found himself flirting with her all the same. It had even crossed his mind to take her up to the apartment and give her something to remember him by. He'd almost done it. He'd been drunk enough, Tatyana was gone, and the world was as cold and harsh and lonely as he'd ever known it.

But she'd said to him, "You can look at me like that, you can look all you want, but don't get any ideas."

It turned out she was married. She didn't wear her ring—she said the metal irritated her skin—but assured him she had a husband at home and that a woman who fooled around deserved all the misfortune she found.

Though, for all that, she did flirt a lot.

He looked at his soup. Now that Tatyana was out of the picture, he was ready to leave the city. He would wait for word from Roth that she was safe, but then he would go.

He had a life of his own in Montana to get back to. He even had a house guest, a girl called Sam. She was the daughter of one of the men in his former unit. That man had taken a bullet for him. In return, he'd promised to keep an eye on the girl, something he couldn't very well do if he was sipping vodka in a dingy Moscow bar with a woman who didn't wear her wedding ring.

He was troubled, though. Something wasn't right. They'd just assassinated three of the most powerful men in Russia, all members of the president's fabled inner circle, the Dead Hand. These were the men behind all of Russia's most aggressive policies. They played with fire, and people got burned. They didn't take to opposition kindly. But so far, there had been no response from the Kremlin. Nothing. Not a diplomatic peep.

Lance felt instinctively that something was going to happen, and it wasn't going to be pretty. The CIA would need someone on the ground. They had to be able to respond swiftly. But, he tried to remind himself, he didn't work for the agency anymore. It wasn't his problem. America and Russia had been at each other's throats since before he was born. The CIA had made it

this far without his help. Surely they'd make it through whatever happened next.

He glanced out the window and saw a beat-up old Volkswagen pulling up outside. There wasn't anything suspicious
about it, but he noticed the girl in the driver's seat. There was
something about her. She was painfully attractive, like something out of a fashion magazine, but that wasn't what caught his
attention. It was something else. Something he couldn't put his
finger on.

He watched her step out of the car and cross the street
toward the bar. He had a gun in his coat, and he moved his
hand slowly from the table to his lap in case he needed to reach
for it in a hurry.

He'd been trained long ago to notice things that were out of
the ordinary. Things that felt *off*. The agency called them
pattern interruptions, and he'd learned more than once that it
paid to be wary of them. This girl was a pattern interruption if
ever he'd seen one.

She wore a white bomber jacket and a skirt that was too
short for the weather. Black fishnet stockings rose above her
shoes, which were brown leather with a short heel and closed-
toe. They reminded him of the sort a tap dancer might wear in
an old movie.

She opened the door, and a gust of cold air whipped into
the bar with her. Everyone but Lance looked her way.

She was young, twenties, with bleached blonde hair and
showy makeup. She was dressed to get attention. Lance looked
down at his soup. She didn't seem to notice him as she walked
up to the bar to order a coffee.

"Is everything all right?" the bartender asked.

"Yes," she said. "Why?"

"You seem in a hurry."

The girl nodded. "I am in a hurry. I'll take that coffee to go."

The bartender began preparing the coffee, and Lance

watched the girl as she waited. He didn't know what to make of her. Nothing about her said GRU. They liked to use attractive women, but they didn't dress them like this. They didn't drive beat-up old cars. They didn't run out for coffee before a job.

He thought about getting her attention but held back.

The bartender brought the coffee with a few packets of sugar and milk, and the girl paid.

Every man in the bar watched her leave. They hadn't taken their eyes off her since she'd entered. A GRU agent couldn't work attracting that kind of attention.

She went back to the car and got in the driver's seat. Then she sat there, sipping her coffee and chain-smoking. She opened her window slightly and flicked ash through the crack.

Lance stayed where he was and watched.

After an hour, she got out of the car. She had her paper coffee cup in hand, and she threw it in a garbage can on the sidewalk. Then she walked up to the door of Lance's building and pressed the buzzer. He couldn't see which button she pressed. It might have been his.

Nothing happened. No one answered.

She carried a large purse and rooted through it. He saw her take a handgun from it and tuck it into the pocket of the bomber. Then she leaned against the wall and lit another cigarette.

When she'd finished the cigarette, she flicked it to the ground and went back to the car. She turned on the engine, presumably to warm up because she didn't pull out of the spot.

Lance watched everything. It was what they'd trained him to do. Above all else—the weapons training, the hand-to-hand combat, the computer hacking, the car hot-wiring, and lock-picking—what the CIA valued most was the ability to wait. To stay still, to remain silent, to watch, and to notice. That was what the job boiled down to.

He looked at the car and memorized the plate.

Who was this woman, he wondered. She could be GRU, but it sure didn't feel like it. The GRU didn't ring your door buzzer and wait outside.

This girl looked like she was waiting for someone.

"She got your attention, didn't she?" the bartender said. She'd come over to refill his coffee.

"Who?" he said.

"Very cute," she said, helping herself to one of his smokes.

"You ever see her before?" Lance said.

"I can't say that I have."

"Why did you ask if she was all right?"

"Didn't you see?"

"No."

"She's been crying."

Lance had only seen her face through the window and didn't notice the tears. "Are you sure?"

"Believe me," she said, "I know what smeared mascara looks like. I've seen more than my share of it."

"Do you think she was a..." Lance hesitated while he chose his words.

"*Prostitutka*?" the bartender said.

"I was going to say *naymit*," Lance said, which meant something more like 'working girl.'

"Aren't you a gentleman?" she said.

"Not really."

"You interested in having a good time?"

"I'm just curious."

The bartender shrugged. "She didn't give off the vibe of a hooker."

Lance looked out the window. The girl was getting back out of the car. She went to the building and lit another cigarette. This time, while she was standing outside, someone let themselves out the front door. The girl let them pass, then caught the door with her foot before it clicked shut. She threw her cigarette on the ground and reached into her pocket for the stashed gun.

Then, glancing up and down the street to make sure no one was watching, she slipped into the building.

15

Tatyana shut her eyes. She'd been anticipating this moment, dreading it. Now that it was there, it was almost a relief.

"Get down on your knees," the voice said from behind her.

She was between the two security barriers, in no man's land, and the Russian guards had dogs. The lights lit up the street like a stadium, bright as midday, and the Belarusians were coming to life too. She guessed there were no more than two Russian soldiers at the post, probably the same number of Belarusians.

The faster she acted, the less blood would be spilled.

She dropped to her knees and, as she did, reached into her coat and pulled out the Browning.

Ahead of her, two Belarusian soldiers came running out of their post. One had a rifle drawn, ready for action. The second stumbled. He seemed to be fastening his belt.

Behind her were the Russians.

She glanced to either side. The trees were densely packed. She could have lost the soldiers among them, but not the dogs. She had no desire to spend the night in the woods killing dogs.

"Just let me go," she said without turning her head. "Believe me when I say I have no desire to kill you."

"Kill us?" the nearer of the two soldiers behind her said.

"Are the dogs still tied up?" she said.

The soldiers stopped. They spoke to each other, but she couldn't make out what they were saying. They were about fifty meters back. She didn't hear the dogs.

Up ahead, the two Belarusians watched the scene unfold as if it had nothing whatsoever to do with them and never would. Had she walked ten yards closer to them, she'd be on their side of the line and would be their problem. But she hadn't.

"Just let me pass," she said again.

"You know we can't do that," the same soldier said. He was doing all the talking, and she listened carefully for the other one. She didn't want him going back to unleash the dogs.

"Just say I was never here," she said.

They laughed, and she could tell they were still together.

"At least take a vote on it," she said. "Your colleague shouldn't have to die because of your decision."

"Put your hands in the air," the speaker said. "That's enough talk."

His accent was like a peasant farmer in an old movie. She didn't move her hands. She knew he wouldn't shoot her in the back, and she felt she owed him one last chance to stand down. "You got a call from Moscow earlier today, didn't you?" she said.

"Stop talking and raise your hands."

"What did they say to you?"

"They said to keep our eyes open. That you were dangerous and a national security threat."

"Well," Tatyana said, watching the Belarusians, "they weren't lying."

"Put your hands in the air right now, or I'll shoot," the second soldier said. He was younger than the first. She could tell from his voice, which had a noticeable tremble. She knew that when she looked at his face—a few seconds hence, dead on the ground, staring at the sky with an eternal expression of surprise on his face—she would be looking at the face of a boy.

Those were the moments that haunted her, that flashed before her eyes when she least expected, that invaded her dreams. This boy's face would be with her forever, and there was nothing she could do to avoid it. "Is it just the two of you?" she said.

"What?"

"In the guard post? Is it just the two of you?"

"What is this?" the older said, his voice betraying doubt for the first time.

"I'm going to give you one last chance to stand down," she said. "Let me pass. Forget I was here. And no one gets hurt."

The man said nothing.

"What's wrong?" the younger said. "Why won't she raise her hands?"

"There's something wrong with her."

"Either I keep walking," Tatyana said, "or you both die here tonight."

The younger laughed nervously. She heard the other step toward her.

"I'm not threatening you," Tatyana said. "I'm telling you what's going to happen. I'm crossing this border tonight. You can't stop that. You can only decide whether you live or die."

"That's enough," he said, pulling a pair of handcuffs from his belt. She heard them clinking in his hand as he took the last few steps toward her.

"Please don't do this," she said.

He came closer, and she waited for his hand to reach her shoulder. Then, she turned suddenly and shot him point-blank in the chest. The look on his face was as if this was the last thing in the world he'd expected. She grabbed him by the vest and held him up to use as a shield. It wasn't her bullet that killed him, but the two in the back, fired by his colleague.

She held out the Browning and pointed it at the other soldier. He was even younger than she'd thought.

He hesitated a second, then fired another shot.

She pulled the trigger, and he dropped to the ground, the bullet cutting clear through his neck an inch above the collar of his vest. She watched to see if he moved, but the only movement was the blood that poured into the snow with the last pulsing beats of his heart.

She dropped the soldier she'd been holding and turned to look at the two Belarusians. "Don't call this in," she said.

The two men stood in the middle of the road staring at her. They didn't know what to do. She was still on Russian soil, and they were prohibited from firing over the line. But they were smart enough to see the inevitable fact that she would be their problem very soon.

She walked toward them. "Let me pass, and you'll never hear from me again."

One of them nodded at the bodies of the two dead Russians. "How do we explain that?" he said.

"Tell the truth. I shot them."

"And how do we explain that we let you walk right by us?"

"It's not your jurisdiction. I'm a Russian, and I shot them on Russian soil."

"Russia is our ally."

"Is that something you want to die for tonight?"

They looked at each other. They were no older than the Russians she'd just killed, and if they insisted, she'd shoot them both dead in an instant. The Browning was still in her hand, and she could see by the whiteness of their knuckles how tightly they were clenching their rifles. She was just a few feet from them, and the panic in their eyes grew with each step. If she stopped walking, even if she slowed down, they'd draw their guns and fire. But she strode toward them, and it was as if her momentum kept them paralyzed.

She was going to walk right past them without a shot being fired. She believed that.

But then the nearer of them panicked. He pulled up his rifle, a laborious maneuver that he didn't stand a chance of completing before a bullet hit his chest.

She dropped to her knee as the second man fired, then shot twice, hitting him both times in the chest.

She'd been expecting them to be wearing body armor, as the Russians had been, but neither was.

The nearer of them was still alive. One look told her he hadn't yet seen his eighteenth birthday. She leaned down and held him while he took his final breath.

"Sleep," she whispered. "Everything's going to be all right."

When he was gone, she stood up and listened to the night. The air was still. Her breath billowed. All she could hear were the dogs, still in their enclosure behind the Russian guard post.

She walked back through the snow to the Russian guard post and put a bullet in the security camera. Inside the office, she found an out-of-date analog tape system that was being used to store the footage.

She took the current tape out of the recorder, unspooled it, and lit it on fire. She searched the office to make sure she hadn't missed any other surveillance equipment.

Then she went to the Belarusian post and searched their office. They didn't even have a tape system. The only surveillance was a logbook with a handwritten record of who'd crossed and when. There'd been no entries since the evening before.

There was a Belarusian police vehicle parked behind the post, and she found the keys in the desk in the office. There were also several detailed maps of the area, which she took and put in her coat. She went out to the car, sat inside, and turned the ignition. It took a few tries, but it started.

She pulled out onto the road slowly—it hadn't been plowed —and headed west.

16

L ance put some money on the table and left the bar. He went out onto the street and crossed to the Volkswagen. It was unlocked, and he got into the driver's seat. Apart from cigarette ash on the center console, it was empty. The glove box was empty also. He reached under the steering column and opened the hood. Then he went to the front and disconnected the battery.

He left the car and walked to the building, letting himself in quietly. No one was in the hall, and he climbed the stairs to the third floor. From the stairs, he could hear the woman on the landing above, her footsteps causing the floor to creak.

He climbed the remaining steps and drew his gun. Peering carefully around the banister, he saw her outside his door, gun in hand. She was looking at the door, and he didn't know if she intended to knock or shoot it open.

He waited.

She raised her hand and rapped on the door.

He stepped up onto the landing behind her and said, "Drop the gun."

She froze.

"Go on," he said. "Put it down."

"This isn't what it looks like," she said.

"Go ahead and put down the gun," he said again.

She held the gun so that the trigger guard rested on her thumb.

"Put it on the ground. I won't say it again."

She bent down and let it fall to the floor.

"The purse too."

She placed the purse next to it.

"Turn around," he said.

She turned to face him, and he almost dropped his gun.

She noticed the shock on his face. "What is it?" she said.

It was his first chance to get a good look at her, and he realized why she'd stood out before. Apart from the bleached hair and provocative clothing, she could have been Tatyana's twin. The resemblance was unmistakable.

His gun was still pointed at her, and she eyed it nervously.

"Please," she said.

"Stop talking."

He reached into his pocket, found the apartment keys, and threw them to her. "Open the door."

She turned around and unlocked it, her hands shaking.

"Get inside," he said.

She stepped forward, and he followed her into the apartment. He picked up her gun and purse on the way and kicked the door shut behind him. "Sit down," he said.

There was a sofa against the wall, and she sat on it, facing him.

"Is anyone else coming?" he said.

She shook her head.

"Tell me why I don't shoot you right now."

"Don't," she gasped. "Please."

"Who are you?"

"My name is Larissa."

"Larissa what?"

"Chipovskaya."

"What are you doing here?"

"Tatyana sent me."

Lance felt his pulse pound. "I don't know a Tatyana?"

"Tatyana Aleksandrova."

"Never heard of her."

Larissa switched to English. "Please," she said again. "Your name is Lance Spector. Tatyana gave me the address of this apartment. She told me to come here and speak to you."

Lance went to the window and looked down at the street below. This could be a trap. Someone else might be watching the entire thing. If it was a trap, they couldn't have found a more perfect bait.

He got some cable ties from the kitchen and threw them to her. "Put those on."

She looked at the ties but hesitated. "Don't make me wear these."

He said nothing and, reluctantly, she put a tie around her wrists and pulled it with her teeth.

"You came looking for me," he said to her.

"This isn't what it looks like," she said for the second time.

"And what does it look like?"

"I came to talk to you."

"With a gun?"

"It's not even loaded," she said. "I don't know how to use it. I stole it from work."

He checked, and it was true. It didn't look like it had fired a single bullet in its life. "You've been crying," he said.

She wiped her eyes awkwardly with her tied hands. "Yes."

"Why?"

"Why do you think?"

"Because you're scared?"

"Of course I'm scared. What are you, an idiot?"

Lance looked at her and tapped his finger against the kitchen counter. "Start talking," he said.

"Tatyana said you'd help me."

"Why should I believe you?"

"Why else would I come?"

"I don't know."

"How would I know where to find you?"

His face grew dark. "If something's happened to her," he said.

"What?"

"If you're part of some sting."

"No. I'm alone. Tatyana told me she was burned. She said I needed help."

"When did she tell you this?"

"Last night."

"How did she contact you?"

Larissa nodded to her purse. "There's a matchbook in there."

Lance looked in the purse and found the matchbook.

"I called the number on it," she said. "Tatyana answered."

"All right."

"Call it for yourself."

"It won't work now."

"What?"

"She'll have destroyed the phone. At least, I hope she has. She's been taking a lot of risks on your behalf."

"You're a friend of hers?" Larissa said.

"Let's figure out who you are first."

"I met her two years ago," Larissa said. "She came to me. She told me our fathers served on the same submarine."

"The sub that sank?"

Larissa seemed surprised that he knew that. Lance looked at her very closely. She was so like Tatyana that they had to be family. "You look like her," he said.

"I know."

"Why?"

"Because..." she said, hesitating.

"Because what?"

"We never really got into it."

"Got into what?"

"Our parents. Our mothers."

"What about them?"

"Our mothers were friends. That much is clear. But Tatyana implied that maybe we shared a father."

"They were both sleeping with the same sailor?"

"It seems that way," she said. The subject seemed to agitate her.

"But you don't know for sure."

"Neither of us ever met our fathers." Larissa hesitated a second, then corrected herself. "Our father," she said.

"I see."

"It seems we're half-sisters."

"But you never found out who your father was?"

"I didn't. If Tatyana knows, she never told me."

"You didn't ask?"

"We only ever met one time—the night she recruited me. Apart from the messages I wrote her, we never spoke again until last night."

"You passed her messages?"

"Yes."

"Where?" Lance said, already knowing the answer.

"There's a locker at Leningradsky Station."

"What platform?"

"The Khimki platform."

He nodded. It made sense. It was certainly one way of doing things. If Tatyana was afraid of being betrayed, why not turn to someone related to her?

"What made you valuable to Tatyana?"

"We trusted each other."

"I mean, what access did you have that she was interested in?"

"I work at a gentleman's club close to the Kremlin."

"You're a stripper?"

Her eyes flashed. "I'm a dancer."

"I beg your pardon," Lance said.

Larissa noticed the sarcasm and fixed him in her gaze, a challenge in her eyes that dared him to say more.

"So, Tatyana told you she was burned?" he said after a pause.

"Yes. She said she was leaving Russia and that I should too. She said if anyone found out I'd been helping her, they'd kill me."

"And she said I would help you get out?"

Larissa shook her head.

"She didn't say that?"

"That's not why I'm here."

"Then why are you here?"

"Because of what I heard."

"Which was?"

She took a breath. "There's going to be a major attack on the American embassy in Moscow."

"What?"

"It's true."

"How do you know that?"

She didn't answer.

"Larissa!" he snapped.

"The club I work in," she said reluctantly, "powerful men go there. Politicians. Businessmen. It's very close to the Lubyanka."

"And you worked there when Tatyana came to you?"

"Yes."

"You just happened to be working where the most powerful men in Russia blow off steam?"

"Yes," she said.

"That's convenient."

She was agitated. She hadn't expected to be challenged like this. "It's the truth," she said. "I worked there when she found me. If you think this is some kind of setup, fine. I'll leave, and you'll never see me again."

He looked at her. Something in the eyes. He knew it wasn't a lie. He knew what it was like to be tricked by appearances, and this wasn't that. This girl shared a father with Tatyana. He'd stake his life on it.

He put the gun back in his coat and took out a small folding knife. When he stepped toward her, she recoiled, and she resisted when he grabbed her arm. He ignored the protest and cut the cable tie from her wrists.

"Thank you," she said, rubbing them.

"You overheard someone planning an attack on the embassy?" he said.

"They weren't planning it," she said. She was breathing rapidly. Scared.

"Take it easy," Lance said. "I'm not going to hurt you."

She cleared her throat. "The man I met was Chinese. He was bragging about the attack. He said he'd been in the Lubyanka and that America was going to pay for its arrogance."

"And you went to the locker."

"Yes. I went to tell Tatyana, and that's when I found the matchbook. That was our signal that she'd been burned and that I was to walk away."

"Walk away from what?"

"Everything. It meant she was done, and I was alone."

"And you panicked?"

"Of course, I panicked. And that's when I saw the phone number. We'd never discussed that, but when I saw it, I knew she meant for me to call."

"Did it ever cross your mind that this was all a trap?" Lance said.

"What sort of trap?"

"Someone comes in and gives you the scoop of the century? Just like that, for no reason? This could be a ploy to get to Tatyana or to get to me."

"I don't know," Larissa said. "You're the professional. If it looks like a trap to you, then do what you need to do. I'm just a stripper."

"A dancer," he said.

She weighed what he said, unsure whether it was meant as a compliment or an insult. "So what do we do?" she said.

"I say we both leave this building, walk away in opposite directions, and never see each other again."

Larissa looked at him blankly.

"Doesn't work for you?"

"This isn't a trap," she said.

"You don't know if it is or not."

"Maybe," Larissa said, "but I know men. I might not be a spy like you, but you can bet your ass I know men better than you ever will."

Lance raised an eyebrow. "Maybe you have a point."

"This guy wasn't lying," she said. "I saw how much he drank. I felt how his body reacted to the alcohol. His clammy skin. His breath. His flaccid—"

"I get the picture."

"I'm just saying, it's hard to lie to someone when they're that close."

"But you manage to do it."

"I'm a professional."

Lance sighed. This wasn't good. It was unexpected, out of the blue, and he did not like surprises. But he couldn't turn this woman away. It wasn't just loyalty to Tatyana. If she was right, if someone really was planning an attack on the embassy, then he had to look into it.

There was a chair by the sofa, and he sat on it, facing Larissa. He pulled his cigarettes from his pocket and lit one.

"Do you mind?" Larissa said.

Lance gave her the one he'd just lit and put another in his mouth.

"You understood," he said, thinking how to put it. "You knew that the information you were passing to Tatyana...."

"I understood that it was off the books if that's what you mean. I understood that we were fighting against Russia. Not for it."

"How did you know that?"

"How does anyone know anything?"

"What does that mean?"

Larissa exhaled smoke. "We understood each other. We didn't have to spell things out."

"So, you called the number on the matchbook?"

"I knew I was supposed to walk away, but the information I have, it's big. It could lead to war."

"Tell me exactly what you heard," Lance said.

She looked around the room as if suddenly afraid someone might be listening.

"We're alone," Lance said.

"What I heard..." she said, then leaned up and looked out the window behind her.

"Are you expecting someone?"

"No, I'm just...."

"Scared?"

She sighed. "I trust Tatyana. That's the only reason I'm here."

"Then tell me what you heard because we don't have time for games."

"All I know is they're planning an attack."

"Who is?"

"The man at the club. He said he was at the Lubyanka with someone named the Polar Bear."

"The Polar Bear?"

"A big guy."

"A Russian?"

"He never said he was Russian, but that's what I assumed. Who else would meet him at the Lubyanka?"

"All right, so he met with this big guy."

"He's albino."

"The Chinese guy?"

"No, the Russian."

Lance nodded. "All right," he said. "He's a big, Russian albino who works in the Lubyanka?"

"Do you know him?"

"No," Lance said, "but it won't take a team of detectives to find him."

Larissa nodded.

"What about the Chinese guy?" Lance said. "What did he look like?"

"Like a typical businessman. Nothing out of the ordinary. His suit was expensive, but his manners weren't fancy. He was really drunk."

"What else?"

"He sweat. A lot. The more he drank, the more he sweat."

"What else?"

"He had money. I recognized the watch."

"Did he give you his name?"

"No, but he said he was from Beijing."

"What about age, weight? I need everything."

"He was like your average guy. Fifty maybe. Not in perfect shape but not too out of shape either."

"All right, so he told you there was going to be an attack on the Moscow embassy?"

"He said it was going to start a war. He was happy about it. Like that was the point."

"Anything else?" Lance said. "Anything at all? Try to think."

Larissa shrugged. "He said America was going to be put in its place."

Lance's eyes narrowed. "Well," he said, "we'll see about that."

17

T he Russian president, Vladimir Molotov, looked at his watch irritably.

Medvedev was late.

He tapped his cigar against the edge of a gold ashtray, and an inch of perfectly formed ash broke off. The ashtray was unique, a treasure handmade in the Vuelta Abajo by Cuban artisans. It had been a gift from Fidel Castro to Nikita Khrushchev after the Cuban missile crisis and, if the legend was to be believed, was made of Incan gold plundered by Pizzaro himself.

The president cracked his knuckles. He didn't know what to do with himself. He was a man who waited for no one, and no one dared make him wait.

No one, that was, except the insolent Mikhail Medvedev.

Thirty minutes already. It was unheard of. If it had been anyone else, there was no way he would have tolerated it. Medvedev was arrogant, he was power-hungry, his greed was legendary, outstripped only by his ambition. There were times the president seriously fantasized about killing him. He was a cancer, and all cancers metastasized eventually. But he served a purpose. He was useful. For now.

The president looked again at his watch and flicked more ash in the tray. Russia was not the power it had once been. The economy was a shambles, riddled with corruption. The military was outdated, a shadow of its former self. But had he allowed things to slip so far that a common thug could keep him waiting?

He was still president, and he had something other world leaders completely lacked. He had *real* personal power. He could extend his term of office at will. He could plunder the nation's coffers. He could kill his enemies, reward his allies, piss on the graves of national heroes, and there wasn't a man in the country who could say one word about it.

He cared nothing about polls, votes, campaign contributions, or the news cycle. He didn't worry about impeachment, parliamentary oversight, human rights, civil rights, or protests. He was a king. An emperor. There was no other leader on earth like him. And yet, here he was, twiddling his thumbs.

He wondered if the US president waited for his underlings, then scoffed aloud to himself. Of course they did. American presidents were impotent eunuchs. Their navy may have had more aircraft carriers, but what use were those to men who were voted out of office before they ever grew the balls to use them? Presidents didn't rule. They couldn't fire a single bullet without congressional say-so. And when their term came to an end? Hah! They were nothing. Less than nothing. A former president would struggle even to get his wife an invite to a naval academy luncheon.

There was nothing so pathetic. American presidents were a dime a dozen. He had nothing but contempt for them, and had already, in his twenty years in office, sat across the table from four of them. They came and went like the seasons, and so did their administrations, their strategic thinking, their entire doctrine. How could they fight like that? How could they think for a second it was enough? The contest between Moscow and Washington was a chess match, decades in the making. Every time the Americans held an election, it was as if their player had to relearn all the rules of the game from scratch.

And what was more, everything they did, every move they made, every battle they fought, and soldier they put in the field, was predicated entirely on short-term domestic issues. The Pentagon frittered away fortunes basing procurement decisions on which arms manufacturers were located in electoral battleground states, and which senators sat on which committees, and which corporations made the largest campaign contributions.

And they had the nerve to speak of corruption.

They put everything backward. They put politics and money above even the lives of soldiers. If that was what they meant by democracy and the rule of law, they could keep it.

Russia was on a path to reclaim not just its ability to threaten the West, but to fight and win. The democracies were in terminal decline, their war-fighting capability eroding by the day, giving way to decadence and weakness. If America were Athens, Russia would be Sparta. Where they had lawyers and politicians and activists, he would have soldiers.

Vladimir Molotov believed he'd been put on earth to achieve one thing—to restore Russia to greatness. He would rebuild its vast army, the army of Stalin, the army that defeated Napoleon and stopped Hitler in his tracks, and when that goal was achieved, he would use it to crush the Americans, the West, and their entire way of life.

He was a warrior, a man ordained for greatness, a god, and his opponents were nothing more than pencil-pushers, lawyers, *servants* of the people. They were mascots, utterly irrelevant, like the mayors of small towns who were hauled out to cut ribbons and wave from parade floats at the fall fair.

They were not lions, they were sheep, weaker than weak, and everything they held dear would turn to ash in their mouths.

Vladimir looked at his watch again and couldn't believe how long he'd been waiting. He should make an example of Medvedev, he thought. Teach him some manners. How could he expect to be treated like a king if he did not act like one? How could he expect respect if he did not punish the disrespectful?

His cigar was coming to an end, and he threw it into the ashtray and went to the bar cart. He had a selection of the finest vodkas in the world, lined up in crystal bottles and decanters that glittered in the sunlight from the window. He chose one and called his servant for ice. Then he slumped into his leather chair by the fire and stared at the flames. Sitting there in his flamboyant suit, the glass elegantly balanced in his hand, he looked like a mafioso in a Hollywood movie. He'd always had a weakness for gangster movies. He believed Scorsese was a genius. When Vladimir pictured power, he pictured Robert De Niro in *Casino*. Indeed, he'd spent years modeling his public persona on De Niro's portrayal in that film. Every mannerism, every tick, every facial gesture, he worked on in front of a mirror until he had it down.

To Vladimir, a man was only as powerful as he acted, and that included the way he held himself, the way he drew from a cigar or swished his vodka so that the ice clinked on the glass.

Photos over the course of his career showed a gradual shift from a stiff KGB officer to the swaggering world leader of today, famous for his slicked-back hair and flamboyant gold jewelry.

He was the first man since the days of the tsar to walk the corridors of the Kremlin dressed in anything other than bland, anonymous proletariat business suits. Instead, he had Gucci and Tom Ford send tailors to conduct personal style consultations. At a recent summit, he stunned audiences in a wine-red velvet blazer, matching pants, and yellow shirt. During the photo-op afterward, he posed with the bland German Chancellor, deliberately making zero effort to keep his cigar smoke from her face.

That was what power looked like.

The image sent a carefully crafted message to the world. It said, watch your back. Russia's humiliation is over. Change is coming.

American presidents went on tours kissing babies and shaking hands with old ladies outside churches. Vladimir, just in the previous month, had been filmed for national television driving a forty-six-ton T-90 tank across a frozen lake in Nizhny Tagil. He trained for three weeks to do it, even learning to aim and fire the 125mm smoothbore cannon, which he did for the cameras, successfully hitting a target five kilometers away.

In Russia, strongmen always ruled. That was what the people understood. That was what they demanded. And if, like the tsar, the leader was overthrown, it only meant he had never been strong enough to hold the position in the first place.

It was the Russian way. It created strength where there would otherwise be only weakness and humiliation. But it also meant men like Medvedev were needed. Such men were distasteful. They were ugly. But there was dirty work to be done, and they weren't afraid to do it. Men like Medvedev culled the herd. They took out rising threats and made it impossible for newcomers to challenge the prevailing regime. Molotov surrounded himself with such monsters. The Dead Hand was a nest of them, a nest of utter vipers, and Medvedev was the worst of the lot. He was a vicious dog, and Molotov had no doubt, none, that one day, he would try to bite the hand that fed him.

Molotov watched carefully for that day, the day he brought Medvedev out to the cold and shot him like the dog he was.

The servant arrived with the ice bucket, and Vladimir picked up two perfect cubes with the tongs and dropped them in his glass. He heard vehicles outside and went to the window. A bodyguard stood outside, his back turned, watching over the snow-covered lawn of the Novo-Ogaryovo presidential estate. Six armored cars were coming down the driveway, preceded by federal police cruisers, their lights flashing.

It was Medvedev's convoy.

The dog had finally arrived.

18

Sandra Shrader had been NSA director precisely one week and still wasn't sure she was up to the job. On a technical level, she was the best of the best, but the politics, the intrigues, the senate hearings—that was a world she had no knowledge of. The president had gone to bat for her, coming out strongly in support of her confirmation, but that didn't stop the nagging doubts in the back of her mind.

The NSA was responsible for overseeing the collection of a truly staggering amount of data, more than any other organization on the planet, and interpreting it felt at times like trying to divine the future from tea leaves.

Those at the top of the intelligence community were now convinced that the next major attack against the United States could be foreseen in the terabytes of data gathered by the NSA every second. But Sandra knew the challenge wasn't in getting enough data but in making sense of it.

The agency had completed construction of the Mission Data Repository in the Utah desert, and expectations were sky-high. The chairman of the Senate Intelligence Committee just wrote an op-ed for *The Times* in which he said that given the nation's upgraded data gathering abilities, a repeat of 9/11 was now inconceivable.

Sandra almost threw up when she read it.

A server farm in Utah was going to do precisely nothing to stop a terrorist attack. But the politicians were too star-struck by all the zeroes and ones in their technical reports to use their own common sense. They heard that their shiny new facility was capable of processing more than twelve exabytes of data, more data than had yet been created in all of human history, and thought it was going to magically make all their problems disappear.

It did give them power, after a fashion, but not the kind of power they thought it did, and certainly not the kind that would make newspaper headlines.

It was true they could track everything. Every swipe, click, tap, keystroke, camera movement, weather development, GPS location, transaction, timestamp, price change, radar blip, flight path, truck route, cab ride, and facial recognition match on the planet. Their ability to gather data was near infinite.

Their thinking was that with all that data, when the next big attack was being planned, the prelude, the build-up, the warning signs would be all too easy to spot. Money would move from one account to another. Plane tickets would be purchased. Explosives would be transported. Everything would have a number. Everything would have a row in a database. They were looking at what happened on 9/11 and preparing for it. It was said that all armies made the mistake of preparing for the last war, not the next. And that, Sandra believed, was the mistake they were making now.

She'd seen the data, the exabytes, raw zeroes and ones, racking up at an uncountable rate like the number on the national debt clock in New York City. It was gibberish. No one could make sense of it.

And yet, that was precisely what she'd been hired to do. Just seven days ago, after a fiercely contested confirmation hearing, she'd stood in front of the Senate Intelligence Committee, raised her right hand, and sworn to God and country that she would execute the role of NSA Director truthfully and faithfully.

It still felt surreal. She'd never been overly ambitious. She'd gone into intelligence work because the president had asked her to.

Before working for the government, she'd developed some of the most sophisticated algorithms ever to be deployed by Silicon Valley. The kinds of things that allowed computers to detect when a criminal suspect was lying, or a commercial pilot was drunk, or a teenage boy was looking for a specific kind of pornography.

She was good at what she did. She was good with numbers. But not with people, and certainly not with politics. Sure, she watched the news like any normal person, but the world of espionage and intrigue and national security was a foreign language to her. Her staff had spent the months leading up to her confirmation giving her a crash course in world politics. They'd succeeded in showing her that essentially anyone in the world could be considered a threat to the United States, and that she should therefore use the NSA to watch everything, everywhere, all the time.

A job that was easier said than done.

But at least that was a language she understood. As far as she was concerned, her job was pure data aggregation, divorced from any attempt to predict what outcomes that data would lead to. She would gather the information, but she would not interpret it. Making sense of the data, adding the names, the faces, the motives, seeing the specifics—that was the job of the CIA. She'd made the argument to the president and the senate, and her nomination had gone through nonetheless.

So here she was.

She wasn't one of those institutional warriors who wanted to destroy the CIA, although she knew some of her colleagues felt that way. In her view, it was the CIA who got the raw deal. They were the ones who had to strap guns to their waists and get on airplanes. They were the ones who said goodbye to their families when they went to work, not knowing if they'd come home.

The NSA was more of a digital weather forecaster, working from the safety of a government office, giving warning of brewing storms, trying to determine exactly where they would make landfall, but leaving the job of responding to others.

If the NSA was the National Weather Center, the CIA was the Coast Guard, the ones who actually got wet in the storm.

And Sandra was content to keep things that way.

It was five a.m., and she was staring at the vaulted oak ceiling above the enormous bed in the master suite of her new, six-bed, seven-bath, colonial home in Annapolis, Maryland. She'd been shocked when she saw how high home prices were in the area. Like everyone else in the tech industry, she'd thought nothing could compare to San Francisco's prices. But Annapolis was a place where the charm of the colonial era combined perfectly with proximity to Washington. Throw in the prestige of the Naval Academy, the best yacht clubs in the world, and some of the most exclusive golf courses in the country, and you had yourself a real little enclave.

Sandra went to the gym in the basement and spent forty minutes on the treadmill, flicking through cable news channels, only half paying attention to the latest round of disasters that kept the twenty-four-hour news cycle churning.

If there was one thing her prep for the senate hearings taught her, it was that the world was changing fast. The prevailing world order was being completely upended.

Not everyone in Washington saw it yet, but the counter-insurgency footing US forces had been on since 9/11 was out of date. When the Soviet Union collapsed in 1991, America emerged as the world's last remaining superpower. The nation's military strategists looked at the world and genuinely weren't sure where to direct their attention. The two Boeing 767's that flew into the World Trade Center on that September morning in 2001 gave them their answer.

For the next two decades, America saw the primary threats to its security coming not from other powerful states but from terrorist organizations. The Pentagon directed research into countering asymmetrical threats from fanatics, and took its eye off the rising military power of its main strategic rivals.

Russia and China had taken advantage of the intervening years to build their militaries, so that today, they posed a far greater challenge to America's long-term security than Islamic terrorist cells ever did.

The nation was transitioning from a position of unrivaled global power to one of being forced to compete with a rising China and a resurgent Russia.

The CIA's new director, Levi Roth, was making waves by reorienting the intelligence community to this new superpower footing. Many in the Pentagon did not appreciate being told they'd squandered the last twenty years chasing bogeymen in the Afghan mountains when they should have been watching China, but as far as Sandra could tell, Roth was correct. The future threat came from Moscow and Beijing, not caves in the Hindu Kush.

She showered and went to the kitchen, where her new automatic coffee maker had just finished brewing a pot of rich dark roast, supposedly customized to all her preferences. She poured herself a cup and took a sip. It tasted the same as every other cup of coffee she'd ever had.

She went to her office, opened the safe in the wall, and took out a blue file. In red ink, stenciled by hand on the cover, just like in the movies, were the words *'Top Secret'*.

It had been sent the night before by Roth himself and had been drafted by a young specialist named Laurel Everlane.

Roth had highlighted a section stating that within a decade, the US would no longer be able to rely on the presumption of overwhelming military might to sway its negotiations with rivals. It said that while Russia had lost its superpower status in the early nineties, it was well on its way to reclaiming that position. Decades of investment in capabilities aimed solely at harrying American influence in Eastern Europe, the Black Sea, the Baltic, the Caucasus, and the Middle East were paying off. At the same time, it was expected to continue acting as a rogue state, refusing to play by the rules of the international community, while simultaneously interfering heavily in American domestic affairs.

While it was not too late to contain Russia, the report regarded China as a power that the US would ultimately be unable to contain.

China had already broken out of its role as a regional power, and the report found that over the coming years, American influence in the Far East would steadily recede as China continued its blistering growth. In strategically contested flashpoints like Hong Kong, Taiwan, and the South China Sea, America would eventually have to come to terms with a China that was able to make demands and back them up with the threat of force.

Sandra noticed that the title of the next section had been changed. Previously, it read:

The USA vs. China
    A Statistical Comparison

Now it read:

Battle Scenarios China Could Win

It was a dramatic headline, and as she sipped her coffee, she wondered where this Laurel Everlane had come up with the balls to write such a report.

There were still powerful voices in the Pentagon who would destroy the career of anyone who dared suggest America could lose a war. Sandra knew they would come down particularly hard on a woman. They would bury her career beneath a mountain of vitriol, making her unhirable anywhere in Washington for the rest of her life.

The report went on to spell out exactly how China might win a hot war in certain contained scenarios. Taiwan was the one that jumped out most provocatively.

Since the Carter administration, the American position on Taiwan had been that if China made any move to retake it, the US would respond with force.

In 1996, the last time China seriously tested that commitment, President Clinton sent the largest naval force since the Vietnam war into the Taiwan Strait. Two carrier groups, Nimitz and Independence, entered the hundred-mile stretch of water that separated Taiwan from mainland China.

The Chinese had absolutely no way of standing up to such an overwhelming show of force and retreated to their own waters almost immediately.

The crisis garnered relatively little attention in the US, but in China, it was seminal. China had been humiliated by foreign powers for centuries. Its entire national trajectory since the end of their civil war in 1949 had been one long road back to regaining international respect. That a centuries-old nation of a billion people could be forced to back down because of just two foreign carrier groups was a humiliation Beijing could not accept.

In the years that followed, a huge portion of China's military investment went toward strengthening its position in a potential Taiwan Strait conflict. Demonstrating supremacy over that small stretch of water, which was right on its own doorstep and had the major cities of Xiamen, Quanzhou, and Fuzhou on its coast, was the first step toward claiming a position of global military power.

It became the litmus test of China's military rise. The day it could beat the Americans in the strait would be the day the world stopped belonging to the United States.

Sandra had to admit that the numbers spoke for themselves. Fourteen hundred ballistic missiles. Eight hundred cruise missiles. All with sufficient range to hit every US base in the region. China's missile capability could render Kadena Air Base on Okinawa, the most important American base in the region, unusable for the entirety of a four-month conflict.

That meant, despite US fifth-generation fighters being superior to their Chinese counterparts in every respect, the US would be unable to field them in sufficient numbers to achieve air supremacy.

Over China itself, the prospect of air supremacy was slimmer still. In 1996, the US had an airspace penetration capability that allowed it to fly jets over mainland China with impunity. Enormous upgrades to the Chinese surface-to-air missile system meant that even with their enhanced stealth capabilities, US supremacy over mainland China airspace was no longer a feasible objective.

The undeniable truth of the matter, which the report sought to hammer home, again and again, was that in any future conflict over the Taiwan Strait, America's options would be dramatically reduced from those that had been open to President Clinton in 1996.

America could still ultimately win such a fight, but the cost had risen so dramatically that it was doubtful the American people would pay the price of it. It would be akin to the war in Vietnam. The military would argue it was capable of delivering victory, but the people at home would stop supporting the fight before that victory could be achieved.

Sandra finished her coffee and put the report in her briefcase. Then she went to the window and checked the driveway. Having a Secret Service detail was something she still wasn't used to, and waiting for the driver to show up in the morning made her feel like a kid waiting for the school bus.

The black Cadillac sedan had pulled up a few minutes earlier, and she gave the driver a brief wave. He nodded back awkwardly.

"Lizzie!" she called out, making her way to the bottom of the staircase. "The driver is here."

Her fourteen-year-old daughter called down from her bedroom, "I told you I'd walk."

It was January, but it was a nice morning.

In San Francisco, Sandra would have had no difficulty allowing Lizzie to walk the few blocks to school. Now, she wasn't even sure it was allowed. She made a mental note to find out the full security protocols for her daughter.

Sandra was a single mother. Her husband had died of a rare form of cancer when Lizzie was four. Her daughter's well-being had been her only concern when the president offered her the job. She'd agonized over uprooting her at such a crucial time and moving her across the country, starting her in a new school, forcing her to make all new friends.

Thankfully, though, it appeared Lizzie was adapting to the change well and had already made a few friends.

Sandra went back to the kitchen and poured Lizzie a bowl of Cheerios. They looked so good she put her diet aside and poured herself some too.

When Lizzie stepped in, Sandra looked up at a daughter whose appearance was decidedly more mature than she'd expected. "Are you wearing makeup?" she said.

"Mom!" Lizzie gasped as if the very question was an affront to all things holy.

"Lizzie, you're fourteen. Is it even allowed?"

"All the girls wear makeup here," Lizzie said. Sandra was skeptical, and Lizzie added, "It's true, Mom. Girls are different here. They're more worldly."

Sandra doubted that too, but she didn't have time to argue about it. She had a full schedule when she got to the office, including a call with the president. "Eat up," she said. "We're sharing a ride."

"I said I'm going to walk."

Sandra sighed. "Are you walking with someone?"

"Yes, Lydia."

"Who's Lydia?"

"A friend."

"Fine," Sandra said, relenting. "You can walk today, but I'm going to have to find out what the rules are with the Secret Service. You know we have to obey certain safety protocols now."

Lizzie nodded.

Sandra was proud of her daughter. She'd done everything asked of her without complaint.

Lizzie shoveled cereal into her mouth and picked up the bowl to slurp down the last of the milk.

"I told you that's unladylike," Sandra said.

Lizzie put down the bowl and leaped from her stool. Her phone beeped, and she glanced at the screen. "Lydia's here," she said.

"What about my kiss?" Sandra said.

Lizzie came back and kissed her mother.

"Don't forget your coat," Sandra said.

Lizzie left by the front door, eyeing the Secret Service agent as she walked by. He gave her the same official-looking nod he'd given Sandra.

Sandra watched Lizzie go down the path and tried to see the girl she was meeting, but the hedge blocked her view.

She put on her own thick coat—January in Maryland was still something she was getting used to, grabbed her briefcase, and stepped out to the government-issue sedan in her driveway.

"Fort Meade?" the driver said when he got in.

"Thank you," she said.

19

President Molotov felt a shiver run down his spine as he watched Medvedev step out of his car. He dreaded these tête-à-têtes. Just the sight of the man gave him the creeps.

Mikhail Medvedev was known inside the depths of the Kremlin's national security apparatus by two nicknames. To most, he was the Polar Bear. He was seven feet tall, had a nose like a snout, and his skin and hair were as white as the driven snow. That, combined with the fact that his name was derived from the Russian word for *bear*, made it inevitable.

The president watched his every move, his thick mane of white hair, his face covered in coarse, unnaturally white stubble. It was the eyes that were the worst.

Were it not for his medical condition, they would have been blue. But they'd been stripped of so much pigment they appeared more red. Not just bloodshot, it was the actual iris. Those beady red eyes kept the president up at night, but there was something even darker about Medvedev, and that was the source of his second nickname.

To those who knew of his origins, of his pathological

inability to form human relationships or feel any sort of empathy, Mikhail Medvedev would always be known as the Orphan. There was only a handful of people who knew him by that name, and none of them, not the other members of the Dead Hand, or even the president himself, used it to his face.

Medvedev came from a dark chapter in Soviet history, a place that, even during the worst years of the Stalinist purges, was spoken of in hushed tones.

That place was the *Dom Rebyenka*, otherwise known as the Child's House, and it was from this abyss that Medvedev, the Orphan, had slithered.

His very existence put lie to the claim that the USSR had ever been a socialist paradise.

Mikhail's Child's House was Volgograd State Orphanage 161.

At the time of his birth, there were many reasons a child might end up in such a place. It could be as simple as both parents being dead, although there were better places to send such a child. It was more likely they were dissidents, accused of subversion, and as such, undeserving of the privilege of parenthood.

But in Mikhail's case, it was the fact he'd been deemed hopelessly and irredeemably defective.

The Children's Houses were a crime, a violence, a blot on the nation that was so shameful the government still refused even to admit they had existed.

Mikhail was brought to 161 from the maternity ward of the nearby children's hospital. Located in the same compound, the two buildings were separated by scarcely a hundred yards. In that distance, all the laws of man and nature ceased to apply, as if the two facilities were located in different universes, created by different gods.

Mikhail grew up knowing nothing of the world beyond the

walls of his ward other than what he could see through a small, barred window.

His mother, a seventeen-year-old factory worker, suffered chemical poisoning during her pregnancy. When Medvedev was born, he looked so unnatural that the nurses thought they were being kind when they refused to let her even see him.

He was taken directly from the mess between his mother's legs to the defectology lab at the hospital's eugenics department. There, a ruling was made on sight, and a two-page form was completed in triplicate by the lab nurse on duty. This brief document was enough to commit Mikhail to the Child's House for what was expected to be the entirety of a short, unhappy life.

The president first met Medvedev many years back when they were both still on the rise to power. Medvedev had applied to work for him, and after their initial meeting, Molotov immediately ordered up Medvedev's file. He'd been told the basic outlines of it before—everyone he hired was thoroughly vetted —but when he met the man face to face, he knew he had to see the file for himself.

When it arrived, it proved to be a rabbit hole. He read it a dozen times, then ordered up more documents—juvenile criminal reports, two unsolved murder cases, and even old tapes of state-made films documenting the practices in the Children's Houses.

He wanted to understand everything he could about this man before bringing him into the nest. He saw in him a unique tool with the potential to be uniquely useful in his rise to power. His curiosity in Medvedev became a compulsion, a morbid addiction. For some reason, he couldn't stop ordering more documents. It was like staring at the sun.

One of the government films had been made right there in Orphanage 161. It depicted row upon row of nurses, working like assembly-line workers, picking up babies with machine-like efficiency, taking off their diapers and replacing them with fresh ones before putting them back in their identical metal cots.

The president watched the film over and over. Late at night, when he was supposed to be sleeping, he was watching the tape, rewinding it, watching it again.

The nurses didn't coo. They didn't sing. They didn't smile or laugh or speak to each other. And the babies, one of which must have been Medvedev, didn't laugh or coo either.

In one scene, he caught a glimpse of a specially built attachment on the side of each cot, a pair of metal prongs with rubber covers. A formula bottle was placed on the prongs and held at an angle so that the babies, no matter how young, learned for themselves to suck at the nipple.

As they got older, the feeding method didn't change. The food changed, but not much, so that by the time he was four, Mikhail was sucking a gray-colored gruel from the same bottle, the nipple of which had been snipped to allow bigger chunks of food to pass through.

Mikhail spent the first years of his life entirely confined to his steel cot. Seasons came and went, but he remained, lying on his back, staring at the ceiling and sucking on the rubber nipple like a piece of livestock in a production facility.

The president remembered the first time he saw the American movie *The Matrix* and thought the directors hadn't been so very imaginative as they were given credit for.

Mikhail was walking from his limousine to the steps of the palace, and at the foot of the steps, he looked up at the president's window as if he sensed him standing there and gave him a perfunctory salute.

The president let go of the curtain, blocking the view.

Mikhail was a strong man, powerfully built, but his muscles never formed correctly. Lying on his back for years, he never learned to walk normally. As he made his way to the steps, his gait was more hobble than stride. He shuffled, or rather lumbered, like a bear.

The new Volgograd Children's Hospital was in the same compound as Orphanage 161, and as he grew older, Mikhail stood on his cot and looked out a fourth-floor window, fitted with prison bars, and watched the children play outside. He never knew or even thought to question why he was not among them. He was so divorced from the reality of his existence that to his malformed mind, they were as different from him as the cockroaches beneath his cot. They were what they were, and he was what he was.

The state health officials came to the same conclusion.

Even though the Children's Hospital was one of the best in the country, Mikhail could never be brought there, no matter how sick he became. It was as if he was a different species. When he got sick, or agitated, or hysterical, he was given an adult dose of the strongest tranquilizers available in the Soviet Union.

For six years, he lay in his cot and watched the children around him slowly lose their minds. They rocked back and forth incessantly, shouted gibberish, smacked their fists in their faces, or smashed themselves against the steel frames of the cots. Many died of self-inflicted wounds, and when they did, their non-human status was reconfirmed by the fact that no death certificates were issued. No coroner's report was requested. The bodies weren't brought to the funeral home. Rather, they were incinerated without ceremony in the same furnace used for the hospital's hazardous waste.

There was a sound at the door, and the president turned.

"Mr President," Medvedev said, knocking the door aside as he burst in. "The assassin fucked up. Tatyana Aleksandrova is still alive."

The president recoiled at the sight of Medvedev. It was the

same every time. No matter how often they met, he never got used to it.

As Medvedev hunched under the doorframe, habitually used to ducking his head, the president found it hard to concentrate. He could think only of the things he'd read in Medvedev's file.

It was through Medvedev that he learned the truth that it was possible to know too much about a man. There was a limit to what could be gained. At a certain point, the information became a distraction, a fog that hid more than it revealed.

The only thing the president needed to know about Medvedev was whether or not he would remain loyal. And all the orphanage reports in the world couldn't answer that question.

Would the fact he'd spent all those years in a cage make him obedient? He didn't know. What he did know was that he would never underestimate Medvedev. This was the child that survived when all around him were bashing their heads in.

When they lost their minds, succumbing to the drone of the ward, yelping a gibberish unintelligible even to themselves, Mikhail learned to speak. He learned how to get out of that place, to rise to the top, to hunger for power. The president hated to admit it, but the man scared him.

"Which assassin did you use?" he said.

Medvedev was cagey. He hated to report failure. "Genadi Surkov."

"He's a competent man," the president said.

"Well, he'll be sucking the end of a gun soon enough," Medvedev said. "I'm going to put my best man on it—Sergey Sergeyev."

"I don't care who you put on it," the president said. "I want Tatyana Aleksandrova dead."

"I understand, sir."

The president sighed. Medvedev was so obsequious. So

deferential. So obedient. It was hard to imagine he'd ever turn against his master.

But then, those were the ones you had to watch most closely.

According to Medvedev's file, it was a nurse named Yanina who marked the turning point in his life. She spoke to him. She gave him a book from her home. It wasn't kindness that motivated her, at least not any kindness that would be understood outside the four walls of that orphanage. In fact, it turned out she was something of a sadist. But to Medvedev, she was everything.

Years later, when she'd had four children of her own, none of which survived past infanthood, she was convicted of child abuse and murder and sent to prison for life.

Medvedev's file showed that in the orphanage, she'd made a practice of smacking him on the mouth with the sole of her plastic slippers until his lips bled. She dosed him with tranquilizers and knocked him around the ward, telling him if he could stand up straight, she'd stop beating him. She jabbed so many unsanitized needles in his feet and hands that he almost died of Hepatitis B.

But when the president asked Medvedev to serve him, to become one of his most intimate, trusted allies, to help him secure absolute power over every aspect of the Russian state, the only thing Medvedev asked in return was that Yanina be granted a pardon for her crimes.

The president granted the request and watched carefully what happened next. If Medvedev killed Yanina, if he tortured her and had her thrown into the river as he had countless others, it would be a clue to the inner workings of his mind. It would speak to his future and to whether he would one day turn on his master.

But Medvedev didn't have Yanina killed.

Instead, he installed her in one of the most expensive

mansions in Moscow, a fifty-hectare estate that included stag hunting grounds and a garden famous among horticulturalists. He bought her jewels and diamonds and the most expensive clothes her corpulent frame could carry. He gave her a tiara that had once belonged to the tsarina and had the occasion marked by a spectacular ball, inviting hundreds of the most important people in the country.

And when the president finally succeeded in getting surveillance cameras installed in the mansion, the tapes showed the most masochistic sexual displays imaginable. Medvedev worshipped Yanina. He licked the soles of her leather boots. She made him wear a dog collar and eat his food from a dish on the ground. She whipped him until his back was a shredded, bloody mess.

But just as with the reports from the orphanage, the president couldn't look away. He couldn't bring himself to delete the tapes or remove the cameras, and there were nights when he found himself in his secure room, logging into the surveillance system and having a technician patch him through to a live feed of Yanina's dungeon.

The conclusion he reached—Medvedev had the soul of a slave.

The president lay awake at night thinking about this man, this hound he'd brought into his service, about what his existence meant, what it said about God and human nature, and the limits of what might one day come for him out of the darkness.

If Medvedev existed, others like him must also exist. And if monsters were out there, it was best to have one of his own on a leash.

"You kept me waiting," he said.

Medvedev's eyes narrowed. He was always calculating, like a lizard.

He never knew what people meant. He couldn't understand nuance. He lacked intuition of any kind. He was a man who saw the world solely as cause and effect. To him, there was no why. Things either happened, or they did not. He had no conception of other people's motives, of how they felt, or how that might influence their actions.

And yet, his predictions of human behavior were prophetically accurate. Maybe his way of looking at the world was better. To him, people were insects, cockroaches, and could be predicted as easily.

"I'm sorry," Medvedev said.

The president threw his cigar in the ashtray. The sooner this meeting was over, the sooner he could forget about Medvedev. "Take a seat," he said.

Medvedev eased himself into the chair opposite the desk. It creaked under his weight, and the president wondered if it would hold him. "I had the meeting with Liu Ying," Medvedev said. He took some photos from his briefcase and slid them across the table. The president looked at them. They were black and white surveillance images of the US embassies in Moscow and Beijing.

"So he agreed?" the president said.

"He said China is ready to start flexing its muscle," Medvedev said.

"This is more than muscle-flexing," the president said. "This could unleash a nuclear war."

"Ying said the time has come for the American sun to set and a new sun to rise in the East."

"But are they willing to commit?" the president said. "Are they willing to carry out this plan?"

Medvedev picked up one of the photos. It was of the embassy in Beijing. "I gave him this very photo," Medvedev said, "and asked if they were ready to go all the way."

"And what did he say?"

"He wrote down a date and time and said it would be the biggest explosion in China since the Second World War."

"And he has Beijing's backing?"

"He said the government was united behind him."

"We're going to need some sort of guarantee," the president said.

"Of course, sir."

This plot was risky. It had the potential to blow up in their faces, to drag them into a war with America they couldn't win, but if it worked, it would change everything.

Naturally, Medvedev had calculated all the angles in his lizard brain. He'd decided that there was no way America would go to war with Russia and China simultaneously. Not over two buildings, no matter how much symbolism they carried. To Medvedev, it was nothing more than a simple cost-benefit analysis. With the withdrawal of US marines and the contracting out of embassy security, the time was ripe for an attack of this nature.

Vladimir knew the truth was more complicated.

"You realize you have blind spots?" he said to Medvedev. "When it comes to calculating human nature, to predicting how ordinary people will react to things, you're not normal."

"I understand that, sir."

"You don't see the world the way other people do."

"You are correct, sir. But just because I see the world differently doesn't mean I'm not right."

The president nodded. He knew that was true. It was the only reason he'd even given his permission to approach the Chinese. Liu Ying set the agenda of the Chinese Central Committee. If he said Beijing was going to do something, he had the power to make it so.

Unless he was lying.

"There are two things we need to worry about," the president said.

"The Chinese," Medvedev said, "and the Americans."

"Let's start with the Chinese."

Medvedev pulled another photo from his briefcase. It was of a young Chinese girl in a school uniform. She was walking on a street with a backpack on her shoulders.

"Who's this?" the president said.

"This is Liu Ying's daughter."

The president's blood ran cold. He couldn't show it. He couldn't let Medvedev see him falter even for a second. But if he was about to say what the president thought he was going to say, then this operation was locked in. There could be no turning back.

"You've kidnapped her," the president said.

"We're afraid the Chinese won't hold up their end of the bargain," Medvedev said. "If we blow up the embassy in Moscow, and they don't do exactly the same thing in Beijing, we're done for."

"We're not just done for," the president said. "It could be the end of our entire existence as a nation."

"Which is why we need to make sure Ying isn't planning any surprises."

"When did you take the girl?"

"While he was in Moscow, playing with Russian strippers and getting so drunk he barely made it back to his hotel room."

"Where is she being kept?"

"Somewhere safe."

"Not our embassy?"

"Of course not, sir. A hotel room in Beijing. We were very careful. You have complete deniability."

"We'll see how much good that does me if something goes wrong," the president said.

"Nothing will go wrong, sir."

"Like nothing went wrong with Tatyana Aleksandrova's assassination?"

Medvedev looked down.

"I never gave you permission to do this," the president said.

"Sir, you told me to secure Ying's agreement."

The president shook his head. He looked closely at Medvedev, trying to gauge if this had been some sort of willful defiance or if he genuinely thought this was what had been asked of him. "What did you tell Ying?"

"I said that if he makes a promise to Moscow, he'd better keep it."

"And if he doesn't?"

"Then his daughter will have a very fruitful career in the red light district under my personal supervision."

The president let out a long sigh. His heart was pounding in his chest, but he couldn't show that to Medvedev. Not now. This plan was happening, the force was committed, and for the duration of the battle, he couldn't afford to flinch even for a second. "You've raised the stakes," he said. "The Chinese aren't going to let us get away with this."

"They'll forgive us if they emerge with the world knowing America is no longer top dog."

"If anything goes wrong…" the president said.

"Sir," Medvedev said, "with all due respect, I would rather have the Chinese jumpy, worrying about this little girl, than looking for a way to fuck us."

The president leaned back in his chair. This had the potential to go seriously wrong. They needed the Chinese. They couldn't pull this off alone.

But Medvedev was right. It was the only way. It was too big a thing to trust Ying without leverage like this. And when the girl was returned, the leadership in Beijing would be pragmatic. They'd make Ying swallow it.

They were committed then. Both nations.

Both embassies were going to be attacked simultaneously.

He needed something to calm his nerves. He opened the humidor on his desk and pulled out two thick Cohiba Robustos. He cut them and handed one to Medvedev. "That still leaves the problem of the Americans," he said, lighting his cigar. His hand quivered ever so slightly as he held the flame, and to hide it, he leaned forward and gave Medvedev the lighter rather than lighting it for him.

"When these two embassies go up," Medvedev said, rolling the cigar between his thumb and forefinger, examining it as if he was going to be asked to pay for it, "America will have two options."

"Either they'll declare war, or they won't," the president said.

"And you're worried they'll go to war," Medvedev said.

"If they go to war with us, Mikhail, they will win."

"But they won't do it, sir. Not with us and the Chinese simultaneously."

"You don't know that," the president said.

"You think I'm mentally deficient," Medvedev said, "but I know this. I know self-interest. I know how people act when their back is against the wall. The Americans will not go to war over this."

"They won't have a choice," the president said. "They've been number one for so long, and their prestige, their honor will be at stake."

"The Americans won't go to war over two buildings," Medvedev said.

"They're not just two buildings, Mikhail. They're the symbols of US power, of US hegemony, of the entire post-war global order. These two buildings prove America won the Cold War."

"It's two buildings," Medvedev said again.

The president sucked on his cigar and blew out a long cloud of smoke. He shook his head. "There's no point making this attack more provocative than it needs to be," he said.

Mikhail was lighting his cigar. He looked up. "The whole thing is an act of provocation, sir."

"Mikhail, I want to make sure this doesn't lead to an all-out response."

"You don't trust my judgment?" Medvedev said.

"Not when the stakes are this high. We need to guarantee they don't go to war over their honor. We need to give them an out. A way to save face when they fail to stand up to us."

"But the whole point of this is to make them lose face."

"We'll still do that, but politically, we have to give them an out. Otherwise, they'll call our bluff. I know it, Mikhail."

Medvedev shrugged. "Maybe you're right," he said.

"We make these look like terrorist attacks. You tell Ying the same thing."

"Everyone will know we were behind them," Medvedev said.

The president smiled. "Exactly," he said. "They'll know that, and we'll know it, and the public around the world will know it, but officially, we'll all say it was terrorists and that we're cooperating, and that's how they'll shy away from war."

Medvedev shrugged. "All right," he said. "If it makes you feel better."

"It does make me feel better," the president said curtly.

"I suppose," Medvedev said, "if the American president has to choose between blaming the attacks on terrorists or admitting he's too afraid to stand up to us and the Chinese, there's no question which way he'll go."

"And the world," the president said, "will still know America backed down. Their dominance will be over. The age of American hegemony will be finished."

Medvedev leaned forward and tapped his cigar on the gold ashtray. "I'd say that calls for celebration," he said.

"Not so fast," the president said. His mind was racing through all the ways this could still go wrong. "If two simultaneous attacks are being planned in Moscow and Beijing, the Americans will find out."

"Sir," Medvedev said. "I'm handling the preparations personally. This is not going to be leaked."

"They just got the Mission Data Repository online. I don't want to risk the NSA picking up on chatter."

Medvedev scoffed. "A computer is not going to be able to prevent this," he said.

"If the US finds out about these attacks before they go off, this entire thing goes off the rails," the president said. "The Chinese will bail. We'll be left holding the bag by ourselves."

"All right," Medvedev said. "How do you propose we prevent that?"

The president picked up the photo of Ying's daughter again. "The new NSA director," he said. "She also has a daughter."

20

Sergey Sergeyev was the Russian equivalent of a linebacker. At six feet eight inches, and a weight somewhere in the three-hundreds, he wasn't the type of man anyone wanted to run into. That wasn't to say it was all muscle, at least not these days. He was a man with appetites, and they'd started to show, but he'd been an athlete in his day.

He'd started out in ice hockey, moved on to wrestling, but found his true calling in competitive weight lifting. He even tried out for the 1980 Russian Olympic team. The games were held in Moscow that year, but Sergey failed to qualify when his trainer set his opening snatch weight too high. Sergey couldn't lift it, and since it was his opening lift, it meant a final score of zero.

His father beat him with a crowbar for the disgrace of it. A week later, the trainer's body was found in the Moskva River.

Sergey spent the next twenty years as a metallurgical worker, rising to the rank of foreman in Moscow's Sickle and Hammer plant. He oversaw the electric foundry workshop and turned out tram cars for cities across the Soviet Union and Eastern Europe.

When the plant shut down, he got a job as a security guard for a man whose prospects were on the rise. That man's name was Mikhail Medvedev, and he was one of the few people in the city who had a size to match Sergey's.

When the two rode around together—they drove a specially modified Mercedes G-Class—they looked like two clowns in a toy car. And that was after the roof had been heightened, the chairs customized, and the entire suspension system ripped out and upgraded to handle their abnormal load.

Sergey was sitting in the Mercedes now, waiting outside the Lyublino district medical center, watching children ice skating in the park across the street.

He saw Genadi Surkov come out the front door of the hospital with a lit cigarette in his mouth.

"Genadi," he called out. "Genadi Surkov."

Genadi froze. "Sergey," he said, recognizing him, "what are you doing here?"

"Relax, Genadi. I'm just here to give you a ride."

"A ride where?" Genadi said.

He was scared, as he should be. Their boss wasn't in the habit of arranging rides for people, especially when they failed their missions, and Genadi knew that as well as anybody.

"Just get in the car, Genadi."

Genadi looked around the parking lot. There were a few cars but no other people.

Sergey could already tell there was going to be trouble. Genadi was a trained assassin. He wasn't going to make this easy.

"Either you come in peacefully," Sergey said, "or I bring you in *unpeacefully*."

Genadi's arm was in a sling. He was fit, athletic, and a lot faster on his feet than Sergey, even with the injury. He was also unarmed. Sergey knew because this medical center used metal detectors.

Sergey waited for it, and the instant Genadi made to run, he pulled his gun from inside his coat and fired three times. Genadi was faster than he'd expected and somehow managed to dodge the bullets and leap behind a low wall for cover.

Sergey watched the wall, but Genadi didn't reappear.

"Damn it," he muttered. He hated it when people made him run.

He got back in the Mercedes and swung a u-turn in front of the hospital entrance, then drove along the length of the wall, picking up speed as he approached the edge of the parking lot. At the last second, he jammed the brakes and swerved around the wall, blocking the path. As he did so, Genadi leaped across the hood of the car and out of the parking lot into the street.

Sergey opened his window and got off another few shots. Windows smashed, cars swerved, but Genadi kept running.

Sergey put his foot down and crashed through the parking lot barrier into the street. He accelerated toward Genadi, forcing traffic to swerve out of his way, and tried to hit him as he ran.

Genadi saw him coming and slipped through the gap between some parked cars. He continued to run along the sidewalk, knocking people out of his way, and Sergey followed in the street, the parked cars blocking him from getting a clear shot. Genadi turned and entered a park, and Sergey followed, ramping onto the sidewalk and through the pedestrian gates, knocking over a garbage can.

Once in the park, Genadi made his way for a treed area where the large Mercedes would have trouble following him.

Sergey floored it, the powerful engine kicking in and catching up to Genadi in seconds and ramming him from behind at forty miles per hour.

Genadi flew up over the hood and hit the windshield hard, cracking it. Sergey jammed the brakes, and Genadi fell off the front of the car onto the ground.

Sergey opened the door and stepped out. "I told you to come peaceful."

Genadi rolled on the ground in pain.

Sergey pulled him up by the collar and hit him hard with a single punch to the face. Genadi swung his leg and caught Sergey with a sharp kick to the knee. Sergey's leg collapsed, and he fell to one knee. The grass stained the tan slacks he was wearing, and he swung around and hit Genadi on the chin with another punch. He pulled his gun from his coat and smacked Genadi with it, over and over, until his face began to give way to a mush of flesh and blood that was scarcely recognizable.

Sergey didn't stop until he was out of breath. He winced when he saw what he'd done. He looked around the park. There were people everywhere, staring in horror at the scene.

He picked up Genadi's lifeless body and dragged him to the vehicle, loading him into the backseat. He checked for a pulse, and to his surprise, Genadi was still alive. He secured his wrists with a cable tie and slammed the door.

When he got to the park gate, he pulled his GRU credentials and told the horrified crowd to get out of his way. "Police business," he grunted hoarsely as he drove past them.

Next to the park was a wide boulevard lined with cheap concrete high-rises. He took it south toward the river and turned into the industrial area in Brateyevo. The land there was all scrub, and he pulled into an abandoned parking lot by the river.

He stopped the car and pulled Genadi out of the back seat by the ankles, letting his head knock the floor of the car and then the concrete pavement with two thuds. He pulled him a little further from the car so the spatter wouldn't get on it, then took out his gun and put a bullet in Genadi's forehead. Looking down, still breathless from his exertion, he spat on the corpse.

He dragged it to the edge of the river. The icy water flowed by fast, and Sergey rolled the body into it, not bothering to do anything to weigh it down.

Then he went back to the car and, cursing, wiped the blood from the upholstery on the backseat.

21

"Mr President," Sandra said, picking up the phone.

"Sandra, how are you?"

She was sitting in her new office at NSA headquarters in Fort Meade, Maryland. Outside was a view of the National Vigilance Park, a memorial to the downed spy pilots during the Cold War. It contained several aircraft, a U-8D Seminole, a Hercules C-130, and a Navy Skywarrior, all propped up on concrete plinths like statues. Beyond the park, the traffic on the Baltimore-Washington Parkway flowed smoothly.

"I'm very well, sir," she said.

"Settling into the new role?"

"Absolutely."

"I hope they're not treating you too badly."

"Not at all, sir."

"And the move? Your daughter's settling in?"

"It's a process, sir. She's still getting used to the security protocols. We both are, to be honest."

"I understand completely," the president said. "After the election, it took four months for the First Lady to move the kids to Washington. 'Security be damned,' she told me. 'We're not pulling the kids from school midway through the year.'"

Sandra laughed politely. "If I may, sir," she said, "I'd like to thank you for stepping in during the confirmation process."

"Your record warrants it," he said. "We just built the biggest computer in the world, and there's no one better qualified to run it than you."

"Thank you, sir. Your confidence is the only thing keeping me going right now."

"Well," he said, moving on to the topic he wished to broach, "I wanted to tell you that someone's going to be reaching out to you today."

"Who's that, sir?"

"Levi Roth."

"CIA Director Roth?"

"The one and only."

"I saw him a few times on TV last week," she said. "His confirmation hearings were even more heated than mine."

"Well, he's a controversial figure."

"I saw that."

"Real old school."

"Yes, sir."

"He likes his spies to be spies."

"As he should, sir."

"Not to say he doesn't believe in what you're doing, Sandra. He's one hundred percent behind your appointment. He views your work as essential."

"Very glad to hear it, sir."

"With the two of you heading things up, we're really going to give our enemies something to worry about," the president said.

"We'll knock 'em dead, sir."

The president laughed.

"Not literally," she added.

"Knock them dead all you want, Sandra. You have my personal seal of approval."

President Ingram Montgomery had always had a rebellious streak. As a senator, he'd gotten into more than his share of trouble. The recent shakeup of the intelligence agencies was only his latest gambit.

"Sir," she said, "would you mind telling me why Roth is calling?"

"Oh, he's not calling, my dear. He's stopping by."

"In person?"

"In an hour."

Sandra glanced at the clock on her wall. "An hour?" she said.

Roth had been one of the most influential figures in American intelligence for thirty years. He'd had the ear of presidents for decades. Meeting him was intimidating.

"He wants to talk about one of his specialists."

"I see."

"But don't worry," the president said. "I'm sending you a file now. It will level the playing field."

"Level the playing field?"

"Read it before he arrives."

The president hung up, and Sandra checked her inbox. There it was, a classified file sent directly from the Oval Office.

Internal Memo:
Levi Roth
Special Operations Group

She read the file, which explained that the Russians had just infiltrated one of the most clandestine and secretive operations in CIA history.

Levi Roth had been running a Top Secret team known as the Special Operations Group out of Langley. The group was responsible for some of the most sensitive and high-profile assassinations ever attempted, and its success rate was unprecedented. Its assassins were the president's secret weapon, giving him a critical third option when diplomacy failed, and military action was impossible. They'd allowed the US to avoid wars, neutralize enemies, and at times, realign entire nations that were otherwise on fatal trajectories.

Like everyone in the intelligence community, Sandra had heard the rumors about Roth. According to agency lore, he'd been offered the directorship so many times that a box had been set aside in the Langley archive building solely for his rejection letters.

She saw now the real reason he'd never stepped up to the role. His work with the group was so sensitive that any attention his promotion attracted would put the lives of his assets at risk.

He'd practically written the book on twenty-first-century espionage, and Sandra now learned that his small group, working out of the sixth floor of the CIA's headquarters building at Langley, was legendary among those at the very top echelon of US military leadership. Only a handful of people knew of the group's existence, and with this memo, Sandra had just joined them.

Roth's group was small, but it had the highest levels of access and authority. His field agents, known officially as Paramilitary Operatives, and within the group as assets, were recognized as the most elite units in the nation. They were recruited exclusively from Navy's SEAL Team Six, Air Force's 24th Special Tactics Squadron, Marine Corps' MARSOC, and Army's Delta Force.

Until a few weeks ago, there had been four of them on active duty around the globe. But somehow, the Russians had infiltrated the group and took out three of the four assets in simultaneous hits.

The sole remaining asset, Lance Spector, was missing in action. He was AWOL. Off the radar.

He was last seen in Moscow, where he'd assassinated Evgraf Davidov, the head of the GRU's Prime Directorate and the suspected leader of the sinister Dead Hand, the Russian president's secret organization for maintaining power through terror.

The report said that Spector had a complicated relationship with Roth. Roth was the one who'd recruited him, and there had been periods in their lives when they'd been extremely close.

The report finished by stating that, while Spector had been the most effective assassin in US history, he was henceforth to be considered *persona non grata*. He was to be permanently banned from the territory of the United States, his citizenship revoked. He was also prohibited from working, directly or as a contractor, for any branch of the federal government.

Sandra raised an eyebrow. That was a harsh punishment by any standard, but given the fact Spector had just single-handedly taken out one of Russia's most dangerous leaders, it almost didn't make sense.

That was, unless there was more to Spector and Roth's relationship than the file revealed. Maybe it was personal.

Sandra realized that the idea of meeting Roth face to face was making her nervous. She'd just spent the last six months studying his strategic concepts and operational doctrines. She'd been impressed by his ability to filter information and analyze situations. As a programmer, she'd always thought there was no way human intelligence could ever keep up with the ever-growing power of supercomputers. Roth had shown her never to underestimate the value of human intuition.

She was grateful they saw eye to eye on the nature of America's future threats.

He'd spent the better part of his career arguing that Russia and China were more serious adversaries than terrorists and Islamic militants could ever be.

From the secure terminal on her desk, she had access to possibly more information than any other person on the planet, and she typed Roth's name into her search terminal. There were literally thousands of classified documents containing his name, and she narrowed the search by cross-referencing Lance Spector.

It took a few minutes, but she found what she was looking for—a quantum-encrypted subnet containing secret communications between Lance and Roth. As she began to scroll through them, there was a knock on the door. It was her secretary.

"Ma'am, Levi Roth is in the visitor's lobby."

"Already? He's early."

The secretary shrugged.

Sandra exited the secure terminal and shut her laptop with a snap.

She made her way to the visitor's reception, where Roth was sitting elegantly on the sofa. There was something about the way he held himself, his clothing, the designer sunglasses, and the way his thick hair was brushed back that made him look exceedingly sophisticated. He would have fit right in with the venture capitalists back in Silicon Valley. He was surprisingly athletic for a man his age, and she found herself wondering if he dyed his hair. He wore a long, black raincoat, and she recognized its Burberry lining.

"Mr Director," she said, extending her hand.

"Madam Director," Roth said, getting to his feet. "And please, call me Levi."

"Only if you call me Sandra," she said.

He followed her to the front desk, where she asked for an available conference room. She was given a keycard, and when the receptionist asked if they needed anything else, she asked for coffee and pastries to be brought up.

"You're rolling out the red carpet," Roth said as they walked to the room.

"Well," she said, "the president did just call to announce your visit. That's got to mean something."

"He insisted I didn't come down here unannounced," Roth said. "He wants no ambushes while you settle in."

"That's very considerate of him," Sandra said, not sure where this was leading.

They took their seats in the secure room. The receptionist brought in a fresh pot of coffee and a tray of pastries, then left, shutting the door firmly behind her.

Sandra pushed a button, and they heard a sound like an airlock being sealed. A green light above the door came on. It was now impossible for anyone to eavesdrop on them.

Roth cleared his throat. "I'm sure you're dying to know why I'm here."

"The suspense is killing me," she said, pouring the coffee.

Roth picked up his cup and took a sip. "You read the file the president sent you?" he said.

She nodded.

"As you know, the Special Operations Group was a very important part of our covert operations."

"I saw that."

"The NSA looks at the big picture, gathers data," Roth said.

"And the CIA gathers the human intelligence, fields agents, cultivates sources," Sandra said.

"Exactly," Roth said. "And the Special Operations Group, until we were targeted last week...."

"Sends in the assassins," Sandra said.

Roth looked at her. "That's correct," he said.

"Are you going to re-form the group?" Sandra said.

"Before we get into that, I want to make sure you and I see eye to eye on things."

"What things are those?"

"Assassinations."

"Assassinations?" Sandra said, surprised. She hadn't been expecting a debate of that nature. "Assassinations are your jurisdiction."

Roth looked at her. "All right," he said, "but is there anything else you want to say?"

"What are you worried about, Roth?"

He looked very serious. "I can't do my job without the data you intercept," he said. "If you're going to hold that back because you have qualms about my methods, I need to know now, before people die."

Sandra thought about that. As far as she was concerned, assassinations had nothing to do with her. "Roth," she said, "the way I see it, my job is to send you and the president information. What the two of you choose to do with it, that's on you."

Roth nodded. He seemed satisfied with that. "The Group is being re-established," he said, "but with a new leader."

"You couldn't possibly continue to head it up in your new public office," Sandra said.

"No, I couldn't," he said. "That's why I've assigned the role to one of my brightest young specialists, Laurel Everlane."

"I see," Sandra said.

"You've heard of her?"

"I read her report last night."

"The one about us losing a war?" Roth said.

"The one and only."

"And your thoughts?"

"I'm a realist, Roth. If someone's got an advantage on us, I want to know that sooner rather than later."

"There are people who call this new doctrine defeatist," Roth said.

"If they want to go around playing make-believe," Sandra said, "telling themselves we have nothing to worry about, building our foreign policy on nothing more than rainbows and lollipops, that's up to them."

Roth nodded. "You know," he said, "the main reason I came here in person was to size you up."

"Oh really?" Sandra said. "And how do I measure?"

He thought for a moment, then said, "There's always been a rivalry between the CIA and the NSA."

"I hope that's not something that will affect our working relationship."

"I can assure you," Roth said, "if you're looking to play nice, you won't find any resistance from me."

"I'm looking to identify the wars we might have to fight," Sandra said, "and ensure we're in a position to win them."

Roth nodded. He looked impressed. He finished his coffee and stood up.

"Before you go," she said, "there's one thing I'd like to ask."

"What's that?" Roth said.

"It's about Lance Spector."

"Lance Spector?"

"Yes," she said. "Lance Spector."

"What do you want to know?" Roth said.

"Why do you have half the government trying to track him down if you already know where he is?"

22

Tatyana sat in the back of a black Cadillac Escalade and waited. She'd called Roth from Paris before getting on the plane, and his driver was waiting for her at Dulles when she landed.

"You ever brought anyone here before?" she said to the driver.

He looked at her in the rearview mirror but said nothing.

He wore a driver's uniform. The car was official, black with tinted windows, bullet-proof glass, and enhanced communications equipment.

"This is a nice car," she said, giving the driver a hint of her accent. "We don't have cars like this in Russia."

"It's the boss's personal vehicle," he said.

She pressed the window button, but it was locked. She knew if she tried the door, it would be locked too.

"Fancy place," she said.

"You should see his house," the driver said, then stopped himself from speaking further.

"I have seen it," Tatyana said.

The driver said nothing.

They were on an old cobblestone street in Georgetown, about a mile west of the White House and just off Wisconsin Avenue. Outside, wrought iron lampposts lit up the stately entrances to colonial townhouses. They were among the most expensive homes in the city.

Someone walked up to the car and rapped their knuckles on Tatyana's window. The driver opened it, and a woman stood there.

"Tatyana Aleksandrova," the woman said. "I'm Laurel Everlane."

"I remember you," Tatyana said.

"Last time we met..." Laurel said.

"We were both shot," Tatyana said, finishing her sentence.

"Well, let's hope that doesn't happen tonight."

Tatyana nodded. She got out of the car, and Laurel led her through the gate. Two french doors led into one of the grandest hallways Tatyana had ever seen.

"What is this place?"

"This is where the magic happens," Laurel said.

They walked across a checkered marble floor into a large sitting room decorated with exquisite antique furniture. The room extended to the back of the house, where another set of french doors led to a formal garden with illuminated plants around a stone swimming pool.

"This is a nice house," Tatyana said.

Laurel nodded. "You should see the suites upstairs. It's like a five-star hotel."

"So, are you going to tell me why I'm here?" Tatyana said.

Laurel nodded and told Tatyana to sit on a sofa that looked like it had been purchased from Sotheby's. Laurel went to a glass wine rack that covered the far wall of the room, floor to ceiling, with LED-illuminated wine bottles.

"Bordeaux okay?"

"Bordeaux would be perfect," Tatyana said.

Laurel opened the bottle and placed it with two wine glasses on the table in front of Tatyana. There was a fireplace, and she flicked a switch, bringing it to life.

"This is starting to feel like a first date," Tatyana said.

"Wait until you hear what I have to say," Laurel said, sitting across from her.

Tatyana poured the wine, and they each took a sip.

"To new beginnings," Laurel said.

Tatyana raised her glass. "I'll drink to that."

"I'm sorry we left you behind," Laurel said.

Tatyana looked at her. They'd both been in Moscow. Laurel was flown out by the CIA from a secret airfield outside the city. Tatyana's route had been a little more circuitous.

"You didn't leave me behind," she said. "I never made it to the extraction point."

"Because you were looking for Lance."

"He told me where he was. Krasnye Vorota. A park by the metro station."

"But you didn't find him?"

Tatyana took a sip of her wine and looked out toward the pool. "The water is heated?" she said.

"All winter," Laurel said. "Now, getting back to Lance."

"I can't talk about what happened," Tatyana said.

"I'm not asking as a friend," Laurel said.

"He wasn't there," Tatyana said. "I went to where he said. All I found was a puddle of blood."

Laurel looked at her. Tatyana had a feeling she knew more than she was letting on.

There was a sound, and Laurel looked toward the door.

"Are we waiting for someone?" Tatyana said.

Laurel hesitated, and Tatyana grew apprehensive. "You don't think...." Tatyana gasped.

Laurel shook her head, getting up from her seat and reaching out to her.

"You don't think I did something to Lance?" Tatyana said.

"Of course we don't, Tatyana."

"I looked everywhere for him."

"I know you did."

"I risked my life," Tatyana said

"Tatyana, calm down. We know that. We know what you did. We know everything."

"Then you know I can never go back to my country."

Laurel looked at her watch.

"Who are you waiting for?" Tatyana said. Then her voice dropped, and she said very clearly, "Laurel, if someone's coming here to kill me, have the decency to tell me."

"Tatyana," Laurel gasped. "We're not trying to kill you. We're trying to recruit you."

Tatyana took a breath. She had to calm down before she made a fool of herself. "Roth wants me in?" she said.

"It doesn't matter what Roth wants," Laurel said.

"What does that mean?"

"I'm the one recruiting you."

"What are you saying, Laurel?"

"I'm the new director. The Special Operations Group. Roth gave it to me."

"To you?"

"What's so strange about that?"

Tatyana shrugged, and a sly smile stretched across her face.

"What?" Laurel said.

"You know what they say," she said. "Hell hath no fury...."

Laurel smiled. "I can't imagine what Roth said to get them to give a team of assassins over to a woman."

"I'd have thought they'd rather see it in the hands of the Russians," Tatyana said.

Laurel nodded. "Me too."

Tatyana took a breath. "Did you find Spector?" she said. She knew she was on shaky ground. Roth might already know she and Lance had been together in Moscow, and even if he didn't, keeping a secret was an even bigger cause of death than bullets in their line of work.

She would have preferred to come clean to Laurel, but she'd given Lance her word. Also, she'd sent Larissa to him. Whatever he was up to, she needed him to keep doing it. If Larissa didn't make it out, she'd never be able to forgive herself.

She also knew that Lance was done with the CIA. He'd said if he never saw Levi Roth again as long as he lived, it would be too soon. Tatyana had said he'd reconsider, but Lance was adamant he'd made up his mind for good. When he got back to the States, the only thing he wanted was to go back to his home in Montana. He'd found peace there. And he'd said he had someone waiting for him there.

"We're still looking for him," Laurel said. "But between the two of us, I have a suspicion Roth knows more than he's letting on."

"And you're working out of here now?"

Laurel nodded.

"Not Langley?"

"The group was burned pretty bad."

"I know it was."

"All assets but Lance are dead."

"And you think there was a leak from Langley?"

"I don't know," Laurel said, "but one thing's clear—Roth doesn't want the same mistakes being made a second time. This time, everything is off the grid. We work out of this house. We sleep in this house. We give up all personal and social connections. We go deep. We have no connection to Langley, we're outside the CIA's chain of command, and the only person we answer to is Roth."

"I see," Tatyana said.

"It's daunting, I know."

"It's not daunting," Tatyana said. "My life is already off the grid. Now that I'm a defector, I'll be looking over my shoulder until the day I die."

"You might as well do it from the inside then," Laurel said.

Tatyana took a sip of her wine.

"Does that mean you're in?" Laurel said, unable to hide her eagerness.

"I won't come cheap," Tatyana said.

"I didn't think you would."

"I may cost more than you had in mind."

"Name your price."

"Not now," Tatyana said. "When the time comes, I'll name my price. And it will be non-negotiable."

23

W hen Sergey got back to the Lubyanka, he was in a foul mood. His pants were ruined, the leather on the backseat of his car was stained, and as he was driving home to change outfits, the boss called.

He walked through the lobby, past the FSB security checkpoint, and toward the restricted elevator at the back. While the rest of the building was occupied by the FSB, Sergey's boss had taken over the top floor for his own operation.

Sergey waited for the elevator, and the soldier standing by the door looked at him. Sergey saw his eye drop to the grass stains on his pants.

"What are you looking at?" he said.

The soldier snapped to attention. "Nothing, sir," he said.

The elevator opened, and Sergey stepped in.

When he reached the top floor, Medvedev's secretary, a pretty little thing by the name of Svetlana, directed him to the sofa in front of her desk.

"How are you today, sweetheart?" Sergey said.

She didn't look up from the document she was reading. That was all right. She could ignore him all she wanted. She was wearing a bright red scarf around her neck and a tight, white dress. Her outfit brought to mind a schoolgirl, or perhaps a nurse. Sergey imagined the sound it would make if he gave her ass a sharp smack.

He stared at her and grinned. She did her best not to notice, but he saw the blush. She couldn't hide from him. He knew all her secrets. If she had even the faintest idea of the things he'd seen, she'd have fled the room.

But her innocent little mind had no clue. And she just sat in her seat placidly, the national flag hanging from a gold pole next to her.

Sergey watched her work. He liked to make her uncomfortable.

There was a sound in the office, and Sergey turned to the door. "Who's he inside with?" he said.

Svetlana looked up at him over the top of her glasses. "I'm not at liberty to say."

Sergey shrugged. "Get off your ass and get me a coffee then."

She got up, went to a fancy capsule coffee machine, and put a cup in the receptacle. She pressed the button, and it whizzed to life. "You take milk?" she said.

"If you're offering," Sergey grunted.

"I thought so," she said, and something about the way she said it bothered him.

"Excuse me?"

"I thought you took milk," she said.

"What's that supposed to mean?"

"Nothing," she said in her saccharine voice, but there was something defiant in her eyes.

She had spirit. He'd grant her that much. He'd have liked to bend her over the counter right there, pull up her skirt, and teach her a lesson.

Of course, he could do nothing of the kind here. Not to her.

This was hallowed ground, and she was already claimed

by the boss. Sergey knew better than to mess with that. His boss, Mikhail Medvedev, was, apart from the president, possibly the most powerful man in the country. He'd just been named head of the Dead Hand after the previous holder of the title found his head on the wrong end of a high-powered sniper bullet. Every plot and plan to increase the president's personal power would be under his direct oversight.

No one messed around here.

One slip up, and the president could be dethroned. He had so many enemies gunning for him that the threat was constant.

This was where the Russian leadership was secured, and where it could all be lost.

So even a man like Sergey remembered his manners in the waiting room. He watched her make the coffee, her neckerchief neatly tied like a proper little Young Pioneer. *Pionerskiy galstuk*, they used to call them when he was a schoolboy. They weren't seen much any longer, but he'd never seen Svetlana without it.

"Why do you wear that?" he said when she came over with his coffee.

"The boss likes it," she said. "Reminds him of his childhood, he says."

"You always wear what he likes?" Sergey said, allowing a lecherous smile to cross his face.

She ignored him. "I see you had an accident," she said.

As well as the grass stains, some blood splatter had gotten on his white shirt.

"You watch your mouth," he said.

He began opening the buttons at his cuffs to roll up his sleeves. It was a gesture people always found threatening, especially women. The door to the office opened, and three men stepped out. One was Medvedev, towering over the other two, who were both Chinese.

And the Chinese were not happy. They stormed past Sergey

toward the elevator, and Svetlana had to jump from her seat to push the button for them.

Medvedev lumbered after them like a sickly ogre, his red eyes darting toward Sergey.

Sergey made to stand, and Medvedev practically pushed him back into his seat as he passed.

"Gentlemen," Medvedev said, "don't be like this. We're friends."

"You've crossed a line," one of the Chinese said in his atrocious accent. "Bringing Ying's daughter into this? It's despicable."

"We needed an absolute guarantee you were going to follow through," Medvedev said.

"And you got it, but at what cost to our relationship?"

The elevator arrived, and as the two men entered, Medvedev spread out his enormous hands. "It is what it is," he said as the doors shut.

Sergey was a man whose life depended on his ability to identify threats. This was a situation he wasn't sure how to read. Something was brewing. That much was clear. Whenever the Chinese were in town, something was in the works, and with Yiu Ling, and now these two, he sensed it was going to be something big.

And as everyone knew, anything big also had the potential to be very dangerous.

Medvedev wasn't about to let him in on all the plans, but that didn't mean he couldn't pay attention.

He already knew Ying was from MSS. The Ministry of State Security was the Chinese equivalent of the GRU or the CIA. If he had to guess, these two were MSS too. They'd been dressed in the expensive tailored suits that the MSS lackeys all seemed to like. They carried the obligatory Mont Blanc briefcases.

"Look at yourself," Medvedev said, turning to him. "You look like you just walked in from the fields."

"Sorry, boss."

Medvedev brushed past him back into his office, and Sergey got up and followed.

He stood by the door, waiting to be offered a seat. The boss was in a mood, the meeting hadn't gone well, and it wasn't the time to take liberties.

Medvedev slumped into his enormous leather throne and ran his hands through his white hair. "It's done?" he said.

Sergey nodded. "Yes, sir."

"No problems?"

"He ran. I had to follow him into a park."

"But the prick's dead?"

"Dead and in the river, sir."

Medvedev nodded. He reached into a drawer in his desk and pulled out a small grocery store bottle of vodka. He unscrewed the cap and took a long swig.

These were the moments Sergey knew to be careful. He'd spent many years in Medvedev's service and had seen too often how quickly things could turn. One minute, it would be all laughs and jokes and shots of vodka, and the next, someone would be lying dead in a pool of blood. The violence was sudden and unpredictable. It kept you on your toes.

One thing he had to admit about Medvedev—the man wasn't afraid to do his own killing.

Medvedev took another sip from the bottle and wiped his mouth. "Your little friend's incompetence cost us," he said.

"Genadi Surkov was no friend of mine," Sergey said, betraying no hint of emotion.

"You two drank together," Medvedev said.

"I drink with a lot of people," Sergey said, not moving a muscle. He stood still as a statue while Medvedev's beady eyes crawled over him.

Then Medvedev nodded. "I remember the two of you," he

said, wagging his finger as if he'd caught Sergey in a lie. "Thick as thieves, you were."

Sergey said nothing. He had his gun beneath his coat, but it was unthinkable to draw it on the boss. He came from the old school. He knew what it took to survive in the service of a man like Medvedev. He was the type of boss who, if he decided he wanted to kill you, you let him. You'd rise farther if you thought like that, and Medvedev was the type who knew how to tell the difference.

"Tatyana Aleksandrova is still alive," Medvedev said.

Sergey nodded. He'd figured as much.

"Two border guards were found dead last night," Medvedev went on. "It looks like she slipped into Belarus. She could be anywhere now. London, Washington, New York."

"I see," Sergey said.

"She received a phone call before she crossed the border."

"Did we intercept it?"

"She used an encrypted exchange to mask the route. We're working on it." Medvedev pulled two glasses from the drawer beneath his desk and poured a little of the vodka into each. "Sit," he said, pushing one of the glasses toward Sergey.

Sergey sat and picked up the glass. He waited for Medvedev to drink, then did the same.

"You saw the Chinese I was meeting with," Medvedev said. "We're working on something with them. Something stressful."

Sergey said nothing. He knew better than to ask questions. The less he knew, the safer he was.

Medvedev drained his glass, and Sergey did the same. The boss poured two more. "I'm sending you to America," Medvedev said. "Something important for the president. Do not screw it up."

Sergey nodded.

"We've had enough screw-ups lately."

24

S vetlana Tolkalina was born in Moscow's Belyayevo district to working-class parents. She was a shy girl, well behaved, did well in school, and graduated with honors from the local secretarial college. When she landed an administrative job at the prestigious Lubyanka, her family was thrilled.

Her mother always feared she was plain, with pale skin and dark hair, but she had the effect of growing prettier to people over time as they got to know her better. She had soft, delicate features and her expressions were mild. She laughed quietly. She ate quietly. She never flirted.

If there'd been a boy she liked, she avoided him like the plague. It meant that when she entered Medvedev's service at the age of twenty-two, she had yet to lose her virginity and had only been kissed once in her life. She was an innocent, a child. Even the kiss had been an unmitigated disaster.

The boy, a high school classmate named Ravil, invited her to the graduation ball. Svetlana said no, but when her mother found out, she forced her to call him back and apologize for her rudeness.

Her school wasn't fancy, but somehow, someone's father had

managed to rent a boat that would host the party as it cruised up and down the Moskva River. The girls in her class took the event seriously. They spent thousands of rubles on dresses and shoes and then spent the day of the event getting manicures, pedicures, and fancy hairdos.

None of that was in Svetlana's nature, and she refused to waste her father's money. She borrowed a dress from her older cousin, did her own hair and makeup, and the only money she brought to the party was cab fare. She wouldn't have brought anything, but she regarded the cab fare as an emergency precaution, something she might need if Ravil turned out to be less of a gentleman than her mother thought he'd be.

Svetlana dreaded the night for weeks. When it came, she was very quiet. She spoke little to Ravil in the taxi. At the party, she danced only when she couldn't avoid it. She drank a little of the sparkling wine that was provided by the school, far less than Ravil, and on the upper deck, as the lights of the city sparkled along the river banks, he planted his mouth on hers in a moment of madness that he somehow thought would be romantic.

She objected. He was drunk. He didn't immediately take no for an answer, and she had to push him away.

She spent the rest of the night with her back to the wall, watching the dance floor as Ravil and his friends snickered and made fun of her. In the pocket of her dress, her hand clutched the cab fare like her life depended on it.

When the boat finally docked, she swore she'd never be put in a compromising position like that with a man again. In secretarial college, she took the bus home as soon as class was over and avoided all dates and social gatherings.

It was a cruel twist of fate, then, that a girl who'd been so careful in college ended up in the office of a man like Mikhail Medvedev. When he saw her walk into his office, he didn't see an office employee. He saw a sex toy, a human doll, something he could toy with, frighten, experiment with. He couldn't form even the most basic of human relationships, but possession was something he understood with crystal clarity.

He made up his mind he was going to torture this girl, abuse her, use her to fill the void in his psyche that made it impossible for him to understand emotions.

By the time Svetlana realized, it was too late. Quitting was not an option.

Medvedev was one of the most powerful men in the country, and he'd decided that she was his personal property.

She couldn't refuse. She couldn't run. And she couldn't tell anyone.

If there was any redeeming factor at all, it was that Medvedev was so utterly emotionally stunted that the games he played often resembled more the acts of a child than the fully developed fantasies of a sexual predator. His torments were simple. Not because he wanted them to be, but because he couldn't conceive of anything more complex.

He liked to tell her what to wear. He took control of her bank account and told her what to buy. He told her to ask his permission any time she wanted to eat, or use the restroom, or shower.

He had dozens of cameras installed in her parents' home, watching every aspect of their life, and he left her in no doubt that if she ever tried to escape, he would have every member of her family murdered in cold blood.

He was a dichotomy. A paradox.

In his political machinations, he was one of the president's most astute and cunning advisors. He could look at a complex strategic situation and see all the nuanced facets at once.

But when it came to Svetlana, he revealed a psyche so stunted that she came to think of him as a sort of monstrous child.

25

L ance sat alone in a bar in a Russian coat, sipping a stale beer, frequently checking his watch. His face was unshaven, and he still had a slight limp. His leg was healing, but it would be a few more days before he'd be putting on his dancing shoes. He chain-smoked and never said more than two words to the waitress.

Across the street was one of the most secure and surveilled buildings on the face of the planet—the US embassy in Moscow. For seven decades, it had served as America's Cold War fortress. It held more operational espionage equipment than any other place on earth. The top two floors had been correctly identified by Russian intelligence as a giant antenna, capable of sucking up every signal, digital or analog, the airwaves could carry. They called the building the Electronic Vacuum Cleaner because of the amount of information it could gather.

Not that the Russians weren't playing games of their own. Since 1953, Geiger counters and other detection equipment inside the building had been going haywire. It turned out the Russians were blasting so many microwaves at the embassy, at times reaching up to four gigahertz, that DARPA had to recommend their staff wear gonadal protection. They even designed a lead-lined jockstrap for the men, although it was never put into use.

Instead, six-inch-thick lead shielding was installed along the entire west side of the building. No one on the American side knew how the Russians used the rays, but it was suspected they triggered covert listening devices.

There certainly was no shortage of bugs. When the work was being carried out to install the lead shielding, the building's concrete was found to be so riddled with microphones that Congress ordered an entirely new building be built from the ground up. The new twelve-story embassy was built right next to the existing structure, and every part of the construction was carried out by American contractors, flown in on diplomatic jets, and given full consular status and protection.

All the building supplies, the sand used for mixing concrete, the drywall, the lumber, the steel, even the paint, were flown in from the States and processed by the US diplomatic warehouse at Sheremetyevo under full diplomatic protection. As the press boasted at the time, the only Russian material used in the entire project was water, and even that was filtered three times by US equipment.

The old building, the building Lance could now see from the window, remained in use but only for routine consular functions. All sensitive business was conducted in the new building, immune to all known Russian espionage capabilities.

Lance had picked up some false embassy credentials from an old drop box of Roth's. He would use them to get in and out of the embassy compound, but he didn't know who to approach once he got inside. He couldn't just walk in and ask for the ambassador. That would raise the alarm, tip off the Russians, and completely waste the intelligence Larissa had risked her life to get.

The last thing he wanted was to tip off the enemy. He had seen it play out that way too many times. Some inept station chief would find out about a planned attack and run around with his hands in the air, raising the alarm. Everyone would congratulate him for preventing the attack. Nine times out of ten, he'd get a promotion. Meanwhile, the plotters would go back underground, draw up new plans, and attack somewhere else.

Tipping your hand didn't save lives—it only warned the enemy of what you knew.

If you really wanted to prevent an attack like this, the only way was to kill everyone involved—the plotters, the clients, the moles, the henchmen, everyone. You pulled the weed out by the roots. Otherwise, you were wasting your time.

And any failure was paid for in blood.

Osama Bin Laden started out bombing embassies. The CIA thought the solution was to protect the embassies. The only solution was to kill Bin Laden, a lesson they learned when two jets plowed into the World Trade Center.

Getting every single conspirator in a plot was not easy. It was a dangerous game of watching and waiting, and at any moment, a bomb could go off in your face.

But if you didn't do it right, well, watch the newsreel from 9/11.

Lance had to find the right person in the embassy, someone willing to play the long game, to sit on the information and wait. That was how you caught and killed plotters.

Finding someone willing to think like that was hard enough. For Lance, it would be next to impossible. They'd never listen. His current status was AWOL, and for all he knew, he was a wanted fugitive. He was hiding out from the agency and had zero wish to be pulled back in.

The front door was not an option.

Across the street, an armored truck drove by and stopped at

the lights. It was marked like the vehicles Russian banks used to transport cash. It waited for the green light, then turned into the embassy's Garden Ring security gate. The guards waved the driver through without even checking his ID.

The guards looked formidable with their Kevlar vests and assault rifles, but Lance knew who they were.

Two weeks ago, that gate had been manned by US marines. Now the guards were employees of a Russian security contractor called Diamond Logistics, a company wholly owned by a former KGB officer with close links to the Kremlin.

How had the US embassy's security been put in the hands of a former KGB officer?

The answer to that question, as always, was politics.

In response to the latest round of US sanctions, the Kremlin had recently ordered the US embassy in Moscow, and the consulates in Saint Petersburg, Yekaterinburg, and Vladivostok, to reduce personnel by seven hundred. That meant pulling out the marines usually charged with protecting the embassy. The Russian government then refused to license a single US company to provide the security, and a no-bid contract worth three million dollars was awarded by the State Department to Diamond Logistics.

It was a travesty, a joke, putting security for the embassy in the hands of the very people most likely to attack it. Lance had already hacked the Acquisitions Office network and tried to read the congressional oversight report for the contract, but someone had deleted it.

You didn't have to be Sherlock Holmes to know something wasn't right. He'd waited until Larissa was asleep, then left her alone in the apartment to come to this place.

As soon as the truck entered the compound, he stood up, leaving money for his drink on the table.

He went outside and crossed the street to the embassy entrance, carelessly flashing his badge as he passed the guardhouse. The Russian guards gave it a cursory glance, barely looking at him before waving him through.

He walked into the compound and scanned the area. He was in a large square surrounded by buildings. The old, original embassy building was on the south side of the square, visible from the street. Next to it, further from the street, was the much larger and more sophisticated new building. Around the square were the many administrative and support buildings. Lance had just entered through the main gate, but there were other, smaller entrances to the compound for state department staff, diplomatic visitors, and deliveries. There was also a separate entrance to the old embassy for members of the public needing consular services. Lance had no doubt security was even worse at all those points.

He scanned the high perimeter wall and the entrances to each of the buildings. There wasn't a single marine on the premises. The only security was Diamond Logistics rent-a-cops in civilian uniforms. On their sleeves was a small patch of the Russian flag. If someone was going to attack, they couldn't have asked for better circumstances.

Lance spat on the ground and kept walking.

There'd been a time when this embassy was the most secure overseas diplomatic facility in the world. There'd been a time when the federal government cared even about the purity of the water being used in the concrete.

Those days were gone.

26

S ergey stepped out of the jet onto the tarmac at Teterboro Airport. It was a small facility in New Jersey that catered mostly to private jets. The Russian Consulate made heavy use of it.

He put a cigarette in his mouth and shielded it with his coat while lighting it. The sky was overcast, the clouds low. He walked to the customs building, where he was required to show his passport and sign in. The Russian government had arranged diplomatic clearance for the flight, and Sergey was traveling under false diplomatic credentials.

He went through the modest customs process and lit another cigarette on the terminal's front steps.

A black Mercedes with tinted windows pulled up in front of him, and he got in.

"Mr Sergeyev," the driver said in Russian.

"Take me to the consulate," Sergey said, opening his window.

The Russian Consulate was on the Upper East Side, just off Fifth Avenue. It was a beautiful limestone house, originally built by a New York real estate mogul as a wedding gift for his daughter. Its transfer to the Russian government had been a sensitive process.

Back in the thirties, the Russians had a consulate on Sixty-First Street. The Soviet government made a habit of snatching up dissidents who'd escaped to America and holding them there against their will. When one of these unlucky people, a young English teacher from Ukraine, leaped from the fourth-floor window to her death, there was public outrage. The New York Attorney General's office was forced to step in and shut the place down.

For forty-seven years, there was no Russian consulate in the city until this one received permission to operate in the nineties. Since then, there'd been multiple complaints that it was being used in ways that contravened the agreement signed with the city.

Sergey didn't like being in New York. Everything was bigger and brighter than in Moscow. The buildings were taller, the restaurants more expensive, the cars newer, and the women better dressed. It fired up his inferiority complex.

"First time in New York?" the driver said.

"No," Sergey said.

The driver nodded. "How's your English?"

Sergey lit another cigarette, ignoring the no-smoking sign, and blew the smoke in the driver's direction. He caught the driver's eye in the rearview mirror and looked at him. "What about me gave you the impression I wanted to make small talk?"

The driver looked straight ahead.

Sergey chain-smoked in the backseat as they navigated the evening rush hour, and when the car pulled up outside the consulate an hour later, he made the driver get out and open the door for him.

He was escorted through consulate security and taken in a private elevator to the fourth floor. There, he entered a carpeted hallway where a lady at a desk told him to take a seat. He sat by her desk and read the name on the door behind her.

It was the office of the consul-general, Jacob Kirov.

"Can I smoke?" he said in Russian to the woman at the desk.

"Of course," she said.

She got up from her seat to bring him an ashtray, and he noted the curve of her thighs under her skirt.

A few minutes later, the consul-general appeared at the door and beckoned him in. Sergey stubbed out his cigarette and entered the office. It contained an ornate desk facing an expansive view of the park just across Fifth Avenue.

"Sergey Sergeyev," Kirov said, taking his seat. He indicated for Sergey to do the same and said, "You come very highly recommended."

"Thank you, sir."

"Medvedev says you're his best man."

"He's too kind," Sergey said.

"Well, I hope you're as good as he says because the top brass is watching this job."

Sergey nodded. "Whatever they want, sir, I'll get it done."

"What they want," Kirov said, "is leverage over their American counterparts."

"A little leverage never hurts."

"That's exactly right," Kirov said.

Kirov pressed a button on his phone, and the woman from the lobby appeared at the door. "Yes, sir?" she said.

"Bring us something to drink, my dear."

She left and returned with a bottle of vodka on a tray. It was accompanied by two Bohemian crystal glasses and a matching ice bucket. She placed the tray on the table and left.

Kirov poured them each some vodka and offered Sergey the ice. Sergey shook his head.

Kirov waited for the woman to shut the door, then took a sip of the vodka. Sergey did the same. Kirov then reached into a drawer in the desk and pulled out an envelope. From it, he removed a black and white surveillance photograph. "Do you know who this woman is?" he said, showing Sergey the photo.

Sergey shook his head. He'd never seen her before.

"This is the sitting director of the US National Security Agency."

"The NSA?" Sergey said.

"Her name is Sandra Shrader."

"I see," Sergey said, looking at the photo. The woman wasn't bad looking—slender, early fifties—although she had that smug look American women got when they were given too much power.

"I think," Sergey said, then remembered where he was and held his tongue.

"Think what?" Kirov said.

"Nothing, sir."

"Relax," Kirov said, pouring more vodka. "This isn't a job interview. You're still Medvedev's man. I'm just borrowing you for a few days."

Sergey shook his head. He let out an embarrassed laugh. "I think," he said, "maybe she buys her clothes at the same store as Hillary Clinton."

A smirk crossed Kirov's face. "It's a sure sign of decadence when you see so many women wearing pants," he said. He held out his glass, and Sergey clinked it.

"You want me to take care of her?" Sergey said.

Kirov shook his head. He took another photograph from the envelope and slid it across the desk. It was a girl. She looked about fourteen, dressed in a school uniform. "This is her daughter," Kirov said.

"I see," Sergey said, letting his tongue wet his lips.

"We want you to kidnap her."

"I can do that."

"She attends a fancy school in Annapolis. No special security precautions, as far as we can tell. You shouldn't have too much trouble getting to her."

"I'm sure I won't."

"Discretion is paramount. You have to take her in such a way that no one but the mother knows it's happened."

"She'll squeal soon enough," Sergey said.

"You leave me to worry about that," Kirov said. "The child lives only with the mother. There's no father in the picture. No boyfriend. The mother receives Secret Service protection, but, as I said, there are gaps in coverage when it comes to the child."

"Is that normal?"

Kirov shrugged. "It's not unheard of. She's a new appointment. Technical role."

"So you want me to get the child without the Secret Service noticing?"

"Exactly," Kirov said. "Have you been to Annapolis before?"

Sergey shook his head.

"It's a small town near Fort Meade, where the NSA is based."

"I see."

"Fancy neighborhood. Nice houses. An oaf like you will stand out if you're not careful."

Sergey nodded.

"We've had the girl under surveillance. If you take her after school on Friday, no one will know she's missing except the mother."

"I see."

"The mother will keep it secret. I'll see to that."

"And the father is dead?"

"Yes," Kirov said.

"What about staff?"

"Staff?"

"Rich people have housekeepers, nannies, drivers."

Kirov shook his head. "Not in Maryland," he said. "The

mother's Secret Service detail is the only thing you need to worry about."

"How long will we keep the disappearance off the radar?"

"For as long as Moscow tells us," Kirov said.

Sergey nodded. "Fair enough."

They finished their drinks. Kirov put the photos back in the envelope and handed it to Sergey. "You've got a room at the Four Seasons tonight," he said. "Tomorrow, you can get to work."

It was Wednesday. They wanted him to grab the girl on Friday after school. "I'd prefer to go to Maryland tonight," he said.

Kirov nodded. "Eager to get started?"

"Familiarize myself with the neighborhood," he said.

"There's a house in Baltimore," Kirov said. "It's where you'll be bringing the girl. You can stay there."

Sergey nodded. He made his way to the door and stopped.

"Is there something else?" Kirov said.

"This girl," Sergey said. "Is she...?" He paused, searching for a way to put it. "Is she off-limits?"

Kirov looked at him. He said nothing for a moment, discerning Sergey's meaning. Then he said, "What limits are you talking about?"

Sergey shook his head. "Nothing," he said. "Never mind."

Kirov looked a little pale, like the vodka wasn't agreeing with him. "You'd better get going," he said.

27

Tatyana sat across the desk from Roth. They were in his office on the second floor of the house in George-town. Bookshelves lined the wood-paneled walls, laden with attractive, leather-bound tomes. She wondered if they were his books or if they'd come with the house but didn't ask.

"I'm sorry I didn't make it last night," Roth said. "Something detained me."

"I understand," Tatyana said. "Laurel took good care of me."

"I trust you were comfortable."

"Very," Tatyana said, and she wasn't exaggerating.

The third floor contained three guest suites, each with a luxurious king-sized bed and its own bathroom, complete with a jacuzzi bathtub and walk-in shower. Each room had its own access to a balcony overlooking the pool, as well as an outdoor dining area and cedar sauna.

"It's not a bad setup we have here," Roth said.

"It's very nice," Tatyana said, "but who's paying for it?"

"Who do you think?"

"Laurel said you made her head of the group."

"That's correct," Roth said.

"If this is some glorified security agency you're setting up on the government's dime to provide services to corporate clients, I'm not interested."

"It's not that," Roth said.

"Then what is it?"

"You know what it is," Roth said. "You know what the asset program was. You know what Lance did for us."

"He was more than an assassin," Tatyana said.

"Exactly," Roth said.

"And you want me to be that?"

Roth looked at her. "If you're willing," he said.

Tatyana looked out the window. A pigeon had landed on the iron lamppost. "I discussed all this with Laurel last night," she said.

"And she said you had a price you wouldn't name."

"And that's why you're here?"

"The US government doesn't sign blank checks," Roth said.

"Sure it does," Tatyana said.

"Well, if you don't want to tell me what you want...."

Tatyana shook her head. "I want to tell you," she said, "but I need to know you're not going to use it against me."

"That's not what this is," Roth said. "I'm not going to force you to do this job. You really are free to say no."

"That's a first."

"This isn't the Kremlin, Tatyana. We're different here."

"That remains to be seen, doesn't it?"

Roth spread his hands. "We've both been around the block," he said. "I think you know the parameters of what I can offer you."

Tatyana nodded. She looked at him closely. His being in this room with her said a lot. He was one of the longest-serving spies in Washington, the puppet master who pulled the strings, the man who whispered in the ears of presidents and who assassinated tyrants.

He was a patriot, but he would always be a spy first. He'd never sell his services to the highest bidder. He believed in something, he had an idea of the world, and that idea was what the CIA would pursue under his leadership.

To some, Tatyana was just another Russian doll with expensive taste. The fact Roth was here said he saw her as more than that. And she had an ax to grind against the system that killed her family.

In Russia, they had a saying: *When the devil himself failed, he sent a woman.* Tatyana aimed to be that woman.

"Laurel's operation here," Roth said, "answers to me and the president. No one else."

"Who knows it exists?"

"So far, only the three of us."

"That's it?"

"For now."

"And your first recruit is a Russian?"

"Everything I built at Langley was compromised. The assets are dead. I don't want a repeat of that."

"What about Spector?"

"He's the only one left alive, but I don't have him yet."

"So you do want him?"

Roth said nothing. He wasn't going to get into that.

"If I join," Tatyana said, "what protection do I have if things go south?"

"What are you looking for?"

"I can never go back to Russia."

"We'd never send you back."

"I'll need some sort of guarantee."

"You'll have citizenship, a new identity, birth certificate, the works."

"The president authorized that?"

"The Attorney General already signed off."

"That was presumptuous."

"Was it?"

She looked at him and shook her head. "You know I'll join you," she said.

"You're not going to regret this."

"We need Spector."

"Yes, we do," Roth said. "And I've found him."

"Where?"

"In Moscow."

"How?"

"He came to us."

"He turned himself in?"

"Not exactly."

Tatyana was thinking of Larissa. Her safety was the only thing that mattered. All of this was to ensure she got out, and whatever she'd said to Lance, it seemed it had caused him to put himself back onto Roth's radar. "Have you spoken to him?" Tatyana said.

"Laurel's afraid that if we approach him, he'll go underground."

"Maybe," Tatyana said.

"He doesn't want anything to do with me, and she doesn't want to push him further away."

Tatyana knew that was a risk. There'd been a time in Moscow when she first found him. He'd taken a lot of medication and was delirious, and he started talking. He told her Roth had killed one of his first handlers, a woman named Clarice Snow. But what Roth hadn't known at the time was that Clarice was pregnant with his child.

"I looked for him," Tatyana said.

"I know you did."

"I searched everywhere. I stayed in Moscow even though the GRU was scanning every network for me."

"I know," Roth said.

"I couldn't find him."

Roth looked at her in a way that made her think he didn't fully believe her. "Even if you had found him," he said, "that's not something you would have been able to tell Laurel."

"Why not?" she said defensively.

"She would have been jealous."

"Why?"

"You know why," Roth said. "You and Lance, alone in Moscow all that time, totally off-grid."

"Whatever you're suggesting..." Tatyana said.

"I'm not suggesting anything."

"Sure you're not."

"I don't care what the two of you got up to," Roth said, "but Laurel will."

"Don't tell her then," Tatyana said.

"She's the head of the program."

"So what?"

Roth looked at her. From the expression on his face, she could tell he knew more than he was letting on, but if he thought for one second that she and Lance had been together sexually, he was very sorely mistaken.

She knew she should tell him the truth, tell him she'd stayed in Moscow to get word to one of her sources, but once she did, Larissa's fate would be sealed. Roth would know she meant something to her, something more than an ordinary source. Then he'd start looking, and, eventually, he'd find the birth certificates.

Roth wasn't an evil man, but he inhabited a cruel world, a place where betrayals were commonplace, where the currency was lies, and where innocent people ended up alone in dark alleys with bullets in their backs.

The moment he found out about Larissa, she would become

a pawn in his game, a piece of leverage, and there would be no pulling her back out.

Tatyana made up her mind. She would tell Roth about her sister only if it became critical to do so. She didn't know what was going on in Moscow, she didn't know what Larissa had told Lance, and she didn't know if the two of them were still together. If Larissa could get out of Russia without getting involved with Roth, without him ever learning of her existence, that would be safer than any of the alternatives. And whatever Larissa had found out about a potential attack in Moscow, or something involving the Chinese, or someone named the Polar Bear, that wasn't her responsibility. As far as she was concerned, her hands were clean of it. She owed Roth nothing. She looked at him.

"What are you thinking?" he said.

"I'm thinking I'm in."

"You won't regret it."

Tatyana let out a weak laugh. "We'll see about that."

"Come with me," he said, standing up. He led her out of the room and down two sets of stairs to the building's basement. There was a secure door at the bottom of the stairs, and Roth entered a code.

Inside was a command center filled with computer screens, communications equipment, servers, the works. It had everything a fully equipped operations center would have and more.

Laurel was standing in the middle of the room, looking up at a wall-sized screen. The glow of it gave the place a ghostly blue haze.

"When was this taken?" Tatyana said, looking at the screen.

Laurel turned to her.

In the center of the screen, a high-resolution image stretched across eight feet of monitor in all the brilliance of Imax. On it, disheveled and wearing a fleece-lined coat, stood Lance Spector.

"Is this live?" Tatyana said.

"No, it isn't," Laurel said. "It's the last time he was seen. Days ago. We've been scouring Moscow ever since."

28

Sergey didn't drive straight to Baltimore but instead left the I-95 at Wilmington and drove south through Delaware, taking the Chesapeake Bay Bridge into Annapolis. It was night, and the town was quiet.

The girl's school was in Eastport, just across Annapolis Harbor from the Naval Academy, and Sergey was amazed at how prim and proper the rows of houses were. Everything was perfectly orderly, just like in a TV show, with white picket fences, neat rows of elm and cherry trees, and American flags hanging over every porch. It was nothing like Russia. Even the sidewalks were paved nicely, with crosshatched brickwork rather than straight concrete. It irked him.

He wasn't an idealist. He didn't work for the boss because he believed in the cause. He didn't believe in anything. He did it because it was his job. Because he'd always done it. And because Medvedev would have him killed if he ever tried to quit.

But being in America, the evil empire, the place against which ninety-nine percent of his work was directed, put a strong desire in him to see it all go up in flames.

He pulled his car up outside the school fence and lit a cigarette. It was a clear, cold night, and he opened the window.

The kid attended a fancy prep school. He pictured the schoolgirls in their skirts and backpacks arriving in the morning. He made a note of the access points, the traffic flow, and the position any Secret Service detail was likely to take up. Then he got out of the car and walked down the street in the direction of Sandra Shrader's house.

The daughter's name was Elizabeth. She went by Lizzie.

The small surveillance pack he'd been given showed her walking home by this route with a friend. The two separated at the corner of Chesapeake Avenue, and Lizzie walked the last block alone.

If Lizzie was with anyone, Sergey was under strict orders not to make a move. It was essential that no one know she'd been taken. It had to remain a secret. Kirov would arrange for someone to call the mother immediately after he took her. They would tell her in no uncertain terms that if she ever wished to see her child alive again, she had to keep her mouth shut.

The moment US authorities found out the girl was missing, Shrader would become useless to them. The Secret Service would take her into protective custody, remove her access to sensitive data, and assign a hostage negotiator to get the girl back.

Sergey had no qualms about any of it. He didn't know why they wanted the girl or what leverage they sought over the mother. It didn't bother him that the target was a child. If the bosses ordered it, he'd have killed the girl without hesitation.

He followed the route to the house and stopped outside. Strictly speaking, he shouldn't have been there—there could have been cameras—but if no one knew the girl was missing, then no one would watch the tape either.

The house was big. He was no real estate expert but guessed it cost a pretty penny. Around the property was a four-foot-high iron fence with ornamental posts. There was a sign warning prospective intruders that it was protected by a security system, but all the houses on the street had that sign.

The government would have performed a security audit, but given that Sandra had only just moved in, no changes would have been made yet. He doubted there was anything about the house that would pose any trouble.

He went back to the car using an alternate route, there was no guarantee a schoolgirl would walk the same way every day, and when he got to the car, he drove back to the highway in the direction of Baltimore. He reached the city and went to the address he'd been given in the city's Fairfield neighborhood.

It was an industrial area, with an interstate rising above scrap metal yards and car wreckers. Oil storage containers were stacked along the shoreline, and a few tankers floated on the water, fenced off by a maze of chain-link barriers.

On Frankfurst Avenue, nestled between warehouses and an enormous toll plaza for the Baltimore Harbor Tunnel, was a beat-up old house with an overgrown lawn and boarded windows.

He parked his car out front and marveled at the decrepitude of the place. It couldn't have been more different from Annapolis.

Inside, the house was serviceable. It had an old sofa and a Sony television set with a built-in VHS cassette player. In the bedroom, there was bedding and clean towels. The refrigerator had been cleaned and left empty.

He made up a bed in one of the rooms and then went back to the car. He'd passed a Chinese takeout place on his way in and noticed it was open all night. He bought shrimp chow mein, spring rolls, and four beers, and brought them back to the house.

As he sat on the sofa and spread his food out on the table, he realized he'd forgotten to ask for chili sauce.

He turned on the TV and flicked through the channels. He let the voices dust up his English and tried repeating some of the phrases he heard. If he had to speak, his accent would make him stand out. He planned not to speak at all.

When he was done eating, he lit a cigarette and killed the four beers, one after the other. Then he went to the bedroom and lay down on the bed, fully clothed.

In the morning, he drove to a Walmart and bought American jeans, an American shirt, and an American coat. He went back to the school and watched the morning intake. He saw Lizzie arrive with a friend. There was no sign of a Secret Service detail.

He watched Lizzie enter the school.

Sergey had a daughter of his own her age. She lived with her mother. He saw her once or twice a year, always at the same cheap restaurant near her mother's house. They'd make awkward small talk. He'd try to ask the right questions but somehow would always fail. At the end of the meal, he would give her cash in an envelope as if paying for the company.

She attended a school like this in Moscow.

As he thought of her, he reached into his coat and caressed the handle of his gun.

"What happened?" Larissa said when Lance got back to the apartment.

He went straight to the window and pulled back the curtain. "We can't stay here any longer," he said.

Fear flashed across her face. "Did someone follow you?"

"No, but it's not safe to stay. The embassy was riddled with surveillance. If the GRU didn't spot me, the CIA will have."

"Weren't you careful not to lead them back to us?"

"Nothing's a hundred percent," Lance said.

"How much time do we have?"

He looked at his watch. "We can eat, but then we have to go. We have to clean the place down too. Make sure we don't leave behind any clues."

Larissa looked around the apartment. "Where will we go?"

"I'll find us something."

"What about my place?"

He looked at her. "Larissa, I don't think you realize what you've gotten yourself into."

"I've been risking my life for two years," she said. "I'm the reason you even know about the plot against the embassy."

"The life you knew is over. You can never go back to your apartment. You can never use your phone. You can never access your bank account. You can't even use your real name."

She knew the things he was saying were true, but she hadn't fully allowed them to sink in yet. "How will I live?" she said, a quiver in her voice. "What will I do?"

"You'll have to leave the country."

"Without a passport or money?"

"I'm going to help you."

"Really?"

He took a step toward her. "We're on the same side now, Larissa. I won't leave you behind. The agency will look after you."

"What agency?"

"The CIA."

Her head was spinning. She went into the kitchen and put the kettle on the stove. "Do you want coffee?" she said.

Lance nodded. "I bought groceries."

She looked through the bag and unpacked what he'd brought. Some chicken, an onion, mushrooms. There was pasta and a jar of pasta sauce too. "I suppose you want me to cook this?"

"I can do it," he said.

She shook her head and began filling a pot with water.

Lance began packing their things. He'd also bought a bottle of household bleach, and he soaked a rag in it and wiped down all the surfaces. It made the place smell like a public restroom.

"There's a hotel across the street from the embassy," Lance said. "We can watch what's going on from there."

Larissa nodded. "What did you see when you were there?" she said. "Do you think the threat is real?"

"Well, one thing's for sure," Lance said. "If someone is planning an attack, they're not going to have to work very hard.

Security is so lax you could drive a circus through that place and they wouldn't pick up on it."

"Is there someone there you can speak to?"

Lance shook his head. "It's not going to be as simple as that."

"But you have contacts there, right? You work for the government. You can go to them."

"It doesn't work like that," Lance said. "I work outside official channels. There's no one there who knows who I am, and if they did, they wouldn't believe what I had to say."

"Well, we can phone it in. Tell them there's a bomb threat. At least get the compound evacuated."

"There's only one way we can protect that embassy," Lance said, "and that's by finding out who's planning the attack."

"So we watch?" Larissa said.

"We watch."

"What if they go through with the attack while we're watching?"

"We'll have to see it coming."

She was cutting the onion, and it made her eyes water. She dabbed under her eye with her sleeve, careful not to mess up her makeup. "I think you should pass this up the chain," she said. "Walk into the embassy and tell whoever's in charge that an attack is coming. Give them a chance to evacuate. Otherwise, you're just using them all as bait, risking their lives so that you can catch the plotters."

She made the coffee and brought it to the table.

He drank it while she finished making the pasta. She worked very precisely. Each ingredient was important and had to be handled correctly.

They ate at the wooden table in the kitchen and afterward gathered their things, gave the apartment a final sweep, and left.

"I don't have any clothes," she said on their way down the stairs.

He looked at her. "We can fix that easily."

They took her car to a department store and picked up some clothes and toiletries. Then he asked her where she usually parked when she was at home.

"I have a space behind my building," she said.

She'd been driving, but Lance asked her if he could take the driver's seat. They went to her part of town and drove by her building without stopping. It was a large high-rise in a residential area with a parking lot in the back.

"What are we doing here? You said I couldn't come back," Larissa said.

"Is there a specific spot where you leave your car?"

"Yes, there, by the lamppost."

He pulled into the spot, and they got out of the car.

"What are we doing?"

"As far as we know, no one's looking for you yet."

"Right."

"If we leave your car here, where it belongs, it will tell them nothing when they start the search."

30

Sergey parked outside the school fifteen minutes before the final bell. The sky was clear, and he kept the sun to his back. He was a block from the gates and waited, smoking with the window open, until he saw the students filing out. Some went to cars, others to the waiting busses, and some walked.

He pulled out his phone and called Kirov.

"We're still on?" he said.

"Yes, but be careful. You have to make certain there's no Secret Service detail at the house. If she disappears on their watch, the alarm will be raised immediately."

"I thought there was a surveillance team on the street," Sergey said.

"They had to move," Kirov said. "The van was drawing attention."

"Fuck," Sergey said.

"You'll figure it out."

"I have to pull this girl, in broad daylight, without anyone noticing, and you can't even keep eyes on the house?"

"Just figure it out," Kirov said. "And don't screw it up, or it will be both our necks."

Sergey hung up and inhaled deeply from his cigarette. Hundreds of girls in identical uniforms were walking through the front gate of the school. He waited until he saw Lizzie, then threw his cigarette out the window and turned the ignition.

She came out the front gate with the friend he recognized from some of the surveillance photos. Sergey let them cross the street, then pulled out of his spot and followed. They turned onto Chesapeake Avenue, and he drove right by them without slowing down or turning his head.

When he reached Lizzie's street, he turned and passed the house. There was a black Cadillac sedan nearby, and he pegged it as a government vehicle, but when he drove by, it was empty.

He drove around the block, back onto Chesapeake, and passed Lizzie and the friend a second time. The sidewalk on Lizzie's street was lined with pruned cedars, giving some cover from onlookers. When he got back onto her street, he parked at a spot where the trees were particularly thick.

He got out of the car and looked up and down the street. He checked every house, every window. He didn't see anyone. There was no one in any of the yards. There were no cars other than those crossing the intersection at Chesapeake every minute or two.

It looked good.

No security detail, no onlookers, no traffic.

He walked to the back of the car and opened the trunk. Inside was a plastic case. He took it out carefully and brought it into the car. He sat in the passenger seat and opened it on his lap. Inside the case was a bottle of distilled water. There were also two glass vials and a pair of surgical gloves. He put the gloves on and opened the bottle of water. Then, very carefully, he took the two vials from the case and stuck a syringe through the lid of the first. He extracted the contents and added them to the bottle of distilled water, then repeated the process with the other vial.

The first vial contained carfentanil, and the second, remifentanil, both of which were derivatives of fentanyl. They were extremely potent, completely untraceable, and could be easily purchased illegally in every city in America.

When he was satisfied that the substances had mixed, he took the lid off the bottle and replaced it with a store-bought plastic spray pump.

Then he watched the sidewalk in his rearview mirror and waited.

It was a few more minutes before Lizzie finally rounded the corner. The friend was still with her.

That was not good.

With Lizzie, there was a plan. With this other girl, he didn't know how long it would be until she was noticed missing.

He couldn't take her. If the Secret Service heard that the classmate of the daughter of the NSA director was missing, they'd be all over it.

That meant he couldn't take Lizzie either.

He sat still and let them walk past his car. He watched them enter the house and checked his watch.

He didn't know how much time he had before the mother returned, and he considered calling Kirov. He held off, hoping the friend would leave before Sandra got back. He sat another thirty minutes, but the two girls remained in the house.

When an hour had passed, he finally dialed Kirov's number.

"Do you have her?" Kirov said.

"No. She brought home a friend."

"What friend?"

"I don't know. A girl from school."

"Where are they?"

"In the house."

Kirov was quiet for a minute. Then he said, "You have to abort."

"I could take them both," Sergey said.

"No."

Sergey said nothing. He lit a cigarette. He was fucked.

"Do you hear me?" Kirov said. "Do not make a move. I'll get further instructions from Moscow."

"You'll tell them I failed."

"I'll say the plan was flawed."

"I'm going to wait," Sergey said. "Maybe the friend will leave."

"What time is it?" Kirov said.

Sergey looked at his watch. "Almost five."

"The mother will be home soon."

"I know," Sergey said.

He hung up the phone and remained in his seat, watching the house. About an hour later, three black Cadillac Escalades pulled up to the gate. They waited for the gate to open, then entered the driveway in a procession.

Sandra Shrader got out of the front vehicle, and her driver escorted her to the door. They exchanged a few words, and then he went back to the car.

She entered the house alone.

The three Escalades stayed for about fifteen minutes before two of them came back down the driveway and left.

Sergey stayed where he was, watching everything. Sandra's driver was the only Secret Service presence at the house. He sat in the Escalade for about forty-five minutes until Lizzie and her friend came to the front door.

Sandra came out and spoke to the driver. Then the friend got in the car. It reversed down the driveway, the gate opened, and it drove off.

Sergey wasted no time.

He got out of the car and walked up to the gate of the house.

It was open. He walked through it and up the path to the front door. He rang the doorbell and took a step back.

He saw Sandra's outline approach through the frosted glass and looked down at his watch nonchalantly. She was looking at him through the peephole. He sighed and turned around, taking a few steps away from the door as if giving up.

The door opened, and Sandra said, "Can I help you?"

Sergey turned immediately and charged right at her, knocking her flat on her back inside the hallway. He sprayed her in the face with the spray bottle, then kicked the front door shut behind him.

He put his massive hand over her mouth, keeping her quiet as she lost consciousness.

"Who was it, Mom?" a voice said from upstairs.

Sergey crept up the stairs and could see by the lights which room the girl was in. He strode into the room, and as she turned to look, he sprayed her with the bottle and watched her collapse.

When she was out, he took a roll of tape from his coat and wrapped it around her wrists. Then, he put her over his shoulder and carried her down the stairs. He stepped over the mother's unconscious body and looked outside. The Cadillac hadn't returned, and he brought the girl down the path to the gate.

He put her on the ground in the shrubs, went to his car, and pulled it up to the gate. Then he laid the girl on the backseat and covered her with a blanket.

He looked up the street. Still no sign of the Cadillac, but he knew he was cutting it close. If he left Sandra the way she was, she would die of an overdose. He had to go back and revive her.

He went back to the house and checked her pulse. It was very faint. He rolled her on her side and pulled a naloxone device from his jacket. He tore off the packaging and placed the tip in her nostril. He pressed the pump, and it administered a dose of the nasal spray.

Instantly, Sandra gasped for air as if she'd just been brought back from the dead.

He sat over her and watched her come to. She was disoriented, and when her eyes focused and she saw him, she panicked. "Who are you?" she cried.

Sergey was sitting on his haunches, looking down at her, and as her maternal instinct kicked in, she realized immediately that this was about her daughter.

"Where's Lizzie?" she said, tears filling her eyes.

"Listen to me very carefully," Sergey said in his broken English. "If you ever want to see her alive again, you say nothing to no one. Your guard will be back soon. You tell him nothing. If anyone finds out we have your daughter, if the government finds out, we kill her."

"What are you talking about?"

"Someone will be in touch with further instructions. Do what you're told, and you will get your daughter back. If anyone finds out we have her, she loses all her value."

"Loses her value?"

Sergey stood up and walked out the front door. He went back to his car and checked on the girl. She needed naloxone too, but just as he was about to give it to her, he saw a car turn the corner off Chesapeake Avenue.

He got into the driver's seat, turned on the ignition, and pulled out onto the street. At the same time, the Cadillac passed right by him and stopped outside the gate.

As he drove off, Sergey prayed the woman had the wherewithal to follow his instructions.

He drove a few blocks, pulled over at a dark spot, and gave the girl the naloxone. As consciousness returned to her, her eyes grew wide with terror. She didn't know where she was or what was happening but couldn't scream because of the tape on her mouth.

He grabbed her and wrapped more tape around her ankles and wrists. He also covered her eyes with it. She kicked and struggled but was soon reduced to passive whimpers.

He got on the highway toward Baltimore and dialed Kirov's number.

"What is it?" Kirov said.

"I have the girl."

31

The cab pulled up outside a hotel on the Garden Ring, directly across the street from the American embassy, and Lance and Larissa stepped out. He put his arm around her as if they were a couple. A pretty Russian with an American wouldn't arouse the slightest bit of suspicion in this neighborhood.

They entered the hotel, and he made sure they got a room on the top floor overlooking the embassy. He told the receptionist he didn't know how long they were staying, and they declined assistance with their bags.

"We have to be ready to leave this place at a moment's notice," Lance said in the elevator.

Larissa nodded.

"We're hiding in plain sight here. The slightest mistake, and we'll be found."

They made their way to the room, and only when they got inside did they realize how small it was.

"Don't worry," Lance said. "I won't make you share the bed."

Larissa looked like she was going to say something but stopped herself.

Lance went to the window and looked out at the embassy. It was formidable, designed to be one of the most secure places on earth. Getting in and out should have been next to impossible. High walls surrounded the entire compound, and the world's most advanced security systems monitored every movement. Lance knew from classified files that there were underground sensors to protect against tunneling, surface-to-air missile silos to protect against aircraft, military-grade signal blockers to prevent surveillance, and full-spectrum sensors that could detect motion, temperature distortions, and sound with the sensitivity of scientific laboratory equipment.

The problem wasn't in the design of the compound or even with the outfitting of the security systems—it was the fact that some idiot in Washington had given the job of monitoring those systems to a Russian company.

They should be tried for treason, he thought.

The Moscow Embassy was more than just another government building. It had stood in the very center of Moscow through the entirety of the Cold War, during all those years when the specter of nuclear holocaust hung over the world like a low fog. It was a symbol of America's commitment during that conflict, and it was an insult to the memory of every serviceman who died in the Cold War that its security was compromised now.

An attack on the embassy was an attack on America's Cold War legacy. It would challenge the very notion of American hegemony.

Larissa was sitting on the bed watching him, and he said, "Do you want anything? Coffee?"

"I wouldn't mind a drink."

He went to the minibar. It had a selection of liquors in miniature bottles, some wine, and a few bottled beers. "What would you like?"

"How about wine?"

He took out the red and looked for a corkscrew. It was next to the TV. He opened the bottle and poured two glasses.

"Thank you," she said, taking a sip.

She was wound up. He felt like he should reassure her.

He sat on the chair next to the bed and took a sip from his glass. He looked at her. It was the first time he'd had a chance to really look. Her eyes, her mouth, the shape of her lips. He saw Tatyana in every feature.

"What?" Larissa said, looking back at him.

"I was just...."

"Staring."

He smiled. "Tell me again what you heard the Chinese man say."

She took another sip of the wine. "Well," she said, "he told me where he was from."

"Beijing."

"That's right."

"What else?"

"He said he'd been in the Lubyanka."

"Speaking to someone."

"Someone he called a real-life polar bear, with skin so pale he looked ill."

"And what did he say about the embassy?"

"He said there was going to be an attack. He said it would change the world. Make the world realize that the American age has come to an end. Something like that."

"Did he say when?"

She shook her head.

"Did he specifically say it was the Moscow embassy?"

She thought a moment. "I don't remember. Maybe he just said 'embassy,' and I assumed."

"All right."

"Could it be another embassy?"

Lance shrugged. "Moscow is a fair assumption."

She nodded. "He said something about throwing dirt in both eyes."

"Both eyes?"

"Like in a fight. Throwing dirt to blind the enemy."

"I see," Lance said.

"His Russian wasn't good," she said. "He was very drunk. He could have been talking about anything at that point. Maybe it was all in my mind."

"I'm sure you heard what you thought you heard."

She shrugged. "Who knows? Maybe he was crazy."

Lance nodded. "But you went to Tatyana immediately?"

"As soon as I could."

"And what did she say?"

"She said to go to you."

Lance leaned back and took another drink. He prayed Larissa was right in what she'd heard. Otherwise, he was about to create a whole lot of trouble for nothing.

"I've been thinking about what you said earlier," he said.

"What did I say?"

"That it's not fair to treat the embassy as bait. That we have to warn them."

"So you're going to do that?"

"I'm going to try."

"You don't look happy about it."

"Right now, I don't know if I'm someone they'll even listen to."

"They won't believe you?"

"They won't believe me. They won't know who I am."

"And you won't tell them?"

"I guess it doesn't matter," he said. "Bottom line is, if they receive word of a threat, they'll have to step up security."

"Will that be enough?"

He shrugged. "It will make whoever's plotting the attack adjust their plans."

"They'll postpone?"

"Postpone. Change targets. It's no way to catch them, which is why I don't like it."

"But you don't have a choice?"

He shook his head. "I don't think we do."

Larissa stood up and looked out the window. Then she turned to him. "Lance?"

"Yes."

"You said you're a fugitive."

"I might be a fugitive," he said. "That depends on Roth."

"What if you don't come back out?"

"I'll come back out."

"If you're a fugitive, a criminal, and you go in there talking about a bomb, lying about who you are, telling them all these things—what if they just arrest you?

"I'll come back out, Larissa."

She didn't look convinced. She stepped toward him and leaned forward. For a split second, he thought she was going to try to kiss him, but then she picked up the bottle of wine by his side. "If you don't come back out," she said, "I'm as good as dead."

He nodded. He hadn't thought about it from that angle. He'd thought she was worried about him.

She filled her glass.

"I should go," he said.

"All right," she said, turning to the window.

He got up and went to the door. As he opened it, he turned back. "If anything does happen to me...."

"You just said nothing would."

"Larissa," he said, "if anything does—if I don't come back, for whatever reason, you have to get out of Russia."

"And how do I do that without you?"

"You keep a low profile. Leave by train. No airports. Don't run. Don't panic. Go west. Get to Germany. Get to the American embassy in Berlin. Once you get there, tell them you need to speak to Levi Roth at the Central Intelligence Agency. Tell him I sent you."

32

L ance flashed his credentials and entered the embassy compound through the front gate. Roth was meticulous in providing all documents that might be of use on a mission. He said the papers were more important than the weapons in most cases, and kept drop boxes for them in every major city in the world. Lance wasn't sure he agreed, but this wasn't the first time he was glad to have them.

The compound was quiet, it was late, and most staff had left for the night.

The Diplomatic Security Service was located in the new building across the courtyard, and Lance made his way to it.

The building was impressive, he thought, like the offices of a tech company, and a wall of glass stretched four stories above him at an oblique angle.

Inside was an additional security check, complete with x-ray scanners and a metal detector, and Lance was relieved to see that this role was still in the hands of marines. The Marine Embassy Guard, as far as Lance was concerned, was the only proper security force for an embassy as important as Moscow. A long-standing memorandum between the State Department and the Marine Corps said the same thing.

"Evening," one of the marines said to Lance, motioning for him to step forward.

"You guys still perform building security?" Lance said, entering the scanner.

"That's correct," the marine said.

"But they gave perimeter duty to a contractor?"

"A Russian company, that's correct."

"What do you fellas think about that?"

The marine looked at his supervisor. "We're not paid to think," the supervisor said.

Lance nodded. He walked past them to the elevators and swiped a magnetic card. The keycard was CIA property, issued by the Special Operations Group, and its use was monitored closely by a branch of the agency that liaised closely with the NSA. Using it was like sending up a flare, it would tell everyone in Washington exactly where he was, but he had no choice. He needed to get this warning to someone who had the power to prevent an attack, even if that meant getting himself sucked into it.

He saw on the directory that the Diplomatic Security Service was on the third floor and pushed the button. When the elevator doors opened, he found himself in a small lobby with some sofas and a desk. Sitting at the desk was a serious-looking woman in a silk blouse.

Most people had left the office, and her job consisted mainly of sitting in her seat, surfing social media, and playing solitaire. She didn't appreciate Lance's interruption to her routine. "Yes?" she said with a strained sigh.

"I'm from upstairs," Lance said. "We just had something big come in, and I want to get it in front of the station chief immediately."

"I'm sorry," the woman said, looking up from her screen. "Who did you say you were?"

"Anderson," Lance said, sliding a plastic ID across the desk.

The credentials were standard issue and gave him a false name, diplomatic cover, and CIA clearance without referring to a specific role. They were great for gaining access to the embassy or getting through an airport security check, but using them here was risky. There was a good chance this woman knew everyone with clearance in the building by name.

"I just shipped in," Lance added. "Still getting used to this cold. Got any tips?"

She smiled thinly and swiped his card through an electronic scanner. "I'm sure you'll figure it out," she said.

They waited awkwardly while the scanner did its thing. There was a large window overlooking the central courtyard of the compound, and Lance looked out through it. "Quite the view," he said.

She nodded disinterestedly.

There seemed to be some sort of delay with the scanner, and Lance began to worry his credentials had already been revoked. "I really need to see him," he said. "It's urgent."

She looked up from her screen, her smile telling him that she really couldn't have cared less about the hurry he was in. "Just waiting for the security check to pass," she said. "It seems to be acting up."

"Can you put a call through and let him know I'm here?"

"As I'm sure you can appreciate, Mr Rapaport is a busy man."

"He's going to want to hear what I have to say."

"It's also the middle of the night," the woman said. "Maybe this is something you could come back with in the morning?"

"This can't wait."

"Well," the woman said with a shrug, tapping her fingers impatiently on the security scanner.

"Look," Lance said, "I've got information about an imminent security threat, and I need to speak to him immediately. This is something credible. It's serious, and it's urgent."

"If it's urgent, you can take it to the security officer at the front gate."

"I'm not taking this to a Russian guard. I need someone with authority."

"Well, I don't know what to say to you, but I'm not calling Rapaport at home. If it's so important, you can call him yourself."

"Give me his number."

"I'm not allowed to hand out private numbers."

Lance looked around the office. He was beginning to lose patience. He took in a deep breath and tried again. "Listen," he said. "We seem to have gotten off on the wrong foot."

"Not at all, Mr Anderson."

"Why are you being so obstructive? All I want is to speak to someone in charge of security."

She glanced at her screen, and he saw she was beginning to get nervous.

"What does it say?" he said. He could tell from her face it wasn't good.

"Listen," she said. "I can give you the number of the RSO. He's in charge of security for the night. Anything you said would go through him anyway."

"I need to speak to the CIA," Lance said.

"Do you want the number or not?"

"This is ridiculous."

"It's the best I can offer."

"Fine," Lance said. "Give me the number."

The woman wrote a name and phone number on a notepad, and Lance leaned over her, pretending to read what she was writing. He looked at her computer screen and saw the reason she was suddenly becoming more cooperative.

A bright red box on the screen read:

Known Security Threat. Highly Dangerous. Assistance Called.

He leaned back before she realized he'd seen the screen. She handed him the note, and he glanced at it.

"You've been very helpful," he said, putting the paper in his pocket.

He looked around the lobby for an exit. Security was already on its way, and he couldn't use the elevator. He looked at the window again. Three floors down to the courtyard, which was paved in cobblestones. He wasn't going to survive that fall.

"Where's the stairwell?" he said.

She was visibly alarmed now. "That way," she said, nodding down the corridor.

Lance started walking down the corridor as the elevator dinged behind him. The elevator door was opening, and at the same time, the door at the end of the corridor leading to the stairwell opened. Four marines stepped out. Lance turned to the elevator, where four more marines were exiting.

"That's him," the receptionist said, pointing at Lance.

"Halt!" one of the marines shouted.

They drew their guns. Lance was unarmed. He looked up and down the narrow corridor, four armed men at either end. He considered his options and decided he wasn't about to fight eight US marines. Getting arrested might turn out to be a faster way of getting in front of Rapaport anyway.

"Hands in the air!"

Lance put his hands up. The marines closed in, their guns pointed at him. They definitely had him flagged as a high-level threat.

"I'm unarmed," Lance said, trying to de-escalate. He was going willingly. The last thing he needed was a bullet from a jumpy marine.

"Down on your knees," a marine shouted.

Lance dropped to his knees and put his hands behind his head. He knew there was no point in saying anything to these men. Their system said he was a threat. They wouldn't listen to a word he said. He waited, remaining still, and when they got close enough, two men rushed forward and knocked him to the ground, twisting his arms behind his back and slapping on a pair of steel cuffs.

"That's it," the marine said. "Nice and easy."

33

Medvedev stood in the doorway of his office, ogling his secretary. She was wearing a short skirt and a light silk blouse that he'd personally chosen for her. The fabric of the blouse was so thin he could see clear through it, and she squirmed in embarrassment under his gaze.

He was about to say something lewd when the phone rang.

She picked it up and answered, her voice as mild as a kitten. Then she pressed the receiver against her chest and looked at him. "Your call to the NSA Director is ready, sir."

"Tell them to put it through."

It hadn't been easy getting Sandra Shrader's personal cell, but this was an emergency. It was the whole reason he'd dragged himself back to the office in the middle of the night.

Levi Roth's golden boy was at it again, threatening the entire operation. If he didn't get this situation dealt with in the next couple of minutes, the entire attack would have to be called off.

He went back into his office and shut the door, then sank into his enormous leather chair. As he picked up the receiver, he ran his tongue over his lips. "Sandra Shrader," he said in his heavy accent, "I hope I didn't wake you."

"Who is this?" Sandra said, her voice frantic. That was understandable. Her daughter had just been kidnapped, and she had no idea what was going to happen to her.

"This is the man who is—how should we say? *Babysitting* your daughter."

"What have you done with her, you sick bastard?"

"My goodness, Sandra. Mind your language, please."

"Where is she?"

"You'll get her back soon enough."

"If you harm a single hair on her head, so help me God."

"She'll be right as rain, Sandra. So long as you do exactly what I say."

"I'm calling the president right now. The Secret Service will be all over you."

"You make that call, Sandra, and Lizzie ceases to be of any use to me."

"You're going to hell, you sick, rotten piece of—"

"Now, now, Sandra. Let's not get crude. This is a simple business arrangement. A quid pro quo. No need to make it more complicated than it has to be."

There was silence on the other end of the line and then the sound of a stifled scream. He pictured her screaming into a pillow. She took a moment to let out all her rage, then came back to the phone. "What do you want from me?"

"Nothing too complicated. Just a little favor."

"What sort of favor?"

"You'll hardly notice it. The type of thing you do all the time. I have a situation that—how should I say this? Needs to be resolved in a way that conforms to my interests."

"You want to influence a situation?"

"That's correct."

"Regarding US national security?"

"I wouldn't go that far, Sandra. I just need a little nudge."

"What you're asking is treason."

"It's nothing of the sort."

"I could go to prison for the rest of my life if I don't report this call."

"Yes, yes. We've been over all that. You call it in. I slit your daughter's throat. I might even have her brought to Moscow so I can do it myself. I take a lot of pleasure in such things. I like to draw them out. Make a meal out of them."

Sandra began sobbing uncontrollably.

"Maybe I'll send you a memento," he said. "A finger, perhaps. Or a toe. Or her head on a platter with an apple stuffed in her mouth." Sandra was crying so hard he was afraid she'd hurt herself. "Breathe," he said. "Deep breaths."

He could hear her trying to pull herself together. He waited while she cleared her snot and composed herself. He had to get this next part just right. If she got even a whiff of what was going on, everything would be finished. He had to keep her off balance, make her believe his problem was personal, that Levi Roth was his target.

He had a lot of ground to cover. It would be tricky, but he knew she would want to believe what he was saying. Her brain would do anything to avoid having to choose between her daughter and her country. And as long as she could tell herself this was nothing more than the usual jockeying for power, the political tug-of-war of a new CIA director and his Russian counterparts, he might just be able to convince her to do what he wanted.

She was a mother, and her daughter's life was on the line. Mothers were curious creatures. They possessed instincts that should have made them so powerful but instead only seemed to make them weaker. They were so easy to threaten, so easy to manipulate. She cared only for Lizzie. She'd sell out a thousand Levi Roths for her daughter. Any mother would.

"The other man," she stammered. "The one who was here. He said—"

"My man, yes. He's very reliable, Sandra."

"He said if I did everything perfectly, Lizzie would be returned."

"So you're ready to talk?" Medvedev said. "You're done crying?"

"Yes," she said uncertainly.

"I don't want to hear any more of this silliness about going to the Secret Service."

"Okay."

"You do what you're told, and everyone gets to walk away from this happy."

"All right," she said again, her voice barely above a whisper.

He nodded to himself. She was defeated, ready to surrender, the spark of rebellion gone.

He still had to be careful, of course. There were limits to what she would do for him. She wouldn't out and out betray her country. Not yet. That would take time.

But Levi Roth? He could get her to betray him.

"Listen carefully," he said. "We don't want any misunderstandings."

"I'm listening," she said.

"The first thing, the most important thing, is that you need to sound absolutely normal. If anyone suspects even the slightest thing is wrong with you, if they think you've been compromised in any way, it's game over."

"All right."

"Little throats will get slit."

"I said, all right," Sandra cried, the tears coming back.

"You can do that?"

"I can try."

"Oh, you'll have to do better than try, my dear. Lizzie's depending on you."

Sandra went through another round of sobbing, and Medvedev waited impatiently for her to pull herself together.

"I'm ready," she said. "I'll do what you want."

"Good," Medvedev said. "This is quite urgent. I need you to act quickly."

"Okay."

"There's an incident taking place right now at the embassy in Moscow."

"The American embassy?"

"Yes. A CIA agent has just been arrested. He used fake credentials, and he was flagged."

"Okay."

"He's being taken to a secure interrogation room in the embassy as we speak."

"I have no jurisdiction whatsoever over the—"

"Hold on," Medvedev said. "This agent is very important to Levi Roth. Roth's been looking for him. He's going to want to speak to him."

"Okay," Sandra said.

"I need you to make sure that doesn't happen."

"If he's CIA, he's under Roth's jurisdiction."

"Not if you say he's a potential terrorist."

"What?"

"You heard me."

Sandra thought for a moment, then said, "Is this agent's name Lance Spector?"

"Oh, look at you," Medvedev said. "You've been doing your homework. Already researching the opposition."

"Levi Roth's not my opposition."

"You tell yourself that."

"Listen to me," she said. "There's nothing I can do here. Spector is Roth's man. They go back years. The president knows he's no terrorist."

"Does he?"

"Yes."

"Without a doubt?"

"Nothing is without a doubt."

"Exactly. You tell them that you know it sounds far-fetched, but you have real data that's raising flags on every circuit board between Fort Meade and US Cyber Command."

"They'll be able to verify that's not true."

"This will all be behind us by then. Just hint that you've got intelligence suggesting this, Sandra. Don't give details. It's a diversion. You can say later it was a false alarm. I just need you to buy me some time. I must have Spector alone in that interrogation room."

"And Roth can't speak to him at all? That doesn't make sense."

"Say no one can speak to him. Not the ambassador, not the senior diplomatic staff, not the lieutenant colonel at the embassy."

"What are you playing at?" Sandra said.

"That's between me and Levi Roth," Medvedev said. "We go back a very long time, and believe me when I say I have good reasons to want to get this asset away from him."

"You were behind the attack on the Special Operations Group, weren't you? The deaths of those other assets?"

"I have my fingers in a lot of pies, Sandra."

"And what pie are you getting me into here?"

"Listen. We're not here for a history lesson. You don't care about these petty rivalries. You don't care about Levi Roth's career prospects. He's a big boy. He'll look after himself. You need to concentrate on getting your daughter back."

"Anything that harms Roth harms American interests."

"You can't honestly believe that," Medvedev spat.

"He's the CIA Director."

"CIA Directors come and go. What do you care who sits in his seat?"

Sandra sighed. He could tell he almost had her. Just another little push.

"It will never go to plan," she said. "This will blow up in your face. And then it will blow up in my face."

Medvedev did have more leverage. He had secrets Clarice Snow had given him that Roth didn't even know existed. He would have liked to keep them in his back pocket—there was no knowing when he would need them—but if he had to give them to Sandra now, it was a price worth paying. "Listen," he said. "I've got documents that are going to seal the deal for you. Things that will blow the lid wide open on Levi Roth. Just do as you're told. Whatever happens can't be as bad as what I'll do to your daughter if you don't."

"No," she said. "It's ludicrous. If Roth wants to speak to his own asset, I won't be able to stop it. The president won't believe for a second that Spector's a terrorist."

"He doesn't have to believe it, Sandra. He just has to hear that you've heard enough chatter on the airwaves to raise the threat level. Say your people need a couple of hours alone with Spector. Even just one hour. All you want is to keep him isolated—no visitors, no phone calls. It makes sense."

"And Roth's going to just sit by quietly and let that happen?"

"What can he do about it?"

Sandra sighed. "Even if Roth believes I have something real on Lance, he's not going to let the NSA interrogate the single most valuable asset in the entire CIA. There are too many skeletons in the closet."

"That's why you have to tell the president it's time to stop listening so closely to everything Levi Roth says. Point to recent events. This Spector agent went rogue on Roth's watch. He hasn't come in from his last mission. He's not responding to communications. He's supposedly Roth's best man, and now he's just waltzed into the embassy throwing around bomb threats."

"Did he make bomb threats?"

"That's what you need time to investigate. A few hours in an interrogation room. The president won't think that's too much to ask."

"And Roth just has to back off?"

"He's too close to Spector to look at this with any degree of objectivity. That compromises the entire CIA. This threat is based on NSA intelligence, and the NSA needs to be allowed to control the interrogation room."

"Control the interrogation room? The NSA doesn't even have personnel in Moscow."

"Send in the RSO. He's responsible for embassy security. This is his job."

The RSO was the most senior member of the Diplomatic Security Service stationed in Moscow. He was responsible for overall embassy security, and that included authority over the marines.

"The RSO doesn't answer to me," Sandra said.

"You don't have to worry about that. You just convince the president to give you the room. Keep everyone else out. Once you get the room, send in the RSO."

"The RSO?" Sandra said doubtfully.

"He's impartial. He's a civilian. He doesn't work for you or Roth. It will look like you're just trying to get to the facts."

"You're forgetting," Sandra said, "that Levi Roth is one of the president's most trusted advisors. He's spent more time in the Oval Office than anyone in Washington. There's no way the president's going to side with me over this."

"You've got to convince him, Sandra. Look at Roth's recent mistakes. The Special Operations Group was blown wide open. Three of the nation's most valuable assets were killed in a single day. The entire project is in the process of being disbanded. Maybe it's time to reassess Roth's position. He's been around a long time. Maybe he's becoming a liability."

"You're trying to use one rogue agent to pull down Roth's

entire career. It's just not possible. The president and Roth are closer than brothers."

"Read the Bible, Sandra. Even brothers turn on each other eventually."

"Not these brothers."

"Listen to me. If there's ever been a time the president's been ready to cut the cord with Levi Roth, it's now."

"You're wrong on that."

"Everyone loses their value eventually, Sandra. You'll learn that soon enough. Mark my words, you plant this seed in the president's ear, and it will grow. Roth's loyalty to a rogue agent. The implication that there's a terrorist plot. The president won't be able to ignore that."

"But none of it's true. They'll find that out."

"That doesn't matter. I'll have what I want by then."

"Which is what?"

"I thought you were smarter than that, Sandra."

"Who are you?" she said.

"Who am I?" Medvedev teased. "Think, Sandra."

"It's Spector," she said. "The RSO is in your pocket. You're going to kill Spector."

"*Brava*, my dear. I'm going to kill Spector. Getting rid of him, and hurting Roth at the same time, that's critical."

"You want to burn to the ground everything Roth's built."

"Is that so bad? Isn't it time for a change of the guard? Nothing lasts forever."

"You're asking me to tear down the career of a man who practically built America's intelligence apparatus. He's a legend here. They'll name a building after him when he's gone."

"What do you care for Roth's career?" Medvedev said, getting nervous. If she suspected for a second that this whole thing was about anything more than disgracing Roth and killing one of his assets, she'd go straight to the president. All the threats in the world wouldn't make a difference then. "I think you need to focus," Medvedev said. "Worry about what's important to you. Your job isn't to protect Roth. It's to protect your country and your family. And what I need is for you to keep Roth out of that interrogation room. It's one hour, Sandra. Surely you can manage that."

"You want Spector to sit tight in a cell until the RSO arrives? That's it?"

"That's it. So simple. And when it's done, you get your daughter back."

She was so close he could feel it.

"All right," she said at last. "Let's say I do everything you want. Let's say the president buys everything I say and gives me full control of the investigation. How do I stop Roth from simply going around my back? The CIA has multiple personnel stationed in Moscow. I don't have anyone. If the marines posted to Spector's room let Roth's guys in, there's nothing I can do to stop it."

Medvedev nodded. She was right. Everything depended on keeping Spector isolated, but the damned RSO was with his Russian mistress at a dacha outside the city. He'd been sent for but was still an hour away. It was a vulnerability that Sandra had no power to remedy. Medvedev realized he would have to deal with it personally.

He didn't know exactly what information Spector had, but the fact he was at the embassy at all proved he'd found out something. Just letting him sit in the room for an hour while the RSO made the drive back was too risky.

The mission was too important.

Medvedev grabbed his coat and put it on. He was going to break one of his cardinal rules. He was going to go out into the open. He was going to expose himself. If he wanted Spector to eat a bullet in that interrogation room, he was going to have to deliver it himself.

"Just do what I told you," he said to Sandra. "You know what happens if you don't."

34

L aurel told the cab to pull over outside the first bar that looked halfway decent. "Right here. This is fine," she said impatiently.

She swung her legs out of the cab and, as soon as she tried to stand, realized her stiletto heels were higher than she'd thought. The shoes had been sitting by the door, and she'd grabbed them impulsively on her way out of the house and put them on in the taxi.

They were Tatyana's, of course. That woman could walk on stilts if she had to.

Laurel hadn't had the benefit of GRU training in that regard, and she wobbled on them like the simple Alabama girl she was.

She felt like a mess. She'd slipped into a tight black dress back at the house, and her makeup had been hastily applied in the cab, in the dark, with the aid only of her compact mirror.

This had been a hasty decision, a spur-of-the-moment jaunt. She'd wanted to get away without Tatyana seeing her. She planned on doing a few things she did not particularly want Tatyana's judgmental eye to witness. She wanted to get drunk, she wanted to have fun, and she wanted to get fucked. In that order.

She walked past the bouncer, grabbing hold of his arm for support when she almost broke an ankle on the step, and went straight to the bar.

The place wasn't particularly busy, and she didn't have to fight for service. "Tequila," she said.

The bartender put a shot glass in front of her and filled it. Laurel didn't have time to waste on lemon and salt. She knocked the shot back neat and shut her eyes, relishing the burning sensation in her throat as she slammed the glass on the bar. "Again," she said. She was ready to blow off some serious steam.

"My kind of girl," the bartender said, eyeing her up.

"Oh, buddy," she said. "I'm just getting started."

She'd already decided she was going home with someone. Anyone. She wasn't going to be picky. As long as he had all the right equipment and knew how to use it, she was all his.

This bartender looked like a perfect candidate.

She caught his eye as she knocked back the second shot. Already, she could feel the tension releasing from her body.

She and Tatyana had been cooped up in the house together for too long. If they stopped to eat, it was takeout in front of their keyboards, and when they slept, it was in rooms separated by only a narrow hallway.

She was beginning to feel claustrophobic.

They hadn't been able to find Lance. He was completely off the grid, as if he'd disappeared in a puff of smoke. Laurel was beginning to fear something very bad had happened.

And the whole time, while they performed hour after hour of tedious search routine, locked together in the command room with only each other for company, Laurel had the distinct impression Tatyana was lying about something.

She'd have bet her life Tatyana knew more than she was letting on.

She and Lance had been off the radar for over a week in Moscow. The more Laurel thought about it, the more convinced she made herself that the two of them had been together during that time.

She couldn't get the thought out of her mind. She hated herself for it, but she kept picturing Lance with Tatyana in some dingy apartment, the two of them awake into the wee hours of the morning, sweating and moaning and heaving on top of each other like two feral animals. It made her want to scream.

And it was so stupid. Laurel and Lance weren't even an item. They never had been. Probably never would be. They barely knew each other, and what time they had spent together, they'd fought.

"Another shot?" the bartender said.

"Hit me."

She hated that she was jealous. She prided herself on her professionalism. Her job came before everything in her life. It wasn't just about her career. The work they did was personal to her. She'd cut ties with family, given up relationships. She'd decided long ago she'd never marry or have kids. And now she was acting like a jealous schoolgirl with a crush.

It drove her nuts.

She didn't even like Lance. She never had.

Roth had brought her in to bring Lance back. Lance was his most valuable asset, the most effective assassin in Special Operations Group history, and the future of the group was at stake if someone didn't lure him back.

Her job was to be the bait.

She'd maybe compromised a little too much in what she'd agreed to. She'd signed every waiver and consent form Roth put in front of her, and before she knew it, she was undergoing cosmetic surgery to increase her resemblance to a woman Roth thought Lance loved.

Maybe they really were all as messed up as Lance said.

For Roth to even think he could replace a dead woman, a woman he'd ordered killed—what did that say about his psyche?

And the really sad part was that the surgery was Laurel's idea. She'd seen the pictures of Clarice, had noticed the resemblance, and had been the one to initially suggest enhancing the resemblance artificially. It was supposed to be a way of tipping the scales, so to speak. Make it impossible for him not to come back.

Maybe it was impossible to do a job like theirs without being screwed up in some fundamental way, she thought.

In any case, it all backfired. It never worked the way she'd thought it would. Lance didn't care who she looked like. It seemed to Laurel that Russian women were more his type.

She knocked back another shot.

That's what their job did to people. They started out spying on other countries but ended up spying on each other.

Laurel only had herself to blame for any of it. She'd signed up willingly. She hadn't had all the facts, but she'd known the world she was getting involved with.

The surgeries, the attempt to manipulate Lance, made her feel cheap. Like a whore. Like a cheerleader forced to sleep with the quarterback to keep him playing at his best. But it was too late now to undo any of it.

Her phone buzzed, and she pulled it out of her pocket. It was Tatyana.

"Oh, get lost," she muttered to herself, knocking back another shot and ordering a refill.

The thing about Tatyana, the thing that bothered Laurel, was that none of it was her fault. Tatyana had nothing to do with any of it. And even if she and Lance had been together, why should anyone even care?

She picked up the phone and answered. "What is it?" she said impatiently.

"Laurel, you need to get back here."

"I just borrowed them," Laurel said, looking at the shoes she'd taken.

"Laurel," Tatyana said in her flawlessly sexy Russian accent. "You need to get back here right now. Do you understand me?"

"Why? What's happened?"

"We've got a hit."

"What do you mean, a hit?"

"It's Lance. He just popped up out of nowhere."

"Where?"

"We shouldn't be talking on the phone."

Laurel was feeling the effects of the tequila and said, "Just tell me, for God's sake."

"The embassy."

"What embassy?"

"The US embassy in Moscow. He just walked in off the street and asked to speak to the head of security."

35

Larissa watched the embassy from the hotel room window with a growing sense of dread. Ten minutes turned into an hour, and then two hours, and there was still no sign of Lance. She kept glancing at her watch as if that would somehow bring him back sooner.

She knew that if he didn't re-emerge soon, she would be on her own. She wasn't ready for that. She couldn't make it all the way to Germany alone. She wasn't built the way Tatyana was. She needed Lance's help.

When two hours and ten minutes had passed, and there was still no sign of him, she knew she had to do something.

She grabbed her coat and purse and left the room. In the elevator, she wanted to cry. She could feel the knot of emotion in her chest, but she held it back. She would need it for what was coming.

She went out of the front of the hotel and stood on the steps, looking at the embassy across the street. It was almost dawn, and the morning traffic was beginning to pick up. There were some taxis by the curb, and the doorman asked if she wanted one.

"No, thank you," she said, her gaze fixed on the embassy gates. She pictured the moment, just a few hours earlier, when Lance had disappeared through them.

She knew now that it had been a mistake to let him.

Armed guards stood in front of the gates and in the small heated guard post. They wore black uniforms and body armor and carried assault rifles. Headsets were attached to their helmets.

Two guards leaned on a concrete barrier by the gate, smoking cigarettes. A black limousine pulled up, and they waved it through. Larissa watched as the gate opened and the limousine drove through to the courtyard. When it stopped, a driver got out and opened the back door, letting out an enormous, white-haired man. As the man hobbled toward one of the buildings, the driver held an umbrella over his head. Larissa thought that was strange. It was dark. It wasn't raining. She wondered what the umbrella could be shielding him from before realizing it was overhead satellite surveillance.

She knew then that something very bad was about to happen.

Without deciding what her plan was, without even stopping to think, she crossed the street toward the gates.

When she reached the guard post, she went up to the window and started screaming at the guard inside. The words came to her spontaneously. "You took my husband!" she screamed in Russian. "You bastards took my husband!"

The guard, a Russian contractor, didn't have the faintest clue what she was yelling about. "We took no one," he stammered.

"My husband!" she screamed. "You took him! You took him!"

The man looked around desperately for backup. The other guards were as taken aback as he was. "I don't know what the hell you're talking about," he said.

"My husband! You took him! You dragged him inside, and he never came back out."

"What is this?" a senior guard said, approaching the post from inside the compound.

"Sir, this woman says we took her husband."

Larissa was getting more frantic by the minute. She let her emotions take over. She was already terrified Lance wouldn't come back out, and all she had to do was give full voice to those fears, and the role came naturally. "My husband!" she screamed. "He did nothing wrong. He's a Russian citizen. They can't just take him."

"There's no one in there," the senior guard said to her. "It's the middle of the night. The embassy isn't even open."

Larissa grabbed him by his vest, and he shoved her off. "Get rid of her before she creates a scene," he said to the other guards. "Get her the hell out of here. She's crazy."

Two guards came at her, grabbing her by the arms. They half-carried, half-dragged her back toward the sidewalk.

"You can't do this," Larissa yelled. "My husband is in there. He's Russian. Let him out."

"Get out of here before you get in serious trouble," one of the guards said, shoving her across the sidewalk.

She stumbled into the street and was almost hit by a passing cab. It swerved to avoid her, and the driver jammed his brakes. He'd seen the guards shove her and got out of his car to see what was going on. He was a big guy with a stubbled face and thick arms, and he was angry. "What the hell is going on here?" he demanded. "You could have killed her."

His car was blocking one of the three traffic lanes, and cars were already getting backed up behind it. They weren't shy with the honking, but the cab driver didn't pay them the slightest attention. He stormed up to the guards, looking ready for a fight.

"Get back!" one of them yelled at him, raising his weapon.

The driver wasn't fazed in the least and said, "You guys ought to be ashamed of yourselves."

He turned to Larissa, and she started blabbering frantically. "They took my husband," she said, feeling every bit as desperate as she sounded. "He's Russian, and they took him into the embassy. They just took him."

"What?" the driver said, outraged.

Someone rolled down a window and yelled at him to get his car out of the way. The cab driver yelled back.

Larissa knew she needed to do everything she could to add to the commotion. She went into the street and blocked more of the traffic. Cars honked, and some drove around her, but enough stopped that a backup became inevitable.

"They have my husband!" she yelled at the cars, and some of the drivers began to get out. "The Americans. They took my husband. They kidnapped him."

As more people heard what she was saying, a crowd began to grow in front of the embassy gates. People were shouting at the guards, demanding an explanation, outraged that a foreign embassy would dare snatch a Russian citizen off the streets of Moscow.

"She's crazy!" one of the guards shouted from inside the post.

The next moment, a large cobblestone smacked against the plexiglass window in front of his face.

"Don't believe them!" Larissa yelled to the crowd.

More rocks started flying, forcing the guards to take cover behind the gates.

As the crowd got increasingly aggressive, it only served to attract more attention. It wasn't long before a city police cruiser pulled up, and an officer stepped out.

Larissa was at the front of the crowd, whipping up the people's emotions, and the police officer approached her. "What's the problem here?" he said.

"Officer," Larissa said, making sure as many people as possible heard what she was saying, "these guards dragged my husband into the embassy, and now they refuse to let him back out."

"What?" the police officer said. If anything, he was even more outraged than the people in the crowd. "They can't do that."

"They snatched him!" she yelled.

When the crowd saw the officer's reaction, they grew even more emboldened.

"Let him out!" someone cried.

"Storm the gates!" someone else shouted.

"Your husband is Russian?" the police officer said.

"Yes," Larissa cried. Her story evolved as she told it, and the crowd grew angrier and angrier. It wouldn't be long before they had a full riot on their hands.

"These guards whistled at me," Larissa yelled. "They called me a prostitute."

"What?" the officer said.

"Some Americans joined them and called me a Russian whore."

"And then the guards took your husband?"

"They dragged him through the gate. A Russian man in the middle of Moscow! They took him, as if the whole city belonged to them."

The police officer started relaying the story on his radio. A minute later, five more squad cars had arrived, backing up even more traffic and creating a show of lights that attracted more attention.

"They're arrogant," Larissa yelled. "They think they own everything. They think they can do whatever they want."

"This is still Moscow," someone in the crowd yelled.

"Show them who's in charge here," someone else yelled at the cops.

The embassy guards were getting very worried. They'd all retreated behind the safety of the high gates, and riot gear was being distributed. They lined up in a show of force, and the situation looked so serious that the marines were being called from inside the buildings. Even embassy officials, the few who were on-site, began to come out of their offices to see what was going on. Larissa saw them speaking to each other nervously in the courtyard, trying to figure out what had happened to create such a dramatic situation right on their doorstep. Some shouted into their cellphones. Others spoke to the marine commander, or the head of the security contractor, desperately trying to determine how they would protect the embassy.

And then, just when Larissa thought the atmosphere couldn't get any more heated, and the crowd looked like it was ready to storm the gates, the sound of low-flying helicopters filled the air.

36

Sandra entered the White House for her first face-to-face meeting with the president since her appointment. As the aide showed her to the Roosevelt Room, she was keenly aware that she was there not as a patriot, sworn to defend the nation, but as a traitor, compromised by a foreign power.

Medvedev had made her options very clear. She could get the president to turn against Roth and Spector, or she could let her daughter be murdered in cold blood by a Russian assassin.

"Coffee?" the aide said.

"What?"

"Coffee?"

"No," Sandra said, and belatedly, "thank you."

The aide left her in the room alone, sitting at a large conference table surrounded by ornate wooden chairs. She rapped her fingers on the polished wood nervously. Every second counted. She'd already taken steps to hijack the situation in the embassy. Still, if she didn't secure the president's authorization in the next few minutes, the orders would be rescinded, and Spector would be released.

The aide returned. "The president will see you now."

Sandra stood up too quickly and almost knocked over her chair.

"Are you all right, Ms. Shrader?" the aide said, looking at her curiously.

"I'm fine," she said, following the aide to the Oval Office. She felt as if she was in a dream. She couldn't allow herself to think. She couldn't hesitate. The slightest sign of doubt and the president would see right through her.

"Sandra!" the president said, rising to his feet as she entered the room.

She shook his hand firmly, looking him in the eye. Then she cleared her throat and said, "Mr President," in as steady a voice as she could muster. Outside on the South Lawn, she could see that it had begun to snow. A Secret Service officer stood on the porch and rubbed his arms for warmth.

"Can I offer you anything?" the president said.

She shook her head. She didn't have time for niceties. "Sir," she said, "we've got a serious situation."

"What's that?" he said, taking a seat on the sofa in the center of the room.

Sandra sat across from him and pulled a folder of documents from her briefcase. The documents were a prop. They contained nothing but raw data, ordinary SIGINT streams from communications networks around the globe. It hadn't been analyzed and had nothing to do with the embassy in Moscow.

"It's urgent, sir."

"All right."

"We don't have time to go through the data right now, but I need you to authorize the NSA to take control of the embassy in Moscow."

"What?"

"Yes, sir. I'm gravely concerned that unless we act immediately, something catastrophic is about to happen."

"What do you mean?"

"An attack, sir."

"Sandra!" the president said, his face suddenly ashen. "What are you coming to me for? There are far faster channels."

"Because, sir," she said, and she glanced around the room, "this attack is coming from our own side."

"What?"

"Sir, what I'm telling you is alarming. I understand that. But there are factions in Washington that want to go to war with Moscow."

"Of course there are," the president said. "There are factions in Washington for everything."

"But this faction is taking action, sir. They're making a move."

The president looked at her very closely as if trying to read her mind. She shifted uncomfortably under his gaze. "What faction are we talking about, Sandra?"

"Sir," she said, "before we go any further, I need to know the embassy has been secured."

The president said nothing. She could see the cogs in his mind working. He didn't like what he was hearing. That much was clear. "I need to speak to Levi," he said at last.

"Sir," she said, thinking only of Lizzie and what was going to happen to her if she didn't pull off this ruse successfully, "that would be a very bad idea."

The president pulled out his phone. Roth was just a call away.

"Please, sir," Sandra said.

The president gritted his teeth. He pushed a button on the phone, and the aide entered immediately.

"Yes, sir?"

"Get Roth down here," he said to her. "I don't care where he is or what he's doing. You tell him to get his ass to the Oval Office pronto."

"Yes, sir."

"Sir," Sandra said, almost in a whisper. She was thinking of her daughter, and the terror in her voice only added to the veracity of her performance. "Roth is implicated in this."

The president became very still. For a moment, Sandra thought he was going to kick her out of the room. There was no turning back now. She was ruining her career, committing treason against her country, and probably securing a life sentence in a supermax prison. The president would see this for what it was, a bald-faced attempt to lie to his face.

He looked at her, eyeing her very closely, then said, "Whatever you've got in your little binder there, I think it will have to wait for Levi to get here."

"Sir," she said, and even to her own ear, her voice sounded false. "The threat to the embassy is from the CIA."

"I beg your pardon," the president said, outraged that she would even dare utter such a claim in his presence.

"The data streams," she stammered, opening the documents as if they could somehow make him believe the impossible. "We're getting indications from all directions that Roth's most trusted asset, a man named Lance Spector—"

"I know Lance Spector," the president said, almost daring her to impugn him.

"Sir, he just walked into the embassy in Moscow, threatening to blow the entire compound sky-high."

"I don't know where you're getting this *data*," the president said, shaking his head.

"And that's not all, sir," she said, her words getting faster and faster. "Spector, he's receiving his orders directly from Washington."

"Sandra, stop this."

"From Roth, sir. From Levi Roth." She pushed the papers toward him, and in her haste, they fell to the floor. "It's all here," she said, reaching for the scattered pages.

"Sandra, you need to stop talking."

She knew she'd gone too far. She'd destroyed her credibility. Ruined herself in his eyes. How would he ever trust her again when all this proved to be a bunch of nonsense?

But she had no choice.

The president got up from his seat. She could tell from his body language that he was about to have her removed from the room. He walked over to his desk and very deliberately reached underneath to where his security button was located.

"Do I understand this correctly?" he said. "Levi Roth, trusted advisor to generations of American leadership at the very highest level, is plotting to blow up an embassy he's spent the better part of his life protecting?"

"I know it's far-fetched, sir."

"Far-fetched? Sandra, were you aware that twenty years ago, Roth almost lost his life rushing into the embassy in Nairobi before it was blown to pieces."

"Sir, I know that's in his file."

"Over two hundred people died that day, Sandra."

"Sir," she said.

He paused to give her a chance to reply, but she had nothing. "Enough," he said. "Whatever your *data streams* purport to show, you can save it until Roth gets here. I won't hear another word of it until he can defend himself."

Sandra felt her entire world collapsing. She'd lied to the president and feared her reputation was ruined. And worse, Lizzie, her dear Lizzie, was going to lose her life because of it.

She couldn't even come clean now. She couldn't ask for help. She'd be in a prison cell long before anyone asked about her reasons.

She was a traitor.

The entire nation would despise her when it came to light.

The door flung open, and she expected to see security guards, ready to manhandle her out of the office. But it was the aide, a distraught look on her face. "Sir!" she blurted before realizing she'd opened the door without knocking. She looked from the president to Sandra, then back.

"What is it?" the president said impatiently.

"Multiple reports, sir. The embassy in Moscow is under attack."

The president looked at Sandra. His face went pale with shock. "Good God," he said quietly.

"Sir," Sandra said, sensing that she'd just been given one last-ditch chance to save her daughter's life. "You need to order the CIA to stand down immediately. It's a matter of life and death."

37

L aurel kicked off the high heel shoes and went down to
the control room barefoot.

The control room was a work of art. Roth had
spared no expense. In complete secrecy, without using any CIA
resources, he'd created a completely secure facility with full
satellite communication links, onsite encryption, quantum-
based cyberattack safeguards, backup systems for power and
communications outages, and direct tie-ins to Pentagon, CIA,
and NSA real-time intel streams. The result was a control center
as effective as anything they could have had at Langley.

Laurel typed in her passcode and entered the room. There
was a fresh pot of coffee at the machine, and she poured herself
a cup.

Tatyana was at a satellite terminal and looked up at her.

"I've been drinking," Laurel said.

Tatyana scanned her, taking it all in—the bare feet, the
short dress, the makeup. Then she pulled up some footage to
the main screen.

Laurel just stared at it. "What...?" she said, lost for words.
"That's...."

Tatyana nodded. "This is live," she said.

The footage showed Lance being arrested at gunpoint by marines. "Why are they arresting him?"

"His credentials," Tatyana said. "Roth had them flagged."

Laurel looked at the screen in disbelief. There he was, larger than life, his face in perfect high definition. And he was on his knees, letting marines handcuff him.

"Why did he turn himself in?" Laurel said. "It makes no sense. He's been hiding out for weeks. Now he just walks into the embassy and gets himself arrested?" She turned to Tatyana and again got the feeling there was something she wasn't telling her. "Where's the sound?" she said.

"This feed is coming from the NSA," Tatyana said. "They're saying there's something wrong with the buffer."

"So, we can't get sound?"

"Not until they fix it."

"We can't get sound on what's happening inside our own embassy?"

Tatyana shrugged. "NSA's got control. I can't access it."

Laurel shook her head. "We need to speak to Lance immediately. He wouldn't just turn himself in like this without reason. Something's going on."

"Agreed," Tatyana said.

"Whatever brought him in, it's going to be something big. Get the station chief on the line."

Tatyana hit some keys, and a dial tone came over the speaker. It was followed by the voice of the CIA Station Chief in Moscow, a man named Rapaport.

"This is Laurel Everlane," she said to him, "calling under authorization Alpha, Lima, Alpha."

Tatyana sent the security verification, and they waited while Rapaport checked his phone for confirmation.

"Ms Everlane," he said after a moment, "I take it this isn't a personal call."

"Are you at the embassy?" Laurel said.

"I am, and before you say anything, I've got to tell you something very strange is going on. There's a riot brewing on the street outside, and we've just been ordered to stand down."

"What?"

"The entire CIA operation in Moscow."

"Under whose authority?"

"The authority of the president."

"The president?" Laurel said. She looked at Tatyana.

"NSA," Tatyana mouthed.

Laurel nodded. It had to be.

Rapaport said, "Do you know what's going on?"

"A CIA asset just walked in," Laurel said. "He's on the third floor. He's been arrested."

"Why would NSA lock us out of that?" Rapaport said. "It makes no sense."

"You've got to get to him," Laurel said. "Find out what's going on. Why he came in."

"My hands are tied," Rapaport said. "They've got marines at our door. Whatever's going on is way above my pay grade."

"You're the CIA Station Chief," Laurel said. "That man is a CIA asset. Get your ass to the third floor and give this phone to Lance Spector. We've got to speak to him."

There was some noise in the background, someone telling Rapaport to get off the phone. Then the line went dead.

Laurel looked at Tatyana. "What the hell?"

"NSA is up to something," Tatyana said. "They're trying to kick me off the video feed now too."

"What?"

"Whatever brought Lance in," Tatyana said. "They don't want us to know what it is."

Laurel's mind ran over the permutations. None of them made any sense. "We need to speak to Roth."

Tatyana hit some keys, and a moment later, Roth's gravelly

voice filled the room. "Laurel," he said immediately, "are you getting this?" He sounded out of breath.

"Are you all right?" Laurel said.

"Something's going on. What have you got?"

"A live feed from the embassy. Lance is in custody. The stream's being buffered by NSA, and they're trying to kick us off."

Roth cleared his throat. He sounded rattled. "The president's just ordered in-country CIA to stand down."

"We spoke to the station chief," Laurel said.

"Any way he can get to Lance?"

"It sounded like the marines took his phone from him."

"Jesus," Roth said.

"What's going on, boss?"

"Shrader's making a play. I'm not sure what her game is, but she claims Lance is involved in a bomb plot."

"Against the embassy?"

"Yes."

"That's ridiculous."

"Well, the president just gave her jurisdiction over the whole thing. I've been summoned to the White House. The president is not happy."

"What does he think is going on?"

"It sounds like Shrader's fed him some crock of shit about us being too close to Lance to see him for what he is."

"And what is he?"

"A traitor."

"Shrader said that?"

"I'll know more when I get out of the Oval Office. Although I doubt it will be good news."

Tatyana pulled up satellite footage of the embassy compound. A crowd was gathering outside, and it looked angry.

"You've got to find out what brought Lance into the

embassy," Roth said. "He's not there for the coffee. Something's coming."

"Sir," Laurel said. "A mob is gathering in front of the embassy."

"Fuck me," Roth said. "I'm at White House security. I've got to go. See what sense you can make of all this. And see if you can get that audio feed running. I want to know what Lance was saying before they arrested him."

The line went dead, and Laurel turned to Tatyana. "I don't think I've heard him swear before," she said.

Tatyana shrugged.

Laurel pulled the satellite footage up to the primary monitor and zoomed in. The crowd was about a hundred strong, and growing. Traffic on the Garden Ring was backed up, and people were getting out of their cars to see what was causing the commotion. Whatever it was, it was about to get a whole lot worse.

"There," Laurel said. "What's that?" Someone was standing at the front of the crowd, riling them up. "Zoom in there."

Tatyana zoomed in on the person's face and then suddenly jerked her hand as if she'd gotten a shock from the console, knocking over her coffee. The cup fell to the floor and shattered all over Laurel's feet.

"Oh my God," Tatyana said. "I'm so sorry." She bent down to pick up the pieces, and Laurel got down next to her.

"Are you all right?" Laurel said.

"I'm fine," Tatyana said. "Just jumpy."

Laurel noticed Tatyana's hand was shaking. She took the pieces of porcelain from her and put them in the trash.

Tatyana went to grab a rag to mop up the spill, and Laurel turned her attention back to the screen. She zoomed the camera in on the person at the front of the crowd. It was a young woman. She was addressing the crowd, getting them worked up, making them angrier and angrier. Some of the men picked up rocks and flung them over the gate. The embassy guards were forced back, and Laurel saw that some of them had their guns drawn, aimed at the crowd. The situation was headed for disaster.

She zoomed in on the woman's face and turned to see that Tatyana was white as a ghost. She was staring at the screen, her mouth open, her eyes as big as saucers.

"What's wrong?" Laurel said.

Tatyana shook her head.

Laurel looked at her, then back at the screen. "Tatyana!" she said. "Who is that woman?"

Tatyana said nothing. She was nervous. Hiding something.

"Please don't lie to me," Laurel said.

Tatyana shook her head again. She looked like she was going to cry. "This is my fault," she said.

"Whatever you're hiding," Laurel said, "it's time to stop."

"I never meant to lie to you."

This was it, the conversation Laurel had been dreading. "I knew it," she said.

"Laurel," Tatyana said, her voice quivering with emotion. "It's not what you think."

Laurel looked away. She didn't want to hear it.

"Lance didn't want to be found," Tatyana said. "He made me promise not to say anything."

"I see."

"But he and I...."

Laurel shook her head.

"We didn't, Laurel. Not once."

Laurel felt her face flush. She couldn't believe the conversation had come to this, but she couldn't hide her emotions any longer. "Whatever you and Lance did, that's your business," she said, turning to the screen. "But if you know something about this, what's happening on this screen right now, I need to know."

The young woman's face still filled the screen. Laurel zoomed out, and they saw that the crowd had continued to grow.

"You've got to stop lying to me," Laurel said. "You've been hiding something since you got here. You either start talking or...."

"Or what?" Tatyana said.

Laurel could see she was shaken. She kept looking at the screen like she was afraid of what it would show. Laurel brought it back in on the young woman, and then she saw it. The way she held her head. The shape of the eyes. The movement of her mouth as she worked the crowd. She looked exactly like Tatyana.

"You know that woman," she said.

Tatyana shook her head.

"Who is she?"

"She has nothing to do with this."

"Nothing to do with this?" Laurel said. "She's inciting a riot outside the front gates."

"She's..." Tatyana said.

Laurel knew it before she even said it.

"She's my sister."

Laurel had to sit down. "You'd better start explaining right now," she said, "before I start to lose my shit."

"She was an informant of mine," Tatyana said. "In Moscow."

"And what is she doing with Lance?"

"I told her how to find him."

"When?"

"It was just before I left Moscow. I was trying to get word to her that I was burned. I had to let her know it was time to flee. I couldn't just leave her behind, Laurel."

"Okay."

"That's why I stayed in Moscow. I wasn't with Lance. I swear."

"I don't care about that."

"Yes, you do," Tatyana said. "I know you do. You're jealous. And that's fine. I get it. You like him."

"I do not," Laurel said, feeling her face flush again as she said it.

"It doesn't matter. It shouldn't get between us. I was in the city so that I could get word to my sister. It's my fault she's involved in all this, and I couldn't leave her behind."

"So, you sent her to Lance?"

"I left her a message. And I gave her a way to contact me. I had a line. I carried a cell."

"And she called it?"

"She said something about an attack at the embassy. That a Chinese and a Russian were involved. They'd met at the Lubyanka and were plotting something."

"You knew about this the entire time you've been here?"

"I couldn't verify any of it," Tatyana said. "It was just something she'd overheard. I sent her to Lance because I wanted him to get her out of the country. I wanted to keep her safe."

"And now the NSA is claiming he's plotting to blow the whole place up."

Tatyana nodded.

"I can't believe you didn't tell me this."

"I was only thinking of my sister," Tatyana said desperately. "She's the only family I have left. She doesn't belong to this world. It's my fault she's involved, and now I've fled the country and left her behind."

Laurel stared at her. She couldn't believe they'd been watching this scene unfold, trying to figure out what Lance was doing at the embassy, and Tatyana had been sitting on this trove of information the whole time, saying nothing. "Is there anything else I should know?" she said.

Tatyana shook her head. "Larissa said something about an embassy attack. I sent her to Lance. That was it. I swear."

"You swear?"

"I didn't even know if she'd connected with him until now," Tatyana said.

"And you don't know anything more about this alleged attack?"

"Nothing," Tatyana said.

Laurel could see that she was close to tears. She was worried about her sister. Laurel reached out and touched her shoulder.

"I'm sorry," Tatyana said. "I should have told you about Larissa's message. I figured she'd tell Lance, and he'd look into it. I didn't know it would come to this. I only wanted her to get out of the country."

"It's all right," Laurel said.

Tatyana looked up at her.

Laurel sighed. "I'm sorry too," she said. "I thought you and Lance...."

"We didn't."

"I know," Laurel said, looking back at the screen. The crowd outside the embassy was getting increasingly out of control. Someone had poured gasoline in front of the gates. It was only a matter of time before it was set on fire, and black smoke was billowing into the air like a beacon to the entire city.

She switched the feed back to the view of Lance inside the embassy. He was still handcuffed in the interrogation room. Marines entered, and it looked like they meant business.

"Still no audio?" Laurel said.

Tatyana shook her head, wiping tears from her face with the back of her sleeve.

"We'll get to the bottom of this," Laurel said.

Tatyana nodded.

"We'll get your sister out too," she said. "You have my word."

Tatyana looked up at her. "Thank you," she said quietly.

And then all the feeds, the live footage of Lance inside the embassy, the external camera angles, even the satellite feeds from the CIA's own secure network—all of them went dark.

38

The marines brought Lance to a windowless third-floor office and sat him on a chair. The room wasn't secure, just an ordinary office, but his wrists were still cuffed behind his back, and he'd been searched for weapons.

"I need to speak to the CIA Chief of Station," he said.

The marines ignored him. They left and locked the door, and a moment later, he heard them arguing out in the corridor. There seemed to be some debate going on as to what they were supposed to do with him. The commanding marine was on his radio, speaking animatedly with someone, while the others butted in with interruptions.

Lance sat and waited. Someone would have to come and speak to him eventually, either the station chief, the embassy RSO, or the marine lieutenant colonel. As the wait grew longer, he wondered if maybe they were bringing the ambassador himself.

The higher up they went, the better it was for him. He needed to pass on the threat information, and it would be preferable if the person he was telling it to had the authority to do something about it. He figured that, at the very least, the embassy would need to bring in additional marines from outside the country. With information like this, there was no way in hell they could leave security in the hands of a Russian contractor.

Lance was aware that this little stunt had put him right back on the CIA's radar. He'd have to answer to the station chief, and likely to Roth too, soon enough. Roth would try to bring him back into the fold, but Lance still wasn't sure what he thought of that.

Whoever came to speak to him, the first thing they'd want to know was what his motives were. They'd want to know why he'd failed to report back after his last mission, why he'd tried to pass off false credentials. They'd accuse him of being part of the very threat he was there to warn them about. They'd also want to know where he'd gotten his information. Lance knew he wouldn't be able to give them satisfactory answers. He certainly wasn't going to give them Larissa.

They'd be suspicious. It would take time for them to piece things together—time they couldn't afford—but he was sure they'd beef up security while they looked into it. The compound already had some of the most advanced security systems on the planet. If they flew in the marines who were supposed to be manning those systems in the first place, that alone could be enough to ward off any potential attack.

There was no clock in the room, and he was estimating how much time had passed when two marines showed up at the door. They pulled him to his feet and shoved him forward.

"Easy, fellas," Lance said. "I came to you, remember?"

"Keep your mouth shut," one of them said.

They escorted him to the elevator and pressed the button for the basement level. Lance knew that was not a good indication of what was to come. He considered giving them the slip, but he couldn't. He still hadn't told anyone in power about the threat, and if he tried to escape now, that would only divert what security resources they had toward apprehending him. It would play directly into the hands of any would-be attackers. What he needed to do was keep his cool and pass on the message.

In the basement, they walked through an underground tunnel that led to a hardened receiving bay. The reinforced concrete gave way to stone, and Lance realized they were entering the underground portion of the original embassy building.

This was the building the Russians had blasted with so many x-rays that every part of it had been upgraded and reinforced multiple times. A set of eight-inch thick steel doors led to a narrow, dingy corridor. Lance was beginning to have second thoughts as the marines led him into yet another elevator. He realized that once he was fully secured and locked away in this place, getting out wasn't going to be easy.

He felt the elevator descend, bringing him deep below ground level, and when the doors finally opened, the marines took him down another stone corridor, narrower and darker than the one previous, passing multiple sets of thick steel doors in the process. Lance looked at the doors as closely as he could. Their only weakness appeared to be their age. They clearly weren't in regular use.

The marines were taking him into some disused part of the embassy, a dungeon that had all the charm of a CIA black site.

They stopped outside some doors, and one of the marines began unlocking them with a set of old keys. The guy wasn't familiar with the keys. It looked like it might have been his first time using them. The seventh key he tried unlocked the door. He leaned his weight into it, and the thick steel swung open with a groan.

"What is this?" Lance said.

The room was a dark, sealed box, about twelve feet by twelve feet. There was a ventilation duct in the ceiling, too small to fit a man. The air was heavy and damp, and mold had started to take over. The only light came from a recessed light fixture in the ceiling. The cover was plastic and had a large brown stain at its center in the shape of a fluorescent bulb. There were two wooden chairs and a rickety wooden table in the center of the room. On the table, a shackling iron had been screwed into the wood.

The room was a holdover from the darkest days of the Cold War. Lance knew exactly the kinds of things that had been done there. "You want to lock me in here?" he said.

The marines looked at each other, then nodded.

"Why?"

They had no answer.

"I'm an American citizen," Lance said. "I came into this embassy of my own free will. I wanted to speak to someone in charge of security because I think there's going to be an attack."

"We don't know anything about that," one of the marines said. "We're just following orders."

"Following orders?"

"Yes."

"Have you ever brought anyone down here before?"

They shook their heads. The two men had their hands on Lance's back, but they'd stopped short of shoving him into the room. Lance was tense. They were tense too, ready to draw their weapons if he tried to resist.

He was beginning to regret getting into this position. There wasn't much he could do about it now, though, with his hands cuffed behind his back and two armed men holding him.

"Tell me this," Lance said. "Who's coming to speak to me?"

The marines looked at each other. "The RSO," one of them said.

The other gave him a look that said he should have kept his mouth shut.

"Who's the RSO?" Lance said.

"A guy from Florida. Goes by Stilton."

"Like the cheese?"

"Like the cheese. He's a slick guy. Likes his toys. Always with a new Russian girl."

Lance nodded. The man didn't sound like the best bet for preventing an attack, but it was what it was. "Is he a stand-up guy?" Lance said.

The two men shrugged. That told Lance all he needed to know.

"We're just following orders," the talkative one said again, and then they shoved him into the cell. "Stilton will be here in an hour. I'm sure this will all be sorted by then."

Lance shook his head. "This doesn't feel right," he said, turning to them as they prepared to shut the door. "If I was going to be speaking to the RSO, this is the last place you'd be taking me."

They looked at him one last time and said nothing. They knew what he was saying was true, but there was nothing they were prepared to do about it.

"At least let me out of these cuffs," he said, but to no avail. They shoved the heavy door, and it groaned shut, the locks clanking loudly behind them.

Lance sat on one of the chairs as best he could, his wrists still cuffed behind his back, and stared at the wall in front of him. Black mold was in the process of spreading across the plaster like an invading army. He waited, and it wasn't long before he heard footsteps in the corridor outside. He knew an hour hadn't passed as the big door swung open once again.

An enormous man appeared in the doorway, his eyes as red as blood and his skin pale as a corpse. He didn't look right. He was a ghoul, something out of a nightmare. As he entered the room, ducking his head, Lance knew he was the albino Larissa had spoken of from the Lubyanka. A giant Russian albino, he thought. The man she'd called the Polar Bear.

Lance suddenly realized how remarkable it was that this man had managed to stay off the CIA radar for so long. If he hadn't, Lance would surely have seen pictures of him. He certainly didn't have an appearance anyone would easily forget. The security measures he must have used to achieve that anonymity would be extraordinary.

At over seven feet tall, he walked with a pronounced limp. Lance didn't even want to guess what he weighed.

Lance looked at the two marines standing in the corridor behind him and said, "Hey, I thought I was waiting for the RSO."

"The RSO has been detained," the Polar Bear said in heavily accented English. "You'll have to deal with me instead, I'm afraid."

"You can't leave me in here with this guy," Lance shouted to the marines, but there was nothing they could do about it. This had clearly been authorized from the top.

The Polar Bear shoved the door with his enormous foot, and it groaned shut. "Lance Spector," he said in his hoarse, guttural voice.

Lance weighed him up. He had no doubt the man was armed. If he'd come to kill him, he wasn't going to have to work very hard. He took the seat opposite Lance, and from the sound it made, Lance was sure it would collapse under his weight.

"Tell me, Lance Spector," the Polar Bear said, laying a document on the table, "what is it you came here to achieve?"

Lance had no intention of telling this man anything, but listening to his questions might provide him with some clues as to what was coming. "I'll tell you what I didn't come to do," he said. "I didn't come to talk to some Russian thug."

The Polar Bear let out a long sigh, like he was very sad to have to deliver this news. "I'm afraid I'm the only one you'll be speaking to today."

Lance said nothing. He looked down at the document on

the table. It was on fax paper, an executive order bearing the presidential seal, and it gave jurisdiction over Lance to the NSA.

The Polar Bear played with the iron ring at the center of the table. It had been used in the past to secure detainees by their handcuffs. If Lance's arms weren't behind his back, they might have used it on him.

"I understand you have concerns for the security of this embassy," he said again. "If you tell me what they are, I can assure you they'll be handled with the highest degree of urgency."

"Really?" Lance said.

"Yes. But first, I'll have to take steps to verify that what you're telling me is true."

"Verify? What I tell you?"

The Polar Bear nodded. "I'll need to know exactly who told you about the threat, who else knows about it, and where I can find them."

"You're asking me to just hand over my sources?"

"How else will I know if what you're telling me is true?"

"Because I'm telling you it's true."

"Yes," the Polar Bear said, "but I have to verify everything."

Lance looked at him incredulously. Was this a game, or did this freak of nature really think he was that naive?

He was a strange man. There was no denying that. But it wasn't just his appearance. It was his words. The questions he chose to ask, and the way he responded to the answers. He foresaw nothing. He intuited nothing. He calculated probabilities and made his moves the way a computer played chess. "You won't tell me anything?" he said.

Lance shook his head. The expression on the Polar Bear's face brought to mind a scientist examining bacteria in a petri dish.

"I want to speak to the ambassador," Lance said. "Or the CIA Station Chief. An American."

The Polar Bear's expression changed. He was like a machine, an artificial intelligence, jumping from one strategy to the next. He took a pack of cigarettes from his coat and put one in his mouth. Lance knew he was going to offer him one before he did it. "Can I offer you one?" he said.

Lance shrugged. "All right," he said.

The Polar Bear leaned across the table and put a cigarette in Lance's mouth. Then he held out the flame of his lighter, and Lance leaned into it.

"I know things about you, Lance Spector," he said.

Lance tried to make himself look comfortable. Getting this man to talk was the only way he'd be able to figure him out. "What do you know about me?" he said.

"I know you're Levi Roth's man."

Lance shrugged. "Maybe I was, for a time."

"Oh, you still are," the Polar Bear said smugly. "He'd never let you walk away."

"And why's that?"

"Come on," the man said. "You know why."

"What are you talking about?"

"You fucked your handler."

Lance remained motionless. This man was a calculator. He didn't say anything unless there was a reason. What was the reason for this? To taunt him? To provoke a response? To remind him that Clarice had sold all her secrets to the Kremlin?

"That's right," the Polar Bear continued, wagging his finger in Lance's face. "You diddled her. I don't blame you. She was an attractive woman."

"Fuck you," Lance said.

"Did you ever stop to think why Roth had her killed when he did?"

"She was selling secrets to the likes of you," Lance said. "She was a traitor. She got what was coming to her."

"But what made him execute the order? What made him pull the trigger when he did?"

"What are you talking about?"

"You've been too easy on him, Lance Spector. Too forgiving."

"I forgive nothing."

"He knew Clarice was carrying your child when he had her killed, Lance. Stop fooling yourself into believing he didn't. You know better than that."

Lance spit his cigarette into the Polar Bear's face. The Polar Bear swatted it away with a mirthless laugh. Lance jumped to his feet, knocking his chair to the floor in the process. He leaned over the table so that their faces were just inches apart.

"There you go," the Polar Bear said, grinning.

If Lance's hands weren't cuffed, he'd have wiped the smile off his freakish face. "You better stop talking," he said.

"Temper, temper," the Polar Bear said calmly.

"You conniving, pasty, freak."

The Polar Bear exhaled a long plume of smoke directly into Lance's face. "Now," he said, "is there anything else you'd like to tell me before I put a nice Russian bullet in your thick American skull?"

39

L ance leaned back in his chair and looked across the desk. The Polar Bear's unblinking, red eyes stared back at him like the eyes of a lizard. If it weren't for his enormous size, the paleness of his skin might almost have made him look vulnerable, like a furless newborn baby, unequipped for the world in which he found himself.

Lance tugged at the chains around his wrists but knew it would do no good.

The man reached into his coat, pulled out an enormous pistol, and pointed it at Lance's head.

Lance shut his eyes.

This was it.

It seemed about right.

On some level, he'd always known it would end with something like this. He might not have predicted the seven-foot-tall albino, but the rest of it—the dungeon beneath Moscow, being sold out by his own side, Roth nowhere to be found—that all felt about par for the course.

He was resigned to it.

"Open your eyes," the man said. "Look at me when I pull the trigger."

Lance opened his eyes.

The ten-inch-long steel barrel of a pistol stared him down.

"A Desert Eagle?" Lance said. "A fucking Desert Eagle?"

"What's wrong with that?" the Polar Bear said.

In his hand was a Mark XIX, one of the largest and most powerful handguns ever made. It weighed in at over four pounds and was chambered in the .50 AE. Each of its seven bullets was an inch and a half long.

"Nothing, I guess," Lance said.

"You don't like it?"

"It won't be an open casket, that's for sure."

The Polar Bear smiled. "Americans," he said, "always with the jokes." He stood and took a few steps back from Lance. "Shame to ruin a fresh shirt," he said.

Lance nodded. He was ready.

The Polar Bear aimed.

And then, the room's steel door swung open, and a big guy in a leather jacket came in. He looked from the Polar Bear to Lance and back again.

"What is it?" the Polar Bear said impatiently, and Lance heard his accent in Russian for the first time. It was unusual. Lance couldn't place the accent. It sounded almost as if this man had learned to speak Russian only at an older age.

"Sir," the man said, coughing, "we've got to get you out of here."

"What are you talking about?"

It was only then that Lance realized what was happening. The air vent above his head was blowing thick, black smoke into the room.

"There are rioters inside the compound, sir. The building is on fire."

The Polar Bear took one look at the air vent, then at the thick walls that separated him from the outside world in four floors of thick concrete, and saw the danger.

He gave Lance one final glare, then pulled the trigger.

40

Th crack of the bullet, its sound amplified in the confined space, echoed and ricocheted around the room, causing Lance's ears to ring painfully.

The same instant that the bullet was fired, he dropped to the ground and caught the chair behind him with his legs. He flung it straight up, smashing the single light in the ceiling above.

The room was plunged into darkness.

The Polar Bear swore and fired three more bullets into the room. Lance rolled until he reached the wall, pulled his left arm from its socket, and, wincing from the pain, got the handcuffs down under his feet and back up in front of his legs.

Smoke rapidly filled the room, and the Polar Bear and his henchman were coughing violently. Lance briefly saw their silhouettes in the doorway against the dim light of the corridor.

"We have to get you out of here," the henchman said.

The Polar Bear looked into the room and said to the henchman, "You're not going anywhere. You stay right here."

"What?" the henchman said.

The Polar Bear fired twice more, aiming into the darkness at the spot where Lance had been sitting. "Stay here and make sure Spector doesn't get out alive," he said.

The henchman was already coughing from the smoke. "Boss, what are you doing?" he gasped as the Polar Bear shoved him into the cell. The Polar Bear pointed his gun at the henchman, forcing him away from the door, then slammed it shut, its lock clanking behind it.

Lance was alone with him in the room. The air was running out, and the darkness was complete. He got to his feet. "He's a heartless bastard, isn't he?" he said in Russian. He took two steps forward to where he knew the chair was and picked it up.

The henchman lunged at him, missing by inches.

Lance, holding the chair with his cuffed hands, swung it hard, hitting him in the head. The chair shattered, and Lance ducked instinctively. He felt the rush of an arm above him and jabbed the man in the gut with two rapid blows. The man doubled over, and Lance stepped around him, catching him around the neck with the chain of his handcuffs.

The smoke made it difficult to breathe, and both men coughed and gasped as Lance held the chain tightly around the man's neck. The man clawed at Lance as he slowly dropped to his knees. Lance put his knee against the man's back and pushed him mercilessly against the chain, applying so much pressure he was afraid the chain would snap. The man's struggling grew weaker until, eventually, it stopped.

Only then did Lance let go.

The smoke had grown so thick that Lance had stopped taking breaths entirely. Even if there'd been light, it would have been impossible to see through it.

He went to where he knew the iron ring was screwed into the table and wrapped the chain of his cuffs around it. Then he yanked, over and over, to pry it loose. The table was old, and the wood had softened over time. When the ring came loose, the steel pin holding it in place fell to the ground with a loud clang.

Lance got on his hands and knees and felt around for it desperately. He needed it to break the handcuffs, but his fingers couldn't find it.

He needed air. He refused to breathe, but he knew that at any moment, his lungs could rebel against his will. The muscles in his stomach were already spasming involuntarily, trying to force in air.

Giving in to the temptation would be a fatal mistake.

He forced his mind to focus, and his fingers crept over a long, steel pin. He'd found it.

The cuffs on his wrists were a modern ratchet design, and he'd paid careful attention to the position of the pawl, the metal prong that prevented the ratchet from turning backward on its gear. He held the steel pin upward between his feet, then brought the cuffs down hard, trying to strike the spot where the pawl caught the gear.

It took a few tries, but on his third attempt, the pin struck the pawl, and the ratchet slipped open.

He shook his hands free, his shoulder still in agony, and the cuffs fell to the ground. Then he went straight to the door and pulled. It didn't budge.

Fighting the urge to breathe, he leaped onto the henchman's body and began rifling through his pockets, searching desperately for anything that would help him escape. He found a pistol in one pocket and a keycard in another.

Going back to the door, he searched with his hands for the lock, then held the pistol right up to the keyhole. He pulled the trigger twice. The door was still jammed, so he fired six more times, emptying the magazine.

With a groan, the door swung open, and Lance fled into the corridor. It, too, was filled with smoke, but the forty-watt bulbs overhead provided just enough light to make out a few vague shapes through it.

In the direction he'd come from, he could make out the red

light of the elevator button. At the other end of the corridor was an emergency exit that he thought led to a stairwell. He didn't have enough air to try both. He ran in the direction of the emergency exit and burst through the steel door.

It led to a concrete stairwell, and he made it up one flight before his body began to give up. He couldn't go any further. He had to breathe. He pulled his shirt in front of his mouth and allowed himself to take the smallest breath of air.

Immediately, he began coughing.

Struggling, on the edge of consciousness, coughing and choking at every step, he managed to climb one more flight of stairs before taking another desperate gasp.

The air was getting clearer as he got closer to the surface. The ventilation system had sucked the smoke to the lowest levels first. He continued to climb, and by the time he got to ground level, he was almost able to breathe normally. He took a few seconds to catch his breath and figure out what to do next.

Before him was a black metal door with a card reader on the wall next to it. He swiped the keycard he'd taken from the henchman, and it unlocked. He opened it carefully, expecting cold, clean air to flood his lungs, but his first gulps gave him the distinct, acrid taste of tear gas.

He peered cautiously around the door and saw chaos. Embassy guards were running in every direction. Some were armed with the launchers they used to fire tear gas, while others held large riot shields and batons. Above them hovered a phalanx of metro police helicopters, their high-powered spotlights lighting up the predawn compound like a prison yard on high alert.

Lance slipped out the door and rounded the old embassy building toward the back of the compound. There, a twenty-foot-high wall separated him from the Moscow streets.

Keeping low, he ran along the wall to the first corner, where he was able to leap against one wall, push off it to the other, and climb the full height going back and forth between the two.

At the top, he triggered the sensors, and the security flood-lights came on, lighting up the entire perimeter like a baseball diamond at night, the power supply kicking in with a loud hum. Given the chaos, it hardly mattered. There were also CCTV cameras along the perimeter, and Lance knew he was being recorded. The footage would already be shooting its way along thousands of miles of fiber-optic cable, straight to the desks of every analyst and specialist from Langley to Fort Meade to Quantico.

There wasn't much he could do about that either.

He lowered himself over the outer wall of the compound and dropped to the ground, absorbing the impact. He was on a narrow lane and made his way along it. When he reached the main boulevard, police cruisers blocked the entire street in both directions, their blue and red lights flashing in the morning mist. Behind them, traffic was backed up as far as Lance could see.

He approached one of the police cruisers and spoke to the officer present in fluent Russian. "What's going on?"

"Arrogant Americans," the cop said. "They took someone."

"What?"

"There's a girl down there who says they took her husband."

"What? Into the embassy?"

"Shocking, I know," the cop said.

"They think they can do whatever they want," Lance said.

The cop nodded.

Lance hurried on toward the gate, where a crowd was still flinging rocks over the fence. Some people were trying to climb the gates. The guards inside were firing tear gas out of the compound in full violation of the embassy's arrangement with the Russian government.

When Lance saw Larissa at the front of the group of rioters, provoking the guards and screaming at them to release her husband, he made a mental note not to underestimate her. She'd created all that commotion on her own.

He made his way through the crowd, shielding his face from the cameras. When he reached her, she was about to throw a full-blown Molotov cocktail over the gate. "Easy tiger," he said, holding back her arm.

She took one look at him, and tears flooded her eyes.

41

When Roth arrived at the White House, he sensed he was already too late. He'd thought he was going to the Oval Office, but the aide made him sit in a waiting room for an hour before coming for him. When the aide finally arrived, he brought him not to the president's office but to the Roosevelt Room.

"Oh," Roth said when the aide stopped outside the door.

The change in rooms was a signal. It was less personal, and as Roth approached the door, he felt a distinct chill in the air.

He was about to knock when the aide said, "They're expecting you."

"Are they?" Roth said.

He opened the door. Before him, arrayed around the conference table like King Arthur's knights, was the White House Chief of Staff, the Chairman of the Joint Chiefs, the Secretary of the Department of Defense, the Attorney General, and NSA Director Sandra Shrader. The president himself was standing at the head of the table.

"Levi," he said, indicating the chair at the far end of the table, "take a seat."

Roth stood as tall as he could. He saw this for what it was, and if he was going down, he would do so with as much composure as he could muster. "I wasn't expecting the whole gang," he said, taking his seat.

"Sorry for the ambush," the president said. "This was arranged hastily, as you can imagine."

Roth nodded.

The president cleared his throat as he took his seat. He knew what this looked like, a stab in the back, and he was embarrassed.

"Well," Roth said, "let's get started. I'd hate to keep so many important people waiting."

Shrader, seated next to the president, had her eyes on Roth like a tiger ready to pounce. The expression on her face was tense, as if her life depended on the outcome of this meeting.

Roth had to admit, she'd played him like a flute. At their previous meeting, she'd been all smiles, so ready to build a cooperative relationship. He prided himself on his ability to read people—his job depended on it—but he had not seen this coming.

"As you are aware," the president began, "I've just ordered all CIA personnel in Moscow to stand down."

Roth nodded. "I was notified."

The president looked at him. It was as if he couldn't believe what he was about to do. He fiddled with the papers in front of him, tapping the remote control for the presentation screen against the desk. He was stalling, as though he thought the delay might make his task easier.

Roth remained perfectly silent. If someone spoke, it wasn't going to be him. If the president wanted to accuse him of something, he would have to come out and say the words.

"It seems," the president continued hesitantly, "that your asset, Lance Spector, just entered the embassy making very serious threats."

"That doesn't sound like anything Spector would do," Roth said, "but if you have verified footage of it happening with audio, I'd be as interested as anyone to see it."

That was a gamble. Laurel had said something about the NSA cutting the audio feed. He guessed the president hadn't been given the full story either.

The president looked at Shrader. She shook her head. He sighed and clicked the controller in his hand. A screen began to descend slowly from the ceiling. It seemed to take a very long time, and everyone waited patiently for it.

"The following footage," the president said when the screen was finally in position, "is from inside the Moscow embassy. It's barely two hours old and, I think everyone will agree, is quite damning even without audio."

"Why is there no audio?" Roth said before it began.

"Technical problems," Sandra said.

"Technical problems," Roth said. "I'd say that's convenient."

The president was about to press 'play' when Roth interjected again. "A fifty-billion-dollar intelligence budget, and we can't get audio on this?"

"Please, Roth," the president said, hitting the button. "We don't need audio to see that this agent has gone rogue. Your own office pulled his security clearance, which is the only reason this incident was even flagged."

Roth watched the footage. It did not show anything suspicious as far as he was concerned. No altercation. No threatening gestures. What it did show was Lance Spector speaking to a secretary at the embassy's main security desk. "They could be talking about anything," he said.

"And what do you think they were talking about?" Shrader interjected. "The weather?"

"I don't know," Roth said pointedly. "There's no audio. No one knows."

"The report says he threatened the embassy," Shrader said.

Roth fixed her in his gaze. "And who wrote the report?"

The president turned to Shrader. Everyone around the table was looking at her.

She said nothing.

"I would also like to know who wrote the report," the Chairman of the Joint Chiefs, a stern-faced general by the name of Elliot Schlesinger, said.

Shrader sighed. "NSA wrote it," she said. "My people."

The footage was still running and now showed Lance leaving the desk and making his way down a corridor toward a fire exit. Before he reached it, he was stopped by marines. He didn't resist arrest but got on his knees and let them take him at gunpoint.

"Why," Roth said, "would the most valuable asset in CIA history walk into a US embassy and make threats? It doesn't make any sense."

"We're going to get to that," Sandra said.

"I mean," Roth went on, speaking directly to the president, "you've seen what he's capable of. With all due respect, sir, he could have taken out those men if he'd wanted. He let them take him."

The president sighed again. He was clearly uncomfortable. Something wasn't adding up, but somehow, Shrader had managed to convince him to go down this path. What Roth needed to figure out was why.

"Sir," he said, "you know as well as I do that Lance Spector is no traitor."

Again, Shrader interjected. "We know for a fact he refused to come in after his last operation," she said. "Your own office flagged him."

"I wanted to speak to him," Roth said. "He was lying low in Moscow, and I couldn't contact him to find out why."

The president threw up his hands. "Come on, Levi. Don't give us that baloney."

"There could be any number of reasons he remained in Moscow," Roth said.

"And he makes that decision? Without explaining it to you? That man is government property, Levi. He's not allowed to make decisions. He's not allowed to go off the grid."

"He's complicated," Roth said.

"His job is to follow orders, Levi, and he's refusing to play ball."

"I'm managing him."

"You're allowing him to get away with insubordination. You're letting him walk all over you and all over the program."

"Sir!" Roth said.

"The man is a fucking liability, Levi, and you know it. He's out of control. How's that for a security risk? Is it any surprise the Russians blew open the program, with men like him calling their own shots?"

"There are reasons—" Roth said, but the president kept speaking.

"He's the only asset still alive. He refuses to report for duty. He refuses to even speak to you or his handler. Does someone need to explain to him the terms of the agreement he signed?"

"He understands the agreement, sir."

"These guys don't get to retire to Montana, Levi. You know that. He knows that. And he's living in la-la-land if he thinks there's any way he gets out of his contract that doesn't end with a bullet in his skull."

Roth was surprised by the president's words. Of course Lance didn't get to just walk away. Of course he couldn't hide up in Montana forever in the cabin he'd built. The agreement he'd signed with the government was for life, and there was no getting out of it.

But at the same time, it was understood by everyone that these assets could be temperamental. They were inherently unstable. Anyone who signed a contract to become an assassin for life clearly wasn't playing from the same deck as everyone else. They were messed up, but they were worth the trouble. The results justified it. The lives they saved justified it.

Roth's job was to keep them on task, to keep them under control, but to do that, he required a certain amount of leeway. If the government wanted to protect the nation, it needed men like Lance Spector. Men who broke the rules. Men who defied their superiors. In short, men who were a little crazy.

"There's been nothing," Roth said, "not now and not at any point in Lance's past that would suggest he's capable of something like this."

"Every man's got his breaking point, Roth."

"Not this man," Roth said and instantly regretted it.

Shrader stepped up. "It seems to me," she said, "that your loyalty to this rogue agent is clouding your judgment."

"And what do you know about it?" Roth snapped.

The president was about to speak but stopped himself. He looked around the table. The silence grew to the point where Roth thought it would consume the room.

"I'm sorry, Levi," the president said, at last, handing Shrader the controller for the screen. "I always told you your loyalty to Spector was going to be your downfall."

"What is this?" Roth said, sensing the change in tone.

Shrader clicked a button, and a photo came up on the screen. When Roth saw it, he realized this was more than a power play. Shrader was going for the jugular.

On the screen was a face Roth had not seen in a long time. It was the face of Lance's former handler, Clarice Snow.

"Who is this?" Shrader said.

"You know who it is," Roth said.

"For the benefit of the others present," she insisted.

"Her name is Clarice Snow."

"Is?" Shrader said, with all the relish of a trial lawyer conducting a cross-examination.

"Was," Roth corrected.

Shrader clicked, and the next image came up. It was of Clarice also, but this time she was lying on the ground in a pool of blood, her lifeless eyes staring straight up. The photo was apparently taken by the killer, and his black boots could be seen at the bottom of the frame, the blood just beginning to reach them.

"She had a tragic end, didn't she, Roth?"

"I ordered her killed," Roth said.

"And could you tell everyone here why that was?"

"She was working for the Russians. Specifically for the Dead Hand, a Kremlin group charged with keeping the Russian president in power."

"She was selling secrets to the Dead Hand," Shrader said, "right under your nose."

"Yes, she was," Roth admitted.

"And it would be fair to say that her betrayal is the reason the Special Operations Group was so severely compromised? The reason three of your four assets were killed in a single night? The reason, in fact, that you've had to re-evaluate the existence of the entire program?"

"It continues to exist," Roth said.

"But in a different form."

"That's correct," Roth said. "I'm rebuilding it from the ground up."

"And Lance Spector is a key part of that plan."

"Of course he is."

"He's the key to the most successful and effective program in agency history. The program that you've built your entire reputation on."

"I'd say that's a fair assessment," Roth said.

"So even if Spector was showing signs of fray—things that should have set off alarm bells and gotten you to pull him from service—"

"By which you mean kill him," Roth said.

"By which I mean kill him," Shrader agreed. "Even if you saw multiple warning signs, you'd have had a very powerful motive not to act on them."

"What are you suggesting? That I saw this coming? That I protected Lance?"

"As you'll see," Shrader said, looking at the faces around the table, "I won't have to say that."

Roth turned to the president. "What is this?" he said. "A witch hunt?"

"Hear her out," the president said gravely. He had the look of a man whose mind was already made up.

"What was Clarice Snow's role at the group?" Shrader continued.

"She was Lance Spector's handler."

"Can you tell us what happened to the man you hired to kill her?"

"That was a separate thing," Roth protested.

"Just tell us what happened."

"He was found dead."

"When?"

"Two years ago."

"It was less than two weeks after he fired the bullet that killed Clarice Snow, isn't that correct?" Shrader said.

"If you say so."

She clicked, and some documents came up on the screen, showing the date on Clarice Snow's death certificate and another death certificate for a John Doe.

"All right," Roth said.

"Did you ever ask Lance if he knew anything about the second man's death?"

"No," Roth said.

"Why not?"

"He had nothing to do with it."

"It never crossed your mind that he might go after the man who killed Clarice?"

"Why would he? She was a traitor. Her death was inevitable. Everyone understood that."

"Were you aware that Lance Spector and Clarice Snow were romantically involved?"

"I was," Roth said.

"You don't think that would be a reason for Spector to have strong feelings about you ordering her death?"

"Lance was sleeping with Clarice," Roth said, "but that's not the same thing as saying they were in love, as I'm sure you're aware, Sandra."

Shrader smiled thinly. "All right," she said. "Maybe Lance and Clarice weren't soulmates. Maybe it was just a casual fling."

"It was a casual fling."

"But shouldn't you have at least looked into the possibility that one of your assets had just murdered someone, in cold blood, without authorization?"

"I didn't look into that possibility because there was no reason to believe that man's death had anything to do with his killing of Clarice Snow."

"Where was Lance when Clarice was killed?" Sandra said.

"On a mission overseas."

"A mission you sent him on."

"I sent him on all his missions."

"Were you making sure he wasn't around to interfere?"

"Are you suggesting he would have tried to stop me from taking out Clarice?"

Sandra smiled. "That's exactly what I'm suggesting, Roth."

"That's preposterous," Roth said. "He'd have killed her himself if I'd ordered it."

"You really believe that?"

"Of course I believe that. It's his job."

"Interesting," Sandra said, a satisfied look on her face. She clicked, and a new slide came up on the screen, this time showing the dead body of Clarice's assassin.

"Where was Lance the day this man was killed?"

"Still on his mission."

"He was AWOL," Sandra said.

Roth shook his head. He knew where she was going. She'd done her homework. She didn't know the entire story, but she knew enough. There was nothing he could say.

"In fact," she went on, "Lance Spector went AWOL the day he found out you'd killed Clarice and has remained so for the two and a half years since. Is that not correct?"

Roth looked at the president. The man's grizzled face was as blank as a stone wall.

"I'd say it's fair to assume," Sandra continued, "that Lance Spector is a little bit *upset* about what happened, wouldn't you, Roth?"

Roth nodded. "It's a giant leap to go from him being upset about Clarice to threatening to blow up an embassy."

"A giant leap," Sandra said, pressing the button again.

The next slide was of an ultrasound. The blood drained from Roth's face when he realized what he was looking at. This was the first time since he'd entered the room that she'd said something he hadn't already known.

"Were you aware," she said, "that Clarice Snow was pregnant at the time of her death?"

Roth said nothing. He had no idea how she'd gotten this information. It didn't make sense.

"Mr Roth?" she said.

He leaned forward to get a closer look. According to the slide, the ultrasound was taken at Johns Hopkins Division of Maternal-Fetal Medicine. Clarice's name was clearly filled in, as was the signature of the obstetrician. It could have been forged, but something told him it was the real thing.

How had he missed this? And what else had he missed? His

mind reeled as he went over the ramifications of what she was saying. Maybe his loyalty to Lance had blinded him. Maybe everything she was saying was true.

"Please answer her," the president said.

Roth cleared his throat. "I was not aware she was pregnant," he said quietly.

He looked at Sandra. She'd beaten him, and the look on her face said she knew it. "Care to hazard a guess as to who the father was?" she said.

Roth looked from her to the president and then around the table at everyone else present.

"It's all starting to make sense now, isn't it?" Sandra said.

"I don't see..." Roth said, but his voice trailed off, unable to complete the sentence.

"You didn't just kill Clarice," Sandra said. "You killed Lance's unborn child."

"I didn't know," Roth said, his voice barely above a whisper.

"I'd say," Sandra said, "that if we were looking for someone with a reason to go off the deep end, someone holding a grudge against our government, we don't need to look any farther than Lance Spector."

"No," Roth said, speaking directly to the president. He was no longer trying to convince anyone. He was just saying what he thought. "I know Lance. What she's saying, it's not possible."

"Isn't it?" the president said. "You killed Lance's child, and in two and a half years, he never said one word to you about it? I think this man is more deceptive than you give him credit for."

Roth's head was spinning. He glared at Sandra. "How did you.... How did you even find out about this?"

"That's not important," she said.

Roth didn't know what else to say. If this were all true, if Clarice had been pregnant with Lance's child when she died, then maybe he really didn't know Lance as well as he thought he did—and didn't know what the man was capable of.

Sandra pulled back up footage of Lance at the embassy. "This is from just a few moments ago," she said, "right before you entered the room, Roth." The footage showed Lance exiting a stairwell and running around to the back of the compound. Smoke and tear gas wafted across the frame, and the sounds of gunfire and helicopters could be heard in the background.

"That's happening now?" Roth said.

"Yes, it is," Sandra said as Lance climbed the wall of the compound.

Sandra switched cameras, bringing up pictures of an angry mob throwing Molotov cocktails over the embassy's front gate.

"If Lance Spector isn't a threat," the president said, "then you tell us what we're looking at here, Levi."

There was nothing Roth could say. He looked at the faces around the table.

He was about to stand up when someone knocked on the door. An aide stuck her head in and said, "Mr President? Sorry to interrupt. There's a coded call from Moscow for Levi Roth."

"Mr Roth is occupied," the president said impatiently.

The aide stared at him.

"Is there something else?" the president said.

"Sir, the call is from Lance Spector."

Roth let out a quiet laugh, as if to underscore what everyone in the room had already decided was the truth. His fate was sealed, and he knew it. And just like he'd always been warned, Lance Spector had been the cause of his undoing.

42

L izzie Shrader lay on her back, staring at the bright fluorescent bulb above her as if staring at the sun. The room was swelteringly hot, and her skin was tacky with sweat. She hadn't moved in hours. Maybe days. She had no idea how long she'd been there, and the only clue of the passage of time was the steady drip in the corner from one of the pipes that ran along the ceiling.

Drip.

Drip.

Drip.

She counted them. A hundred. A thousand. How many seconds in an hour?

When she thought about where she was and what had happened to her, she couldn't breathe and began shaking uncontrollably.

That was when she forced herself to stop thinking.

Back to the drips. The counting. The light of the bulb shining down incessantly like the Eye of Sauron.

She was underground. She could tell by the way the concrete was formed, poured in molds. By the looks of things, it had been a grow-op once. There was thick plastic sheeting on the floor, and on the ceiling, as well as the long fluorescent tubes, were the remains of a pretty heavy-duty ventilation system.

It didn't work now. The room didn't feel like it had seen ventilation of any kind in a very long time.

She was on the ground. There was a bed, a spartan thing with a metal wire mesh beneath a thin mattress, but it was stained so badly she didn't dare go near it.

Next to it was a filthy porcelain sink, something worse than the worst gas station toilet she'd ever seen, and it didn't work. She'd tried it. She was so thirsty she'd drink even from that.

She heard a sound outside the door, and her body flooded with adrenaline.

The man hadn't been back since he'd flung her in there. It sounded like he was coming now.

Last time, he'd forced her to sit still on the bed while he filmed her on his phone. He'd told her to say hello to the camera, but she couldn't. Her mouth wouldn't move. Her voice wouldn't sound. He'd pulled her head back by the hair and made her look at the camera. She'd been crying.

She knew that footage was for her mother. At least, she couldn't think of any other use for it. Ransom footage. That was what it was.

She pictured her mother receiving it, and it made her want to cry all over again.

The man sounded Russian, as far as Lizzie could tell. It could have been something else. She didn't have a lot of experience with accents from that part of the world.

He was massive. There wasn't a snowball's chance in hell of her overpowering him, but she had tried. After he was done with the filming, and she'd thought of her mother watching it, she'd thrown herself against him, clawing, biting, scratching like the cornered little animal she was.

He'd flung her across the room with a single arm, like she was nothing more than a rag doll. She hit her head so hard on the wall that it made her want to throw up. Her vision blurred.

When she regained focus, she saw him, his enormous bulk, standing over her like a bear. He was looking at her, and the smile on his face made her blood shiver. It wasn't right. It wasn't natural. She'd never seen that look on a man's face before, and she realized instinctively what it was he was thinking.

Later, she heard him playing with the little peephole in the door. It had been reversed so that he could watch her.

It made her feel like insects were running all over her body.

43

Lance and Larissa got a few blocks from the embassy before they dared to stop. They could still hear the chaos at the embassy, the helicopters overhead, and the police sirens.

"You really went for it," Lance said.

"I had to get you out of there."

A police car sped by, and Lance turned away from it. "Well, you sure know how to get a crowd going," he said, looking at her. There was a new confidence in her eyes. And it was justified. She hadn't just succeeded in forcing the embassy into lockdown—she'd saved his life. She didn't know it yet, but he did.

"I've always been good at raising hell," she said.

Lance let out a brief chuckle.

"It's true," she said. "You should consider recruiting me. I could be one of those agitators the CIA sends in to destabilize countries."

"The CIA doesn't do that," Lance said.

Larissa smiled. "Sure they don't."

Another police car sped by, and Lance said, "I think you

might have created enough chaos to justify the ambassador in recalling the ejected marines."

Larissa said, "So the embassy's safe?"

"Well, I wouldn't go that far. But at least it's got its guard up now."

"So, what next?"

"We need to find a payphone," Lance said. Going directly to the embassy had been a mistake. He'd gone in to report a security threat to the station chief and had ended up in an underground cell with a Russian trying to kill him. The breach in security went all the way to the top, and he needed to get word of that to Roth.

"There are payphones in the park," Larissa said.

They went to the phones, and Lance dialed a series of secure codes that were handled directly by Langley. When he finally got through, the operator said she couldn't connect him directly to Roth.

Lance gave her a top-level emergency clearance code. The purpose of the code was to ensure Lance direct access to Roth in situations like this, and built into it were secret flags he could use to pass on additional distress messages. Lance gave her the distress code indicating a threat from within. She didn't understand its specific meaning, but Roth certainly would.

The operator typed the code into her terminal and then hesitated.

"What's the problem?" Lance said, sensing distress.

"I'm sorry, sir. It looks like your clearance has been revoked."

"I don't have time to get into that right now," Lance said. "I just need to speak to Levi Roth urgently."

"Sir," the operator said, her voice trembling, "under the standing order granting your status, I am required by law to tell you that this call is being traced and that deadly force has been authorized in your apprehension. You are commanded, by order of the President of the United States, to stand down immediately and turn yourself over to the authority designated under your terms of reference."

"Listen," Lance said, "I understand what you told me, but you have to inform Roth of my call. You have to patch me through."

"They're," the operator said and then hesitated again. "They're tracing your location as we speak."

"I don't care," Lance said. He gave her another clearance code, and another, until she interrupted him frantically, saying, "Roth's with the president. The only way you're going to get through to him is if the White House operator connects you."

"Can you connect me to the White House operator then?"

The phone clicked. There was a tone, and a moment later, he was on a direct line to the Oval Office. Lance gave the White House operator the same clearance codes he'd given Langley, and this time he was told to hold.

When this operator came back on, her tone had changed, and she read to him the same legal message about turning himself in.

"Can you tell Roth that someone at the embassy just tried to kill me?" Lance said.

"I'm sorry, sir," the operator said. "I'm only authorized to read the message I just gave you."

"You want me to turn myself over to the people who just tried to put a bullet in my skull?"

"That's correct, sir."

"What kind of joke is this?"

"I'm sorry, sir."

"Can you at least give me the authorization code for your message, so I can verify it's real?"

The operator read him a valid White House authorization code.

"I need the CIA code," Lance said.

She read him Roth's code, and as Lance suspected, it had

also been appended with a secret distress flag. The flag Roth had given meant 'cut and run'.

Lance hung up the phone, slamming the receiver harder than necessary.

"What happened?" Larissa said.

"They wouldn't put me through. They told me to turn myself in."

"You already tried that."

"Something's very wrong," Lance said. "Someone at the White House is deliberately trying to prevent me from getting a message through to Roth."

"What else can you do?" Larissa said.

"I can try Laurel," he said.

Lance dialed Laurel's private line, very aware it was the first time he'd called her since dropping her from a flying helicopter over the Moskva River. He waited uncomfortably, unsure how she'd react to hearing from him.

"Lance," she gasped when she picked up the phone. "Is that you?"

"Laurel! It's me."

"The embassy is in chaos," Laurel said. "The NSA cut all our feeds. We couldn't get to you."

"That's okay. I got out."

"What's going on there?"

"Something's very wrong. I tried to warn them of an attack, but they locked me in a cell with a psychopath who tried to kill me."

"Tatyana told me about the plot. A threat against the embassy. A Russian albino from the Lubyanka, and a Chinese guy who spilled the beans at a strip club?"

"It's real," Lance said. "I've met the albino, and he's getting help from our side."

"Who's helping him?" Laurel said.

"I don't know, but he was holding a document authorized by the NSA."

"We've been searching all the databases we have access to," Laurel said. "We have no record of an albino at the Lubyanka."

"There must be photos of him somewhere," Lance said. "He's seven feet tall. He goes by Polar Bear."

"Whoever he is," Laurel said, "he doesn't show up on the record."

"He's a strange character," Lance said. "He has a limp. Something congenital. Check hospital records in Moscow. See if any seven-foot albinos received leg surgery."

"I don't know if we can find that."

"He also had a weird accent. I couldn't place it, but I wouldn't be surprised if Russian was not his first language."

"A foreigner? That widens the search."

"Also, start looking at the NSA. Something's off, and I'm thinking the stink is coming from their direction."

"They have a new director. Sandra Shrader."

"Start with her."

"All right," Laurel said. "Anything else you can think of that might be useful?"

Lance hesitated a second, then said, "The guy, the albino, he had access to information that only Clarice Snow knew. Things she must have sold to the Kremlin before...."

"Before she was killed?"

"Yeah."

"What did the albino say? Things about you?"

"Yeah. Me, Roth, her."

"Okay, that helps."

"And check the embassy logs," Lance said. "See who entered the embassy after I was arrested. This guy should have been logged. I was in the old embassy building basement."

"Tatyana's pulling those records now."

"I've got to go," Lance said. "I'm being traced as we speak."

"Good luck, Lance."

"You too," Lance said. "I'll check back with you in a few hours. Hopefully you've got something for me by then. I want to go get this guy."

"I do, too," Laurel said.

"And for God's sake, convince someone that the embassy needs to be evacuated. Whatever's coming, it's going to be big."

"I'll get Roth to tell the president."

"Laurel," Lance said.

"What?"

"I thought you knew."

"Knew what?"

"Roth's in trouble."

"What? He just went to the White House to meet with the president."

"I tried to call him. They wouldn't let me speak to him."

"He was in the Oval Office."

"I sent him a secret distress code when I tried to speak to him."

"Did he get your code?"

"I think so," Lance said, "because he sent one back."

"What was it?"

"He told me to cut and run."

"Fuck."

"I thought you knew."

"If they've gotten to him...."

"You need to be careful, Laurel. Watch your back. Watch that new NSA director."

Larissa tapped Lance on the arm. Two police officers were approaching cautiously, their hands on the guns at their hips.

"I've got to go," Lance said. "I've got company. I let the NSA trace my location, and guess who shows up?"

"Who?"

"Russians."

44

Larissa watched the two police officers approach. "You there!" one of them called out.

They were still a hundred yards off, and she hit Lance again on the arm. "We've really got to get going," she said.

Lance hung up the phone and grabbed her. They started walking through the park away from the cops.

"Hey!" the officer called. "You! Stop right there."

Lance kept walking as if he hadn't heard them.

"What are we doing?" Larissa said.

"There's a gate up ahead. When we get to it, you run."

"What are you going to do?"

"I'm going to get rid of these guys."

"I'm not leaving you again."

"I'll meet you at the hotel."

Larissa didn't like it, she didn't want to split up a second time, but she could hear the police officers getting closer by the second.

"Don't look back," Lance said. "Just slip through the gate and get back to the hotel."

She touched his hand unconsciously and was embarrassed when she realized what she'd done.

"I'll meet you there," Lance said, looking at her. "At the hotel. I promise."

The cops drew their weapons. "Get on the ground, or we'll shoot!" one of them called.

Larissa looked back. They'd stopped, and she was still standing by Lance's side. The cops were approaching very cautiously. They'd clearly been warned of the potential danger.

"Get down!" the cop called.

The two officers spread apart about ten yards from each other. It looked like they'd received tactical training. They were about thirty yards away. One of them spoke into a microphone at his collar, calling for backup. In the distance, she heard yet another police siren.

Lance turned around slowly to face the officers. "Is something the matter?" he said in flawless Moscow dialect.

The officers lowered their weapons just a hair, and Lance pushed Larissa in the direction of the gate. "Go, now," he cried.

Larissa didn't hesitate. She ran for the gate, slipping through it as the sound of two gunshots filled the air.

On the street beyond, two police cars sped past her in the direction of the park's main entrance. Larissa went the opposite way, trying hard not to run as more and more police vehicles sped by.

When four more gunshots went off, each bang felt like a blow to her stomach.

She pictured the bullets ripping through Lance, knocking him to the ground in a mess of blood.

She kept walking, not fast, not slow, and when some cops pulled over next to her, she pretended to be drunk on her way home from a nightclub. She slurred her words and gave silly answers to their questions. She even tried to kiss one of them.

They swore at her and drove on, and she walked all the way to Kiyevsky railway station before she dared stop.

She entered the station and looked at the electronic departure board hanging above the concourse. She looked down the list of international departures leaving in the next thirty minutes—Kyiv, Lviv, Dnipro, and Odesa in Ukraine. Chişinău in Moldova. She could board one of those trains, and all of this madness would be behind her. But not without Lance.

She went back outside and got in a cab, telling the driver to take her to the hotel.

"There's something going in that part of town," the driver told her. "Police everywhere. You'd be faster to walk."

"I don't want to walk."

He turned and looked at her. She knew she looked a fright. Her hair was everywhere. Her makeup was smudged. She'd been crying. She made no attempt to hide the fact from the driver.

He scanned the steps of the train station, looking for a more lucrative ride. There was no one.

"I'll pay twice the meter," she said.

"The meter will be nothing," the driver said. "It'll be backed up for miles. Five hundred rubles tops."

"I'll give you two thousand. I just want to sit."

The driver sighed. "Two thousand?"

"Yes."

"You mind if I smoke?"

Larissa shrugged, and after the driver lit his cigarette, she lit one of her own. It was snowing again, and she opened her window to let in the predawn air.

The traffic was as bad as the driver had said. It took thirty minutes to travel six blocks, and when they finally got to the hotel, she could see that the police were still dealing with the disturbance outside the embassy.

"What happened there?" she said, curious to know what story had been circulating.

"I heard it's a protest against the sanctions," the driver said.

Larissa nodded. She paid, tipping an extra thousand rubles, and walked through the lobby without making eye contact with anyone.

She'd refused to allow herself to think of what might have happened to Lance, but as soon as she was in the elevator, the tension in her chest made it difficult to breathe.

She stepped out of the elevator and got to the door of the room before realizing she didn't have a key.

That was the last straw. She burst into tears.

And then the door opened.

45

"There's blood on your face," Larissa said, looking up at Lance's face.

Lance wiped his mouth with his sleeve, missing the blood, and let her into the room.

She sat on the bed and kept crying. She couldn't stop.

"You're going to be all right," Lance said to her. "Everything's going to be all right."

She looked at him. There wasn't just blood on his face. It was on his hands, his shirt, spattered across his pants.

"What did you do to those police?" she said.

"They weren't police."

She burst into another round of tears, and Lance put his hand on her back. He sat on the bed and let her rest her head on his shoulder. They sat like that, awkwardly, neither speaking until she stopped crying.

Then, Lance got up and put on the kettle.

"Are we sleeping here?" Larissa said.

Lance didn't look too happy at that prospect, but he could tell Larissa needed him to say yes. "We can stay a few hours," he said. "Then we need to go. We're too close to the embassy."

There was only the one bed, and Larissa said, "I can take the couch."

Lance smiled. He finished making the tea while she washed off in the bathroom. When she came back out, she felt more like herself.

He handed her a cup of tea.

"This is good," she said, taking a sip.

Lance was standing by the window, peering through the curtain. She could tell he was concerned. He wanted to leave the hotel, but she needed time. Police were still swarming outside, mopping up the dregs of the protest.

"You should shower," she said.

He looked at himself in the mirror. "You should try to sleep," he said.

"Won't you sleep too?"

He shook his head. He was still on the clock, still alert. He wouldn't stop until he knew where the threat to the embassy was coming from.

"Do you think they'll evacuate the embassy?" she said.

Lance shrugged. "You know Americans," he said. "We don't like to back down from a fight."

"You could call it a tactical withdrawal," Larissa said.

Lance sighed. He wasn't happy. Despite the riot, one of the buildings catching fire, and his attempts to warn embassy security of the threat, nothing had been done to evacuate the compound. It was still full of workers, and more would be arriving very soon.

He went into the bathroom and took off his shirt. He didn't shut the door. He washed at the sink and toweled off.

"You know how long that embassy's been there?" he said.

Larissa got up and went to the window. She looked out at it across the street. The floodlights along its perimeter were lit up, on high alert, and security guards were making a show of force, manning the towers overlooking the walls and doing patrols.

The older buildings in the compound were from the nine-teenth century. She had no idea how long they'd been part of the American embassy.

She shook her head.

"The older building," Lance said. "The US took it over in 1953."

"Okay," she said. Lance was tired. She could tell he needed to sleep.

"Stalin was still alive in 1953," Lance said.

Larissa nodded. It was, in fact, the year Stalin died.

"That's how long that compound has stood as the symbol of American power in this city."

"We should get some rest," she said.

"It's never been evacuated," Lance said. "Not once, in all that time. Not at the height of the Cold War, when the generals liter-ally had their fingers on the nuclear launch buttons."

"I see," she said.

"So evacuating it, leaving it empty, for the first time...."

"It would be a statement," she said.

"Let's just say, it would be difficult to paint that as a *tactical* withdrawal."

"It would have ramifications."

Lance shook his head. "Do you remember the first time you heard that America had won the Cold War?"

Larissa shrugged. "That wasn't exactly the way we looked at things."

"But it was clear, right? At some point? America beat the USSR, and the Cold War was over."

"I guess so," Larissa said.

"But the US and the USSR never fought."

"Not openly."

"So how could it be said that one side won?"

"The American economy was stronger. It provided a higher standard of living."

"Sure," Lance said, "but that was as true in Stalin's time as it was in the nineties."

"Right," Larissa said.

She wanted to stop talking. She wanted to sleep. She wanted to get away from all of this and never think about it again. But Lance seemed to need her to listen, like he needed to say the words out loud.

"The reason America won the Cold War," Lance said, "is because everybody, in Russia and America and around the world, believed they'd won."

"Right," Larissa said.

"It was about perceptions."

Larissa nodded. She poured herself more tea and sat on the windowsill.

"Perception is everything. If people think you're strong, you're strong. If they think you won a war, you won the war."

"And if they see you evacuating the Moscow embassy?"

"If they see you pulling out of a post like the Moscow embassy, well, maybe they start to rethink how powerful you are."

Larissa looked down at the embassy gate. She remembered how it had been a few hours earlier. That seemed like a lifetime ago. The police had completely cleared the area, and embassy staff were arriving for work as if none of it had happened. Two police cars, directing traffic past the gates on the Garden Ring, and a single fire truck in the central courtyard, its lights off, were the only signs of the chaos she'd managed to whip up.

"They're not going to evacuate," Lance said.

"Because of the perception?"

"No president wants to be the guy who backed down."

"But this is because of a bomb threat."

Lance shook his head. "No," he said. "It's more than that. We don't know who's behind this threat. We don't know the timescale of the threat. We don't know if the attack is planned for the next day, the next week, the next month."

"Surely, a mistaken evacuation would be better than a bombing that killed American embassy workers."

"But how long would they keep it empty?"

Larissa shrugged. Her eyelids were growing heavy. She leaned her forehead against the window and looked down the Garden Ring. Traffic was back to normal, heavy in the morning rush, but moving. A convoy of three large construction trucks was coming down the street.

Lance lay on the bed. He'd put his shirt back on and was looking at the ceiling. Larissa would have liked to share the bed with him.

The trucks stopped outside the embassy and signaled to turn. Guards approached and spoke to the lead driver.

"Lance?" she said.

He looked at her.

"You need to see this."

He looked right into her eyes, and without another word, knew what was about to happen.

Everything that followed was a blur.

"Three trucks—" Larissa said, but before she ever finished the sentence, Lance was on his feet, moving like a cat, pure adrenaline fueling his every instinct.

"What are you doing?" she said, but he was already gone.

She looked at the door, open to the corridor, and stared at it as if expecting him to come back.

Outside, the Russian security guards were waving the trucks into the compound.

Below her window, Lance emerged from the hotel, running toward them. "Stop!" he yelled. "Stop those trucks."

Instead of doing what he said, the guards drew their weapons on him.

Larissa had never seen anything in her life like what

happened next. Lance ducked as the guards opened fire, rolling forward on his arm. Bullets sprayed the ground, smashed into vehicles, shattered glass. The guards didn't care at all about collateral damage.

Lance, still rolling, somehow managed to pull a handgun and get off a shot. One of the guards fell to the ground.

Lance stopped behind a car. Hundreds of bullets followed his path. The car's windows collapsed in sheets. The tires blew, and it dropped on its suspension. He waited a few seconds, then leaped out from behind it, hitting another guard in the forehead with a single shot.

He took cover behind another vehicle, ran to the far side, and fired two more bullets before ducking. He repeated the maneuver, and the four remaining guards were on the ground.

Lance then leaped over the hood of the car and closed the rest of the distance to the gate.

The guards Lance had killed were Russian contractors, but as he reached the gates, it was US marines that came at him.

"I'm CIA," Lance yelled. "Stop those trucks. They're loaded with explosives."

The marines lowered their weapons and turned to look at the three heavy construction trucks that had just entered the compound. Instinctively, they realized he was telling the truth.

One of the marines started running toward them.

And then, a blinding flash of light.

Larissa felt as if she was being sprayed with water. The glass in the window flew into the room as if sucked by a vacuum. She fell backward onto the ground.

She didn't know how much time passed then—maybe a single second, maybe thirty. She ran her hands over her body. She was dazed, in shock, but the glass had been coated, and apart from a few cuts, she thought she was all right.

She tried to stand and almost lost her balance. She wasn't sure where she was.

She stumbled in one direction and then another. Cold air came in from the open window. The curtain dangled in the breeze. She went to it and looked out at where the embassy had stood.

There was nothing left.

46

The American embassy in Beijing was located inside a ten-acre compound in the Chaoyang district. The eight-story glass and steel structure, constructed in 2008, included over half a million square feet of office space, making it one of the largest diplomatic missions on the planet.

As relations continued to deteriorate between the United States and China, it had come under increasingly brazen and sophisticated surveillance measures, unlike anything seen at the Moscow embassy during the worst years of the Cold War.

The US government had responded in kind, deploying defensive anti-surveillance measures such as jammers and radio signal blockers. Interior walls had been lined with metallic radio wave reflectors, while the exterior, including the roof, had been coated with an advanced light-absorbing compound that made the building appear as a black blob on satellite photos. In addition, an array of military-grade geostationary satellites was in permanent orbit above the embassy. It meant that, short of a Chinese attack on the US military satellite system, communication between the embassy and Washington could not be cut off.

At DARPA headquarters in Arlington, an entire department spanning four floors had been set up to develop new ways to protect the embassy from Chinese surveillance and ensure its continued operability and usefulness during times of heightened tension.

The reasons for this were simple and well known to the Chinese. The US government used the Beijing embassy as its command and control center for a wide array of operations that defied the ruling communist regime and undermined its most aggressive international and domestic policies. On a wide variety of fronts—including the harboring of political defectors and dissidents, the protection of American technological superiority and intellectual property, and the deployment of cyberattacks against Chinese corporations and government organizations known to have stolen Western technology—the embassy was ground zero.

Taiwanese dissidents and Hong Kong separatists called it the Beijing Hilton because of how supportive it was of their efforts. Internet users across the city knew that if they were anywhere near the embassy, they could avoid the government's Great Firewall and skirt the efforts of official censors.

The US government's enormous warehouse at Tianzhu, which benefitted from the same diplomatic protections as the embassy proper, was used to supply Uighur rebels in Xinjiang while also smuggling out those most at risk from government crackdowns.

In recent months, the Chinese had already forced the closure of US consulates in Chengdu, Guangzhou, and Shenyang. It was only a matter of time before the remaining consulate in Shanghai was shuttered, leaving the embassy in Beijing as the last American outpost in the entire country.

When eight trucks rolled into the embassy compound, just after rush hour on the morning in question, all bearing the markings of a local construction company specializing in the installation of luxury swimming pools, only four people on earth knew what they contained. Those people were Mikhail Medvedev, Liu Ying, Liu Ying's Moscow liaison, and a Beijing customs inspector who'd been tasked with loading the trucks.

Within three hours of the trucks' arrival at the embassy, all but Medvedev and Liu Ying would be dead, assassinated with a single bullet to the back of the head.

The embassy's two thousand personnel, including marines and other military personnel, diplomatic and consular staff, American support staff, and hundreds of carefully screened Chinese support workers, were well aware that the Beijing government was not their friend. They knew they were tolerated rather than welcomed in the city. They knew that relations between China and the US were at their lowest point since the creation of the modern Chinese state, and they were getting worse by the day.

But not a soul would have guessed that they were about to be the target of the greatest act of state-sponsored terrorism in modern Chinese history. There had been zero indication, either from within the Chinese diplomatic mission or from the constant stream of intelligence reports coming from Langley and Fort Meade, to suggest there was the slightest risk of an attack.

The Chinese government was not above acts of aggression against its rivals. Along its disputed border with India in the Himalayas, in Hong Kong, in the Yellow Sea, the East and South China Seas, and in the Taiwan Strait, it had been engaging in provocative paramilitary activities that resulted in real casualties to foreign military personnel. Just two months earlier, forty-two Indonesian naval personnel had been killed in a collision with a Chinese submarine inside the Indonesian exclusive economic zone around the Natuna Islands. On the border with India, dozens of troops on both sides had died in a series of increasingly violent clashes. In Hong Kong, eighteen American journalists were arrested for violating newly enacted national security legislation. Two of the journalists later died while in Chinese custody, with the Chinese claiming they'd succumbed to pre-existing medical conditions. Despite the uproar created by the deaths, none of the other journalists had yet been released. Chinese naval vessels had begun ramming into Vietnamese fishing vessels around the disputed Paracel Islands in the South China Sea, killing hundreds of fishermen.

China was flexing its muscle.

After decades of restraint, it was willing to get a little blood on its hands. It was willing to hurt people. It was the second most powerful nation on earth, rapidly gaining on the first, and was beginning to act like it.

The trucks were loaded with a solid white, Chinese-made cyclonite nitramide, its chemical composition based closely on RDX. It was odorless and tasteless, and entirely undetectable by the embassy security system.

RDX, an organic compound developed by the British military during World War Two, was invented for use against German U-Boats with increasingly thick steel hulls. The British gave the explosive, which was more volatile than TNT, the codename Research Department Explosive. When it was introduced to the United States military in 1946, they shortened that to RDX.

The chemical in the back of the trucks was refined from an exceptionally high grade of RDX known as RDX-II and had a detonation velocity of over nine thousand meters per second. Its RE factor was eight, making it eight times as explosive as TNT.

When six tons of it exploded simultaneously in the embassy's central plaza, it created the largest non-industrial explosion on the Chinese mainland since the end of the Second World War.

The impact of the explosion was instantaneous.

People within the initial blast radius heard nothing. They saw nothing. They were simply vaporized. The shockwave traveled from the explosion at speeds in excess of Mach twenty, creating temperatures above a thousand degrees Celsius.

Those further away heard the explosion, the crashing of glass, and the screaming of victims.

Ten miles away, people heard the blast so loudly that cars pulled over in the streets and stopped traffic. The plume of smoke could be seen from Tianjin and Baoding.

It would take weeks for the US government to get an accurate count of the number of casualties. By that time, American permission to operate anywhere on the Chinese mainland would be revoked, signaling the onset of a new Cold War.

47

The president tossed in his bed. He'd been short with his wife and regretted it. She was lying next to him now, ostensibly asleep, but he knew she was sulking. "I'm sorry, Doris," he said.

She said nothing.

"I'm just stressed." He sat up and swung his feet over the side of the bed. "Will you forgive me?"

Still no answer.

He put a hand on her shoulder. "I'm going to go out to the balcony," he said.

He crossed the room to the humidor he kept by his dressing table and fumbled in the dark for a cigar.

"Ingram. You're smoking?" his wife said, turning on the lamp.

"I can't sleep."

"Whatever is the matter?" she said.

"It's nothing."

"Heavy is the head," she said. He looked at her, and she added, "We talked about the cigars."

He nodded but took one from the humidor anyway. He

snipped it in the guillotine of his cigar cutter before remembering it had been a gift from Roth. It was made of gold and whalebone and had belonged to the captain of one of Nantucket's most renowned whalers.

"They're trying to turn me against Levi Roth," he blurted.

She stood immediately. "Ingram!"

"I know."

"He's your—"

"I know he is."

"You and he...."

"Doris, I know."

She came over and put her arms around him, and he let out a long sigh. "Ingram Montgomery," she said into his ear, "you told me a long time ago to let you know if this place ever threatened to steer you off course."

He nodded.

"There are a lot of dangerous people in this city."

"I know, Doris."

"It's a swamp, Ingram. You don't forget that."

"I'm reminded of it every day."

"There have been moments when you thought you weren't up to the task of running this country. Of protecting it."

He nodded again. This was one of those times, if there had ever been one.

"But no matter what you've faced," Doris said, "whatever storms and tempests and rocky shores you've sailed, Levi Roth has always, *always* had your back."

It was true.

"That man," she said, "he's the watcher on the wall, Ingram."

"I know it, Doris."

"Only you know the things he's done. The sacrifices he's made. The monsters he's faced."

Ingram nodded.

"Whatever they're telling you in the briefings, whatever evidence they're bringing, whatever their spies are coming back with, you look at it very carefully."

"I do, dear."

"You look very long and very hard at any messenger who brings you ill news of Levi Roth."

"I know you're right," Ingram said, "but if the news is coming from multiple directions, all saying the same thing, I can't let personal loyalty blind me to the facts."

"What facts?"

"It's one of his men, one of his assets."

"One asset?"

"His best operative."

"What of him?"

"Everything we're seeing tells us this asset has gone off the rails. He's a rogue agent. No question about it. He's maybe even plotting to attack us."

"Treason?"

"Treason," Ingram said gravely.

"Well," Doris said, "if it's the asset who's doing it, that indicts him, not Roth."

"But Roth keeps defending him. He's so adamant. I can't get him to accept that this is one apple that's threatening to rot the entire tree."

"Well," Doris said, "it seems to me his crime is misplaced loyalty."

Ingram nodded. He looked at his wife. He was a lucky man to have her, and he knew it. "If it's misplaced loyalty he's guilty of," he said, "I don't want to be guilty of the same sin."

Doris looked at him sadly. "Many a great man has been pulled down by his loyalty to lesser men," she said.

Ingram knew that was true. He'd just witnessed it before his very own eyes in the Roosevelt room. Roth seemed determined to be torn down by Spector. It was as if he wanted everything he'd spent his life building to get torn down.

His thoughts were suddenly interrupted by a loud knock on the bedroom door.

"What the hell could that be?" Ingram said, looking at his watch.

"Sir," a voice said from outside the door. "We need to get you and the first lady to the bunker immediately. We're under attack."

48

The bunker, known officially as the Presidential Emergency Operations Center, was a hardened facility deep beneath the White House's East Wing. It could withstand direct nuclear, chemical, biological, and conventional attacks while at the same time allowing the president to maintain full control of all branches of government.

He and Doris had been brought down and shown around when they first took up residence in the White House, and Ingram remembered hoping he would never have to see the place in anger.

As he stood in the steel-plated elevator, his wife's hand in his, he realized that this night was going to be the defining moment of his presidency. What he did next was what he'd be remembered for. What he'd go down in posterity for. He couldn't afford to waver. He couldn't allow old friendships to cloud his judgment. He had to act decisively.

He looked at the four Secret Service agents escorting them and wondered if any of them knew more than he did about what was going on. If they did, they weren't letting on.

"I'm sorry about this," he said to Doris.

The Russian   307

She shook her head as if to say it wasn't his fault.

When they reached the bunker, Doris was escorted to the residential quarters, and he was taken down a hundred-yard corridor to a formidable-looking steel blast door.

Standing by the door was his Chief of Staff, the Attorney General, and the Defense Secretary.

"Ready, sir?" the Defense Secretary said.

"Where's the Vice President?"

"He was at a campaign event in Florida last night, sir. He's safe."

"Can someone please tell me what in God's name is going on?"

Military personnel went through the process of unlocking the blast door, all twenty-five tons of which slid open on its hinges as smoothly as the door of a small safe.

Beyond the door was a fully operational military command center, complete with satellite relay control and nuclear launch capability. The equipment was still booting up, coming to life with the distinctive buzz of the new generation of quantum computers recently delivered by IBM.

The space was compact, and while some personnel already stood at their posts, many were still finding their position, giving the room a chaotic feel.

On the main screen, live conferencing links to the emergency centers at the Pentagon, Langley, and Fort Meade were all online. People could be seen rushing around at all three centers, getting to their posts with clipboards or hastily-grabbed cups of coffee in their hands.

When Sandra Shrader walked into the Fort Meade center, Ingram thought she looked like she'd been throwing up. Her face was white as a sheet, and her hand was shaking so badly she had trouble holding her coffee.

"Will someone please tell me what's going on before I blow a fuse?" the president said to the screen.

"Sir," Sandra said, her voice trembling, "there's been an attack."

"What attack?" the president demanded.

"The United States Embassy in Moscow, sir," she said. "It's been destroyed."

Ingram's mind went blank. It was surreal. Who would dare do such a thing? He looked around the room at the assembled representatives of the nation's highest security agencies.

This was it.

This was the real deal.

Not a drill.

The time had come for all of them to show what they were made of.

"Sir," Sandra continued, clearing her throat, "and the United States Embassy in Beijing."

Ingram looked at her. "Come again?" he said.

In her frail, choked-up voice, she said again, "And the United States Embassy in Beijing."

"What about the United States Embassy in Beijing?" he said, the horror of her meaning slowly dawning on him.

"Sir, the attack—it's against the United States embassies in Moscow and Beijing. Simultaneously."

"Simultaneously?"

"Yes, sir."

"Against both embassies?"

"That's correct, sir."

"Good lord." He had to hold on to the side of the table to steady himself.

His chief of staff rushed forward. "Are you all right, sir?"

"I'm fine, damn it," he said, waving him away. He stood and looked at the faces of his advisors. The effect was the same on everyone—absolute silence. Not a word from anyone. No one even dared move.

The moment stretched for ten, twenty seconds.

It was for Ingram to break the spell. "I see," he said, attempting to sound in command of the situation.

On the screens before him, he had the Pentagon, Fort Meade, and the Site R continuity of government facility at Raven Rock. What he did not see was a live link to the CIA.

"Where's Langley?" he said.

"Sir," Sandra said, and then, instead of speaking, she put her hand in front of her face and doubled over. The terrible sound of her vomiting filled the speakers.

The president looked around at his staff awkwardly.

One of Sandra's assistants came to her aid.

"Can we put Fort Meade on mute, for God's sake?" the president said.

The sound was cut, and the Chairman of the Joint Chiefs, Elliot Schlesinger, jumped in on one of the screens. "Sir," he said, "on a code red from NSA, the CIA has not been looped in on this emergency signal."

"What code red?" the president barked. "I want Levi Roth on this call immediately."

"Of course, sir," Schlesinger said, "but you may want to see something first." Schlesinger signaled to someone off-camera, and a fresh feed came up on the screen. "Sir, this is from directly outside the embassy in Moscow."

"What am I looking at?"

"That's the Garden Ring, sir. Morning traffic. From the time-stamp, you can see it was taken just a few minutes ago."

The footage showed a man coming out of a hotel and opening fire on embassy security, killing several guards.

"Is that...?" the president said, not daring to finish his sentence.

"Yes, sir," Schlesinger said. "Identity has been confirmed. The attacker is Lance Spector."

The president felt as if the wind had just been knocked out

of him. He'd been standing in front of the screens. He pulled up a seat and sat down. "I see," he said.

"Sir, it appears NSA concerns about an infiltration within the CIA are credible."

"So you're saying...."

"There's cause for concern, sir."

The president nodded slowly. He turned to the Fort Meade screen and made sure Sandra was done throwing up her breakfast. "Sandra?" he said.

She looked no better than she had before. "We're still analyzing, sir."

The president gritted his teeth. He didn't know what was going on, but the NSA had come to him with concerns about Spector. The president had listened to those concerns, then done absolutely nothing about them. Now, the Pentagon was showing him footage of Spector killing US embassy security guards just minutes before an attack. "All right," he said.

"All right, what, sir?" Schlesinger said.

"Bring him in."

"Bring him in, sir?"

"Bring in Roth. Get him in custody. And issue a kill order against Lance Spector."

49

Sandra thought she was having a panic attack. The second the president killed the video, she ran from the control room to the nearest restroom and locked herself in a stall.

She dropped to her knees and began retching violently.

"Are you all right in there?" someone said from the next stall, but Sandra couldn't answer.

When she finally came out, her eyes were full of tears, and her makeup was so messed up she looked like a raccoon.

A junior member of the secretarial staff was standing by the vanity with a clump of paper towel in her hand. "Director Shrader," she said, handing her the paper.

"Thank you," Sandra croaked.

"Are you okay?"

"I'm just...." she said. And then, "Something I ate, I think."

"I know you're in the middle of a crisis," the girl said. "I can't begin to imagine the stress you're under."

Sandra turned and looked at her. "What are you talking about?"

"Oh," she said, embarrassed that she'd overstepped a boundary, "the bombings. I thought maybe I could offer—"

"The bombings?"

"Yes, ma'am. The embassy bombings."

"I see," Sandra said. She ran the cold water and washed her face. The girl stood there awkwardly, watching her. "Haven't you got somewhere to be?"

"Yes, ma'am," the girl said, escaping the room as quickly as she could.

The moment she left, Sandra burst into tears. She tried to stop. She knew people would be able to tell she'd been crying, and that could raise suspicions. She had to pull herself together.

But she was afraid she was losing her mind. For a second, she'd actually thought the girl had been talking about Lizzie.

She was so worried about her daughter that she couldn't think straight. And now the nation was in crisis, there were hundreds of casualties, possibly more, and people would be looking to her to respond. And she wouldn't be able.

Her daughter was in the hands of Russian psychopaths.

It was beginning to sink in that she might never see her again.

And whoever had Lizzie had lied. They'd used her. They'd told her to undermine the president's trust in Roth and then used the opportunity to launch the most devastating attacks on US sovereignty since 9/11.

What was she going to do? When the investigators came in later and tried to unravel this clusterfuck, how would she ever explain her actions?

She knew there was a very real chance she might spend the rest of her life in federal prison.

And Lizzie.

She still wasn't back.

Someone entered the restroom, but when they saw Sandra, the state she was in, they apologized and backed away.

She knew she had to get her act together and get cleaned up before she created a scene. She rewashed her face, reapplied her makeup as best she could, and went back to her office.

A large television on the wall showed cable news coverage of both attacks over and over, as if on an infinite loop. There were so many angles. One showed cell phone footage from a tourist in Beijing outside the embassy. Someone was waving at the camera, and then a shockwave, like something out of a science fiction movie, blasted the scene, flattening the person and sending a cloud into the sky far in the distance.

"Good lord," she said to herself.

"Are you feeling better, ma'am?" the girl from the restroom said, placing a hand on Sandra's shoulder.

Sandra wasn't feeling better. That explosion, the explosion in Russia, all those casualties—it was her fault, and she knew it. She'd lied to the president. She'd distracted him from the real issue. And she would have to live with that knowledge for the rest of her life.

Her phone rang. It was an unknown number.

Her heart sank.

She knew it was the Russians, and something told her they weren't calling to tell her where to pick up her daughter.

She shut the office door, locked it, and muted the television. "What is it?" she said, her voice strained almost to the point of breaking.

"Sandra," the voice said, "is that any way to speak to an old friend?"

She felt like throwing up again. She glanced at the waste paper basket as her stomach did backflips. "You lied to me," she said.

"Lied to you? Sandra, I'm offended."

"You said you were going after Roth."

"We are going after Roth."

"The embassies...." She stopped herself and lowered her voice. "Embassies are going up in smoke all over the world."

"That's precisely why we're calling, Sandra. You need to warn the president that he has a rat in his house."

"A rat in his house? Is this some sort of joke?"

"What could possibly be funny about this situation, Sandra?"

She went to the window and shut the privacy blind. "I'm the fucking rat, you piece of shit. I'm the one who did this."

"Now, now, Sandra. You need to calm down. We're getting Lizzie ready to come home, and we can't have her mother in a panic when she arrives."

Sandra shut her eyes. She refused to let this bastard get the better of her. She refused to cry. "Lizzie?" she said.

"She'll be home before you know it, Sandra. But you need to make clear to the president that you have solid intelligence regarding these attacks."

"Like the intelligence you gave me about Clarice Snow?"

"Intelligence that proves Lance Spector is a traitor and that he's the one behind the attacks."

"I don't even know if the president is still listening to me," Sandra said.

"Oh, he'll listen. He's listened so far, hasn't he?"

Sandra felt dizzy. This was a nightmare. She thought about what it would take to smash the window of her office and jump out to her death.

"Why are you doing this?" she said.

"Warning you of traitors? Because we don't want a war to break out between our countries. Russia could gain nothing from that."

"Then why attack us?"

"Don't concern yourself with the big picture, Sandra. Just do as you're told."

"Where's Lizzie?"

"She's close."

"I want to speak to her."

"First, I need one more little favor."

"Favor? What favor?"

"I want Spector."

"If we knew where Spector was, we'd be going after him ourselves."

"Don't do that," he said. "You see to it that I get the information first."

"Why do you want Spector?"

"That's for me to know," he said.

"What if I can't get it?"

"Oh, you'll get it," he said. "You have so much riding on it."

"You sick bastard," she spat. "Give me my daughter back."

"Sandra," he said, his voice so conciliatory it practically oozed.

"Don't you dare patronize me."

"You find Spector, and you get the information to me before anyone on your side can take action. I want him, and I'm going to have him."

"What if I can't?"

"Well," he said, "you've got an imagination. You know what I could do to your little girl here."

"Don't do a thing," Sandra gasped. "I'll find him."

50

Tatyana couldn't take her eyes from the screen. The news anchors didn't know what to say. For once, they seemed genuinely speechless. The embassies were shown over and over, from dozens of angles, and when the helicopter footage started coming in, showing the full scale of the devastation, she couldn't believe what she was seeing.

Smoke rose from the crater at ground zero as if there'd been a meteor strike.

All she could think of was her sister.

Laurel's voice yanked her from her thoughts. "This is how wars start," she said.

Tatyana nodded. This was going to change everything. Larissa had been right all along. Her warning, the conversation she'd overheard, it was all true.

And now, she might have paid for it with her life.

Whoever planned these attacks knew exactly what they were doing. To pull off one would take months of planning and the ability to circumvent some of the most sophisticated security measures on earth.

To pull off both? Simultaneously?

"How could they let this happen?" Tatyana said, her eyes still fixed on the screen. "We knew it was coming. Lance broke into the embassy and laid it out in front of their faces."

Laurel just shook her head.

"How could they be so blind?"

"I don't know," Laurel said.

"This is going to be unlike anything they've ever seen," Tatyana went on. She was ranting, but Laurel didn't interrupt her. "Whatever happened after 9/11, this is another level. Forget the Taliban. Russia and China? That's no insurgency. They're superpowers."

"I know," Laurel said.

"This is going to be the mother of all wars. Americans haven't faced a threat like this in living memory. They've never fought a fight they didn't already know they were going to win."

"We'll win this fight," Laurel said.

"What if you don't?"

"*We* will, Tatyana," Laurel said, emphasizing the 'we'.

Tatyana realized she was crying, tears streaming down her face, and she couldn't stop. "What if she's dead?" she said.

Laurel came forward and took her in her arms. "She's going to be all right."

"How? How is she going to be all right?"

"She was with Lance."

"And Lance ran right into it," Tatyana cried. "We saw the feed. He ran right in, seconds before the blast. There's no way he survived that."

Laurel let go of her, and instantly, Tatyana realized what she'd said. "Oh, Laurel! I'm sorry."

But Laurel shook it off. "We don't know what happened," she said.

"I'm sure he's okay."

Laurel looked at her like she was about to say something but stopped herself. She looked around the room, then made for the door without saying another word.

Tatyana didn't know what to do. In her concern for Larissa, she'd forgotten what Laurel must have been going through. She went to the door. "Laurel, wait."

Laurel had rushed up the two flights of stairs and let herself out onto the balcony. Tatyana followed. When she got out to the balcony, Laurel was leaning on the rail, looking out at the backyard. "I just need a second," she gasped.

"I know," Tatyana said.

Laurel looked at her but said nothing. She wouldn't allow herself to show weakness or vulnerability.

Tatyana pulled out a chair for her, and she sat.

Neither of them said a word. The pool was uncovered, lit up, and steam rose off it. It had started to snow, and the flakes disappeared into the water.

Tatyana reached into her pocket and pulled out a pack of cigarettes. She put one in her mouth. She knew Laurel had been trying to quit but offered her one anyway. Laurel took it, and Tatyana gave her a light.

Then they smoked together in silence.

51

Lance didn't know where he was.

He couldn't breathe. He couldn't see.

The sound in his ears was deafening, like someone had just struck a giant tuning fork right next to his head.

Everything was so black he wasn't even sure his eyes were open. He rubbed them and tried to stand up but stumbled back to the ground.

He began coughing, choking on the smoke, and when he reached up and touched his head, it was sticky with blood.

"Help," he heard someone cry.

Others were shouting too, he realized, and crying. Their words were in English and Russian. Dozens of people.

He got up and stumbled a few feet forward, tripping over the body of a US marine. He crouched down and felt the man's neck for a pulse. There was none.

There was a flashlight next to the marine, and he picked it up.

He shone it through the thick billowing smoke and saw deep craters in the ground where the construction trucks had been.

He kept moving, following the sound of voices, and passed some more marines on the ground. He checked the first. He was unconscious but had a pulse.

"Hey," Lance said to another marine. The man was sitting on the ground with his back to the crater. "Hey, you—you all right?"

The marine looked at him blankly.

Lance crouched down in front of him. "You know this man?" he said, pointing to the unconscious marine on the ground.

The marine nodded slowly.

"Pick him up and bring him that way," Lance said, pointing back toward the front of the compound.

The man struggled to get up, and Lance helped him. He lifted the injured marine onto the other man's shoulder and then sent him in the right direction.

Then, he continued forward into the smoke, passing the three craters.

There were bodies everywhere. Ahead, he could make out the concrete entryway to one of the underground sections of the old embassy building. Everything above it was gone. He stumbled on through the thick smoke. Dust from the rubble was so thick he could hardly breathe, hardly see. It filled his mouth, and he had to stop to cough it up. Somewhere in the distance, he heard the sound of generators coming to life. And then the sirens of dozens of emergency vehicles.

By his feet was another body. A woman. He was about to step over her when she moved her hand and grabbed him by the ankle. Lance bent down. She was alive, but barely.

He recognized her. It was the woman he'd spoken to earlier at the security desk.

He looked around for anyone who could help, but there was no one. Then he lifted her over his shoulder, wincing from the pain, and carried her toward the gate.

Through the smoke, he could already make out the blue

and red flashing lights of ambulances, and he staggered toward them. As he approached, a team of medics came at him, speaking in Russian.

"She's hurt," Lance said, handing over the woman.

The medics put her on a stretcher and lifted her into the back of an ambulance.

"You're hurt too," a medic said to Lance.

Lance brushed the man's hand away and went back into the embassy. He worked in a daze, not entirely sure whether the carnage around him was real or a nightmare.

He found more and more bodies—marines, Russian contractors, diplomatic and consular staff. He checked for a pulse on twenty corpses before he came across another living person.

It was a man in a suit, struggling to make his way toward the gates. His suit looked strangely intact, unsullied by the blast, apart from the fact that his right arm, and the arm of the suit, had been completely blown off.

"Here," Lance said to him. "Let me help you."

The man reached out to him with his one arm and collapsed. Lance caught him as he fell. "I got you," he said.

The man was losing consciousness, and Lance tapped him lightly on the cheek. "Stay with me, buddy."

He opened his eyes and looked at Lance.

"What's your name?" Lance said.

"Rapaport," the man said.

"You're the Station Chief," Lance said.

The man nodded, then looked at where his arm should have been. His uncomprehending eyes rolled back in his head, and he lost consciousness.

Lance could see from the blood spurting from what was left of his arm that he still had a pulse, although it was getting weaker by the second. He pulled off his belt and tied it tightly around the stump. Then he lifted Rapaport over his shoulder and carried him back toward the ambulances.

"Is he even alive?" a medic said as he loaded him into the back of the ambulance.

Lance grabbed the medic by the shoulders. "Yes, he's alive," he said. "And you're going to do everything you can to save him." He grabbed the paramedic's name tag and pulled it from his shirt. "He lives," Lance said, making sure there was no room for misunderstanding, "or I come knocking."

As more and more police vehicles poured into the area, Lance realized he had to get out of there. He walked out onto the street and saw that all the hotel's windows were completely blown out.

Larissa, he thought, for the first time since the blast.

He went into the lobby. The fire alarm was ringing. People were running everywhere. Some were injured, and others were helping them toward the ambulances out front. Lance took the stairs to the room.

When he got there, Larissa was on the ground, her back to the wall, the curtains blowing above her in the shattered window frame.

She was crying.

When she looked up and saw him standing in the doorway, she shook her head as if she didn't believe her own eyes. "I thought..." she stammered but didn't finish the sentence.

52

There was a conference room immediately off the command center, and the president entered it, shutting the door firmly behind him. He needed to clear his head.

The nation was under attack. He'd just ordered the arrest of his most trusted advisor, and placed a kill order on the CIA's most valuable asset.

He felt like he was blundering in the darkness, grasping at straws, and somewhere, deep down, he knew he was being outmaneuvered, manipulated. It was not a comfortable feeling, and his head spun at the endless permutations of what might be happening, and what might be yet to come.

Who was behind the attacks?

What was their objective?

What trap was being set for him?

There was a coffee machine on the side table, and he pushed the button for a dark roast. He took the plastic cup to the conference table and sat down.

Russia and China—America's two most powerful adversaries. They were the only nations on earth that could hope to attain superpower status and displace American hegemony. And they'd attacked simultaneously.

In geopolitical terms, it was by far the greatest challenge since the end of the Cold War. Whoever was behind it was making a statement. But what statement?

If it was terrorists, he could handle that. America had been on a counter-terrorist footing for twenty years. The military was perfectly equipped to go into some remote Afghan mountains and hunt down jihadists. It was strange to think it, but the best scenario right now was for terrorists to be behind this. Religious extremists, political radicals, environmental anarchists. There was a playbook for countering them. A method for fighting back. There was a frame of reference.

More complicated, more destructive to the nation's morale and prestige, would be an attack from the inside.

The president had known Levi Roth for over thirty years. As much as one man could know the soul of another, he knew Roth's. Or he thought he did.

What if he was wrong? What if Roth had been drawn off course?

The president found that hard to believe.

With his own eyes, he'd seen Roth do things for his country that few people would even believe. He had difficulty imagining the man who did those things could become a traitor. But then, nothing was impossible. The NSA's vast surveillance apparatus had been throwing up red flags left, right, and center, raising the alarm about Roth. What if they were right?

And then there was the question of Lance Spector. Who knew how many loose screws that man had rattling around? He'd been so poked and prodded by Langley that it was hard not to imagine him going off the deep end eventually. He was a trained killer who had failed to report for duty. He'd broken into the embassy just hours before the attack, and then, only minutes before, footage showed him killing embassy security guards. The Pentagon and the NSA were both gunning for him, and the president himself had just issued a kill order.

But none of that was conclusive.

It didn't look good for Spector. And it would be convenient for the president if he did turn out to be behind the attacks. But without further data, it was impossible to know for sure what had been going on in Moscow. Not to mention Beijing. Whatever else Lance Spector was capable of, he had not, as far as the president was aware, developed the ability to be in two places at once.

The more he thought about it, though, the more he realized that the Spector angle might be convenient for him politically. It would allow him to explain the attacks in a way that average citizens would understand.

There had been lone gunmen before. Guys went nuts all the time. This guy was the perfect candidate. Military service. Experimental CIA program. It wouldn't be pretty—it would make the CIA look like a disaster and trigger the end of Levi Roth's career—but it would be an explanation Joe Schmo on the street would understand.

And sometimes, finding an explanation acceptable to Joe Schmo was all that mattered. Especially when the alternative was an outcome so bleak that the president couldn't bear to countenance it.

War with Russia and China.

In the nuclear age, that wasn't something that could ever be allowed to happen.

It would change everything. It would alter the international political landscape beyond recognition. It could end modern life as it was known. It could end life, period.

The president sipped his coffee. "No," he said to himself.

War, real war, against Russia and China was not on the cards. To hell with everything else. Ingram Montgomery might not have been the most religious man on earth, but he attended church, believed in God, and was not going to face his maker as the man who unleashed global war.

If war were coming, he would fight it, but he would not go down as the man who started it. Not even after provocation of this magnitude.

There could be no winning in a war like that. And even if there could, even if the world after such a war was something worth winning, Montgomery had access to facts that few people on the planet had ever seen.

He knew what the Chinese and Russian militaries were capable of.

Victory in that conflict was not a foregone conclusion.

While the balance was on the American side, there were circumstances, especially against both rivals simultaneously, in which the US military could lose the upper hand. There were wars that, despite the Pentagon's brave rhetoric and optimistic projections, America could lose.

America versus Russia and China was one of them.

He clenched his fists and reminded himself, as much as it was distasteful to admit, that his job was not to do what was right, it was not to seek justice or retribution, it was not to speak the truth. Above all else, his job was to protect the nation, ensure its continued existence, and preserve the lives of its citizens.

There would be consequences to this attack, almost certainly there would be military consequences, but there was a line beyond which president Ingram Montgomery dared not cross.

He knew what he needed to do, and he knew what he needed to say.

Every news channel on the planet was showing footage of the embassies being blown to smithereens. The footage was being looped incessantly. The images would never be forgotten. The embassies were not in remote, backwater places. They were in the capital cities of America's two greatest rivals for dominance.

This was a crisis like none faced since the Japanese bombing of Pearl Harbor. And after that, Franklin Roosevelt mobilized what ultimately turned out to be over ten million men.

He looked at his watch. The recording studio was being set up next door and would be ready in a matter of minutes.

But what could he, as president, say? What words would reduce the options available to him? What words would bring him closer to danger? What words did the men behind these monstrous attacks want to hear come from his mouth?

He knew his job was not to console the nation, although he would have to appear to do so. He knew his job was not to explain what had happened or to reveal those responsible. His job was not to do the right thing. His job was to maintain order, maintain control of the situation, protect American prestige, and make the country appear as powerful as possible.

His job was to go on camera, address the nation, and save as much face for the United States as possible. Because weakness, even just the appearance of weakness, would cost more lives. Someone, somewhere, would see it and would pounce. He couldn't allow that to happen.

And, of course, there was an opportunity here too. No politician worth his salt let a good crisis go to waste.

His predecessors took the mess of 9/11 and used it to invade the country with the second-largest oil reserves on the planet. What was he going to do?

Ingram Montgomery had always been hawkish on foreign policy. The first thing he read every morning was his national security bulletin. And he didn't read it for threats. He read it for opportunities. If there was a contained, easily won, strategically valuable war to be had out of this disaster, he would take it.

Carl von Clausewitz said that war was just a continuation of politics, and Ingram believed that. He was not afraid of war—so long as it was a war he could control. Something along the lines of the Iraq invasion? That, he could handle.

But he could not allow his hand to be forced. Even now, he recognized that having someone like Lance Spector ready to take the fall was essential.

There was a knock on the door, and it opened. It was his chief of staff holding a phone.

"Not now," the president said.

"Sir, this is a call you're going to want to take."

Ingram sighed. "Who is it?"

"It's Kirov, sir."

The president took the phone and, with a clenched jaw, put it to his ear. "Kirov," he said, practically spitting the word from his mouth.

Speaking to a Russian was not at the top of his priority list right now, but this was a call he could not refuse. A secret addendum to the Moscow Summit agreed by Nixon and Brezhnev decades earlier contained rules for situations like this. Rules to mitigate the risk of accidental war breaking out. Kirov was required to call the president and tell him whether or not this attack was an act of war carried out by the Russian government against the United States. It was a big call. Perhaps the biggest of his presidency.

He held his breath.

From the first dulcet word out of Kirov's mouth, he could tell what it meant.

"Mr President," Kirov said, his privileged Russian accent luxuriating over every syllable. "Allow me to extend the sincerest condolences of the Russian president in the wake of this shocking attack."

"Kirov, what the hell is going on over there?"

"I assure you, Mr President, the Russian government is as taken aback as you are."

"You assure me? You assured me our facilities would be secure when you expelled our marines."

"Sir, this was nothing we saw coming. You have my word on that."

"And why the hell isn't your president telling me this himself? We just suffered the largest attack since 9/11, and it happened in the center of Moscow, on your watch, on your soil, Kirov."

"I know, Mr President, and believe me, our president will be contacting you very shortly himself. I am just calling to discharge Russian obligations under the agreement of 1972."

"And what is your message, Kirov?"

"My message is that this is not an act of war, Mr President, and that Russia is not deploying nuclear or conventional forces against NATO or the United States."

"You're goddamn right it's not an act of war," the president said.

"Quite right, Mr President."

"Because we'd hand your asses to you, Kirov. You're aware of that, aren't you?"

"You would be handing a lot of asses, sir."

"What's that supposed to mean?"

"To us, to Beijing, at the same time. With all those asses, you would really have your hands full."

The president hung up. He looked at the phone to make sure the call had ended, then, speaking directly to the handset, said, "Go fuck yourself, Kirov."

53

The president walked onto the stage, fully aware that the next two minutes were quite possibly going to be the most critical of his presidency.

The world was watching. Allies and adversaries. Russia and China. The slightest sign of weakness, the slightest hesitation, and they would move in for the kill.

And the nation was watching. Congress. The military. The people.

He was the leader of the greatest nation on earth, the most powerful force the planet had ever known. No army from any empire in any era in human history came close to its dominance. Two million active and reserve personnel, thirteen thousand aircraft, six thousand tanks, thirty-eight thousand armored vehicles, two thousand artillery vehicles, and eleven hundred rocket projectors. In the sea, 415 vessels, including twenty aircraft carriers.

And always, in the background, unspoken, four thousand armed nuclear warheads. Effective strike range was ten thousand miles from land, seven thousand from sea.

Nowhere was safe. Nowhere was out of reach. Absolute

dominance could be projected to any spot on the planet.

There was a comfort in that. A knowledge, deep within every citizen of the country, every citizen of the globe, that someone was in charge. Someone held the reins.

And that comfort, that certainty, had just been shattered.

The US embassies in Moscow and Beijing were smoldering ruins. What did that say of America's ability to keep its rivals in check? What did it say of America's role in the international system? What did it say about who really ruled the world?

The cameraman gave him the signal.

He looked around the room. Apart from the cameramen and a few technicians, the room was empty. But no mistake, Ingram Montgomery felt the eyes of the world on him. "My fellow Americans," he began, clearing his throat. He knew he wasn't a physically imposing man. He knew the impression he gave. His gift was in his powers of oration. What his body lacked, his deep, booming New England voice and its archaic mariner's undertones would have to make up for.

"Moments ago, our nation suffered a direct and deliberate attack. The United States embassies in Moscow and Beijing were bombed."

He paused to let the words sink in.

"The United States is viewing these attacks as an act of all-out aggression, and that is why I am declaring as of this moment that we are at war."

He paused again.

He'd spoken to no one of this. There would be a frenzy in Congress. But in his soul, he knew it was necessary.

"Have no doubt, whoever is behind these vile, despicable acts will feel the full might of the American military machine."

If there'd been an audience, he would have been able to gauge its reaction, to modulate his message. In its absence, he had no choice but to follow his instincts and keep going.

"At this moment, we are still uncertain who was behind

these attacks and what objective they were pursuing. As we speak, the National Security Agency is analyzing data from around the globe to pinpoint exactly who did this, and the moment we find out, war plans will be put into effect."

Was he going too far? Was he committing himself too deeply?

"Make no mistake," he said, his voice growing louder, "I tell you now, and I swear it before the nation and before God, that America will not rest until the full fury of her vengeance, the full wrath of her justice, has been meted out."

The room was silent. The technicians knew they were witnessing history.

And then a red light came on above the communications panel. The room was sealed—no one could interrupt the president during a moment like this—but that one panel was present to pass in messages if they were deemed important enough to influence the president's words in real-time.

"No stone," the president said, distracted by the technician reading the incoming message, "will be left unturned in our search for the perpetrators of this atrocity."

From the technician's face, the president knew the information was critical. "I'm getting live updates as I speak," he said. He beckoned for the technician to come forward and hand him the message. The technician looked at his colleagues before stepping forward with a small piece of paper.

The president read it.

Footage of Lance Spector killing embassy guards in Moscow has been leaked to all networks.

The president smiled. The information couldn't have been more opportune if his people had come up with it themselves.

He was talking tough, but he did not want war. The Spector angle was infinitely preferable.

"I'm being informed that new footage appears to show images of the attacker just moments before the first explosion. Let me say this—if these attacks were carried out by a traitor from within our own ranks, by an operative who swore an oath to protect this nation and its constitution, then there can only be one penalty."

He deliberately left a pause to heighten the drama of the moment.

"That penalty is death."

54

"What the hell do they think they're doing?" Roth said to his driver as four Secret Service vehicles got in front of them and forced the Escalade to the side of the road. They were headed north on Sixteenth Street, and Roth had hoped to make it back to Laurel and Tatyana before this happened.

The president was going to pin the attacks on Lance. He was going to blame the whole thing on the CIA. And that meant all of them were going to be arrested.

It seemed Sandra Shrader had her claws so deep into the president he'd arrest his own chief of staff if she told him to.

Roth had little doubt now. Sandra was in league with the Kremlin. There was no other way she could have known what she knew.

It was damning information, that was for sure. Clarice pregnant. The only way anyone could have known that was if Clarice had told them. And the only people Clarice spoke to were in the Kremlin.

And if it was true, it also meant Lance's unborn child had been killed when Clarice was.

"Drive around them," Roth said to the driver, his voice rising. "We have to get back to the house."

The driver tried to pull onto the sidewalk to get around the Secret Service vehicles, but they lurched forward to block his path. He then put the Escalade in reverse, but when he tried to back up, a DC metro police cruiser pulled up tight behind them. The Escalade hit it, and the officers inside got out and drew their weapons.

"I'm sorry, boss," the driver said.

"It's not your fault," Roth muttered as he hastily pulled out his cell phone and dialed Laurel's number.

Secret Service agents, pistols drawn, got out of their vehicles and closed in on the Escalade.

"Pick up, pick up," Roth said. The agents opened the doors of the car and yanked the phone from his hand. "What is the meaning of this?" he demanded, his voice rising in anger as two Secret Service agents pulled him out of the car. "Get your hands off me, you son of a bitch!"

"Don't make this more difficult than it needs to be," an agent said, pushing Roth up against the side of his vehicle.

"Make this difficult?" Roth said. "Do you know who the hell I am?"

"I've been ordered to bring you in, sir," the agent said.

"On whose authority?"

"It's an NSA authorization code, sir."

Roth's driver was being taken from the vehicle, and Roth said, "Don't tell me he's under arrest too?"

"His name's not on the warrant," one of the other agents said.

"I should hope not," Roth barked. "He works for the same agency as you idiots."

The agents let go of the driver, and Roth said to him, "You need to get back to the house. I have a bad feeling about this. Tell Laurel and Tatyana they're not safe."

The driver nodded. He and Roth had worked together a long time, and Roth knew he could be trusted.

The Secret Service agents then shoved Roth into the back of one of their cruisers. Roth watched through the window as his driver pulled the Escalade back onto the road and drove off.

He hadn't expected Shrader to move so aggressively or so quickly. Someone was making a power play, and they had to know that Laurel and Tatyana wouldn't sit by idly while it happened.

That meant they were in danger.

He should have warned them sooner.

The four Secret Service cruisers started moving in convoy formation, and when they pulled onto the beltway, Roth said, "Can you at least tell me why I'm being taken?"

The two agents in front looked at each other, then one sighed and pulled the warrant from his jacket. "Sir," he said, reading the warrant, "you're being arrested by order of NSA Director Sandra Shrader. The order is to take you to NSA headquarters at Fort Meade immediately."

"Fort Meade?"

"Yes, sir."

"Listen to me," Roth said. "Is this something you've ever been ordered to do before?"

Neither of them answered.

"The director of the CIA being brought in at gunpoint to face the NSA director? It's ludicrous."

"Sir, there'll be people waiting to speak to you at Fort Meade."

"This can't be legal," Roth said.

The agent held up the warrant for Roth to read for himself. It had been countersigned in the president's presence by the Attorney General.

"I see," Roth said, reading the signature.

They drove on, remaining mostly silent for the thirty

minutes it took to reach Fort Meade. When they got there, they pulled up to a loading bay at the rear of the main building and brought Roth into a private service elevator. The elevator took them to the second floor, where an anonymous conference room was waiting at the end of a long corridor. Inside the room, Sandra Shrader and a bunch of NSA officials were seated around a table.

"Sandra!" Roth said, as soon as he was brought into the room, and before anyone else had a chance to speak, "what you're attempting to do is treason, and everyone in this room knows it."

From Sandra's reaction and the look on her face, Roth realized it was true. She wasn't acting of her own volition. She was under duress. In fact, judging from her face, she was scared to death.

"Whoever's making you do this," Roth said, "it's not too late to stop it."

"Please stand by for the president," one of the men present said. There was a screen at the far end of the room, and everyone turned to it. The president's face appeared, and Roth saw that he was still in the Emergency Operations Center, surrounded by the same top-level officials.

"Levi Roth," the president said, reading from a sheet of paper in his hands.

"Mr President!" Roth began, but the president raised his hand to stop him.

"I'm declaring," the president said, "that your asset, Lance Spector, is a traitor to this nation, guilty of high treason, and an enemy of the state."

"Mr President!" Roth protested again, but again he was cut off.

"Furthermore, I'm declaring the Special Operations Group officially under investigation for involvement in this attack."

"Ingram!" Roth gasped, but the president kept reading.

"I'm ordering that you and your two operatives, Laurel Ever-lane and Tatyana Aleksandrova, be arrested and taken into custody immediately."

"This is a mistake!" Roth shouted. "This is an outrage!" Before he knew what was happening, he'd been shoved up against the desk and pushed forward. Agents grabbed him by the wrists and pulled them up painfully behind his back. Then he heard the click of the cuffs as they snapped shut on his wrists.

55

S ergey sat in his car and lit another cigarette. He was parked in a disused lot in DC's Navy Yard, and he'd been sitting there so long that the ashtray in the car was beginning to overflow. Every few minutes, he turned on the engine to get the heat going.

He'd been told to bring weapons and await orders, and by the time Kirov finally called, he was antsy to get going.

"Sergey, are you in the capital?" Kirov said.

"I've been sitting here for hours like you told me to."

Kirov spoke with mock sympathy. "Oh, was it all right, Sergey? Not too uncomfortable, I trust."

"Fuck off, Kirov."

"Did you bring the weapons?"

"Of course, I brought the weapons."

"Good. Roth's just been arrested, and Sandra has given us the location of the safe house."

"Where is it?"

"Georgetown. Write this down."

Kirov read off an address on Wisconsin Avenue, and Sergey

did not write it down but committed it to memory. "Who's there?" he said.

"Laurel Everlane and the traitor, Tatyana Aleksandrova."

"Just the two of them? You're sure of that?"

"Reasonably sure. There's a driver who provides a little extra security, but he was with Roth when they arrested him. I doubt you'll be seeing him."

"Very well," Sergey said. "I'm going to enjoy this—especially the traitor whore."

"Hold your horses, Sergey. There's been a slight change of plan."

"What change?"

"The boss wants them brought in alive if possible."

"What? That's too risky. They're trained professionals."

"You can manage it," Kirov said patronizingly. "Medvedev said you're his best man."

"That's only because I killed his other men," Sergey said.

"Exactly," Kirov said. "Anyway, you might have some help."

"The boss knows I work alone."

"Not that sort of help. Federal agents are on their way to arrest Everlane and Aleksandrova as we speak. They're not expected to resist."

"So you want me to take them from the feds?"

"There's a good chance they'll be arrested. That means they'll be in handcuffs. Bringing them in alive should be easy."

Sergey hung up the phone. He did not like changes to the plan. Two bullets, that was what he'd had in mind. Taking the women alive was a whole other ball game, even with police on the scene.

He stubbed out his cigarette and fired up the engine. Traffic was slow, the streets quiet, and as he crossed the Rock Valley Creek into Georgetown, a light snow began to fall.

He approached the address cautiously, circling the block in his car a number of times, making a note of the layout of the surrounding streets. The neighborhood was affluent. Everything, from the cast-iron lampposts to the cobbled streets, exuded American civic virtue.

His fastest escape route would be to cross the Potomac and get on the parkway, but the bridge worried him. The alternative route was to get on the Whitehurst Freeway at Canal Road and drive back into the city.

By the time he turned onto Wisconsin Avenue, he had a good sense of how any potential car chase might go. He pulled into a parking spot a few houses down from the address he'd been given and watched the house. It was a colonial townhouse, well-lit, with a narrow footprint. He had no doubt there was a state-of-the-art security system in place.

He stayed put for several minutes, and when the flashing lights of two black government-issue Cadillacs came around the corner, he got out of his car and went to the trunk.

The boss wanted the women alive, but that depended on whether or not the women allowed themselves to be arrested. If they did, this mission would be as easy as taking candy from a baby.

In the trunk of the car, he had a US military model M-32, six-shot, 40mm grenade launcher. The weapon could be used with a variety of ammunition types, and he'd already loaded it with high explosive grenades. He now removed the first four grenades from the revolver and replaced them with CS gas canisters. The final two remained high-explosive.

He watched as two federal agents entered the house. Two more remained in the vehicles on the street.

As well as the grenade launcher, he took two handguns, checking that they were loaded, and two Axon Taser 7 devices, which were the most advanced conducted electrical weapon available, used exclusively by law enforcement agencies. He checked the tasers carefully. They had a shooting range of thirty-five feet and were able to fire two separate spools. They punctured the skin with barbed darts that remained connected to the device by insulated copper wires. He also had a spray bottle containing the same mixture of carfentanil and remifentanil he'd used on Sandra Shrader and her daughter.

He brought the weapons and a gas mask back into the car and put on the mask.

When the agents came out of the house, Everlane and Aleksandrova were with them, handcuffed and compliant. They hadn't resisted arrest, exactly as Kirov had predicted.

Sergey opened the window of his car and hoisted the grenade launcher out through it. He took aim, switching off the safety, and fired off the four CS gas canisters. They lobbed into the yard in front of the house, emitting thick plumes of smoke. Without hesitating a second, Sergey then fired the two live grenades at the two Cadillacs parked on the street.

The first bounced off the roof and exploded a few yards beyond the car, shattering the windshield. The second went through the windshield and exploded inside the car, raising it a yard into the air with the force of the explosion.

Sergey pulled a gun from his coat and put the car into drive. He could barely see through the gas mask and drove erratically, jamming on the brakes as soon as he reached the house. With his handgun, he shot and killed the agent who was still seated in the car the grenade had missed.

Then he turned toward the house and opened fire on the two agents escorting Everlane and Aleksandrova. They were easy prey, coughing and choking on the gas, firing blindly in his direction. Squinting through the gas mask, he took them out with two well-aimed shots.

Tatyana and Laurel were highly-trained operatives, but with their wrists cuffed behind their backs and both of them choking on the gas to the point they were in real danger of asphyxiation, they stood little chance of evading him.

He pulled a taser from his pocket and walked into the gas

toward them. The first woman ran at him, he had no idea which it was, and he pointed the taser at her and fired. The darts flew out at her at 180 feet per second. They spread out over her chest, completing a circuit that channeled a modulated electric current through her body, disrupting all voluntary muscle control. She fell to the ground immediately, completely incapacitated.

He then pulled the other taser from his coat and fired it at the second woman. She was already on the ground, choking on the gas.

With both women down, he sprayed them with the narcotic mixture he'd used at Sandra Shrader's house, and was about to lift them up and carry them to his car when a Cadillac Escalade came speeding down the street. It jammed to a halt, skidding on the cobbled street and crashing into the back of Sergey's vehicle.

Sergey realized it was Roth's driver. He looked at the man. The driver looked back, confused, still processing what was happening. He opened his door, but Sergey put two bullets in his chest before his foot even touched the ground.

Sergey then walked over to him, as calmly as if he was out for a stroll, and put a third bullet in his skull, right between the eyes.

56

Hidden deep beneath the Kremlin's Sobornaya Square was one of the largest underground complexes in the world. Stalin successfully kept its construction secret for years, no small feat given the scale of the project, by disguising the work as part of the Moscow Metro System's Arbatskaya to Kropotkinskaya line extension. Over half a million cubic yards of concrete and a quarter-million tons of steel were secretly moved to the site, while even more soil and rock was ferreted out under the guise of ordinary construction waste. The project took twenty-two years to complete, and by the time it was finished, it contained more elevators and high-powered ventilation fans than any other building in the USSR.

Deep within this complex was an oval-shaped chamber, large enough to hold about fifty people. Around a table at its center sat the top military leadership of both Russia and China.

The meeting was so secretive that those present had passed through an underground medical facility prior to their arrival, where they were not only subjected to an x-ray, but also a modified MRI scan, to check for surveillance devices.

At intervals ranging from thirty to sixty seconds, the entire chamber was subjected to a low-level electromagnetic pulse designed to make electronic surveillance or recording impossible. It also meant the electric lights flickered in a way that gave the already cavernous room the feeling of being illuminated by candlelight.

The assembled military leaders, eight from each nation, were awaiting the arrival of Mikhail Medvedev and Liu Ying, who at that very moment were standing next to each other in the facility's high-speed elevator.

The atmosphere in the elevator was tense.

"I trust your daughter was returned safely," Medvedev said just before the doors opened.

Liu Ying gave him only the briefest of nods to acknowledge he'd heard him, and then they left the elevator and walked down the corridor to the oval chamber.

"Gentlemen," Medvedev said as they entered the room, "remain seated, please." He spoke in Russian, and his words were translated by an eighty-year-old blind Mongolian man whose terms of service prohibited him from ever leaving the Kremlin.

The words Medvedev was about to share had never been written down. They would not be recorded. No one from either country's legislative or judicial branch would ever know they'd been uttered.

The assembled men were generals, admirals, and intelligence directors. Not one of them was below the age of sixty. The mood was stiff, formal, but some attempt had been made to make it celebratory. At Medvedev's direction, Cohiba cigars and expensive bottles of scotch and vodka had been brought down and placed on the table.

A cloud of cigar smoke now hung over the table like smog over an industrial zone.

There were no laptops, no cell phones, no pens, no paper.

The only electrical devices in the room were the flickering
lights and the fans in the ventilation shafts. Heat came from gas
radiators affixed to the walls. They glowed orange, giving the
room an even more ethereal feel. On the wall was a large map
of the world, and at Medvedev's direction, red stars had been
placed over Moscow and Beijing.

Liu Ying took a seat next to Medvedev and nodded at the
Chinese members present.

Medvedev looked at the assembled faces. Together, these
men commanded over three million active service personnel
and seven thousand nuclear warheads.

The day when they were capable of standing up to the
United States was fast approaching, and the events of the past
few hours had thrown down a gauntlet that the entire world
would not be able to ignore.

"Gentlemen," he began, "I have called you here today to tell
you that the global strategic landscape has been altered dramatically in the last twenty-four hours."

The translator repeated his words, and the generals from
both sides of the table nodded their heads in agreement.

"The attacks on the US embassies in Moscow and Beijing,"
he continued, "were the most overt acts of provocation against
the United States in a generation."

More nodding.

"Hundreds of Americans were slaughtered in plain sight, in
attacks that were clearly orchestrated by the military forces of
the Russian Federation and the People's Liberation Army of
China. We know it. The Americans know it. And the people of
the world know it."

Medvedev looked at Liu Ying, who refused to look back
at him.

"Not even during the darkest depths of the Cold War did we
dare carry out such a brazen attack on American pride or target
such potent symbols of American power."

As his speech continued, Medvedev observed the impact his words had on the generals. They were enjoying it. More were taking up his kind offer of cigars. Some had begun to open the crystal decanters and pour the liquor into the crystal glasses he'd had brought down.

"If the Americans fail to respond to this attack, the era of their global hegemonic dominance will have come to an end." He reached for a bottle and began pouring himself a generous measure of vodka. "If the American president persists in his feeble, pathetic claim that these attacks were the work of one lone rogue agent, the entire world will see that he has backed down from a challenge. They will see that he is too afraid to fight."

He raised his glass. "Please join me in a toast," he said, "as we celebrate the day that Russia and China regain their rightful places on the global stage as military superpowers, capable of acting with absolute sovereignty in their spheres, without any fear of American interference."

To a man, they raised their glasses.

"From now on," Medvedev said, "there are three players in the grand game. America, China, and Russia. And we just showed the world that the Americans are no longer willing to stand up to the other two."

57

L ance and Larissa washed, packed up, and got out of the hotel in a matter of minutes. Out on the street, there were police everywhere, medics, firefighters. There had been hundreds of casualties, and the authorities would be digging bodies out of the rubble for weeks.

They had to walk a few blocks before they could catch a cab, and when they did, Lance told the driver to take them to the Kursky railway station. It was located on the other side of the city center and, at that time of the morning, would be the busiest station in the city. The crowds would provide cover.

They spoke little during the cab ride, and Lance told Larissa to keep her face covered as they entered the station.

They hurried through the enormous concourse, past the waiting area, and down two sets of escalators. Below ground, the passageways gave access not only to the station's platforms but also to the metro system and a warren of shops and eateries.

They walked briskly until they found a dingy bar with neon lights advertising slot machines. Inside, the place was dark, quiet, and had multiple escape routes. A television in the corner was showing pop music videos.

Lance chose a table where he could watch the entrance, and the bartender hauled himself over. He was an unhealthy-looking guy in his mid-forties and didn't seem to take his work too seriously. "What'll it be?" he said.

"Coffee," Lance said.

"Same," Larissa said, then to Lance, "You want to eat?"

Lance knew she was hungry and nodded. They ordered spaghetti and a pizza. Neither of them had high expectations of the food, but when it arrived, they devoured it. Then Lance looked at his watch and ordered more coffee.

"How long are we going to stay here?" Larissa said.

Lance wasn't sure. The place was about as good as any they were going to find, and he went up to the bar and asked the bartender if he could use the phone.

"There are payphones in the station," the bartender told him.

Lance pulled some cash from his wallet and put it on the bar. "I don't want to use those phones," he said.

The bartender looked at him carefully. The cash amounted to about fifty dollars. His instincts told him not to take it.

"Just a quick call," Lance said. "No trouble."

The bartender was still hesitant, and Lance doubled the cash.

Reluctantly, the man nodded toward the curtain at the end of the bar. "Make it quick," he said.

Lance went through the curtain to a filthy little staff area. There was a desk covered in newspapers, a half-eaten container of takeout noodles, and an ashtray with about two packs worth of cigarette butts stubbed into it.

An old landline phone sat on the desk, and Lance picked it up and dialed Laurel's secure line. The call failed to connect, and an automated voice gave back a compromised security code.

That was odd. Ominous even. It was an internal CIA flag indicating Laurel was not to be communicated with.

He tried Roth's line and received the same compromised flag. Roth was the CIA Director. For his line to be flagged, something seriously wrong was going down.

Whatever it was, it would have to wait. The albino was behind this attack, and Lance needed to know how to find him. Any delay and the man could disappear forever.

He hung up the phone. It was time to take a risk. He picked up the receiver again and dialed a CIA automated phone exchange located outside the city. The exchange had been operating in secret since the seventies and worked on antiquated AT&T vertical switch codes.

Lance dialed the exchange, flagged his call as level three priority, enabled full tracing, and had it forwarded to both Roth's and Laurel's central lines at Langley. Anyone who intercepted it would be able to trace his location. It was a risk he had to take. Whatever was going on in DC, someone at the CIA had to be willing to put political rivalries aside in order to get the man behind the bombing.

He went back to the table. Larissa had ordered some pastries, and they sat on a napkin on a blue plastic tray. They had a sugar dusting and were filled with sweetened whipped cream. "I don't know how you can stomach those things," he said.

She put one in her mouth and smiled. "Try them."

He sipped his coffee. "We need to wait here a while," he said. "I couldn't get hold of anyone in Washington."

Larissa nodded. "Is that normal?"

"No," he said. "It's not. But we need to wait here in case someone calls us back."

"From the CIA?"

He nodded.

"Is that safe?"

"No," he said.

She nodded and popped another pastry into her mouth. "Guess I don't need to worry about my figure then," she said.

Lance smiled. "You don't need to worry about a thing," he said and put one of the pastries in his mouth. It tasted like a chemical approximation of sugar and cream.

"Good, right?" Larissa said.

Lance drained his coffee and asked for more. The bartender came over with the pot and refilled their cups. "You're finished with the phone now?" he said.

Lance fixed him in his gaze. "Someone's calling me back," he said. "You let me know when they do."

The man nodded.

Lance looked up at the television. "Would you mind putting on the news?" he said.

"The bombings," the man said. "That's all they're talking about."

"*Bombings?*" Lance said.

The bartender nodded.

Lance looked at Larissa. "Would you mind passing me the TV controller?" he said to the bartender.

The man shrugged and came back with it. Lance flicked to the local news channel, expecting to see images of Moscow. What he saw on the screen he instantly recognized as the skyline of Beijing. "Bombings," he said again as the helicopter footage zoomed in on the site of another massive explosion.

"What happened?" he said to the bartender.

"The embassies," the man said. "Both of them."

"What embassies?"

"American embassies in China and Russia," the man said and made a gesture with his hand like something going up in smoke. "Poof," he said.

"Both of them?" Lance repeated, his eyes locked on the television screen. The bombing in Beijing looked to be at least as big as the one in Moscow—hundreds of casualties, if not thousands. "When did this happen?"

"Same time as the bombing in Moscow," the man said.

"Same time?"

He nodded.

Lance picked up the TV controller and flicked through all the news channels. Everyone was talking about the bombings, comparing them, speculating on who was behind them and what they meant. There was footage of people dying in the debris, bodies being pulled from the rubble, children crying. One strongly pro-Kremlin channel was showing side-by-side images of the US flag burning simultaneously in Moscow and Beijing, saying it was the end of the American era.

The bartender went back to his work, and Lance sunk into his seat. He felt as if he'd just been punched in the gut. "This could have been stopped," he said to Larissa under his breath. "We warned them."

She nodded.

"This is going to mean war," he said. "The Kremlin and Beijing, they went too far. The United States is going to fucking end them."

The footage switched to a televised statement from the US president. It looked to Lance like he was broadcasting from the secure studio in the White House bunker. He shook his head. That wasn't the message he should have been sending. It made it look like he was afraid.

He couldn't hear the president's words—a news commentator was speaking over him in Russian—and he turned up the volume.

The president was giving the usual spiel about bringing the perpetrators to justice, and then, in the middle of his speech, he stopped talking and received a message.

The footage cut to a security camera feed from outside the embassy moments before the bombing took place. Lance watched as the camera tightened in on a man who was killing embassy security guards.

It was him.

His eyes went immediately to the bartender, the only other person in the bar. His eyes were glued to the television. Lance drew a handgun he'd taken from one of the guard's bodies at the embassy, pointed it at the bartender, and said, "I'm going to need you to stay very calm."

58

Medvedev, seated in the enormous seat behind his desk, pressed the large green button that summoned his secretary. He was feeling very pleased with himself. The meeting had gone off without a hitch. The generals were all suitably impressed. The president had just called from his estate at Novo-Ogaryovo and invited him to come out for a personal tête-à-tête. He foresaw some major increases in power and influence in his future. Even Liu Ying had fallen into line. He'd been ordered directly by the top brass in Beijing to suck it up and not raise so much as a peep about his daughter's kidnapping. Medvedev had seen to it that the child was returned unharmed, more or less, and that was the end of the matter.

He'd won. His risk had paid off.

America was on her knees, and in a single stroke, he'd changed the geopolitical landscape of the entire planet.

It was a new beginning. The myth that American power was unassailable was over. He'd proven that, and delivered on his promise to the president a hundred times over. It was time now to bask in the glory of his success.

Svetlana opened the door. She was such a pretty girl, a child really, and so timid. She remained at the door, afraid to venture further. "You called, sir?" she said quietly in her mouse voice.

"Come in, Svetlana, come in," Medvedev said.

He knew she was afraid of him. He liked that. It was, in fact, his favorite thing about her. He liked watching the fear on her face. He could almost feel the rapid thumping of her little heart when he looked at her. It aroused him.

She entered and shut the door, keeping her back to it. So close to the door, he thought, as if it gave her some sort of protection. "How is the new apartment?" he said.

She looked at the floor. She was embarrassed. For a time, he'd had surveillance equipment placed inside her parents' home. They lived in a working-class neighborhood, a forty-minute train ride away. He'd enjoyed watching her there. He'd enjoyed controlling her from a distance.

But the time had come for his control to become a little bit more hands-on, and that meant having her closer. He needed to know he could visit her, *access* her, whenever he wanted.

He thought of it as part of his therapy. Medvedev was a man who was under no illusions. He was well aware of his deficiencies. He'd read the medical textbooks on maternal deprivation syndrome. He knew he had mental abnormalities that would haunt him forever, that followed him into the deepest recesses of his soul, and corrupted every natural instinct he ever had.

In short, he knew that he was a monster.

A child needed more than watery gruel to become a person. It needed more than a steel cot. If there was no mother figure in its early life, no caregiver to latch onto emotionally, the child's development would be perverted so severely that it would lack the empathy that could be taken for granted even in animals.

There had been a slew of research following the collapse of the Ceaușescu regime in Romania, and Medvedev devoured all of it. He invited American specialists and researchers to come and speak to him about it.

It wasn't so much that he wanted to be like other people. He was what he was. A scorpion did not wish to become a butterfly. It was just morbid curiosity.

The apartment he'd purchased for Svetlana was not cheap. It was in one of the more expensive neighborhoods in the city, and Medvedev himself owned several penthouses in the area.

"The apartment is good," she said timidly.

He'd made no effort to hide his cameras. The cameras in the shower and above her bed were so large they were impossible to miss. He liked that she knew she was being watched. It gave his voyeurism, he thought, an intimacy, a mutuality, that hidden cameras would have lacked.

Svetlana was a toy to him, something to be played with, and he liked that she knew it.

Soon after she'd moved in, he started calling her at all hours of the day and night, giving her precise instructions on what he wanted her to do. Do this. Wear that. He would send her humiliating costumes and embarrassing toys and tell her exactly what he wanted her to do with them.

It was taking a toll on her. She'd tried to run away once, but his guards caught her at the train station. He had also learned, from her internet searches, that she was considering suicide. But there was nothing she could do. He'd left her in no doubt that if anything were to happen to her—if she disappeared or hurt herself in any way—every member of her family would suffer so horribly that they'd curse her with their dying breaths. The threat seemed to have done the trick, as she'd stopped resisting, stopped fighting back. She knew the situation she was in and no longer fought it.

She was looking at him now the way someone might look at a lizard in a vivarium.

"I wonder," he said, "if you wouldn't mind going down to the imaging department to pick up a package for me."

She nodded and was out of the office before the last of the words had even left his mouth.

He poured himself some vodka while he waited for her to come back. When she returned, she was holding a sealed pouch containing his photos. As she handed it to him, he reached out and touched her hand. She recoiled as if shocked by a thousand volts. She moved so fast it startled both of them, and he knocked over his vodka.

Without thinking, he swung his arm and backhanded her across the face. He hit her so hard that her feet left the ground as she fell backward. "Bitch," he snarled, mopping up the drink before it wet his documents.

He poured himself some more vodka and knocked back the shot. Svetlana remained on the ground, unmoving.

"Get up," he snarled, pushing himself out of his chair and onto his feet.

When she didn't obey, he walked over and crouched down to check her. She was unconscious. He checked her pulse. That was okay.

He tapped her cheeks, and when she failed to wake up, he went to his desk and picked up the bottle of vodka. Then he pinched her by the cheeks and began pouring the liquid into her open mouth.

She immediately began to cough.

Medvedev smiled. "Drink," he said as she coughed and struggled to get up.

She managed to get to her feet and instinctively backed away from him until she was against the door. She opened it.

"Did I say you could leave?" he said, going back to his seat.

He could see her heart sink as she realized he was going to prolong the encounter. The terror on her face was palpable. Reluctantly, she let the door shut behind her.

"Come," he said. "Pour me some more vodka."

She came forward and poured his drink. He looked at her, her cheek flush from the smack he'd given her, her eye beginning to swell, and handed her back the glass. "You drink it," he said.

She shook her head.

"Go on," he said. "Drink."

She knew she had no choice, and picked up the glass, downing the shot in a single go.

"Good," he said. "Again."

She looked at him.

"Go on," he said.

She downed the shot again, and another, and another. He didn't let her stop until she was throwing up in his wastepaper basket, retching like a teenager after her first party. When he was done, she was so drunk she could barely walk.

"Now clean that up," he said to her.

She stumbled as she bent down, then picked up the trash can and left. Outside, he heard her knock something over as she passed her desk.

He chuckled as he opened the envelope. It contained black and white surveillance photos blown up on thirty-by-twenty-centimeter sheets.

The first was of Levi Roth, his wrists in cuffs, being escorted into the back of a federal police vehicle.

Medvedev poured himself some of the vodka and flicked through the rest of the images.

The next two were of the sluts, Tatyana Aleksandrova and Laurel Everlane, bound like a pair of piglets lying on a concrete floor.

He heard Svetlana outside and smiled to himself as he pushed the button again, calling her back into the office. He was going to have some fun with her.

59

Tatyana woke with her head against a concrete floor. She had no idea where she was or how she'd gotten there. She tried to move, but her ankles and wrists were restrained. The room was humid, pitch black, but she could hear labored breathing close to her face.

"Hello?" she whispered.

It was Laurel's voice that answered. "Tatyana, where are we?"

"I don't know," she said.

"We've been unconscious. He drugged us."

"I remember being in the car," Tatyana said. "He resuscitated us. Then knocked us out with something else."

"How long have you been awake?"

"Not long," Tatyana said. "But I heard him speak Russian. He swore and muttered to himself while he drove."

"We could be anywhere," Laurel said.

"Anywhere within driving distance."

Tatyana heard Laurel struggle against the restraints. There was a sound of kicking, Laurel's feet scuffing the concrete floor, and then she stopped. "We're in trouble," she said.

"We'll get out of this," Tatyana said.

"They beat us in Moscow. They beat us in Beijing. Before this guy kidnapped us, we were being arrested by order of the president."

"Laurel, this isn't over."

"Where's Roth? Where's Lance? They could both be dead for all we know."

Tatyana said nothing. Laurel was upset, but Tatyana wasn't exactly having the best day of her life, either. There followed an uncomfortable silence, and neither of them said anything for some time.

It was Laurel who finally broke the silence. "I'm sorry."

Tatyana turned in her direction. She couldn't see her, but she knew she was close. "For what?"

"I've been giving you a hard time since you got here."

Tatyana said nothing.

"I know you've risked everything to help us," Laurel said. "I do trust you, for what that's worth."

"It's all right," Tatyana said.

"You were right," Laurel said.

"About what?"

"It was Lance. I was jealous."

"That's okay," Tatyana said.

"I just..." Laurel said but didn't finish the sentence. "I've been distracted," she said.

"There's a lot going on."

"Whoever's behind this," Laurel said, "they're kicking our asses."

"We're down," Tatyana said, "but we're not out."

They heard a sound outside the door, and both became silent. It was followed by the clinking of a key in a lock, the sound of a deadbolt, and then the door swung open.

There was light in the hallway, and against it stood an enormous man. He remained still, looking down at them, making sure they were both in the same place he'd left them. He was holding a baseball bat, and he patted it against the palm of a hand that was closer in size to a catcher's mitt than anything Tatyana had ever seen.

Instinctively, Tatyana and Laurel both began squirming against their restraints.

"What have we got here?" the man said in Russian.

"We work for the federal government," Laurel said, "and unless you release us—"

"Federal government?" the man scoffed. "You two are so far up Levi Roth's ass that without him, no one can even confirm you exist."

"What do you mean, without him?" Laurel said.

"Oh, haven't you heard? You weren't the only ones arrested. Roth is in an orange jumpsuit as we speak."

"What are you talking about?"

"It's true. Arrested on the president's orders. For treason."

"Bullshit," Tatyana spat.

"Oh," the man said, directing his attention to Tatyana. "She speaks. And you'd know all about treason, wouldn't you, you treacherous little whore?"

"They're going to come for us," Laurel said. "They're going to find you, and they're going to kill you."

The man laughed. "They're done with you," he said. "I did them a favor, taking you." He came over to Tatyana and prodded her with his foot. "I'm going to have some fun with you, my darling."

She struggled so hard against her restraints that her wrists began to bleed, but there was zero give in them. She couldn't get loose.

"You're going to learn firsthand the price of betraying the Motherland."

"You're the one betraying the Motherland," Tatyana said.

He bent down and grabbed her around the waist. She struggled against him, kicking and squirming as he slung her over his shoulder as easily as if she was a sack of flour.

"Where are you taking her?" Laurel cried as he carried Tatyana out into the corridor, locking the door behind him.

Tatyana struggled furiously, but it was no good. The man was a bear. He handled her effortlessly. He brought her down a dimly lit corridor, past more doors similar to the one he'd just locked, and into another room.

"The boss wants you alive," the man said, "but he didn't specify in what condition."

He slung her off his shoulder and threw her onto the floor, lobbing her like a stevedore unloading a cargo. She hit the concrete so hard that she almost lost consciousness. He came in after her and picked her right back up. There was a wooden chair by the wall, and he propped her up on it.

Then, he caught her chin in his fist and forced her to look at him. In the dim light, she could only make out the outline of his face. And then he spat.

Tatyana convulsed in revulsion.

He drew his hand back and smacked her hard across the jaw. His palm was like a leather bat. Her head jerked back so forcefully that the chair toppled over, and she fell to the ground.

He kicked her then, again and again. She whimpered in pain, and he spat on her again.

Rage filled her. It coursed through every cell of her body, every synapse of her brain. She wanted to kill this man, and in her searing anger, she swung her legs at his feet and tried to trip him up. She managed to get him off balance, but he was so big she couldn't bring him down. He stumbled, and his foot landed right next to her neck. He raised it then.

For a brief second, she thought he was going to stamp down on her neck with his full weight. She was certain he wanted to.

And she was certain it would kill her. But instead, he stepped on her chest, putting his weight there, pressing heavier and heavier, until she heard the unmistakable sound of a rib cracking.

She thought she was going to die.

She heaved and gasped for air.

She screamed in pain, but no sound came from her.

"Stupid bitch," he snarled, bending down to her. He wrapped his fist in her hair and pulled her by it back into the chair. He then broke her restraints and tied her wrists to the back of the chair and her ankles to the two front legs. He leaned into her face, so close she could smell his acrid breath, and said, "You're not going anywhere, my dear. I'm going to put you through living hell. By the time I'm done with you, you won't remember how to spell your name."

He took something from his pocket, and Tatyana realized it was the same taser he'd used before. She knew it packed a punch. He began unspooling the darts, and when he was done, he caught the barbs in her skin, attaching them to her inner thighs, her breasts, and her neck.

He took a few steps back to admire his handy work.

She looked up at him defiantly. "You sick fuck," she spat, and then he pulled the trigger.

Pain flooded through her body in a surge so overpowering she lost complete control of her body. She couldn't scream. She couldn't breathe. Her jaw clenched so tightly that she was in danger of breaking her teeth.

She didn't know what was happening, and when it stopped, she didn't know how long it had lasted. She scarcely knew where she was. All she knew was that the man was still there, still looking down at her, a strange, gleeful look on his face.

She tried to collapse off the chair, but the ties kept her in place.

"How did you like that?" he said.

Her vision was blurry, and when she looked down at her body, she saw she'd soiled herself.

The man smiled. He liked that. And then he pulled the trigger again.

60

Laurel struggled to get to her feet but couldn't. She screamed in the direction of the door but knew no one could hear her. She pulled against the ties at her wrists but couldn't break them.

When she heard Tatyana's muffled screams through the door, she knew she had to do something. She rolled across the ground until she reached the wall, then, using the wall for support, somehow managed to get to her feet. The room was still pitch black, but she knew where the door was, and if there was a light switch, it would be close to it.

Moving carefully along the wall, using it as support so she didn't lose balance, she made her way first to the corner of the room and then to the door. From there, despite her tethered hands, she was able to feel around the wall until she found the switch. She didn't try it immediately. She was too scared it wouldn't work.

Then she heard Tatyana scream again and, without thinking, flipped it.

There was a flicker as the old fluorescent tubes heated up, and then the room was flooded with bright white light. It was blinding. Laurel had to shut her eyes against it. She could only open them after they'd had time to adjust.

When she finally looked, she saw what appeared to be a basement with high-voltage lights hanging by chains from a concrete ceiling. Above the lights was a plethora of disused ventilation equipment, a cooling system, and water pipes attached to sprinklers. The floor was raw concrete, and it sloped slightly to one corner where a drain had been installed to gather excess water. One of the water pipes came down the far wall, turned at the corner, and was attached to a water faucet.

It was easier to move in the light, and even with her ankles still tied, she was able to cross the room to the faucet. The stifling heat of the room had left her parched, and she could already taste the water. She turned the tap, but nothing came out. It didn't work.

She tried to follow the pipe to its shutoff, but there was none. Where it rounded the corner, a bracket held it to the wall. The bracket's edge was a straight, sharp cut of brass, and she began rubbing the ties at her wrists against the corner vigorously.

It was difficult, and several times her hand slipped. The sharp edge of the brass cut into her skin. By the time she'd cut the ties, her wrists looked like she'd been trying to kill herself.

She then got down on the ground and began the same process with the ties around her ankles. When she was finally free, there was so much blood on the ground beneath the bracket that it pooled on the concrete.

She looked around the room for anything that might help her escape. It was not promising. Apart from the water pipe, the only other thing in the room was a small metal bed frame in one corner.

Above the lights, the largest of the air ducts came in through one wall, made its way to the center of the room, then turned ninety degrees. In the duct were two air vents, one near each wall. Laurel thought she might be able to pry them loose.

She looked at the two walls the duct passed through. They were each made of the same gray concrete and offered no clues as to what lay on the other side. Unless she was ready to claw through concrete, the duct was the only way through them. The problem was that the duct was too small for her to fit in.

She pulled the bed frame beneath one of the air vents and tried to reach it. It was too high. She had to lean the frame up against the wall, wedging it in place at an angle before she could use it to reach the ceiling.

Then, using nothing but her fingernails, she began prying at the vent. It was fastened tightly, and it didn't look like the tiny screws were going to budge. She kept clawing at them until her fingers bled, but it did no good. She began to lose hope, but just when she was about to give up, she heard a faint tapping on the duct.

She stopped and held her breath.

She heard it again. A light *tap, tap, tap.*

"Hello?" she said very quietly, speaking into the vent. She waited, then repeated it louder. "Hello?"

There was a brief pause, then a faint, timid response. It was so weak she wasn't sure at first if she'd heard it at all. Then it came again. "Hello?" she heard in the unmistakable voice of a little girl.

"Hello," Laurel said again.

"Please help me," the girl said.

"Where are you?"

"Locked in a room."

"Are you all right?"

"I'm frightened," the girl said. She began to cry.

"Is there a light on in your room?"

"Yes," the girl said between sobs.

"What's your name?"

"Lizzie."

"What age are you, Lizzie?"

"Fourteen."

"All right," Laurel said. "My name is Laurel. Together, we're going to get out of here, all right?"

"All right."

Laurel looked at the duct again and wondered if it might be large enough to fit a fourteen-year-old girl. "Lizzie," Laurel said, "how long have you been down here?"

"I don't know," Lizzie said.

"Days?" Laurel said.

"I think so."

"Everything's going to be all right," Laurel said.

The girl was still crying.

"Lizzie," Laurel said, "we're going to escape together, okay?"

"How can we?" Lizzie said.

"I have a plan. All you need to do is follow my directions exactly."

"If the man catches us, he'll beat us," Lizzie said.

"We won't let him catch us."

"I can hear screaming," Lizzie said.

Laurel gritted her teeth. She could hear it too. She'd witnessed her share of such interrogations in the past. She knew all too well what could happen in an underground cell when a man was left alone with complete power over another person. Whatever that man was doing to Tatyana now, it didn't sound to Laurel like she'd be able to survive it for very long.

"All right, Lizzie," she said. "Tell me what you see in your room."

"A bed," Lizzie said.

"Do you see a duct on the ceiling? A thick one, with vents?"

"Yes," Lizzie said.

"Do you think you could get up to it?"

"It's too high."

"What if you moved the bed under it?"

"I don't know," Lizzie said.

Laurel knew the only way she was getting out of that room, the only way Tatyana had any chance, was if that child somehow got herself into a tiny air duct over ten feet from the ground.

She had to think. She had to put herself in the kid's position. She had to get that child to achieve the seemingly impossible.

"I'll tell you a secret, Lizzie," Laurel said. "I'm a CIA agent. I can kill the man who locked us in here. All I need you to do is move your bed underneath the air vent and see if you can reach it. Can you do that for me, Lizzie?"

61

Somehow, Lizzie managed to do the impossible, and by the time she was in Laurel's room, her hands were bleeding, she'd cut a deep gash in her thigh, and she was sobbing uncontrollably. Laurel coaxed her through the duct and told her how to kick open the vent from the inside.

"Well done," Laurel said as she pulled the girl out of the duct. She wrapped her arms around her and held her for as long as she dared. She knew they didn't have much time. Eventually, their captor would tire of torturing Tatyana and would come back to check on them. When he did, all chance of escape would be gone. "We have to keep working on getting out of this place," she said to Lizzie.

She felt the child's body stiffen.

"Don't be afraid," she said, but she knew there was little use in saying it.

Lizzie wiped her eyes and forced herself to stop crying. "All right," she said.

Laurel smiled. She had to admit, the kid had guts. "I'm going to put you back into the duct," she said. "Did you see any light when you were in there?"

Lizzie nodded.

"All right," Laurel said, flooding with relief. "That light leads to the outside. You have to crawl all the way to the end of the duct. When you get there, you'll be able to kick open the vent and get to the outside."

"What about you?"

"I don't think I can fit," Laurel said.

Lizzie looked at the duct again and nodded.

"When you get outside," Laurel said, "you have to be careful, okay? You have to be quiet. You have to creep away and escape without anyone spotting you. Then you can bring back help."

"What if the man sees me?"

"He won't be looking out there."

"What if he is?"

Laurel held Lizzie tight. She looked into her eyes. "I'm not going to lie to you, Lizzie. If he catches you, he'll do something bad. That's why I need you to be brave right now. I need you to do this even though it's dangerous. Can you do that?"

Lizzie hesitated only a second before nodding.

"Good girl," Laurel said.

"How will I know where to get help?" Lizzie said.

Laurel shook her head. "I don't know. I don't know where we are. Hopefully, there are people around, or a gas station or store you can go to. You need to find someone who'll help us, and you need to call the police and tell them exactly where we are."

"All right," Lizzie said.

"Can you do that?"

"I think so," Lizzie said.

Laurel looked at her again and nodded. Then, she hoisted her back into the duct and told her to go toward the light. The child crawled forward, disappearing into the vent. Laurel waited until she heard Lizzie banging at the end of the duct. Then she heard Lizzie's voice.

"It's stuck."

"Keep trying, Lizzie. You have to get through it."

"I can't open it," Lizzie said, and she started to cry again.

Laurel coaxed her, soothed her, tried to get her to calm down. She talked Lizzie through it for about fifteen minutes, but it seemed that no matter how hard she tried, the vent at the end of the duct was too securely fastened to be kicked off.

With Lizzie growing increasingly distressed, Laurel began to lose hope. She had no choice but to accept the facts for what they were. "It's all right, Lizzie," she said. "Come back to me. We'll find another way out."

Lizzie immediately began coming back. Laurel was watching her when the door of the room swung open. Their captor burst in, a wild frenzy in his eyes, and when he saw Laurel on the bed, her hands reaching into the duct, he lunged at her.

Laurel dropped from the bed at the same moment that the man leaped onto it. His weight dislodged it, and it fell to the floor. Seeing her chance, she darted past him toward the door. He swung an arm wildly at her, and she dodged it, making it to the doorway as he scrambled back to his feet.

With no time to think, she ran blindly down a dark, narrow corridor, the giant of a man stampeding after her like a charging bull. By the time she realized the corridor was a dead end, it was too late. She stopped and turned. The man was bearing down on her, closing the distance between them at a blinding pace.

There was a metal chair against the wall, and in desperation, she grabbed it. He lunged toward her, but at the very last moment, he stumbled and lost his balance, falling forward. She raised the chair, its legs pointing forward, shielding herself from his massive bulk. He fell right onto the chair legs. Laurel ducked, and the chair jammed against the wall under the man's weight.

It buckled and broke but not before the man let out a sudden, jarring wheeze, like the sound of a tire being punctured. When Laurel realized what had happened, she saw that one of the legs of the chair had gone right through his chest.

She was beneath him, and his warm blood poured down on her like the steady flow of a faucet.

The man gasped, then began to slump. He fell onto Laurel slowly, his enormous weight threatening to crush her, and when he stopped, his face was just an inch from hers.

Laurel looked at him, his cold, gray eyes, the horrible final contortions of his face as he gasped for air. She only had seconds.

"Who do you work for?" she said, grabbing his face in her hand. "Tell me who you work for!" She squeezed. "Who sent you? Tell me."

The man said nothing. The life left his eyes. It was too late.

She pushed herself out from under his still warm body with a shudder and got to her feet.

She had to find Tatyana.

62

Consciousness came flooding back to Tatyana in a sudden gasping jolt. She had no idea where she was, and the only sensation she felt was pain. She glanced around, panic-stricken, before realizing she was in the passenger seat of a beat-up car. There were bullet holes in the windshield and windows. The car was moving, and cold air was rushing in through the bullet holes.

"You're awake," Laurel said from the driver's seat.

"How long was I..." she said, but it hurt to talk.

"Shh. You have a broken rib. I've given you something for the pain."

"How did we escape?"

A voice came from the backseat, startling her. "She killed him."

Tatyana turned before remembering the pain in her chest. "Who is this?" she said flatly.

"This is Lizzie," Laurel said.

"Lizzie?" Tatyana repeated.

"Lizzie was in the cellar, too," Laurel said.

Tatyana turned slowly to get a better look at her. The girl

was bruised, there was blood on her clothes, and she hadn't washed in days. Despite all that, the look on her face seemed buoyant. "I see," she said.

They were on a highway, stuck behind snowplows that were raising a spray of slush in their wake. The slush sprayed up onto the hood of their car, which seemed, as far as Tatyana could tell, to be a Nissan. "Is there any heat in this thing?"

"It's broken," Lizzie said.

"This is the car the Russian took us in," Tatyana said.

Laurel nodded.

Tatyana's head was spinning. Between the torture and whatever meds Laurel had given her, she was finding it difficult to concentrate. "How long was I out?"

"Not long."

"How did you kill the Russian?"

Laurel looked at Lizzie in the rearview, then said, "He had an accident."

"He was impaled," Lizzie said, and she ran a finger across her neck for emphasis.

"He won't be coming after any of us ever again," Laurel said.

"Did he happen to tell you who he was working for before he... got impaled?" Tatyana said.

"You sound annoyed," Laurel said. "Maybe I should have left the questioning to you."

"Sorry," Tatyana said. "I'm just—" Without warning, she started to cry.

"What's the matter?" Lizzie said.

Laurel put her hand on Tatyana's shoulder and said, "She's been through a lot, Lizzie. She needs time to process."

Lizzie nodded. Tatyana got herself under control and wiped her face with her sleeve. "I thought he was going to kill me," she said quietly.

"So did I," Lizzie said.

Tatyana leaned back and let out a long sigh. "Where are we going?" she said.

"Fort Meade," Laurel said.

Tatyana nodded. She assumed it had something to do with Roth, but the way Laurel was looking at her said there was more to it. "Are you going to make me ask why?" she said.

"Lizzie," Laurel said, "tell Tatyana who your mother is."

"Sandra Shrader," Lizzie said.

It took a moment for the name to register with Tatyana, then it clicked. "NSA Director Sandra Shrader?" she said.

"The one and only," Laurel said.

Tatyana looked back at the child. "They kidnapped you to get to your mother?"

Lizzie nodded. They didn't have far to go, and fifteen minutes later, they were exiting the highway and approaching the main security plaza of NSA headquarters. "Let me do the talking," Laurel said.

Tatyana put her hand on Laurel's leg. "Wait," she said.

Laurel looked at her. "What is it?"

"Stop the car. Turn around."

"What?" Lizzie cried. "You promised to take me to my mother."

"We will," Laurel said.

"But not yet," Tatyana said. She turned to Laurel. "Get me to a phone."

"Why?"

"I know how the GRU operates. As long as they think they have Lizzie, we have an opportunity."

"What opportunity?"

"We need Sandra Shrader to continue playing along."

"How are we going to do that?"

"We'll get her to come to us. Then we'll explain."

Laurel thought for a moment, then stopped the car. They'd just passed a gas station, and she did a U-turn and drove back to it. It had a small convenience store with a payphone outside. Laurel pulled into the lot and parked as far from the building as possible. She didn't want to draw attention to the car.

Tatyana winced as she tried to get out of her seat.

"Tatyana," Laurel said. "I can make the call."

"I'll make it," Tatyana said.

"No, you won't," Laurel said, searching the dashboard for coins.

Tatyana sighed. "I'm fine."

"You need to get to a hospital."

"I'm not going anywhere."

"Your rib is broken. There could be internal injuries."

"I'm not going anywhere," Tatyana said again, more forcefully than the first time.

Laurel shook her head.

There was a filthy cup holder in the door next to Tatyana, and at the bottom, mixed in a sticky mess of spilled drinks and used ketchup packets, were some coins. Tatyana scooped them up and handed them to Laurel. "Just make sure she understands how sensitive this is. She can't let anyone know Lizzie's back. She has to play it cool."

"I'll make sure," Laurel said.

Tatyana reached out for Laurel's hand and grasped it. "This might be our only chance," she said. "If we play this right, we can lure whoever's behind this out into the open."

"I get it," Laurel said and left, slamming the door slightly harder than was necessary.

When she was gone, Lizzie said, "You two sure don't get along, do you?"

"We get along," Tatyana said.

"You hate her."

"She hates me," Tatyana said.

"No, she doesn't. You should have seen the way she carried you out of that house. She was terrified that you'd die."

Tatyana looked out the window. Across the lot, Laurel was approaching the payphone. She looked like she'd just stepped out of the costume department of a disaster movie. There was blood and dirt all over her clothes, and her hair was completely disheveled. "How about we play the silence game?" she said to Lizzie.

Lizzie sighed but kept her thoughts to herself. They watched Laurel make the call, then she came back to the car and got into her seat.

Tatyana looked at her. "Well?"

"She's coming."

"She's coming here?" Lizzie cried.

"You stay in the car when she gets here," Tatyana said. "No one can see you, do you understand?"

"No," Lizzie said defiantly.

Tatyana shook her head. She leaned back and shut her eyes. This was good. It was a chance. A real chance. She looked at Laurel next to her and noticed her hands were shaking. "You're cold," she said.

Laurel nodded.

"I wanted to say," Tatyana said, then paused while she mustered the will to say the words.

"You wanted to say what?"

"Thank you," Tatyana said hesitantly.

Laurel looked at her. "I didn't know they knew that word in Russia."

"You saved my life," Tatyana said.

"You would have done the same."

Tatyana shrugged. "I don't know."

Laurel smiled.

"I've had my guard up around you," Tatyana said.

Laurel nodded. "We're more similar than we care to admit."

Tatyana bit her lip. There was something that had been bothering her, something she thought Laurel ought to know.

Ordinarily, she would have kept it to herself, taken it to her grave just to avoid having to talk about it, but the pain and the meds were doing a number on her inhibitions. "You know," she said, "Lance was never in love with Clarice Snow."

"What?" Laurel said, surprised.

Tatyana nodded.

"How would you know that?" Laurel said.

"Because he told me."

"When you two were...."

"No," Tatyana said. "He and I never were...."

Laurel looked away. Something in the gas station seemed to have drawn her attention. A customer entered. The customer paid, then went back to his car and left.

"He'd taken a lot of pain killers," Tatyana said. "He thought he was going to die. And he told me that he never loved her."

"Okay," Laurel said, still looking out the window. "I don't know what you expect me to do with this."

"He also told me Clarice was pregnant when Roth ordered her killed."

"Pregnant?"

"With his child."

Laurel turned and looked at her. "Why are you telling me all this?" she said.

"Because I owe you," she said.

"What do you owe me?"

Tatyana said nothing for a moment, and when she spoke, her voice felt dry. She cleared her throat, then said, "Loyalty, Laurel. I owe you loyalty."

Laurel looked like she was going to respond, but just then, a large, black SUV rushed into the lot. Its headlights passed over them like search beams as it pulled up next to them, its engine running.

"That's her," Tatyana said. She looked back at Lizzie. "You stay put. We'll bring her to you."

Laurel got out of the car, but before shutting the door, she looked back at Tatyana and said, "Loyalty?"

Tatyana nodded.

"All right," Laurel said and handed Tatyana a piece of paper that she'd ripped from the payphone's phone book.

"What's this?" Tatyana said.

"Switch codes."

"Switch codes?"

"Someone left me a message."

"What message?"

Laurel shrugged. "We'll find out. Together."

63

Tatyana allowed exactly fifteen minutes for Sandra and Lizzie to get reacquainted. Neither could stop crying, and Sandra kept saying, "Thank you, thank you, thank you," over and over. Tatyana kept looking at her watch, and the moment their time was up, she said, "Ms Shrader, we need to take care of business."

Sandra nodded. She understood the situation. She'd committed treason. She'd failed to report Lizzie's kidnapping. She hadn't known it would lead to the bombing of two embassies, but that was what had happened, and now it was time to punish whoever was responsible. She would never be able to make up for the hundreds of deaths that she'd helped cause, but now that Lizzie was back in her arms, there was nothing she wouldn't do to try and atone for her failure. For her betrayal of office. She was ready to come clean and face the consequences. Disgrace, prison, whatever the president deemed appropriate.

"If I don't bring back the vehicle, my driver will have to report it," she said. She'd come alone without first securing authorization for the SUV.

"This will be fast," Tatyana said. "Whoever took Lizzie, how have they been communicating with you?"

"He calls me."

"And you've tried tracing the call?"

"I put in eight separate requests," Sandra said. "Each went to a different decryption team. None of them could work with it. The calls are being filtered through some next-generation tech. Something they'd never seen before."

"It's always the same man who calls?" Tatyana said.

"Same prick."

"Russian?"

"If I had to guess," Sandra said.

"All right," Tatyana said, "this is where we stand. Right now, he doesn't know Lizzie's free. He doesn't know his man is dead. He thinks you're still doing his bidding."

"It won't take him long to find out," Sandra said.

"But in the meantime, we have an opening."

Sandra nodded. "All right," she said. "It's slim, though."

"Yes, it is," Laurel said, "but it's better than nothing. What's the last thing this guy said to you?"

Sandra thought back. "He wanted me to turn the president against Roth."

"Which you did."

"Yes," Sandra said.

"What else?"

"He wants Lance Spector. He thinks the NSA can find him before the CIA does."

"So he wants you to send him a location? That's what he's expecting?"

"Yes. He wants me to find Spector. He wants him badly."

"Well," Tatyana said, "if that's what he wants, then that's what we'll give him."

"Give him Lance?" Laurel said.

"It's the only thing we have that he wants."

"Use Spector as bait?" Laurel said.

Tatyana nodded.

"Do we even know where Spector is?" Sandra said.

Tatyana turned to Laurel. Reluctantly, Laurel nodded. "I think so," she said. "I checked my analog line right after I called you."

"Langley uses analog lines?" Sandra said.

"They used to," Laurel said. "It's a legacy system. Barely monitored."

"Which is why Lance used it now," Sandra said.

"If he tried to reach me or Roth and couldn't get through, he'd have known something was up."

"So, you can get in touch with him?"

"Well," Laurel said, "the switches he sent, we need to decipher them, but in theory, they can be used to trace the location of the call."

"He left you a traceable signal? Isn't that risky?"

"Extremely," Laurel said. "Any operator at the switchboard could have intercepted the message. He'd only use this if he really needed to get in touch."

"So, we can call him back?" Sandra said.

"I hope so," Laurel said. "It's unlikely he called from a cell. That means, if it's a landline, he needs to still be where he called from."

"When did he leave the message?"

"I can't tell."

"We need to call him back," Sandra said.

"That's where you come in," Tatyana said.

Laurel nodded. "You need to get back to the office and get these switches deciphered. We can't trace the call until you do it."

"What about Lizzie?"

"Leave her with us. She has to remain out of sight in case the Russians are having you watched."

"Leave her? Again?"

"She'll be safe," Laurel said. "You have our word."

"All right," Sandra said reluctantly. She knew she had no choice. "But don't leave this vehicle. Your faces are on every police bulletin in three states and the district."

"They don't think...." Laurel said, her words trailing off.

"Yes, they do think," Sandra said.

"They think that we killed the federal agents who came to arrest us?"

"That's the current theory," Sandra said. "They've got a massive manhunt underway, and you've both been flagged as armed and dangerous."

64

L aurel, Tatyana, and Lizzie sat tight in the car while Sandra went back to headquarters. The car was freezing, even with the engine running, and after a few minutes, Laurel said, "Who's hungry?"

Lizzie raised her hand immediately.

Tatyana turned to her. "You can't go into that store. You heard what Sandra said."

"The gas station attendant isn't going to have seen the APB."

"Your clothes are filthy."

Laurel sighed. "We need to eat something."

Tatyana looked at her. "Take off the jacket," she said. "Take off your top and put it on inside out." Then she cleaned up Laurel's makeup with some spit on her fingers and tidied her hair. "What if there's a camera?" she said.

"This isn't Russia," Laurel said. "We'll be long gone before anyone looks at that footage."

Tatyana sighed. "This is stupid," she said. "A needless risk."

"Define 'needless'," Laurel said, getting out of the car. She looked back at Tatyana defiantly. "Any requests?"

Lizzie had a few suggestions, and when Laurel came back, Tatyana had to admit she was glad for the hot coffee. Lizzie dived into the food, tearing open a packet of tiny doughnuts coated in finely powdered sugar.

"Give me one of those," Tatyana said.

It took fifteen minutes for Sandra to return with the deciphered switch signatures, and they all sat in silence as Tatyana dialed the number of a Moscow landline into Sandra's cell phone.

"Is it on speaker?" Laurel said.

She nodded. The phone clicked, then clicked again, and then the dial tone stopped.

No one spoke.

"Hello?" Tatyana said in Russian.

No response.

Tatyana looked at Laurel and Sandra, then said, "Lance, this is Tatyana."

There was another pause, then Lance's voice came through, loud and clear. "Tatyana?"

"It's me, Lance."

"Where's Laurel?"

"Right next to me."

"I thought you'd never call."

"We had a few kinks to iron out on our end," Laurel said.

"Well, tell me you figured out who my albino is."

"Not quite," Tatyana said, "but we have something else."

"What do you have?"

"Where are you?"

"Hiding out in a bar in Kursky Railway Station. My face is on every news channel from here to Vladivostok."

"Is Larissa with you?" Tatyana said, unable to hide the apprehension in her voice.

"She's here, watching the bartender."

"Will you be able to get around the city?"

"You tell me how to find this guy," Lance said. "And I'll figure out how to get to him."

"We think we can lure him into the open."

"And how do we do that?"

"How do you lure anything?" Laurel said. "With bait."

65

L aurel, Tatyana, Lizzie, and Sandra drove back to Washington in Sandra's government SUV. She'd told her security detail that she had a personal matter to attend to and that she was taking the night off. She'd also sent her driver home early.

Laurel told her to put the heat on full and tuned the radio to a local news outlet. The bombings had the whole country riled up. The story seemed to be snowballing, taking on proportions beyond even what such devastating attacks warranted.

Despite the president's attempt to push the blame onto one rogue agent, namely Lance, there was a frenzy of talk about the attacks being the opening shots of World War Three or the beginning of a new Cold War. Only this time, Russia would have the growing might of a resurgent China on its side. People were calling for preemptive nuclear strikes against the Russians and Chinese. They heard three different senators say that war was inevitable.

Laurel was beginning to see why the president had said what he'd said. As much as it sickened her to admit it, blaming this whole thing on Lance might just have been the best move for the country. If it emerged that the Russian or Chinese governments had even the slightest involvement in the attacks, the president's hands would be tied. There would be no walking things back. War between the three largest nations on earth would be inevitable.

As they got closer to Georgetown, Laurel was careful to avoid any lingering police presence around the house, and they parked a block away. "I'll go first," she said, "and make sure no one's still there."

The others waited for her signal, then hurried down the street toward the house. The front was closed off with police tape, and there was a seal on the front door. Laurel tore the seal out of the way and unlocked the door. She noticed a bullet hole in the wood.

Once inside, they went straight to the basement. Laurel checked the security terminal at the control room door. She could see that the police had attempted to access it, but when they'd realized it was a solid steel blast door, they'd given up. She entered her code and the door opened with the whoosh of an airlock being released. They found the room completely undamaged and went straight to their computer terminals, leaving Sandra and Lizzie to stand by the wall and watch them.

"Tatyana?" Laurel said once her terminal had powered up. "You see about requisitioning a high-altitude drone. I'll plant the location information into the database. If the albino is as connected as we think he is, he'll catch it before anyone at Langley even notices."

Tatyana looked up at Laurel. "For the intel source," she said, "put that it was a Chinese diplomat attending a strip club near the Lubyanka."

Laurel hesitated. "You're sure you want me to enter that?"

Tatyana nodded. "Lance will protect her," she said. "He won't leave her behind."

Laurel typed the words. Since it was true, the information

would make the intel appear more legitimate. The albino was no novice. The slightest hint of a trap and he'd disappear forever.

Given recent events, the CIA and Pentagon both had assets over Moscow, and Tatyana was able to pull up a live drone view of the city. She put it onto the main display. The shape of the Moskva River appeared on the enormous high-resolution screen, surrounded by concentric ribbons of highway a few miles farther out.

"What are we looking for?" Tatyana said.

"Lance picked up a burner cell phone," Laurel said, typing its number into her control terminal. "He texted me from it. It should be traceable."

They waited with bated breaths. Nothing happened. The drone was being recalled by the Pentagon, and Tatyana had to switch feeds to satellite. "We should have seen something by now," she said.

"Just wait," Laurel said. "He said he was leaving central Moscow. Outer cell towers will take longer to filter through."

They stared at the satellite imagery of the city for what felt like an eternity, and then as if by magic, a tiny red dot blipped on the screen.

"There!" Lizzie gasped. "There!"

Tatyana saw the dot. It was in an industrial zone south of the city. She realized immediately that Lance had gone back to the apartment in Kapotnya. She typed furiously on her keyboard, and the view zoomed in, close enough that they could make out the lights of the vast oil refinery that was less than a mile from the apartment.

She quickly set up a router to mask the call, then Laurel typed the cell phone number into her terminal and hit enter. They heard a dial tone. Then, the dot on the screen turned green. "It's working," Laurel said.

It was Larissa who answered the call. "Tatyana?" she said,

her voice so clear on the speaker that it sounded to Tatyana as if she was right there in the room with them.

"Larissa," Tatyana gasped, her voice breaking with emotion. "I'm so sorry. I should have taken you with me."

"You didn't know I was going to cause all this trouble," Larissa said.

Tatyana, laughing and crying at the same time, said, "I never should have left without you."

"You were trying to keep me safe. You didn't know what I'd heard when you left."

"And it was true," Tatyana said. "Everything you tried to tell me, it was all true."

"I told Lance. We did what we could. There was nothing else—"

"Larissa," Laurel said, clearing her throat. "Sorry to interrupt, but is Lance with you right now?"

Lance's voice came over the line. "I'm here, Laurel."

"Lance," Laurel said. "We're ready."

"You leaked the location?"

"The apartment in Kapotnya. We just seeded the source. It won't be long before your little friend picks up on it."

"He's not so little," Lance said.

"Is Larissa going to be somewhere safe?" Tatyana said.

"We're in the bar across the street from the apartment," Lance said. "We can see everything from here."

"Swear you won't let anything happen to her," Tatyana said. "Make sure they don't get anywhere near her."

"You have my word, Tatyana."

Tatyana was quiet for a moment. She was going to ask him to put Larissa back on the line but stopped herself. She looked at Laurel.

"God speed, Lance Spector," Laurel said and terminated the call.

66

Levi Roth, dressed in an orange jumpsuit, sat on a hard bench in a federal prison holding cell, his ass growing more numb by the minute. Three of the walls that surrounded him were made of unfinished cinder block, painted in a thick coat of high-gloss paint. The paint was an institutional pink color that reminded him of chewed bubblegum. The fourth wall was of steel bars. He'd been sitting, staring at the bars for what felt like an eternity and was just beginning to doze off when a cool breeze blew over him, as if a door somewhere out of view had been opened to the outside. His hands were icy cold, and instinctively, he pressed them between his legs for warmth.

In front of him, stenciled on the wall beyond the steel bars in large block-cap letters, was a single word.

Arraignments

Roth knew more than his fair share about appearances

before the Foreign Intelligence Surveillance Court. He knew, for instance, that he would not be speaking to any lawyers. He knew he would not be making or receiving any phone calls. He also knew that he was not entitled to a presumption of innocence or the right to face his accusers. No documentary evidence of any kind would be used in the making of a determination in his case, no witnesses would be called, and there would be no public record of any decision made against him.

He could enter the courtroom an ordinary man, a twenty-first-century citizen of the greatest democracy that ever existed, with all the rights and protections the constitution afforded. And in the space of a few minutes, all of those rights and protections could be stripped away. Centuries of legal progress could be erased with the swing of a gavel. Levi Roth himself could be erased, shipped off to a secret offshore facility that not even the judge in his case knew the location of.

Black holes existed. Legal black holes. And Roth knew he was sitting right at the very edge of one of them, at the event horizon.

His only consolation was that none of that was likely to happen today. Not that he was immune, but the gears of this particular system of justice took time to turn. His hearing today would most likely be postponed without him ever getting near the panel of judges. Then it would be back in his cell before dark and back on this bench first thing after breakfast tomorrow.

And that could go on for months. He was in this for the long haul now. He'd initiated these kinds of proceedings against others, and he knew they were designed to grind down the perpetrator. Relieve him of his strength to resist, his will to fight back.

When he finally got before the panel, it would be his word against the word of the largest and most powerful collective organization known to the entirety of human history, the

Federal Government of the United States of America. That government would be represented by a nameless, faceless attorney, appearing from a nameless, faceless office somewhere deep within the bowels of the justice department. He would appear via conference call, his voice obfuscated to protect his identity.

When it was all over, Roth would be sentenced to a prison term exceeding his natural life expectancy by many decades. His only chance of ever getting out was by presidential pardon or in a pine box.

He wondered what they'd say if he asked for a warmer jumpsuit.

He heard some guards approaching and sat up. They arrived and opened the cell. They were escorting another man in an orange jumpsuit, and they told that man to sit on the bench next to Roth.

Roth moved a few inches aside to make room for him, and the man sat down heavily. "You looking at?" he said to Roth.

"Nothing," Roth said.

They sat still, neither saying a word, neither taking his eyes off the stenciled letters on the facing wall. There was no clock, but Roth felt the passage of perhaps an hour before the man broke his silence. "What did you do?" he eventually said.

"Nothing," Roth said. "I'm innocent."

"Sure you are," the man said.

They sat in silence for another long period until the man said, "Don't you recognize me?"

Roth did recognize him. He'd had nothing to think about for two hours, and while it hadn't hit him at first, it had come eventually. "You're the YouTube guy," he said.

"The YouTube guy?" the man spat. "I'm the biggest independent media outlet in this nation."

Roth nodded. The man was a political commentator of sorts. He broadcast online and on the radio from a high-powered transmitter he'd set up on a ranch somewhere in West

Texas. Strongly anti-government, he propounded several conspiracy theories that had steadily been gaining traction among certain segments of the population. "I guess an election year's a bad time to be in your line of work," Roth said.

"Free speech in this country is a hoax," the man said. "A thing of the past. We live in a fascist state now."

The man's arms were covered in tattoos.

"You served?" Roth said.

"You bet your ass I served," the man said, pulling back his sleeve. It was a tattoo Roth had seen countless times before—an eagle holding a Semper Fidelis banner.

"I guess you're what passes for a domestic terrorist these days," Roth said.

"It's a crock of horse shit," the man said.

Roth nodded. He agreed. He knew that man was there because of his ability to sway voters, nothing more. "You pissed off the wrong pencil-pusher," he said.

"How's this even legal?"

Roth sighed. "Legal's what they say is legal," he said. Gone were the days when the CIA kept clear of domestic affairs. These days, whether you were in Basra or Boise, once they set their sights on you, there was nothing you could do to stop them.

Roth knew better than anyone why it happened and how, but that didn't mean he liked it.

They heard more footsteps approaching.

"This bench is going to get cozy," Roth said.

But when the guards appeared, they weren't escorting another prisoner. They were escorting a blonde woman in a black blazer, black skirt, and black heels. In one hand, she carried a black leather briefcase, and in the other, a large plastic Starbucks cup.

"Sandra Shrader," Roth said. "I never thought I'd be so glad to see you."

67

L aurel pored over the drone feeds. The street in front of Lance's apartment was quiet. It was late. There was no traffic to speak of. The weather was abysmal, but the snow on the ground made it easier for the sensors to pick up heat signatures. A cat in the alley next to the building showed up clear as day.

Her phone beeped. It was Roth. "You're out," she said.

"Sandra came to get me."

"There's a long story there," Laurel said.

"She's been catching me up. Who else knows about the situation with her daughter?"

"Apart from me and Tatyana, no one."

"Let's keep it that way," Roth said.

He sounded tired, which didn't come as a surprise to her, given what he'd been through. She could practically hear the gears in his mind at work now, figuring out how to use the present situation to his advantage. It wasn't every day that leverage over the director of the NSA fell into his lap. If Laurel's instincts were correct, he'd hold this over Sandra for years to come.

"I've already spoken to the president," he said. "The warrants against you and Tatyana have been dropped."

"That's a relief. Tatyana could use a doctor."

"What's wrong with her?"

"Another long story."

"All right," Roth said, "well, I got the president to agree to an extension of your mandate."

"What mandate?"

"We can go over the details later," Roth said, "but it looks like he's going to sign off on the Special Operations Group acting completely outside CIA authority, under your control."

"What does that mean?"

"It means more power," Roth said, "and if you check your satellite feeds, you'll see that you've already been given full access to all NSA, DoD, and even NASA resources."

"Holy cow," Laurel said, typing the coordinates of the apartment in Kapotnya into NASA's high-definition network.

"Nice, eh?" Roth said.

"Very."

"You also have the ability to grant your own top-level clearances," Roth said. "Tatyana, her sister, whoever you want—you can bring them in without going through the CIA's red tape."

"The president said yes to that?"

"I learned a long time ago," Roth said, "that the best time to ask someone for something was right after they learned they'd just fucked you."

"It sounds like he gave you everything you wanted."

"Everything *we* wanted, Laurel."

It was true. If the group really had been granted full access to everything on Roth's wishlist, it was going to be the most formidable, battle-ready, and well-resourced intelligence asset in the history of espionage. "All we need now is for Lance to come back into the fold," Laurel said.

She heard the hesitance in Roth's voice. "We'll have to see

about that," he said. "In the meantime, I want visuals on that apartment of his from every angle. If he so much as opens a curtain, I want to see it."

"I'm requesting the additional satellites now," she said.

"I just sent emails to the Pentagon and the White House bunker, linking them to your control view."

"Why did you do that?"

"I put my neck out, trying to convince everyone Lance was the most valuable asset this country had ever produced. If he's about to give us the people behind the bombing, I want everyone who matters to have a front-row seat."

Laurel's new satellite feeds were coming online, and she zoomed in on a small park two blocks away from the apartment. Three Russian military tactical vehicles, each capable of carrying its own discrete team, had gathered there. "Looks like we've got contact," she said.

Three four-man teams got out of the vehicles and began making their way in tactical formation toward the apartment. Two teams headed for the front of the building, while the third approached the back, taking up overwatch positions.

"Do we have contact with Lance?" Roth said.

"I already notified him," Laurel said. "Eight men from the front. Four at the back."

"Good. Make sure this footage is patched through to the Pentagon and the White House. I want those pencil-pushers to see why I keep standing up for this guy."

68

L ance sat with Larissa by the window of the bar. It was the seat he'd been in the first time he'd set eyes on her. That seemed like a lifetime ago now. She'd pulled up in her beat-up Volkswagen, and nothing had been the same since.

Outside, it was snowing heavily, and the infrequent traffic made its way through the snow cautiously.

Lance looked at Larissa. That first time he'd seen her, he'd thought she was a prostitute. He couldn't understand now how he'd ever imagined that. She seemed constitutionally incapable of giving up that much of herself. Even now, after all they'd been through, she was a closed book.

She glanced up at him.

"Can I get you anything?" he said.

She looked at the empty coffee cup in front of her. "To be honest, I wouldn't mind something a little stronger."

He smiled. "The first rule of being an operative," he said, "is no drinking on the job."

"I'm not an operative," she said. "And besides, I've seen

James Bond. He has enough vodka in his martini to knock out a horse."

"One-hundred-twenty milliseconds," Lance said. "That's how much time you lose after a single drink."

"That doesn't sound like very much."

Lance shrugged. "It's enough."

"You think it will come down to that tonight?"

"To milliseconds?"

She nodded.

"I think it might."

Larissa looked at him uneasily.

He got the bartender's attention. "Two more coffees," he said, holding up two fingers.

"One," Larissa said to the bartender. "I'll have a glass of wine."

"White or red?"

"Red," Larissa said, then looked at Lance. "You don't know Russian women. We have more tolerance than you think."

Lance shrugged. "I won't argue with that."

Larissa leaned toward the window and looked at the building across the street. "That's it, isn't it?" she said, looking up at the apartment. "The third window."

"You don't need to worry about that."

"What do you mean I don't need to worry?"

"I promised your sister I'd keep you safe."

"Armed men are coming to kill you," she said.

Lance sighed.

"What did you think?" she said. "That I'd just sit this out?"

He shook his head. "I'm not going to put you in harm's way."

"At least let me do something."

He took a sip of his coffee.

"Lance!" she said. "I didn't come this far to watch you get killed."

The bartender came over with the wine. Larissa took a big sip.

Lance looked out the window. "Under the table," he said.

She looked at him blankly. "Excuse me?"

He touched her knee, and she realized he was passing her a pistol he'd retrieved from the apartment. "That's a loaded Yarygin," he said. "Standard Russian military issue. Seventeen rounds."

"Seventeen bullets?"

"You ever used one?"

"Once or twice," she said.

"Make sure the safety is off."

"I know."

"Hold it firmly."

"I remember how to use it."

"Watch the apartment window from here. I'll signal when I need you to create a distraction."

"What's the signal?"

"I'll turn the lights on and off three times."

"What sort of distraction do you have in mind?"

"Come out onto the sidewalk, aim at the window, and fire until you hit it."

"That's it?"

"It will buy me some time," Lance said, "but you'll need to get the hell out of there after you do it. Make some noise, then walk away."

"Walk away?"

"Hold the pistol close to your leg. Don't draw attention. Don't run. Don't look back. Just walk."

"Where?"

"You know the hotel we passed on the way in?"

"The one with the strip club?"

"Yes."

"I'll meet you at the bar there after the gunfight."

"All right."

"Just sit there and wait."

"I'll wait."

"If I don't show...."

"You'll show," she said.

He reached into his coat and pulled out an envelope. It contained cash in US dollars and Russian rubles. She'd seen him taking it from a safe in the apartment earlier.

She shook her head.

"Take it," he said. "You'll need it."

Reluctantly, she took the money and put it inside her coat.

"Okay," Lance said.

Larissa looked down at her wine.

"Not so thirsty now?" he said, sipping his coffee.

She shook her head.

He reached out and took her hand. "Listen to me," he said. "If anyone follows you when you're walking away, you'll have to shoot them. Do you understand?"

She looked at him for a moment before nodding.

"They'll look like security forces. They might tell you they're going to arrest you for something. You can't let them do that."

"I know," she said.

"You have to look innocent. Look sweet. And when they get close, draw your weapon and shoot."

She nodded.

"No warnings, just shoot."

"I'll do it."

"They won't be expecting it. That gives you the edge."

She nodded, but her eyes were wide with fear.

He squeezed her hand. Using her to create a distraction might make the difference, but he was putting her at risk. If anything happened to him, they'd scour the neighborhood for her. "Anyone comes at you," he said again, "use the pistol."

He finished his coffee and was about to order another when a beep came from the burner phone.

"Go time," he said.

69

L ance read the message on his way up the stairs.

Eight men from the front. Four at the back.

He entered the apartment and went straight to the back window. There was a courtyard behind the building. It was empty, and the only way to access it was through one of the buildings on the other side. He scanned the windows and balconies of those buildings and knew the team at the back would occupy positions to block off escape.

There were ways he could draw them out, but he didn't have time.

It was the eight men approaching from the front he was more worried about. They would come from both ends of the street and enter through the front door.

They were also the ones who were a threat to Larissa. He hoped he wouldn't need her to create the diversion, that had been his way of getting her to stay in the bar, but that didn't mean she was completely safe. Anything could happen down there, and after the diversion she'd created at the embassy, he had little doubt the Russians were on to her.

He went to the living room and looked down at the street. Larissa's silhouette was visible in the bar window. She was still sitting where he'd left her, watching the street. At intervals, her hand brought her glass to her mouth.

And then, he made a last-second change to his plan. She was too vulnerable. He was too far away from her if something went wrong. He needed to be on the ground floor.

He had planned to take out the men in the apartment—the layout was good for an ambush—but he hadn't counted on there being eight of them on the street. Eight was too many. Some would come up the stairs, but they'd leave at least two outside to watch the front of the building.

Once the fighting started, there was no telling how it would go down. If Larissa came out of that bar with her gun, for whatever reason, they would kill her.

It would be safer to kill the men outside first, then follow the rest up to the apartment.

He had two silenced Beretta M9 pistols that he'd taken from the apartment earlier. They were chambered in the 9x19 Parabellum, and each carried fifteen rounds. Then, he went back down to the ground floor and hid in the corner of the hallway behind the staircase.

He placed a small mirror on the ground, positioned so that he would be able to see what was happening at the door, and waited.

It was another five minutes before anyone came to the door. They used an electronic lock pick to get in quietly, and in the mirror, he counted six men entering the narrow hallway.

They were from the president's own Special Operations Force, an elite unit Lance had encountered before around

Raqqa and Palmyra in Syria. They were among the best-trained units he'd ever come across. They carried PYa handguns like the one he'd given Larissa, and Vityaz submachine guns. Two of them had AK-105s, which were essentially carbine versions of the AK-47.

He knew their hand signals. Four were going straight for the stairs. Two would clear the lower levels behind them. That meant there were two men still out on the street. They were the ones he was worried about.

He knew just how easily a life could be ended. The lightest touch of a trigger. The release of a spring. The strike of hammer on primer. Firing a bullet was about as complicated as striking a match. But once that bullet left the barrel, all the prayers under God's blue sky couldn't pull it back into the chamber.

The two men on the ground floor were coming his way.

He waited. He could hear the other four on the landing above him.

At the very last second, staying as low to the ground as possible, he peered out from behind the stairs and shot both approaching soldiers in the knees. Before their heads hit the ground, they'd each been hit with another bullet between the eyes.

Above him, the other four continued up the stairs. There was a brief pause and then the explosion of a flash-bang grenade. In a matter of seconds, they would realize he wasn't in the apartment. He would have to come back for them.

He ran to the front door, kicked it open, and rolled to a position behind the nearest parked car. He quickly located the two soldiers that were out there. One was on the sidewalk by the open door of the building, and the other was in the middle of the street, looking up at the apartment window.

Lance had a pistol in each hand and pointed them at the man by the door. He pulled both triggers as the man swung wildly in his direction. The man hit the ground at the same moment the second opened fire. Sustained fire from a submachine gun ripped through the row of cars along the sidewalk, shattering glass and popping tires in a ten-yard arc in front of the soldier.

Lance only had seconds to do something. The soldiers upstairs would have a clear line of sight on him when they reached the windows, but he was pinned in place. The seconds passed like eons, and then the distinctive pop of a pistol shot brought the submachine gun fire to an abrupt halt.

Lance rose from behind the car. The soldier lay dead on the ground, a halo of blood in the snow around his head.

Across the street, just inside the door of the bar, Larissa stood with her gun extended in front of her, frozen in shock.

Lance couldn't believe what she'd done. She was supposed to be inside, staying out of harm's way.

But then, even before it happened, he saw in his mind what was to come.

A hail of bullets poured down from the window of the apartment. The glass at the front of the bar shattered into a thousand pieces. In the chaos, the only thing he was aware of was Larissa's slight frame falling to the ground with the excruciating drama of a slow-motion movie sequence.

70

Larissa fell as the world around her shattered. Glass fell everywhere like a sudden downpour of hail. Chips of wood and concrete flew through the air. By the time the gunfire ceased, the bar was so thick with dust and smoke that she could barely breathe. The palms of her hands were cut from glass. Her ears rang as if a fire alarm was going off inside her head.

And she'd killed a man.

In all the chaos and confusion, that one fact stood out in her mind like a beacon.

As the dust cleared, she could see out into the street where the soldier lay on the ground. He was facing her, and his cold, lifeless eyes stared at her as if looking into her soul.

She looked around for Lance but didn't see him.

She just had time to register that the shooting in the street had stopped when more gunfire came from inside the apartment building.

She made an effort to focus.

The hotel. That was where she was to meet Lance.

Walk away, he'd told her. Don't run. Don't look back. Just walk.

But as her senses came crashing back to her, she became aware of something new. The sound of screaming. Someone in the bar was hurt.

She moved through the dust in the direction of the screams. The power had gone out, and it was difficult to see. Shards of glass crunched under her feet. She took a few steps toward the center of the bar and crouched down.

It was the bartender. She'd been hit in the neck, and blood coursed from the wound in time to her weakening pulse. It spread across the ground in an expanding crimson pool.

Larissa held the woman's face in her hands and said, "Everything's going to be all right."

But it wasn't. The woman was going to die. She knew it, and the woman knew it.

The woman looked up at Larissa and stopped screaming. A flash of recognition crossed her face, and she said, "Your man brought this."

Larissa was taken aback. The life in the woman's eyes was fading by the second, but the way she was looking at her made her blood shiver.

Larissa wanted to tell her that Lance wasn't her man, that she didn't think he was capable of belonging to anyone, but the woman, even as her breath grew weaker and weaker, forced herself to say more. "There's a darkness around him," she said. "A cloud. The smell of blood—it's the weight of the wolf who knows it has killed too much and too freely."

Larissa nodded. She knew what the woman was saying was true. There was a sadness to Lance's actions, a certain air of detachment, as if he was no longer part of the world he fought for—like there was nothing at stake for him in the fight. He wasn't a part of it. He was just passing through. He lived his life like it was a sentence that had to be served.

Larissa had once heard that in order for the KGB interrogators to torture their victims, they first had to be subjected to the most brutal tortures themselves. For them to be able to inflict that kind of pain on others, it had to first be allowed to get inside them, to tear their souls apart, to stamp out the empathy and compassion that would otherwise stop them from doing their job to the degree necessary.

Larissa saw now that the same was true for assassins. For killers. Whether they were Russian or American, it made no difference. For them to take life so readily, they first had to die themselves.

She also knew that she was now a part of that group. She'd taken a life.

She held the woman as she took her final breaths, and when the last of her life finally left her, it seemed to just float away, like a falling leaf from a tree.

Larissa's eyes filled with tears. The woman was gone.

And then a voice from behind her broke the spell.

"Get up."

She turned to see a soldier, blood pouring from his forehead, pointing his gun at her.

71

L ance re-entered the building and scanned the hallway. When he was sure it was clear, he made his way to the stairs, carefully checking the landing above as he climbed the steps. The second floor was clear, but as he made his way to the third, a bullet struck the staircase's wooden handrail, missing him by inches.

He swung behind the banister and fired upward without seeing the shooter.

When a flash-bang grenade came down the staircase, he crouched, shut his eyes, and covered his ears with his hands.

He heard the bang and then fired in the direction it had come from without being able to see through the smoke.

He heard a body slide down the stairs. He stepped toward it and put another bullet in the head, then crouched down and took a flash-bang from the man's belt. He continued then to the next level.

He could see the door of the apartment, which had been smashed open. He approached cautiously. Three men were still unaccounted for, and they would be waiting inside, ready to ambush him.

He dropped to his knee, fired three shots at the wall next to the doorway, and a soldier slumped to the ground behind it. He shot the man again in the head and rolled to his right in time to dodge a spray of return fire.

The bullets kept coming, and he had to retreat as far as the staircase. He descended a few steps and threw the flash-bang he'd taken from the dead soldier into the apartment.

He waited for it to go off, then ran for the doorway, diving into the apartment. While still in midair, he knew there was a man running for the door. He turned and fired two shots, hitting the ground hard on his back as he landed.

The man who'd been running fell to the ground, and Lance got up and went to him. He was badly injured—one of the bullets was in his shoulder, and another was in his knee. Lance took his guns. "Where's the other guy?" he said, scanning the room.

Apart from the injured man's breathing, the room was silent.

Lance dragged him across the room to where a heating pipe ran along the floor and restrained him with his own cuffs. He searched him, taking anything he might use to escape, including the keys to the cuffs.

"Try to escape, and you die," Lance said.

"You're too late," the man said.

"What does that mean?"

The man laughed. "You'll see."

Lance put his gun against the man's knee and said, "There should be one more of you. Where's the other guy?"

The man laughed again, and Lance pulled the trigger, sending a bullet into his knee. He writhed in agony while Lance cleared the apartment. The last soldier wasn't there.

His mind went immediately to Larissa.

He picked up the soldier's rifle and ran to the window.

Outside, he could see the eighth soldier. He was standing in the bar, pointing his gun at someone.

Lance had no doubt it was pointed at Larissa.

He took a moment to aim, inhaled slowly, and as he breathed out, let his finger depress the trigger. The gun fired, and a split second later, the soldier fell to the ground, dead.

Lance prayed Larissa was still safe and that she would make her way to the hotel, but he didn't have time to watch.

According to the message from Laurel, four more men were approaching from the back of the building. The gunfire would have drawn them out of their positions, and they'd be making their way toward him.

He made his way to the bedroom, from where he could see the courtyard behind the building, but just as he entered the room, he saw a soldier in the process of climbing in through the window. Lance fired three shots, ran over to him, and shoved him back out. There was another soldier on the fire escape, and Lance quickly pulled back inside as a bullet struck the window frame.

He drew his handgun, reached out the window, and fired blindly. Then he looked around and aimed with his second gun, hitting the man on the fire escape twice in the head.

Below, in the courtyard, the final two soldiers were in retreat. They provided themselves with wild, undirected cover fire, but Lance unslung the rifle from his shoulder, aimed at one and then the other, and took them both out.

He took a breath. He could already hear sirens in the distance and knew more special forces operatives would be on their way. He didn't have much time.

He went back to the living room, where the soldier still lay cuffed to the pipe. He'd lost a lot of blood and was beginning to slip out of consciousness. Lance bent down and tapped him on the face to wake him up. "Ambulances are on the way," he said.

The soldier nodded.

"I don't know if you have a family, but if you want to be alive when the ambulances get here, you have to talk right now."

"Go to hell," the man said.

"That's fine," Lance said. "You have a lot of dead comrades here. If you want to join them, you have thirty seconds to make up your mind. I'll wait."

Lance stepped back and sat on the sofa. He started a timer on his watch and let the man see it. The man still refused to speak.

Lance shrugged. He got up and went to the window, making sure the street was still clear. He would leave through the back but would have to go soon if he didn't want to encounter more trouble. "All right," he said when the timer started to beep. "Make peace with your God because you're about to meet him." He raised his gun and pointed it at the soldier's face.

"Wait!" the soldier said at the very last second.

"Who sent you?" Lance said. "That's all I need to know."

"The albino sent us," the man said.

"Who is the albino?"

"I don't know who he is. No one knows who he is. He's a ghost. A chimera. He appears and disappears as he pleases and answers only to the president."

The sirens were getting closer.

"Everyone leaves some sort of trail."

"This man stays out of sight. He stays out of the sun. It burns his skin. Even if you scoured the entire city with your drones and satellites, you'd never find him."

"Then how *would* I find him?"

"You have to get close to him. You have to be where he is. You need someone on the inside."

"Tell me how I do that," Lance said.

"He works out of the Lubyanka," the soldier said. "You can get to him there."

"That's a lie. We checked the FSB databases a thousand times. He doesn't exist."

"Of course, he doesn't exist. He doesn't work for the FSB. The FSB works for him. He uses the Lubyanka as cover because he can get in and out unseen."

"We've been watching the Lubyanka round the clock. If he was there, we'd know."

"No, you wouldn't," the man said. "He comes and goes by a secret underground entrance. He has his own elevator. His office is on the top floor, and that entire floor is completely sealed off from the rest of the building."

The sirens were so close now that Lance couldn't delay any longer. He had to leave.

There'd been a triage kit among the man's things, and Lance gave it to him.

Then he left.

72

I
t felt strange to Lance to be returning to Tatyana's
hotel. He remembered vividly the night she'd been
attacked and knew it was a place already on the GRU's
radar.

When he arrived, there was no bouncer at the door. The
place was quiet, almost deserted. Inside, a single dancer
performed for a handful of men. Larissa was at the bar, her
back to the stage, a drink in front of her. There was blood on
her coat and hands. As he sat down next to her, he noticed that
she was drinking straight vodka. He let her knock back the shot
before speaking.

"You look comfortable."

"Did I ever tell you what I did before I met you?" she said.
Her hand was shaking.

He knew how she was feeling. No one ever forgot the first
time they took a life. It would stay with her forever, a ghost in
the shadows of her mind.

"Are you all right?" he said, touching her arm.

"That waitress is dead."

"Waitress?"

"The lady at the bar who flirted with you. The bartender. She got hit."

"I'm sorry," Lance said.

"She said you brought it," Larissa said. "You brought the storm. You carried it with you like a curse."

Lance nodded.

"Those soldiers," Larissa said. "The one I...." She couldn't finish the sentence.

"You can't think about that now," Lance said.

"They were ordinary men with ordinary lives. Wives, maybe. Children."

"They were soldiers," Lance said. "That's all we can let them be."

"One of them was standing right in front of me. He wasn't more than ten feet away from me." Her voice cracked.

"I'm sorry," Lance said again.

He got the bartender's attention and ordered two more shots. They didn't have time for it, but Larissa was in shock.

The bartender poured the two shots, and Lance handed him some crumpled bills. There was blood on both of their clothes, and sirens could be heard on every street for miles around. Lance counted out another hundred dollars worth of cash and put the money on the bar.

They knocked back their shots, and Lance said, "We can't stay here. Tatyana stayed here, and they came for her."

"They sent an assassin?"

Lance nodded.

"Like you?"

He nodded again and got up. She remained seated. She stared at the empty shot glass in front of her.

The first time wasn't easy. He knew it. She'd have flashbacks for years. She'd have dreams, nightmares, that felt so real she wouldn't be able to tell them from reality.

"She said something to me," Larissa said.

"Who did?"

"The waitress from the bar."

"Oh?" Lance said.

Larissa hesitated, searching for the right words, then said, "She said that you're a wolf who's tasted too much blood."

Lance didn't know what to say. He looked at the bartender. There was a phone on the bar. It wouldn't be long before the doors burst open, and soldiers poured into the hotel. "We need to go," he said, putting his hand awkwardly on Larissa's shoulder.

She pulled away from him.

"Call a cab," Lance said to the bartender.

They went outside, and Larissa lit a cigarette. Lance put his arm around her and pulled her into him as some police cars sped by, sirens blazing.

When the cab arrived, he told the driver to take them to the closest metro station.

They got out at the station, and Lance immediately hailed another cab, getting the driver to take them to the next metro station.

"What are we doing?" Larissa said.

"Hiding our tracks," Lance said. He told her to take off her coat, which had blood on it, and they left it behind.

They paid each driver in cash, and when they got out at the next station, they got in a third cab, which he let take them all the way downtown.

The albino would be expecting that. He wouldn't know how much the soldier had told Lance, but the bullet in his knee would confirm that he'd been questioned, and the fact he was alive would confirm he'd talked.

Wherever he was, he'd have his guard up now. He'd just walked into a trap, and he knew it. He knew he was being hunted.

They got out of the cab at a busy plaza on the Garden Ring,

and Lance looked around for the cheapest-looking hotel he could find. The cheaper the hotel, the less computerized their systems.

They were in the albino's territory now, and he knew they were coming for him.

He chose a nondescript hotel down a side street with shutters on the windows and gas heaters outside so people could sit on the patio in winter. He brought Larissa into the lobby, and they got a room using false identification papers. Once upstairs, he told her to have a shower and wash off the blood.

When she came out, she dressed and sat on the side of the bed while he had a shower of his own.

Lance came out of the bathroom to find her asleep on the bed, two little bottles of vodka from the minibar empty on the side table next to her.

He pulled out the burner phone he'd been using to make contact with Laurel and typed out a message.

Got a lead on the albino. Need satellite surveillance and schematics on the Lubyanka.

He clicked send and turned off the phone. Then he removed the SIM from the back of the phone and took a lighter from his pocket. He held the SIM over the flame until it began to melt, then threw it in the toilet and flushed it.

He let Larissa sleep for thirty minutes, then woke her.

They went back down to the lobby and left the hotel, walking a few blocks before hailing another cab. The cab took them right into the district of the Lubyanka. It was Larissa's home territory, close to where she worked every day, and she knew it well.

"We need a hotel—small, not a chain. Someplace you've never stayed before."

She knew of a place not dissimilar from the last one, and they got a room.

When they were upstairs, Larissa collapsed on the bed and seemed to fall asleep instantly.

There was a sofa by the window, and Lance shoved it in front of the door. The room was on the fourth floor. It was as safe as they were going to get.

73

Roth hadn't been back to the White House since the ambush in the Roosevelt Room, and he straightened his tie before entering the Oval Office.

"Mr President," he said, "thank you for seeing me."

"Of course, Levi."

It was late. The president was in a gown and slippers, the fire was lit, and Roth was glad to see a bottle of port open on the table.

The president was on the sofa by the fire and rose to his feet.

"Please, sir," Roth said, motioning for him to remain seated.

"Roth," the president said, "my predecessors would be ashamed if they could have seen how I treated you."

"Not at all, sir. You were doing what you thought was best."

"I was a fool, Roth, and I apologize again for my misjudgment."

Roth joined the president by the fire, and the president poured two glasses of port. It was a Flagman's Colheita, the name carefully stenciled on the bottle by hand.

"Delicious," Roth said, taking a sip.

"1952," the president said. "Consider it a peace offering."

They raised their glasses.

"The generals were very impressed with your man's performance," the president said.

"Impressed enough to understand why I stood by him?"

The president shrugged. "They don't understand loyalty in the same way that spies do. Their work is less personal, less reliant on any one man."

"I can see that," Roth said.

The president nodded.

"Well," Roth said, "he seems to have come up with a lead. He sent a message last night."

"What did it say?"

"Not much, but he requested surveillance on the Lubyanka building."

"So it's still all pointing to the Russian government?"

"It is, sir."

"As we feared."

"As we feared, sir."

The president raised his cup to his mouth and drained it. He poured himself another. "Are there really men in Moscow who seek to pull us into war in such a flagrant manner?"

"It appears there are those willing to risk everything," Roth said.

"And in Beijing?" the president said.

Roth nodded. He finished his drink, and the president immediately refilled it.

"I've ordered two Carrier Strike Groups into the South China Sea," the president said. "Two to the Mediterranean. One to the Baltic Sea."

"That's a substantial deployment, sir."

"I think it sends the right message."

Roth nodded. "Of course, we'll need to do more than send messages."

The president topped up both their glasses. Roth could see he was preparing to say something difficult.

He looked at Roth gravely, and Roth said, "If there's something you want to say—"

The president cleared his throat. "The thing is, Levi..."

"Just say it, Ingram."

"I'm afraid I'm not sure what more we can do than send messages in this case."

Roth had been about to take a sip of his drink. His hand froze just in front of his mouth. "Excuse me?"

"You heard me, Roth."

"But this attack, sir. This provocation..."

"I can't pull us into a World War, Roth."

"But we're not talking about a World War."

"I'm not willing to risk any kind of war. Even if it's localized."

"But we have two embassies in ashes. I don't see how there's even a choice here."

"There's always a choice."

"We were attacked, sir."

"We were only attacked if we choose to be," the president said and took a big gulp of his port.

"You're still considering pinning this on my man?"

The president said nothing.

Roth put down his glass and got to his feet.

"Sit down, Roth."

"Even after he risked his life to find out who was behind the attack?"

"Let's not be children about this."

"Children? With all due respect, we were *attacked*," Roth said, emphasizing the word. "We had our asses handed to us."

The president's tone changed. He didn't like this any more than Roth did but was not about to be lectured by a subordinate. "We were attacked by Russia and China, Roth. You know as well as I do what that means."

"It means what it means."

"It could mean the end of everything."

"We can respond proportionately," Roth said. "We focus on their military capabilities. Their espionage infrastructure. Their satellite and cyber systems."

"It's too risky. The Pentagon doesn't like it."

"To hell with what the Pentagon likes."

"Both Russia and China at once, Roth? Think about that."

"I don't need to think about it. It's already happened. They struck first. The thinking's been done."

"No, it hasn't," the president said. "Not as long as we have another person to pin this on."

"I can't believe you're still thinking of putting this all on Lance." Roth was losing his temper. To let these attacks go unanswered would be the gravest tactical mistake in a generation. He knew how the enemy thought. He knew there were some risks that simply could not be hazarded, some costs that could not be paid. An all-out war with Russia and China was probably one of those risks. But to completely deflect this? To blame it on a rogue American when they knew someone in the Kremlin was involved? It showed intolerable weakness.

"When 9/11 happened," the president said, "we knew that the only ones truly implicated were the Saudis."

"Please don't give me a history lesson," Roth said.

"The Saudis, our biggest ally in the Middle East. A three-hundred-billion-dollar arms contract. The most powerful army in the region."

"I understand what happened, sir."

"Did we start a war with Saudi Arabia?"

"Of course we didn't."

"We went after Iraq. We went after Afghanistan. Wars we wanted to fight."

Roth had nothing to say to this. He went to the door.

"We're not in kindergarten, Roth. This is the reality of the situation. This is the reality of the politics."

Roth shook his head. "We were attacked by Russia and China. That's the only reality I know right now." He slammed the door as he left.

He was at the elevator by the time the president caught up to him. Roth looked at him, standing there in his robe and slippers, slightly breathless from having hurried down the corridor.

"Levi," he said, "I'm telling you this as a friend. Do not let your asset go after whoever it is in the Kremlin he thinks did this. You call that hound to heel, Levi. You get him to stand down."

"Even if I wanted to," Roth said, "I doubt I could."

"A simultaneous war with Russia and China could mean the end of the world," the president said. "That's what's at stake here, Roth. You know it as well as I do."

74

L ance spent the morning purchasing fresh clothing and toiletries while Larissa slept. He also picked up a new burner phone and laptop.

He'd heard Larissa tossing and turning during the night and, more than once, weeping. Time would heal the wound, but it would leave a scar. There would be no forgetting what she'd done. He knew she'd learn to live with it, but she'd never truly get over it.

He found himself buying her fresh croissants, strawberries, pastries, anything he thought might give her some comfort.

When he got back to the room, she was awake in bed watching a soap opera.

"Hey," Lance said.

"Hey," she said.

"How'd you sleep?" he said, knowing the answer.

"Okay."

"The first night's the worst."

She nodded.

He knew the shoot-out the night before was all over the local news and was glad she'd found something else to watch.

"I got breakfast," he said. He went to the coffee machine and put on a pot. "We should eat now. Once I make contact with Washington, we'll have to leave quickly."

Larissa spread the food on the bed while Lance finished making the coffee. Then they ate. At first, she picked at the food, but pretty quickly, her appetite took over.

"I think it's time we made a plan to get you out of the country," Lance said while they ate.

"I told you before," she said, "I'm not going anywhere without you."

"It will be safer if you go alone. You'll be harder to find. I can show you how to adjust your appearance to slip through security."

"And what about papers?"

"I'll take care of that. Our best bet is to get you close to the border. Then the CIA can send someone across to get you."

"Who would that be?"

"It depends."

"I'm with you now. Why not just keep it like that? I'll get out with you."

"I've got something to do."

"I know what you've got to do. I'm the one who told you about it."

"Larissa!"

She sighed. She wasn't happy. "Would Tatyana come?"

"That would be risky. They're already looking for her."

Larissa nodded. "You want to get rid of me."

"Larissa..."

"No, I understand. I'm a liability to you now."

"You're not a liability."

"I'm the one who found out about this in the first place. I brought it to you. I started it. Now you want to finish it without me."

"Things are about to get a whole lot more dangerous."

"More dangerous than what happened last night?"

He shook his head. She had no idea. "If we manage to get to this albino," he said, "the Kremlin will come down on us like a ton of bricks. They'll search every hotel room, every railway carriage, every aircraft hold, and ship manifest."

"That never held you back before."

"Every time I do something like this," he said, "I accept the fact that there might not be a way out afterward."

"So, what are you proposing?"

"I'll take you to the train station. We get you as far away from here as possible. When you get to the border, you send a message to Laurel, and she sends someone to come smuggle you out of the country."

"And what happens after?"

"After?"

"When the CIA has me?"

"What do you mean?"

"What use will they have for me then? What future will I have?"

"They're not going to abandon you, Larissa. I'll make sure you get a fair deal."

"A fair deal?"

"A new identity. Protection."

"Witness protection?"

"Yes."

"Like in the movies."

"More or less."

"You want to send me out to the middle of nowhere? Some small town in America, to work in a hardware store or a gas station, spending my life looking over my shoulder, always waiting for the day they come for me?"

"You'll be safe. You'll be able to start a new life."

"What new life?" she said. "I'll be a fugitive in my own skin."

"What did you think would happen?" Lance said. "How did you think this would all end?"

Larissa shook her head. She was close to tears, and he didn't want to push her. He needed her to function.

He knew what she wanted. She wanted a commitment from him. Something personal. And he couldn't give it to her. Anything he said now would be a lie.

"I wish I never heard those words," she said. "That man in the club. The attack. The plot. I should have run a million miles."

"It's too late for that now," he said.

She poured two cups of coffee and handed him one. They drank together, and when they were done, Lance said, "I'm going to make the call. When I get back, be ready to leave."

She nodded.

Lance left the hotel and walked to a nearby park. He found a bench and wiped off the snow before sitting down. He had techniques to mask the route of his call, but there was still a chance it would be picked up by the Russians. They'd be monitoring the Moscow phone system like hawks.

He opened the computer on his lap and looked around to make sure no one was taking any undue interest in him. Then he opened the connection.

He waited while the route was secured, and then, all of a sudden, Roth's face filled the screen. He looked tired, like he hadn't slept.

Roth saw the surprise on Lance's face and said, "Not who you were expecting?"

Lance cleared his throat. "I thought I'd get Laurel."

"I wanted to speak to you directly," Roth said. "The entire joint chiefs saw what you did last night."

"I put on a good show, then?" Lance said. "The emperor is entertained?"

"Come on, Lance."

"No, you come on, Roth. This isn't a game we're playing over here."

"I was just saying...."

"I know what you were saying."

"You know our hands are tied."

Lance let out a hollow laugh.

Roth nodded. "No one in the Pentagon believes for a second you were behind the bombings."

"I couldn't care less what those bureaucrats think."

"You know as well as I do, we can't go after Russia and China on this. If war were to break out between three superpowers, no one's walking away from that. That's game over. That's an extinction-level event."

Lance shook his head. He was used to the constant maneuverings in Washington. The calculations. The politics. He was used to being told what to do by people who'd never left the comfort of their air-conditioned offices, who'd never set foot on the battlefield, who drank soy lattes and ate low-carb veggie wraps while other people risked their lives to carry out their orders. He'd met generals who cared more about advancing their careers and getting their kids into private schools than they ever cared about the lives of the men under their command. He knew that the minutiae of the federal pay scale occupied far more analyst attention in Washington than any war threat ever would.

And it got to him. It got under his skin.

"You know," he said, "there was a time when if someone sucker-punched America, we punched back."

"That's not your decision to make, Lance."

"How is this even up for debate?"

"The president doesn't want to take us into a war that could destroy us."

"We back down from this," Lance said, "and that's it. We lose everything. Our position. Our leadership. Our fucking dignity."

"Since when did you care about dignity?"

"Fuck you, Roth."

"Fuck me? Fuck me?"

"Do you even give a shit about getting the man who is behind these attacks?"

"You listen to me very carefully, Lance. This is coming from the top. You're ordered to stand down. Do you hear me?"

"Stand down? I'm just getting stood up."

"Don't go after these guys, Lance. The president will have your nuts on a platter."

"Someone's got to do it."

"There's a chain of command, Lance. There's a system."

"Your system is going to let this guy get away with the biggest attack on America in a decade."

"Lance, if you go rogue on this, you risk unleashing the most devastating conflict in human history."

"No, Roth. That's what you're risking by letting them off the hook. What do you think will happen if we don't hit back for this? That the Chinese and Russians will pack up their toys and go home? No. They're going to be all over us, everywhere. We need to nip this now before it gets a whole lot worse."

"Lance, stand down. That's a direct order."

"Our nation was built on stronger stuff than an order like that," Lance said. "I'm going after this guy."

He disconnected.

He couldn't believe it. The president wanted to stand down. The powers in Washington preferred to blame this on one of their own than actually go after the man responsible.

He made his way back to the hotel, dumping the laptop in a trash can on the way. He was about to ditch the phone too, when something told him to hold onto it.

He didn't think the morning could get much worse, but then, when he got back to the hotel, Larissa was gone.

T atyana leaned back from the screen and rubbed her eyes.

"You should take a break," Laurel said.

Tatyana sighed. "I know this place," she said, looking at the live feed of the plaza in front of the Lubyanka. It was busy, with workers coming and going in a steady stream. "I've been there. I've worked with these people. I've looked them in the eye. I know how they think."

Laurel had just made coffee and put a cup on the desk in front of Tatyana. "Roth wants us to focus on the armored convoy movements," she said.

They'd managed to track armored vehicles moving to and from the president's country estate outside the city to a tunnel close to the Lubyanka. Judging from the convoy configuration, traffic closures, and air coverage, someone very important was being transported. From public records, they could tell it wasn't the president himself.

"Right now, the convoy is still at Novo-Ogaryovo," Tatyana said. "I'm trying to get higher resolution imagery from its last arrival time, but air security over the facility is even tighter than for the Kremlin." She pulled back to the footage of the plaza.

"What are you looking for?" Laurel said.

"It's just a feeling," Tatyana said. "These people, coming and going, to and from the building. These workers. One of them knows something."

They heard the door open as Roth entered the room. He locked the door behind him and took a seat at the meeting table between the desks. He looked upset.

"Everything okay, boss?" Laurel said.

He sighed. "If I only had to fight our adversaries and not our own people, my job would be a whole lot easier."

"What happened?"

"The president ordered us to call off the operation."

"What?" Laurel said.

Roth nodded.

"How can he not want to get to the bottom of this?" Laurel said.

Tatyana was still staring at the satellite feed, but she said, "Politicians can only ask questions when they know they're going to like the answer."

Roth nodded. "He can't pursue this operation when the only logical outcome is that it will lead to war with Russia."

"And China," Tatyana added.

"And China," Roth agreed. "And maybe he's got a point. War on that scale hasn't been seen in modern times."

"Fuck that," Laurel said. "They hit us, we hit them back. An eye for an eye. It's in the Bible."

Roth let out a brief laugh. "If we're going to do this, we have to keep it completely off the radar," he said. "No new resource requisitions. Give back any assets we're not using. I want it to look from the outside like we're standing down the operation."

"You mean we can continue to hunt?" Tatyana said.

"Continue hunting, ladies," Roth said. "But, like I said, keep it on the down-low. If the president gets even a whiff that we didn't stand down when ordered, he'll have us arrested. And mark my words, no one will be coming to our aid next time."

Roth left them, and the two women sat and looked at each other.

"We need to find something actionable for Lance," Laurel said. "And fast."

"There might be something here," Tatyana said, squinting at her screen. "If I could just get these optics in a little closer."

"What have you got?"

"It might be nothing, but I've cross-checked it with all the known convoy movements, and I think I've got a correlation."

"What correlation?" Laurel said, leaning over her shoulder.

"You see that woman? The red scarf?" Tatyana said. "School children used to wear them in the Soviet era."

Laurel nodded. She'd studied Soviet customs in detail and knew all about the Young Pioneers.

"I don't think I'd have noticed her but for the scarf," Tatyana said.

"What are you saying?"

"I've worked for these men," Tatyana said. "I know the control some of them can exert over the women beneath them."

"And you think this woman works for the albino?"

"She's definitely connected to the convoy movements. She comes and goes at the same time it does. I ran her through the facial recognition system, and apart from a short stint at college, her record has been purged. She never worked for the FSB."

"So maybe she's his secretary?" Laurel said.

"Something like that," Tatyana said.

"*Something*?" Laurel said.

"I don't think any woman would dress like that by choice," Tatyana said. "The Young Pioneer scarf? It's from another era. If I'm not mistaken, it's an outfit selected by a man."

"Her boss?" Laurel said.

"A powerful, lecherous son of a bitch," Tatyana said. "Believe me when I say I know what I'm talking about."

76

The moment Lance left the room, Larissa grabbed what few things she could see that would be of use—her clothes, the pistol Lance had given her, the envelope of cash he'd left by the bed. She shoved the money and gun into her purse and slipped out of the room.

She didn't forget for a second that she was a wanted fugitive, but if Lance's only plan was to send her off on a train and wait for a CIA operative to come get her, she preferred to make her own way.

She needed to get her head straight. She needed time to think. Her mind was in turmoil, and every time she shut her eyes, the image of the soldier she'd shot came rushing back to her.

She took the elevator down to the lobby, her heart pounding with every second that passed, and when the doors opened, she practically ran for the front door. Just as she was leaving, the concierge said, "Your husband went that way if you're looking for him."

"Thank you," she said, then went outside and walked in the opposite direction.

She knew the area well and, by instinct, found herself walking in the direction of the club she worked at. It was something familiar. Something that belonged to her. She didn't stop to think of the forces that were at work trying to track her down.

When she first rounded the corner onto the street the club was on, she could almost imagine her previous life. Life before she'd killed anyone.

As she approached the club, she realized something wasn't right. Someone should have been opening the place up already, putting out the awnings, and turning on the signs. But there was no one there.

That was her signal. She should have turned around, right then and there, and gotten out of there as quickly as possible. But something made her keep walking.

From the street, she could see that the place was empty. There were no lights on, no music playing. As she got closer, she realized the front door hadn't been shut properly. It had always been troublesome. There was a knack to it. Unless you knew what you were doing, the latch wouldn't catch when you shut it behind you, and it wouldn't lock.

She should have turned and run. But instead, as if her actions were being controlled by another person, she put her hand on the door and pulled it open. Then, she stood at the entrance for a long moment, just looking into the darkness of the corridor as if contemplating entering an abyss.

There, she could see nothing, hear nothing. Just an eerie silence.

She reached into her purse and pulled out the pistol. Then, moving very slowly, she made her way into the corridor. She didn't dare turn on the lights for fear of alerting someone. The only light came from the door, and she pulled out her cigarette lighter to use as a torch.

She took a few steps forward, then froze. Her eyes were adjusting to the darkness, and she could see that there was something before her on the ground. It was like a black stain on the white linoleum, and as she got closer, she realized it was a pool of blood. It was coming from the office.

She fought the urge to turn around and kept going, walking all the way to the door of the office. When she peered inside, she saw that the blood was coming from a body. On the ground in the center of the room, facing upward, his eyes staring blankly at the ceiling, was her fat, tattooed, stubble-faced boss.

Between his eyes was a single bullet wound. On one of his hands, three fingernails had been torn from the fingers, their fleshy remains lying on the floor next to the body.

He'd been interrogated, and she realized it was her that the interrogators had been searching for.

In her shock, she dropped the lighter. The room plunged into darkness. She bent down, searching for it and her hands reached straight into the sticky mess of blood. She wanted to gag, but just as she found the lighter, a sound of breaking glass came from the back of the building.

Someone was still there.

She stepped over the corpse, revulsion crawling over every inch of her skin, and hid behind his desk. Footsteps were coming her way.

Then voices. Two men.

"Let's get out of here before people start showing up," one of them said.

Larissa held her breath as they passed the office.

They left, but she remained where she was for a long time, too scared to move. Eventually, she crept out from behind the desk. She flicked on the lighter and gave her boss a final glance as she stepped over him. He'd always been a prick, but he didn't deserve to die like that, at the hands of torturers. It was yet another death, she thought, to add to her conscience.

At the door, she checked carefully that no one was still there, then slipped out of the building as quietly as she could.

Once outside, she hurried along the sidewalk to a small shopping plaza. Inside, she went straight to the women's restroom and locked herself in a stall. No sooner had she turned the lock than she immediately began to hyperventilate. She held onto the walls to keep her balance as she calmed back down.

Then, she let herself out of the stall, expecting at every moment to see a group of GRU agents ready to arrest her. The room was empty, and she went to the sink and washed her hands and face.

As she was leaving the plaza, she noticed some payphones by the food court. She could still remember the phone number that had been on the matchbook Tatyana had left her. It had been seared into her memory. What if she'd never found that matchbook, she wondered. What if she'd never dialed the number on it? She wouldn't be in any of this mess.

She pushed the thought from her mind and went up to the payphones. As she dialed the number, she doubted it would even connect. Tatyana had told her never to call that number again. But she knew that if she didn't speak to someone soon, she was going to lose her mind.

The phone made a number of sounds, like the clicks of an old internet dial-up system, before eventually returning a dial tone. She waited, holding her breath, and then miraculously, as if from a dream, Tatyana answered.

"Larissa," she gasped, her voice full of concern. "This call will be traced. You need to hang up now."

"I killed a man," Larissa blurted.

"You did what you had to do," Tatyana said. "Those men came after you."

"I'm not like you," Larissa said. "I don't think I can do this."

"All you need to do is get out of there and keep moving."

"Every time I shut my eyes, I see his face."

"I know, Larissa. I know what that's like, but you need to save yourself now. Otherwise, it will all have been for nothing."

"How do you live like this, Tatyana?"

"The same way as anything else," Tatyana said. "I take it one day at a time."

Larissa nodded. She knew she should get moving, she knew she was being foolish, but she couldn't help it. "Lance wants to send me away," she blurted.

"What do you mean?"

"Put me on a train. Get the CIA to come pick me up."

"Listen to me, Larissa. You can't let that happen."

"He said it's for my own safety."

"The only place you're safe right now is with Lance Spector. No matter what happens, you stay by his side."

"He doesn't want me."

"Then find a way to make him want you."

"I don't know...." Larissa said, grasping for words.

"You're a resourceful girl, Larissa. Do not let him send you away. I'm speaking from experience."

"What do you mean?"

"I had a chance once to stay with him, a chance to push the issue, so to speak, and I didn't do it."

"You mean you didn't become lovers?"

"I let him slip through my fingers, Larissa, and horrible things happened later. Things that would not have happened if I'd stuck with him."

"I'm not sure he wants me," Larissa said. "In fact, I know he doesn't."

"Then make him want you."

Larissa shook her head. She knew men. She wasn't afraid to use her body to get what she needed, but with Lance, she wasn't sure she had what he was looking for. She wasn't sure anyone did. "Are you in love with him?" she said.

"What?" Tatyana said. "What does that matter now?"

"Are you?"

There was the briefest pause, then Tatyana said, "Don't ask me that, Larissa."

Larissa was about to hang up when Tatyana stopped her. "Wait," she said with great urgency.

"What is it?" Larissa said.

"The albino. He has a secretary."

77

When Larissa got back to the hotel, Lance was packing up the few items he'd taken from the apartment in Kapotnya. She looked at him awkwardly, embarrassed, like a child who'd run away and come home again.

She thought Lance would say something about it but what he said was, "We've got to get out of here."

He kept packing, stuffing the items hurriedly into a small backpack. She wanted him to stop. "Don't you even want to know where I was?" she said.

He looked up at her. "Okay. Where were you?"

"I went to the club I used to work at."

"Did anyone see you?"

"No."

"Are you sure?"

"I think so."

"Were you followed?"

She shook her head. Lance went to the window and pulled back the curtain. "We don't have time for this," he said. "We need to leave."

"My boss was dead on the floor," she said.

Lance nodded. "They know who you are now. They're going to keep coming after you."

He finished packing, slung the backpack over his shoulder, and they left the room. In the corridor, he pushed the button for the elevator, and they waited for it in conspicuous silence.

"Aren't you mad?" Larissa said.

"I don't have time for games, Larissa."

She nodded. "I see."

They stepped into the elevator and watched the doors shut. Then Larissa said, "You were going to leave without me."

He looked at her. "You were gone."

"Maybe someone took me."

"The concierge said you left."

The doors opened, and she followed him across the lobby and out to the street. She felt like everything was unraveling, as if it was spinning out of control, and there was nothing she could do to bring it back together.

Lance hailed a cab, and when they got in, he asked for the closest train station.

Larissa didn't know what to do. She felt her heart pounding faster and faster, and the thought of him putting her on a train and abandoning her made her want to scream.

"I called Tatyana," she said in a burst of emotion.

"They'll have traced the call," Lance said flatly.

She reached out for his hand and clutched it so tightly her nails bit into his skin. "She said I should stay with you," Larissa said.

"Did she?"

Larissa pulled his hand onto her leg. "She said to do whatever it took to stay with you."

Lance looked at her. She could tell he was conflicted. He wanted her. She pulled his hand further up her thigh. She smiled meekly, nodded her head, encouraged him. She felt the weight of his hand as if it was made of iron.

She leaned toward him.

"You can't stay, Larissa," he said. "It would be reckless to keep you here."

"Tatyana said I'd be safer with you, no matter what you said."

Lance shook his head.

"She said if she'd clung to you that first time you met her, a lot of horrible things would not have happened to her."

She pressed his hand onto her thigh, trying to keep it there.

The cab stopped. They were at the Yaroslavskiy train station.

Lance looked at her, then pulled his hand from her thigh. "Change of plan," he said to the driver. "Take us to Sokolniki." It seemed he wasn't going to get rid of her after all.

The cab took them to the nearby park and dropped them off at a café. They sat at a table outside and ordered coffee. The sky was clear, and light from the sun poured through the trees.

"Thank you," she said.

He acted like he didn't hear her.

The waiter came with their coffee. He also brought small silver bowls of olives and candied nuts. Lance cleared his throat when the waiter left and said, "The man we're hunting works out of the Lubyanka."

Larissa nodded. She sipped her coffee.

"The CIA has a dropbox outside the city. I have to get some things from it."

"What kinds of things?"

"Weapons."

78

L ance felt a vibration in his coat pocket. It was the phone, a message from Laurel.

"Wait here," he said to Larissa.

"Where are you going?"

She was jumpy now, shaken up. He understood that. What he didn't understand was why he'd allowed her to stay. Was it temptation? Was it that he thought she'd be useful?

He had no idea if he could keep her safe. Whatever was coming could quickly get out of hand. One thing was clear, though—he couldn't bring himself to put her on a train alone.

"I have to make a call."

She nodded.

"Don't go anywhere," he said. "From here on, we stick together."

She nodded again, looking relieved at having heard him say that.

He went into the café and asked the waiter for the phone. Laurel's message had been sent in the clear, with no encryption, and the return number was a regular open line. He dialed, and Laurel picked up immediately. "What's going on?" Lance said.

"I've got something for you."

"Tell me you found him."

"Do you know where the Russian president spends most of his time in Moscow?"

"The country estate," Lance said.

"Yes," Laurel said. "Novo-Ogaryovo. Armored convoys have been exiting a tunnel close to the Lubyanka and going straight there. From what we've seen, it's got to be your albino."

"Where did the intel come from?"

"Roth got it from NASA and NSA satellites."

"Roth told me to stand down."

"He had a feeling you weren't going to obey his order."

Lance nodded. "Son of a bitch," he said.

"Novo-Ogaryovo won't be easy to get into, Lance."

"I'll figure out a way."

"Be careful," Laurel said.

He hung up the phone and went back to Larissa. "We need to get moving," he said. "We need a car."

She took a final sip of her coffee and left money on the table to pay for it. Then they went to a nearby car rental office, and Lance got them a BMW sedan. They drove across the city to a decrepit-looking, Soviet-era apartment complex. It consisted of eight sixteen-story concrete apartment blocks, all identical, and they towered so high that their top floors disappeared into the mist above them.

Lance looked at Larissa. "Wait in the car," he said. "I'll leave the key. If I'm not back in twenty minutes, don't come looking for me. Drive straight to the train station. You'll need to get out of Moscow as quickly as possible. Do you understand me?"

"Are you expecting trouble?"

"Only if someone's found the stash. They sit here for years. Sometimes they're discovered, and then the GRU watches them, waits for someone like me to come along."

Lance made his way to one of the apartment blocks and checked the elevator. It worked, thankfully, and he took it to the twelfth floor. When he found the door he was looking for, he walked past it. There was no one in the corridor, no sign of GRU surveillance, and the door appeared not to have been tampered with.

Lance had memorized the locations of hundreds of these drop boxes around the world, and accessing them was always a risk.

He walked up to the door, raised his foot, and brought it down hard on the cheap plywood. The door had an upgraded deadbolt, but a few solid kicks, and the frame began to split. By the time he'd broken in, several neighbors had come into the corridor to see what was causing the commotion.

Lance ignored them.

He entered the apartment and found the setup he expected. In the center of the room was a pile of weapons cases. In full view of the neighbors, he began opening them, one by one.

He was familiar with the equipment, it was always packed in the same configuration, and he made his way straight to the Czech CZ 75 semi-auto pistols. He found the guns, the compatible silencers, and the ammo. He also found a sizeable M82 sniper rifle with an accompanying bipod and scope. Its ammo included silver-tipped, armor-piercing incendiary rounds, as well as .50 caliber BMG rounds. From what he knew of the Novo-Ogaryovo compound, his best bet at taking out a target would be a long-range sniper shot.

There was also a plastic folder containing blank documents and the materials necessary to forge passports—American or Russian. He grabbed those too.

He placed the cases for the M82 and the pistols into canvas carrying bags and heaved them onto his shoulder. There was other equipment that would have been useful—flashlights, rope, wire cutters, tools, C-4 plastic explosive wrapped in Mylar film—but the bag already weighed over forty pounds.

Behind him, some men had gathered by the door, watching him. They were dumbfounded by the arsenal of weapons they saw before them. "Help yourselves, fellas," Lance said in Russian. "What have the police ever done for you?"

79

Medvedev loved being at the president's Novo-Ogaryovo estate and reclined regally by the fire, sipping his expensive Bärenfang. It was a honey liquor based on a fifteenth-century recipe used by East Prussian and Lithuanian bear trappers.

He still remembered the first time he'd tasted it, decades earlier in Berlin. He'd been there to train East German secret police in a new class of interrogation techniques that, to this day, remained classified by the German government. Even then, he'd known Bärenfang would be his drink for life.

"Girl!" he cried out to the housemaid. "Bring me another!"

She came running into the library, almost spilling the golden liquid in her haste.

"Wait," he said when she made to leave.

She hesitated.

"Come to me," he said, patting his meaty lap with his hand. "Sit."

She looked at him, terrified, like a rabbit in the gaze of a wolf, then turned and fled.

Medvedev shook his head. She didn't know who he was. None of them did. He was just one more guest of the president here.

And they didn't fear him.

The president's estate was an eminently comfortable place, excellently appointed with all the amenities one would imagine. But it was deadeningly dull. Medvedev pulled his phone from his pocket and dialed Svetlana's number. If the president's staff wouldn't offer him diversion, he would have to bring in his own.

Svetlana answered on the first ring. She always did. "Sir?" she said apprehensively.

She'd thought she'd be rid of him for a few days. He'd noticed the look of relief on her face when he told her he'd be away. Now he was going to relish disabusing her of that illusion.

"Sveta," he said, using the familiar form of her name. It never failed to make her skin crawl. "I'm going to need you out at the estate after all."

"What's that, sir?"

"I need you to come to the estate."

"I'm not cleared, sir."

"I'll get you clearance, Sveta," he said, feeling a rush of pleasure as she digested his meaning.

"Very well, sir," she said after the briefest of pauses.

He picked up his glass and brought it to the window. Outside, a stork coasted over the lawn so elegantly it could have been a cloud, landing next to one of the frozen ponds. "Oh, and Sveta," he added, "I'll need you to pick up a few things on your way."

"Of course, sir."

"There's a man at the concierge desk at the department store. His name is Kuragin. Tell him I sent you." She knew the store well. He sent her there to pick things up regularly.

"What am I picking up, sir?"

"Oh, you'll see, my dear. You'll see," he said, running his tongue over his plump lips.

He hung up the phone and threw another log on the fire. He was content. Everything was going his way. Roth's assassin was still on the loose—he'd gotten the better of the forces sent out to Kapotnya to kill him—but there were limits to the threat one man could pose.

Medvedev knew that if he was safe anywhere, it was there, inside the president's personal estate. The compound was one of the most closely guarded sites on the planet, protected by a full infantry battalion of the Russian Army. In the event of an attack, they could call on the support of a new batch of Su-57 fighter jets that had just been transferred from the 929th Chkalov flight-test center in Akhtubinsk. The jets were capable of going up against any aircraft on earth, even the new American F-22 Raptors. Not only were they armed with an infrared search and track system that the F-22 lacked, but they also had a higher top speed.

Mikhail looked out the window. The estate grounds were well-tended, decorated with pools and ponds and countless statues, but in the winter, no amount of tending could stop the place from looking desolate and barren. There were some soldiers standing outside on the driveway, smoking cigarettes with one hand while the other remained in their coat pockets for warmth.

There was a humidor on the sideboard, and Medvedev opened it, helping himself to a generously proportioned Cohiba Robusto.

When he heard the sound of a throat being cleared behind him, he jumped to attention. "Mr President, sir," he said, hastily putting down the cigar.

"Mikhail," the president said, "I didn't mean to startle you."

"Not at all, sir," Medvedev said, doing up the top button of his shirt.

"I'll be brief," the president said. "I don't want to keep you from your cigar."

"You're not keeping me from anything, Mr President."

"I need to know how big of a problem we have."

"Problem, sir?"

"I was just notified that your man, Sergey Sergeyev, is dead."

Medvedev had been hoping to keep that fact from the president a little longer. What he needed now was for everyone in the Kremlin to hold their nerve. He was so close to his goal that he would tolerate no backpedaling. "Can I offer you a drink, sir?" he said, trying to buy some extra time.

"I only have a few moments, Mikhail."

Medvedev was severely lacking in almost all aspects of interpersonal relations, but there was one area he understood perfectly well, and that was power dynamics. It was what made him so valuable and so dangerous. He took a breath and reminded himself that his time was coming. He would not be the president's lapdog forever. He was so close to his goal that he could almost taste it. He just needed a little more time. "Sergeyev's death is nothing to worry about, sir."

"Wasn't he the one keeping the NSA Director in line?"

"We no longer have a use for Sandra Shrader, sir."

"Correct me if I'm wrong, Mikhail, but isn't she the one who provided the intel leading to the apartment in Kapotnya?"

Medvedev knew he needed to nip this in the bud. "The American assassin is a problem," he admitted.

"Lance Spector is more than a problem, Mikhail."

"I understand that, sir."

"Your name's next on his list, for God's sake."

"Yes, sir. It's likely that is so."

"I want him dead, Mikhail. And I want you out of my house."

Mikhail bowed his head ever so slightly. "Very good, sir."

The president left.

Mikhail picked up his cigar and put it in his mouth. He pictured the look on the president's face when he finally realized he'd been outplayed, outmaneuvered by his own hound, and without realizing, bit clear through the cigar.

80

L arissa sat in the back of the rental car and thought about what Tatyana had said to her on the phone. A secretary, young, pretty, dressed like a loyal communist schoolgirl from the seventies, complete with the short skirt and red scarf. Tatyana had said Roth wanted to focus on the convoy, but something told her that the secretary was the real key. Larissa knew she was right. She felt it in her bones.

Maybe you had to grow up as a girl in Russia to understand it, but something told her that if this secretary was anything like she was, she would be willing to risk her life to see her lecherous boss get his nuts chopped off.

It was more than a hunch. It was instinct.

And Larissa was determined to play her part in it. She wanted her pound of flesh. She wanted revenge. She was going to have nightmares for the rest of her life about the man she'd killed, the people she'd seen die before her eyes, and if there was one thing that would make her sleep easier, it would be knowing that the man behind all of it had paid for his crimes. She was tired of seeing those men getting away with everything. They'd taken over the country. They held the entire population hostage. It was time to make them suffer.

She spread herself across the back seat of the car. Outside, the snow fell on gas pumps and streetlamps and asphalt. They were still in the city's outskirts, the neighborhood where Lance had picked up the weapons from the apartment block, and they were waiting for a signal from Laurel.

Lance was in the front of the car, going over schematics of the presidential compound, and Larissa opened her window a crack and lit a cigarette.

The plan was to get into the compound undetected and take out the albino with a long-distance sniper shot. Larissa was no expert on the subject, but she understood there were several problems with the plan. For one thing, they didn't know for certain that the albino was inside the compound. Secondly, even if he was, there was no guarantee Lance would be able to find him. The compound covered hundreds of acres and multiple buildings, the largest of which was a presidential palace with dozens of rooms spread over three levels.

The entire compound was one of the most heavily guarded facilities in all of Russia, protected by every branch of the Russian military, as well as special sections of the intelligence service, the federal police, and the Moscow metro police force.

Lance didn't seem worried, but she knew his getting in and out alive was not a foregone conclusion.

Which was why they were waiting for the signal from Washington. Laurel and Tatyana were desperately trying to track down the secretary's location before Lance had to start executing his plan. They were using all the satellites and drones at their disposal, but Larissa was worried it would take too long. No one wanted Lance going into the compound unaided, and all three women were convinced that if they could just find the secretary, she'd be the key to coming up with a better option. For all his skills and bravado and willingness to take risk, Lance could never outmatch one young secretary who'd reached her limit and was ready to take revenge on her boss. That was what Larissa, Tatyana, and Laurel all understood.

It was Roth and Lance who'd required convincing.

There was a buzz on the phone.

"Is that them?" Larissa said eagerly. "Have they found her?" She knew that if they hadn't, the order would be for Lance to go in alone.

"It's them," Lance said.

"And?"

"Looks like they found her."

Relief flooded Larissa's body. "Thank God," she said.

"I just hope it's worth it."

"Believe me," she said. "This will be more than worth it. If I know this girl, all she needs is a gun, and she'd gladly put a bullet in her boss's skull for us."

"Remind me never to piss you off," Lance said, firing up the engine.

"Where is she?" Larissa said.

"I don't know yet," Lance said. They drove to a strip mall surrounded by apartment towers and pulled over. There were some payphones in the parking lot, and he stopped next to them. Then, he took a small metal box from the glovebox that looked like an external hard drive and got out of the car.

"Just find out where she is," Larissa said. "I'll take care of the rest. All I need is two minutes with her."

"We'll see," Lance said, walking over to the phone.

She watched him make the call. He unscrewed the cover of the handset and attached the metal box to it before dialing. While he was talking, he made no sign one way or the other, and she couldn't tell how the call was going.

As soon as he got back into the car, she said, "Well? What did they say?"

"Do you know the GUM department store on Red Square?"

"Know it?" Larissa said. "I practically live there."

"Well, the secretary entered that store less than ten minutes ago."

"We'd better hurry," Larissa said.

Lance drove very fast through the Moscow traffic. As they approached Red Square, and the facade of the store rose above them, he said, "That's one big department store."

Larissa shrugged. "It's not that big," she said. "If she's in there, I'll find her."

He pulled over by the front entrance and said, "I'll meet you back here. If you don't see me, leave and come back on the quarter-hour. I'll be here."

"All right," Larissa said.

"And don't forget, the entire city is looking for you."

She pulled her scarf from her purse and tied it the way he'd shown her. It made her feel like a grandmother, the way it covered her hair and came in around her face. She also had sunglasses and a coat they'd purchased with a faux-fur lined hood that provided additional coverage.

She pulled up the hood and stepped out of the car.

"Every fifteen minutes," Lance said. "On the quarter-hour."

81

L arissa was so familiar with the GUM State Department Store—she shopped there all the time—that entering it now was a jarring reminder of a life she'd thought she'd left behind forever.

During the Soviet era, those stores had been an institution. There was one in every city, and she remembered them clearly from her childhood, not that she'd been able to buy anything back then. In those days, they were a place where only the political elites and party members could go. A place where, no matter how bad the Soviet economy got, all the luxuries of the West were on full display. Politicians' wives went there for whatever they wanted—the finest caviars, the rarest vodkas, and plushest furs. Meanwhile, ordinary people, like Larissa and her mother, lined up for hours outside shortage-ridden state dispensaries for the most basic of necessities.

That was why the store meant so much to her and why she frequented it now so regularly, despite the prices. It was a symbol to her of everything she'd overcome, or thought she'd overcome.

The one she was entering now, just off Red Square and

facing the Kremlin, was the most opulent of them all. Located at the very heart of Moscow, it was perhaps the most famous store in all of Russia. It was housed in a fabulous building, and it glowed now with the light of a thousand crystal chandeliers. Its facade extended eight hundred feet along the east side of Red Square, and the most prestigious architects of Tsarist Russia had contributed to its renowned glass-roofed gallery. Before the revolution, it had been a favorite of the Tsarina and her court, and by the time the Bolsheviks executed her in 1918, it held over twelve hundred stores, rivaling the finest anywhere in Europe.

Larissa knew all this and never forgot it when she entered the store's breathtaking foyer. To her, it was more than just a store, it was a part of Russia's history, an emblem of what her country had been, what it later became, and what it might yet be again.

She peered down the long aisle of the store's grand hall and tried to guess where she would go if she'd been sent there by a boss. At the far end of the gallery was an extensive lingerie department with all of the most intricate and expensive designs imaginable. She knew it well and figured it was a good place to start her search.

She hurried up to the second floor and, as she approached the lingerie department, noticed something red out of the corner of her eye. Without realizing what it was, it caught her attention. Then she saw that it was the red scarf of the Young Pioneers. The woman wearing it was young, with a kind face, and the look on that face was one of pure terror.

It was her, the secretary. There was zero doubt in Larissa's mind.

She didn't enter the lingerie department as Larissa had expected but walked up to an anonymous-looking door just off the main hallway. Larissa had never noticed the door before, and it appeared to be made of solid brass with black leather trim. Other than a small brass button next to it, it had no mark-ings or instructions of any kind.

The secretary pressed the button and waited. Larissa watched from behind a pillar on the gallery. After a brief wait, there was a buzzing sound, and the secretary pushed with her entire weight against the door, which slid open on its heavy hinges like the entrance to a stone ruin.

Larissa stayed where she was, watching the door, and when the secretary returned, it was plain from her face that she'd been crying. She made her way to the women's restroom, and Larissa followed.

The woman entered one of the stalls, and Larissa entered the one next to her. On the other side of a thin slab of marble, she could hear sobbing. Then she heard the woman speaking into her phone.

"I picked up the package," she said. There was a pause, the sound of a package being opened, then, "Devices, sir. Toys. All sorts of toys." Another pause, and then, "No, I'd like to. For you. I hope they don't hurt too badly."

The woman hung up and burst into tears. Larissa left the stall and locked the main door of the restroom from the inside so that they couldn't be disturbed. When the secretary came out of her stall, she saw Larissa standing in front of the door.

"Don't be alarmed," Larissa said, sensing that that was exactly what the secretary was going to be. "I'm a friend."

"What is this?" the secretary said. "Let me out."

Larissa remained where she was. She felt she could handle this situation, handle this woman. She knew her better than she knew herself. She knew how scared she was. She knew the powerlessness she felt. The hopelessness. But most of all, she knew the rage. "I'm going to help you to get even," she said.

"What are you talking about?" the secretary said, glancing around the room for another means of escape.

"There's no one here but us," Larissa said.

"Who are you?"

"My name is Larissa Chipovskaya. Up until a couple of days ago, I was a dancer at a gentleman's club close to the Lubyanka."

"I don't know what you're talking about," the woman said.

"I know what kind of man your boss is."

The woman looked petrified. "We can't talk about this," she hissed, keeping her voice barely above a whisper. "We can't talk about my boss."

"He can't hear us here," Larissa said, "and what I have to tell you will only take a few seconds."

The woman tried to shove her way to the door, but Larissa blocked her.

"Let me out," she said. "Please. I'm going to be in trouble."

"Your boss has gone too far."

The woman's eyes darted around the room desperately, like a cornered animal.

Larissa knew she didn't have much time. "He's under surveillance right now," she said. "We're going to strike. We're going to make him pay for the things he's done."

"That's a lie," the woman said. "No one can make him pay."

"He's with the president as we speak," Larissa said. "Is that a lie? He travels back and forth between the Lubyanka and the president's estate in a cavalcade and enters the Lubyanka through a tunnel. Is that a lie?"

"How do you know all this?"

"The Americans want to take him out."

The secretary's eyes widened in fear. She shook her head. "You're lying to me. This is a trap. I don't want anything to do with this. I'm a loyal servant—"

"It's not a trap," Larissa said. "It's real. It's happening now."

"What are you talking about?"

"They're coming for him."

"He's above the law."

"It's not the law that's coming."

"I can't be here," she said, her voice growing frantic. "Please let me pass. I have to get back to him."

"An assassin," Larissa said, knowing she was taking a risk now, laying out all her cards. She had an instinct for this woman, but she was beginning to feel doubt. "An American assassin is going to kill him."

The secretary shook her head. "Why are you telling me all this? I don't want to know. I don't want any part of it."

"Because we need your help. We can't do it without you. We can't get close enough."

"I can't help you with this."

"I know you," Larissa said. "I know what it's like to be in your shoes. I've been there, believe me."

"You have no idea who I am."

"I know you want a chance to do something to this man, to get even with him, to taste revenge."

"He said he'd kill my entire family," the secretary said, her voice cracking under the strain of the emotion. "He said he'd kill everyone."

"Not if we kill him first," Larissa said.

The woman shook her head. "I can't," she mouthed silently. "I just can't. I can't."

"Yes, you can," Larissa said. "You can fight back. *We* can fight back. Now is our only chance."

She kept shaking her head. She was so terrified she couldn't even speak. Larissa stepped forward and took the package from her. Inside were the most depraved and outrageous sex toys she'd ever seen. They were made of sharp-cut steel and looked like they'd been designed more for pain than pleasure.

"This is *your* chance," Larissa said. "You want to get even. You *need* to get even. I know you do."

The secretary said nothing. Larissa tried to read her face but couldn't tell what she was going to do, which way she was going to go. There was a moment's silence, then she made to speak but stopped herself.

"Please," Larissa said, her own voice barely above a whisper either. "We can't do this without you."

When the secretary finally spoke, her voice was so quiet that Larissa had to lean in closer to hear her. "There are cameras," she said.

"There are what?"

"Cameras. He has them everywhere. He watches me. He's always watching me. Even in the bath, even when I'm asleep, he's watching."

"He's not watching here," Larissa said. "I have a car waiting outside. A driver. He'll keep us safe. We can get you away from here."

"What about my family?"

"They'll only be safe when your boss is dead. Believe me."

The secretary nodded. It seemed she agreed with that much. "This is real?" she said.

"This is it," Larissa said. "This is your one chance to break free. Your one chance to show that you're more than a plaything for him. More than a toy. Are you ready?"

The secretary nodded ever so slightly. Tears ran down her face. She reached up and wiped them away with the edge of the red scarf. Then she took the scarf off and threw it on the floor.

82

L ance drove. Larissa sat in the back with the secretary.
"Svetlana Tolkalina," she said when Larissa asked
her name.

She was the personal secretary of a seven-foot-tall albino
man named Mikhail Medvedev, who did not work for the FSB,
but maintained an office on the top floor of the Lubyanka
because of the security afforded by its tunnel access route.

"Who does he work for?" Lance said.

"I don't know that he works for anyone," Svetlana said. "All I
can say is he reports directly to the president."

"What about the Dead Hand?" Lance said.

Svetlana nodded. "Yes, I've heard talk of it."

"And he's at the presidential compound at Novo-Ogaryovo?"

"He relocated there after the bombings."

"Which he orchestrated," Lance said.

Svetlana nodded.

"Including the attack in Beijing?" Lance said.

She nodded again. She seemed ashamed for her part in it.

"It wasn't your fault," Larissa said to her, putting a hand on
her leg.

"I'll have to answer for it," Svetlana said.

"How can we get to him?" Lance said.

"You'll have to get into the compound."

Lance nodded. That was what he'd expected, although it was easier said than done. The entire estate was surrounded by a twenty-foot-high wall equipped with motion detectors and cameras. In the ground were highly sensitive tremor sensors, and the airspace above was monitored by a sophisticated, high-definition, localized radar system. If you fired a rocket from outside the compound, it would be intercepted and shot down before reaching its target. There were even stories of birds being shot down.

"I can help," Svetlana said.

Lance looked at her in the rearview mirror. They were headed out of the city on one of the main arteries, and traffic was backed up. "Come again?" he said.

"Medvedev obtained clearance for me to get into the compound. He wants me to come spend the night."

"When's he expecting you?"

"In a few hours."

"How were you supposed to be getting there?"

"He was to send a car."

"To your home?"

She nodded.

"Where do you live?"

She told him, and a chorus of car horns accompanied Lance's sudden u-turn. "Before we go any further," Lance said, "I need to know you're certain you want to do this."

"Do what?"

"Help us."

Svetlana looked at Larissa. Larissa was nodding her head in encouragement. "I think so," Svetlana said.

"You *think* so?" Lance said.

"Will it be dangerous?"

Lance looked over his shoulder at the two of them. He pulled the car over and stopped, then turned to face them again. "Will it be *dangerous*?" he said.

Larissa jumped in. "She didn't mean that, Lance. She knows what she's getting into."

"Ladies," Lance said, "let's be under no illusions. What we're considering is breaking into one of the most closely guarded facilities on the face of the planet, the private residence of the President of Russia, protected by specialized divisions of every major military and intelligence organization in the country."

"We understand that," Larissa said.

"We're going to break in, and then we're going to kill a man who appears for all intents and purposes to be one of his most senior and trusted advisors."

They both nodded.

"You'd be hard-pressed to come up with something more dangerous than what we're about to do."

"I understand what you intend to do," Svetlana said.

"The chances of us all getting in and out alive...." Lance said.

"We know," Larissa said.

"Svetlana, if you agree to help us get into this compound, there's a very real risk it'll be the last thing you ever do."

Svetlana turned to Larissa.

"You too, Larissa," Lance said. "Nothing about this is guaranteed."

"I made up my mind a long time ago," Larissa said.

"Are you ready to die for this?" Lance said.

"I'm willing to risk my life," she said.

"I am too," Svetlana said.

"You're both certain?"

"You don't know the things I've been through with this man," Svetlana said. "You couldn't imagine them. But if you could, you'd understand that I'm willing to die to bring down Mikhail Medvedev."

Lance nodded. He knew the risk they were taking. The chance was all too real that it would cost someone their life. He didn't want to sugarcoat it. He pulled the car back into the street, and they made their way toward Svetlana's apartment.

"There's only one way into this compound that won't set off the alarms," Lance said. "The front gate."

Svetlana nodded. "And I can get us right through it."

83

Svetlana went into her apartment to get ready as if she was still planning to meet with Medvedev. She showered, shaved her legs, and put on her lingerie and makeup exactly as she would normally have.

Lance and Larissa were seated outside in the car, waiting. "If something happens to me in the compound," he said, "you have to get her out of the country with you."

Larissa nodded.

"We don't hang people out to dry," Lance said.

"I understand," she said, "but nothing's going to happen to you."

"You'll have to show her how to dye her hair and adjust her eyebrows, the way I showed you."

"I will."

"The makeup, the lips."

"I remember," Larissa said. "The scarves, the sunglasses. I've got it."

"Get a train to another major city. Lie low for a few days in a hotel room. Don't take any risks."

"It's not going to come to that," Larissa said.

Lance had already made false passports for himself and Larissa, and he went to the trunk of the car and got a false Russian identification card that had been prepared by the CIA. It was an older style document, and he wrote in Svetlana's height, eye color, and date of birth on it. It didn't have a photo and couldn't be used to board aircraft, but it would do at some of the less sophisticated land borders.

"No airports," he said, handing it to Larissa.

She nodded and put the card in her coat pocket with the false passport Lance had already given her. Then she opened her window a crack and lit a cigarette. He could tell she was nervous, and it didn't surprise him. The plan was to wait for Svetlana's ride, kill the driver, and then for Lance to take his place. That would get him inside the compound.

It meant leaving Larissa behind somewhere at a nearby hotel. She'd wait for them there, and if everything went according to plan, Lance and Svetlana would come back safely and meet her there. Then they'd get out of the country together.

If Lance and Svetlana weren't back after twelve hours, for any reason, she was to leave without them and get to the US herself. She'd find her sister there.

It wasn't the best-laid plan by any stretch, but they didn't have time to come up with something better, and Lance was adamant they didn't miss this opportunity. He intended to dress in the chauffeur's uniform, drop Svetlana at the mansion, and then remain in the compound. At some point, someone would wonder about the car and its driver, but he would be done by then. If he could kill Medvedev without implicating Svetlana, then she'd be shuttled out of the compound in the ensuing chaos. No one would suspect her involvement. They'd think she was just in the wrong place at the wrong time.

She'd get back to Larissa, and then, regardless of what happened to Lance, at least they'd have each other.

A black town car pulled up to Svetlana's building, and a uniformed driver got out and buzzed the door.

"Are you seeing what I'm seeing?" Larissa said. They were about a hundred yards from Larissa's building, but in the light from the doorway, there was no mistaking it. Svetlana's driver was a woman. "There's no way you're going to fit in that uniform," Larissa said.

Lance nodded. He got out of the car and walked up to the building. He hadn't expected a woman. He'd intended to kill the driver, but when he reached her, he said, "Stay calm. No one's getting hurt."

"I'm just a driver," the woman said, seeing his gun and raising her hands.

"Put down your hands. Get in the car."

She did as he said, and he got into the backseat next to her. Larissa got into the driver's seat.

When Svetlana came down, she was dressed to the nines in a black sequined gown, heels, and a provocative pair of fishnet stockings. She was surprised to see Larissa in the driver's seat and even more surprised to see Lance and the driver in the back.

Lance handed the gun to Larissa. "Everyone wait here," he said. "I've got to get the other car."

"Can't we use this one?" Larissa said.

It was a nice car, a black sedan like the BMW he'd rented, but he needed the seven-series for a particular reason. He went to get it and pulled it up next to the town car. When he rejoined them, the three women were sitting in the car, looking at each other in silence.

Larissa and the chauffeur got into the back of the rental, Svetlana sat up front, and Lance drove. He pulled out of the parking lot and headed toward the highway for Novo-Ogaryovo.

Svetlana looked across at him. She looked a lot more sophisticated in the new makeup and clothing—more dangerous. "I thought the plan was to kill the driver," she said.

"We're not killing the driver," Lance said.

"Because she's a woman?"

Lance shook his head.

He got off the highway at Odintsovsky, the closest exit to the presidential estate, and found a motel. Larissa checked in while he brought the car to the room, backing up as close to the door as possible. Then they brought the driver into the room and sat her on the bed.

"Do you know the man you work for?" Lance said to her. He had a gun in his hand, and she was so terrified it was all she could do not to burst out crying.

She nodded her head. "I know the secretary too," she said.

"I'm going to pretend you didn't say that."

She looked at the ground.

"I'm going to drug you," Lance said. "Then we're going to tie you to the bed. This will all be over when you wake up."

Lance had some oral tranquilizers in his bag, and he gave them to her with a glass of water. "Take these," he said. He watched her swallow the pills, then left the three women in the room to remove her uniform.

When he came back, the driver was out cold. He secured her to the bed, put a blanket over her, and shut all the blinds.

Larissa was in the bathroom, and when she came out, she was wearing the driver's uniform.

Lance arched an eyebrow. "It suits you."

"Shut up," she said.

He went out to the car and fully reclined the back seat. The car had a special executive package that allowed the back seat on the passenger side to recline fully, like the first-class seat on an airliner. He knew from experience that it was possible to modify the seat to create a compartment beneath. It was large enough that a person could hide in it. He loaded the M82 sniper rifle and some other weapons into the compartment, then slid a plastic tube through a gap in the seat to allow for air.

He showed the compartment to the girls and told Svetlana she'd have to play the diva. "Just lay back like you're used to the good life," he said. "The guards will take one look at you and think—"

"That I'm a whore," she said.

Lance looked at her awkwardly.

"Don't worry about it," she said. "It's basically what I am."

"Not after tonight," Larissa said.

He showed them how to set up the back seat, creating a hidden airtight compartment.

"Don't use a blanket," he said to Svetlana, "and whatever you do, don't block that tube. I'll be breathing through it."

He climbed into the compartment and curled himself into a tight ball.

"Everything okay?" Larissa said.

"Yup," he said.

Larissa put the air tube in his mouth and then sealed the compartment shut.

Lance couldn't see a thing. Other than the engine, he couldn't hear anything either.

There was a lot that could go wrong. If the guards knew the chauffeur or recognized that the car had been switched, they were in trouble. If the guard dogs realized someone was hidden in the seat, they were in trouble. If the air tube got blocked, or he was discovered for any reason, he was dead. But there was no other way of getting into the compound without setting off the alarm. And he knew that if there was even the slightest hint that someone was coming for Medvedev, the Russians would have him evacuated before Lance got anywhere near him.

He felt the car begin to move and waited. It was fifteen minutes to the compound, and his only clue as to the vehicle's progress was the motion.

When the car stopped, he knew they were at the first security checkpoint.

Svetlana was reclined above him, looking like a good-time girl, used to the high life. She was expected. Medvedev himself had sent a car for her. Her name was on their list. Getting past shouldn't create any difficulty.

Larissa wasn't the chauffeur Medvedev had sent, but she looked the part. She could pass for the driver at a casual glance. The guards likely wouldn't notice the difference.

He knew they were doing a security pass on the vehicle. Running mirrors along the undercarriage, letting their dogs get a good sniff.

A minute passed.

Then another.

It was excruciating.

Lance had told Svetlana to lay back as if she was trying to sleep but not to cover herself with a blanket. She couldn't look like she was trying to conceal anything.

After what felt like a very long time, the car began to move again.

He'd gone over the satellite photos of the compound with Larissa, and they'd agreed beforehand on the best place for her to let him out. There was a second security checkpoint closer to the presidential palace, but the driveway between the two wasn't particularly well lit.

It provided an opportunity for him to slip out of the vehicle undetected.

The car was moving along the driveway when Svetlana slid across her seat and released the clamp that sealed Lance's compartment.

"We're in," she said, opening it up.

Larissa was driving as slowly as she could without arousing suspicion, and Lance didn't waste any time pulling his canvas bag out of the compartment and rolling out of the car onto the driveway.

Svetlana pulled the door shut behind him, and the car kept moving seamlessly. Lance crawled through the snow-covered lawn to a landscaped area filled with sparse shrubs and topiary that had been covered with burlap netting for the winter. In the bright moonlight, he welcomed the extra cover. There were sensors throughout the grounds, and if he tripped one, he'd be lit up like a firecracker.

He moved through the shrubs to a stand of trees. From that position, he could see the entire east wing of the palace, the part of the building most likely to house a guest.

He opened the canvas bag and removed the rifle, scope, and bipod. Lying on the ground, he focused on the second-floor windows of the building and began his watch.

vetlana gave Larissa one final, wistful look before stepping out of the car and making her way toward the mansion. She was at the visitor entrance on the east wing and had to climb a set of steps to get to the door. Soldiers in the livery of the president's Elite Guard stood at the sides of the steps, their eyes staring directly ahead as if they hadn't noticed her. Beneath their ceremonial helmets and luxurious, fur-lined coats, she saw that they were wearing the full Kevlar armor of a modern tactical unit.

Just inside the entrance was a fully-equipped security checkpoint, like at an airport, with metal detectors and an x-ray scanner. She put her purse on the conveyor belt for the scanner, aware that the soldiers would see the full outlines of the metal sex toys Medvedev had ordered.

She put her phone and watch in a tray, and the guards placed them in a plastic envelope and gave her a token to pick them up on her way out.

She walked through the metal detector and a full x-ray scanner and was thoroughly patted down by a fresh-faced soldier before being issued a visitor's lanyard. Outside, Larissa drove back down the long driveway on her way out of the compound.

Svetlana took a deep breath. It had worked. She was in. And she suddenly felt very alone.

As she entered a grand hallway, its floor decorated in an intricate nineteenth-century parquet pattern and the walls ornately carved in marble, she was painfully aware that she was entering a place where the ordinary laws of society did not apply. No one would be answerable here. Anything could happen. The men in this place operated with impunity, and if things started to go badly, there would be no one to turn to.

The guards standing by the walls were as motionless as statues. Not a hair moved on their heads, their eyes were as still as corpses, but somehow, she knew they were all watching her. A shiver ran down her spine.

She looked down the long hallway, its magnificent marble pillars stretching three floors up to a domed roof inlaid in gold, and realized she had no idea where she was going.

She glanced at the guards. They offered no clues.

She kept walking toward the enormous round window at the far end of the hall, the only sound the click of her heels on the parquet. The chandeliers above were supplemented with candelabras that made the shadows around her move like ghouls. She looked back at the guards at the security post, then ahead at the round window, and felt like she was making a journey that could only be one way.

And then, from a massive wooden door at the end of the hallway, Medvedev emerged. He was wearing a black silk gown that was strangely feminine, something a geisha might wear, and silk slippers with the president's seal sewn into them in gold thread. In his hand was a long leather bullwhip, something that looked truly depraved, and on his face was the most lascivious smile Svetlana had ever seen. A sickening feeling came over her as she began to realize what was in store for her.

"I've been waiting for you, my dear," he said.

She felt a knot form in her throat that prevented her from responding.

"Did you bring the toys?" he said.

Her stomach turned as she nodded.

"Then don't be shy," he said, ushering her through the doorway. "Come along. Everything's ready."

She walked through the door, her skin crawling as she passed him, and found herself in another grand hallway. While the last one had been lined with heavy wooden doors, the rooms off this one were open, and she could see into them. They walked past antique statues, and she saw into a magnificent library, its leather-bound tomes lit by a chandelier that must have been the size of a small car.

"I have a very well-appointed suite," Medvedev said, scuttling ahead of her in his slippers and gown like some strange, dressed-up crab.

Svetlana was terrified. She'd been through a lot with Medvedev, things she'd never have imagined she'd allow to happen. He'd violated her in ways she wouldn't have believed possible. But she already knew this was going to be different. It was going to be worse.

She'd heard of men who fantasized about death, who craved the moment when life left the body of a woman. She knew Medvedev took pleasure from her suffering. The more she feared him, and the more terrified she became, the greater his excitement grew. But up until this point, he'd never crossed the line into actual torture.

Something told her that was about to change.

As they arrived at the door to his suite, carved in mahogany with the presidential seal embossed at its center, her heart pounded in her chest. She realized she was entering a room she might never come back out of.

"After you," he said, standing behind her.

Other than the guards and Medvedev himself, she hadn't seen a single soul in the palace. She wondered if anyone else was there. Any women? The president?

She wondered if Medvedev would be permitted to kill her in a place like this?

"I…" she stammered, her voice catching in her throat.

"You?" Medvedev said playfully, shutting the door behind him.

She began to cry. It wasn't an act. It was a spontaneous outpouring, like the tears of a child. "I want to go home," she said quietly through her tears.

Medvedev laughed, a hearty, fulsome sound that came from the depths of his enormous chest as if from a barrel. "Don't be stupid, my dear. You just got here."

"No," she said, shaking her head. She realized she was about to put everything at risk, to jeopardize the mission. Lance was inside the compound, relying on her to play her part. But she couldn't go through with it. Her body rebelled. It refused to comply.

She turned around and faced Medvedev.

"It's too late to change your mind," he said. "You're a fly in a web. A rat in a cage. There's no escape."

She didn't know what to do. She wasn't thinking clearly. Her mind went blank, her vision dimmed, and the only thing she was aware of was the set of doors at the far side of the bed.

Acting purely on instinct, she ran for them. She had to climb across the enormous bed, past the flames of a stone fireplace, and without knowing if Medvedev was behind her or not, she grasped the brass handles on the doors and pulled them open.

They led to a curved staircase, and she fled up the steps, not knowing where they led.

Behind her, she could hear Medvedev down in the room, still laughing. "You can't get away from me here," he roared.

Svetlana kept fleeing. At the top of the stairway was another door leading to yet another hallway. She ran past door after door, all identical, all with the same seal carved into the paneling. At the end of the corridor were two palace guards, standing in front of draped Russian flags, and as they watched her run toward them, they remained as motionless as stone.

Svetlana lost her shoes. She dropped her bag. She was running, stumbling, and when she looked back, she saw Medvedev's hulk emerge from the stairway. He was lumbering after her with surprising speed, like a freight train gaining momentum, and she realized there was nowhere for her to run.

As the end of the hallway bore down on her, the two guards stepped forward to stop her from reaching the enormous, gold-plated doors.

"Help me!" she screamed as she approached them. "Help me!"

In her final steps, she fell to the floor in front of them and slid forward. They grabbed her, their cold, lifeless faces showing not the slightest hint of emotion.

"Help me!" she cried again. "He's going to kill me!"

The guards pulled her to her feet. Their fingers gripped into her flesh. Their hands were as cold as ice. She already knew they were going to hand her back to Medvedev.

"Give her to me," Medvedev barked at them, breathless from the pursuit. "She's mine."

"No!" Svetlana cried. "You can't!"

The guards brought her toward him. She struggled in their grip, pounding her fists against them, but it was as if they didn't feel her punches and didn't hear her pleas.

Medvedev reached out and grabbed her by the hair, yanking her toward him. She hit his chest and fell to the ground.

"You're going to pay for this," he snarled.

And then, as if by a miracle, light flooded into the corridor.

Svetlana turned. Behind the guards, the gold doors drew

slowly open like the gates of a castle. As her eyes adjusted to the light, she made out the silhouette of a short, muscular figure. He seemed to be holding a crystal tumbler in one hand and a cigar in the other, and his arms were slightly outstretched.

His build was stocky, but his pose, the light behind him, and the way the guards bowed their heads gave him an aura that bordered on the messianic.

Svetlana knew immediately it was the president himself, Vladimir Molotov, in all his glory.

"What is the meaning of this?" he said, his voice neither quiet nor loud.

"Mr President," Medvedev started but then stopped.

The president took one look at him, at Svetlana on the ground by his feet, and said, "Medvedev, you are a guest. You were not brought here for this debauchery. You were brought to wait. Your presence is tolerated, but not for very much longer."

Svetlana looked from the president back to Medvedev. She didn't understand what was happening. And then, as suddenly as he'd appeared, the president retreated to his room and the doors shut. Medvedev was humiliated. He looked furious as he turned, marching back in the direction he'd come from empty-handed. Svetlana, it seemed, had escaped his clutches. For now.

The guards pulled her to her feet and began walking her down the hallway. "Not a word of what you saw here tonight," one of them said as they handed her over to the guards on the lower level. "What happens in the palace, stays in the palace, understood?"

85

L ance watched through his scope as two guards escorted Svetlana out of the palace. He could see she'd been crying but, apart from that, appeared to be unharmed. A military vehicle pulled up, and she climbed into the back. He watched as it brought her all the way to the main security gate and out of the compound. That was good. If she'd figured out a way of getting herself ejected from the compound, it was one less thing for him to worry about. For now, she was out of harm's way.

Larissa had left in the car earlier too, which meant Lance was the only one of them still inside the compound. That meant that if for some reason, he couldn't make it out, Larissa and Svetlana would at least have each other. With the identification papers and cash he'd given them, their chances of getting out of the country alive were about as good as he could have hoped.

Svetlana had exited from the east wing of the building, and Lance scanned it, searching for a sign of Medvedev's presence. From the schematics, he knew that was where the guest suites were located, but from the distance he was at, he couldn't see anything. He needed to get closer.

He slung the strap of the rifle over his shoulder and began making his way closer to the palace. It was dark, and he had to proceed with extreme caution. The entire area was under heavy surveillance, and his heat signature would show up under even the most cursory scan.

He reached a stone-tiled patio that contained a long swimming pool. The pool had been emptied for the winter and was covered with a canvas tarp. Beyond it was a gravel path that went the whole way around the palace. Apart from some sparse shrubs and a few lawn ornaments, there was nothing else between him and the palace's exterior wall.

He checked his ammunition and silencers and took a few final items from the canvas bag.

If he got much closer to the palace, his movements were likely to trigger a motion sensor that would flood the area with light from high-powered floodlights attached to the roof. The sensors weren't perfect. He'd read reports of them being tripped so frequently by critters, or an errant security guard, that they were often turned off.

That wasn't a chance he could afford to take, though.

A steel case on the roof contained the electronics for the security system. It was located on the southeast corner of the palace and measured about two feet by four feet. Lance could see it from his position and knew it was one of four such boxes required to keep the security system operational. Taking it out would alert the guards that they had an intruder. That would, in turn, cause the evacuation protocol to be initiated and would leave Lance with mere minutes before helicopters full of soldiers began landing on the lawn.

But it would also leave the security forces blind while the system went through its reboot cycle. That gave him about five minutes with the sensors and cameras offline.

He lay down on the stone patio and set up the M82 for a shot. It was the right tool for the job—a long-range anti-materiel gun with a five-inch, .50 caliber slug. It was loaded with the silver-tipped, armor-piercing incendiary rounds, and Lance aimed carefully, then exhaled as he pulled the trigger. It was a simple shot, and the sound rang out so loudly that every man, woman, and child within five miles would have heard it.

The floodlights came on with an audible snap as power surged through the electrical system. They bathed the entire compound in so much light that the grounds were brighter than they would have been in full daylight.

Lance remained on the ground, motionless. He heard barking dogs in the direction of the main gate, and from a tower above the palace came the high-pitched wail of a manually activated air raid alarm. Somewhere close by, military forces were being mustered, including evacuation helicopters for the president and his guests, and air superiority aircraft to fight back any potential aerial assault.

Every single guard in the compound now knew they had a breach, but until the sensors rebooted, they would have no idea where it was coming from.

Lance counted to ten, then, leaving the heavy sniper rifle where it was, took rope, a grappling hook, and the silenced handguns and made a mad dash for the east wing palace wall. Once there, he swung the grappling hook at the second-story window ledge. The first try missed, and as he swung for a second time, the glass in a nearby window shattered, and a hail of bullets narrowly missed him. Lance turned and put two bullets in the head of the guard who'd fired them.

Then he swung the grappling hook, and this time it caught the ledge. He climbed the rope to the second floor and broke the window with his elbow before climbing into the building. Once inside, he found himself in a long corridor lined with thick mahogany doors, each bearing the seal of the Russian president. To his left, two guards were running toward him, and to his right, at the far end of the corridor, he saw the gold inlaid doors that led to the presidential suite. Between him and the suite, another pair of guards was preparing to open fire.

Lance dove to the floor and rolled, dodging multiple bullets. He fired twice, and the two guards to his left fell to the ground. In front of him was a set of wooden doors, and he crashed through them, finding himself in what appeared to be an enormous dressing room. Black leather shoes, suit jackets, shirts, and ties filled the shelves. Countless mirrors lined the walls, and they crashed and collapsed as gunfire from the corridor followed him into the room.

He ducked behind a thick wooden bench as bullets flew everywhere, sending shards of glass and splinters of wood in all directions. From behind the bench, he returned fire, killing another guard as he tried to enter the room. The last guard threw a smoke grenade through the doors. It arched in the air, leaving a trail of gas, before landing on the floor at Lance's feet.

He held his breath and ran for the door, taking quick aim at the last guard as he entered his field of view. Within minutes, the entire corridor would be overrun with fresh soldiers, but for now, apart from the men he'd killed, it was empty.

He looked up and down. The corridor was enormous. There were dozens of doors leading to rooms, staircases, and more corridors. There was no way he was going to find Medvedev in time.

There was only one chance.

He needed leverage.

He made a dash for the presidential suite and threw himself against the enormous golden doors. They burst open, and Lance crashed into a room built entirely of marble. Ahead of him was an enormous fireplace, a log fire raging in the hearth, and all around were the treasures of the Tsars, plundered and kept hidden by generations of Russian oligarchs.

A man stood by the fire, and when Lance looked at him, he realized it was the president. In his hand, pointed at Lance, was a gun that glimmered as if made of silver.

In Lance's hand was a gun of his own, pointed at the president.

On the president's face was a strangely contented smile, almost like he was glad of the intrusion. "What have we got here?" he said.

"Tell me where Medvedev is, and I won't kill you," Lance said.

The president let out a mirthless laugh. "Maybe if you weren't flat on your face, I'd be more worried."

"Oh, you should be very worried," Lance said, getting to his feet. He scanned the room. They were at the corner of the building with windows facing west and south. He was rapidly running out of time, but he needed to know where Medvedev was before he left the room. Not for a second did it cross his mind to actually kill the president. That was against the rules, unwritten though they were.

Those rules were so deeply ingrained on both sides that they would not be set aside, even in a situation like this.

The Russian president was no friend of America. He'd been a thorn in the side of US leadership for decades. He'd exceeded his term limits, refused to relinquish power, amassed one of the largest private fortunes on the planet, rearmed the Russian military, and strangled domestic opposition with a brutality not seen since the Cold War. And yet, every CIA asset ever to step off the Farm knew not to even think about taking his life.

That rule wasn't just some holdover from a bygone era of statesmanship and etiquette. It wasn't a misplaced belief in some international moral code. It was an amoral calculation of self-preservation, rooted in the very bedrock of modern *realpolitik*. The cold, hard fact of the matter was that the Russian president's finger rested on a button capable of ending life on the planet. That was the final deterrent. You did not kill a man with that much power, no matter how much you wanted to. There was simply too much uncertainty. For one thing, a failed attempt could trigger a nuclear response from Molotov. If he knew the CIA was targeting him personally, then what incentive did he have to preserve the peace? But even if an assassination attempt succeeded, there was no telling what it would lead to. There were known dead hand provisions that dictated the Russian military respond aggressively to an attack on Molotov. And beyond those provisions, there was the uncertainty as to who would step into his shoes if he was killed. Who would succeed him? And what temperament would that man have, knowing that his predecessor had been taken out by an assassin?

There was simply no scenario in which the American military could foresee an advantage in taking out a sitting Russian president.

"You're Roth's man, aren't you?" the president said. "Spector something."

"Lance Spector," Lance said.

"Lance Spector," the president repeated, stepping forward. His gun was stretched out in front of him, his finger caressing the trigger.

Lance backed away so that he couldn't be seen from the hallway or through the windows, his gun trained on the space between the president's two calculating eyes.

"Surely, you must know that killing Medvedev will make no difference to anyone in the grand scheme of things," the president said. "It won't bring back the lives that were lost in the embassy bombings. It won't undo the cataclysmic blow to your country's prestige."

"This isn't about my country's prestige," Lance said.

"Sure it is," the president said. "Everything boils down to prestige, sooner or later."

"This is personal," Lance said.

The president nodded. "Of course. I almost forgot. That's *your* face on all the news channels, isn't it? You're the one they're pinning all this on."

"As long as Medvedev's in a coffin, I'll be able to sleep at night."

"You tell yourself that," the president said sarcastically. Soldiers in the corridor were gathering by the door, but they held back from entering the room out of fear of causing the president's death.

"Tell them to stand down," Lance said.

"They won't stand down."

"Then tell them to bring Medvedev."

"You know I can't do that."

"I'll pull this trigger if you don't," Lance said.

"You shoot, I shoot," the president said.

Lance glanced around the room. "I'm going to go out on a limb here and say you've got more to lose from this exchange than I do."

The president couldn't argue with that. "Your orders preclude you from killing a man like me," he said.

"Fuck my orders," Lance said. "You tell your men to bring Medvedev right now, or you're a dead man. I'm done worrying about the consequences."

For the first time, a flicker of doubt crossed the president's eyes.

"Do it," Lance said.

"You won't kill me," the president said. "You're a dog, and a dog obeys its master."

"If you've read the reports on me," Lance said, "then you already know how well I obey my master."

The president stared at him, his beady eyes calculating the permutations, assessing the odds. They reminded Lance of the eyes of a crow.

"How much longer are you willing to risk your life for Medvedev?" Lance said.

Another moment passed, the president's gaze darting from Lance's gun to his eyes and back again. Then the tension seemed to leave the president's body. He lowered his weapon a fraction of an inch. His finger moved from the trigger. "This doesn't have to happen today," he said.

Lance smiled. "It's happening today."

The president shrugged. "It took ten years to track down Osama bin Laden."

"I'm not coming back to finish this job in ten years. We do it today."

The president knew it was over.

"Come on," Lance said. "You're not having a shootout with me. Give me what I came for."

The president shook his head. He turned to the corridor. "Bring Medvedev," he called out. "Bring him now."

Lance nodded. "Was that so difficult?"

"Not so difficult," the president admitted, "but a shame, nonetheless."

Lance kept an eye on the corridor, the windows, and the ceiling. Every second that passed brought them a second closer to the moment the president's elite guard mounted an armed response.

"He was an intelligent creature," the president said.

"You'll find a new pet," Lance said.

The president shook his head. "Not like this one. A truly unique creation."

"No one's unique."

"He could read people," the president said. "Read situations. He foresaw everything. He told me your president didn't have the balls to go to war over these embassy attacks."

"There might be war yet," Lance said.

"No," the president said, shaking his head. "There will be no war. Your president will put the blame for this on you, Lance Spector. You'll see. You'll go down in history as a terrorist. A crazed mad man."

"I've got more pressing concerns than my page in the history books," Lance said.

The president shrugged. "If I can be so bold as to give you some advice, Mr Spector. You need to alter your priorities."

Lance shrugged. The president was playing for time. "Tell them to hurry up," he said.

Suddenly, there was an explosion from the adjoining room. A set of wooden doors were blown off their hinges. They came flying into the room, followed by a fireball and a wave of thick, black smoke. Simultaneously, the glass in the windows shattered, and Lance saw the bright beams of tactical lights dancing around in every direction as an assault team prepared to breach.

He'd been blown back against the wall by the blast but still had his two guns in his hands.

While the soldiers could see nothing but the smoke in front of their faces, Lance could follow the beams of light right to them. He fired off two shots and rolled, fired two more, and altered position again.

In the space of ten seconds, he'd killed every soldier in the tactical team without a single shot having been fired in return. As the smoke cleared, he got behind the president, knocked the gun from his hand, and grabbed him. With his gun to the president's temple, he said, "Tell your men in the corridor to stand down."

The president was in a daze, disoriented, blood flowing from his ear from the shock of the blast. In the dust and smoke, he couldn't see anything. He couldn't hear because the blast had deafened him.

"Tell them," Lance yelled, his mouth an inch from the president's ear. "Tell them to stand down."

"Stand down!" the president cried. "Stand down, for God's sake. That's an order."

"Give me Medvedev, or it's game over," Lance yelled. "I'm not fucking around."

A voice came from the corridor. "Medvedev's here."

With the windows shattered, the smoke was clearing quickly, and Lance could make out the shape of the doorway. In the dim light from the corridor, he saw two soldiers standing there, and between them, restrained in their grip, was the enormous hulk of the albino. Even in the darkness, his skin seemed to have a translucent glow, like the skin of a cephalopod.

"Bring him closer," Lance said, holding the president firmly in front of him as a shield.

The soldiers pushed Medvedev forward, and Lance reached out and pulled him by the collar.

"We meet again," Lance said. "The man himself. The albino. The Polar Bear."

"The orphan," the president added.

"I have nothing to fear from you," Medvedev spat, the contempt in his voice so guttural Lance could almost taste it. "Your nation has peaked. It is past its prime. What I did marked the beginning of a new world order, and my president will honor—"

Lance unceremoniously pulled up his gun, pressed it against Medvedev's pallid forehead, and pulled the trigger. In the same motion, he pushed the president forward into the two soldiers who'd been holding Medvedev and ran straight for the window to his left. Even as Medvedev's enormous bulk was still falling to the ground, thumping the floor like a fallen sack of sand, Lance was in the air outside the room.

He fell a single story and hit the ground using all four limbs to spread the impact. Along the length of the palace, soldiers were rushing to windows, opening fire, and there were more ahead, out on the snowy lawn, forming a perimeter around the palace.

Lance opened fire on the closest of them, then ran back to the palace, fired two bullets at a ground-floor window, and crashed through it into an enormous library.

There was a soldier there, and Lance shot him, all the while moving, crossing the library in seconds. He dove through another window on the far side of the building and was back outside in the snow. From his knowledge of the compound, he knew there was a row of fir trees leading from the west face of the palace to a forested area used for hunting. He found the trees against the sky and followed them as far as the forest, leaving chaos and commotion back at the palace as the soldiers tried to figure out which way he'd gone.

The security system was coming back online, and as soon as the floodlights kicked in, he was completely lit up. Helicopters and fighter jets were flying by overhead, and one of the choppers spotted him and opened fire. Lance just had time to make it into the forest, where the tree canopy at least gave him some cover.

The forest led to the compound perimeter. The trees outside the perimeter had been felled for security, but no one had thought to clear the trees inside the barrier. Lance leaped up and climbed the nearest of them. Its limbs stretched out toward the wall, and as soon as he was above it, he let go and dropped down onto it.

He landed on coils of razor wire and had to grab onto them to prevent himself from losing his balance. The blades cut deep gashes in his flesh. He couldn't hold on, and a moment later, he was on the ground outside the perimeter, bleeding from a dozen razor cuts.

Helicopter searchlights panned the area. He could hear dogs and the sounds of men shouting. There was a small, fast-flowing river a few yards ahead, and he scrambled toward it. A thin layer of ice had formed along the shore, but in the middle, the icy water flowed with a strong current.

Without a thought, he jumped into the water.

86

Roth waited impatiently as his car cleared White House security. The president had called him in, and it was so late that it could only mean one thing.

The president had found out what Lance had done.

That could only mean one thing. Trouble.

When he got to the Oval Office, he found the president dressed in his robe and slippers, sipping brandy. "Mr President," he said.

"Roth," the president said, the expression on his face revealing nothing.

"I take it there's a problem, sir."

"A problem?" the president said. "Only if you consider outright insubordination to be a problem."

"I ordered him to stand down, sir."

"You *ordered* him? What does that even mean to a man like this?"

"I know," Roth said, feigning dejection. The truth was, he'd decided to allow Laurel and Tatyana to keep feeding Lance the information needed to complete the mission. It was necessary. You didn't let a man like Medvedev get away with what he'd done. But it wouldn't do any good, not for himself or for Lance, to let the president know that now.

The president shook his head. He poured Roth a glass of brandy and said, "Have a seat, Levi. We need to talk."

Roth sat on the sofa and took a sip of the brandy. It had a rich bourbon aroma.

"You like this stuff?" the president said.

"I do, sir," Roth said, taking another sip.

"Kentucky," the president said, holding up his glass. "Aged in old bourbon barrels. Good as any cognac."

Roth took another sip. It was good. He leaned back on the sofa and told himself to enjoy the drink while he could. Whatever the president had in store for him would not be good.

"So," the president said, leaning forward, "I won't make you guess why I called you in."

"I'm sure I have an idea," Roth said.

"You're not going to like it."

"I'm a big boy, sir. I can take my punishment."

The president inhaled deeply, buying himself time before saying, "I hear Spector's already on a flight back."

"He's scheduled to land at Dulles in a few hours," Roth said.

"My people tell me the flight was out of Kyiv."

"That's correct, sir," Roth said, surprised the president had taken the time to familiarize himself with the details.

"And he's got two Russian citizens with him."

"Correct, sir. Two women. They helped him complete the mission. One of them was the initial source of the threat information."

"Larissa Chipovskaya," the president said.

"Correct, sir," Roth said, growing increasingly worried at how much the president seemed to know about the operation.

"The sister of your recent defector, Tatyana Aleksandrova."

Roth cleared his throat. "Half-sister," he said, "but yes, sir. That is correct."

"And together, Spector and these two Russian women masterminded their way into the presidential palace at Novo-Ogaryovo and killed the man behind the embassy bombings."

"Mikhail Medvedev, sir."

"The Polar Bear," the president said.

"Correct, sir."

The president leaned back and took another sip of his brandy. "So we're in agreement as to the essential facts?"

Roth nodded. This was bad. He'd served under several administrations, and one rule stood as a constant—the greater the detail a president was aware of, the more trouble it meant.

"First off," the president said, "I'd like to know what information Lance Spector had about the bombings before they occurred, and why he did nothing to stop them."

"Sir," Roth said, "Lance tried to raise the alarm. Our people locked him in a cell. In fact, the man they sent to question him was the same Medvedev who later turned out to be the bomber."

"How was it that a Russian interrogated a CIA agent in an American embassy?"

"Sir," Roth said, "embassy security was placed in the hands of a Russian contractor months ago."

"And who authorized that?"

Roth didn't want to tell the president he'd authorized it himself, so he said nothing.

The president sighed. He knew well what had led to that situation, and it had nothing to do with Roth or Lance Spector.

There was a humidor on the table, and he opened it. He took out two cigars and offered one to Roth. Roth didn't like where the conversation was going, but he took the cigar.

"Roth," the president said, his tone taking on a more conspiratorial tone, "I want you to answer me bluntly."

"Of course, sir."

"Under the present circumstances, would military intervention against Russia and China be justified?"

"Justified, sir? *Absolutely,* it would be justified. They attacked us. There's no doubt. If we don't respond to this provocation, we're giving them free rein. We're telling them, and the world, that they can do what they want to us and get away with it. Who knows where that will lead? Or how many more deaths would come of it?"

"More deaths?" the president said.

"Yes, sir."

"But surely, risking a war with such powerful adversaries also risks more deaths."

Roth was getting heated. He could see the argument the president was gearing up to make, and he didn't like it. "With all due respect, sir, when someone punches you in the gut, you hit back. Otherwise, you're inviting them to treat you like a punching bag."

"Like standing up to a schoolyard bully."

"Exactly, sir."

The president nodded. He raised a hand to warn Roth that he would not like what he was about to hear. Then he said, "And what if the Kremlin and Beijing were not behind the attacks?"

Roth shook his head. "They were behind the attacks, sir. Beyond a doubt. Spector faced down Medvedev in person. The Russians initiated it. The Chinese went along with it."

"From what I hear, he came face to face with the Russian president, too."

Roth nodded. He'd known that little detail would become a bone of contention. There was nothing he could say to smooth it over. It had been CIA policy, and the policy of every US administration since at least the days of Harry S. Truman. The Russian president was untouchable. He knew it, the president knew it, the Russians knew it, and Lance Spector definitely knew it. He should never have been anywhere near President Molotov. It risked triggering a nuclear response of apocalyptic proportions.

"Look, Roth," the president said, "this is just you and me talking here. Spitballing, if you will."

Roth sighed. There was only one way it could go. "Please don't back down from this, sir," he said. "This is a challenge. The Russians are testing us. They're seeing if we still have the stomach for a fight. If we don't stand our ground, who knows what they'll do. Invade Ukraine? Invade Moldova? Invade the Baltic States, Poland. We'll be in World War Three before we know it."

"I disagree," the president said. "If we find evidence, incontrovertible proof, that Russia and China were not behind these attacks, then there is no challenge to the prevailing order."

"But there will be no such evidence," Roth said. "There can't be."

The president shrugged. "Still spitballing," he said, "what would the benefits be if we were to find such evidence?"

"Sir!" Roth protested. "I don't want Russia and China to be behind the attacks any more than you do, but they are. That's the fact of the matter. They did this. The generals in Moscow, the generals in Beijing, they hit us, and they hit us hard. If we back down now, we're telling the world we're no longer the dominant superpower. It's like a pack of wolves, sir. The moment the alpha lets down his guard, that's the moment every other wolf in the pack makes his attack."

The president grimaced. Roth knew his words had struck a nerve, but the president persisted. "Just answer the question, Roth."

"Any benefits to our two largest rivals not being the ones behind these attacks?"

"Humor me."

"Where to begin?" Roth said. "We'd avoid war. Fighting

Russia would be a nightmare. There's no question about that. Not only do they have a nuclear arsenal capable of destroying the entire planet, but they've also shown an egregious willingness to break long-standing international norms. They've tampered in our elections and sought to foment domestic unrest. They've hacked into our infrastructure and cut power to entire sections of the national grid. They've used paramilitary and mercenary forces to directly challenge our positions in the Middle East...."

"So they'll fight dirty?" the president said.

"They'll fight dirty, and they'll fight hard, sir. They've already shown a brazen willingness to challenge us around the world. It's as if they no longer fear us."

"And if we were to initiate a conflict now, with the elections so close?" the president said.

"Everything we've seen, they'd ramp up a hundredfold, sir. Cyber attacks, disinformation, voter tampering—all of it would go into overdrive."

"They could sway the outcome."

"They could pull down your entire administration. Not just your career but every single member of the cabinet. They've been gathering dirt for decades. I've seen some of the kompromat, sir. Our military leaders, key House and Senate leaders, even you and me—they could tear us all to shreds with the things they know."

The president nodded. He knew all this. He knew Roth knew it too. He was merely making his point. He wouldn't fight Russia because it would cost him his presidency. That was what it came down to. It would cost him his job. And it would cost Roth his job.

"And you haven't even begun to discuss actual war-fighting, Roth, have you?"

"No, sir," Roth admitted. "Warfare against Russia would be like nothing in living memory. In terms of raw numbers, Russia has never ceased being a superpower. It has two million active and reserve personnel and sufficient conventional forces to make a ground invasion unfathomable. And in terms of budget, taking purchasing power into account, they have about one dollar to spend for every three dollars we give the Pentagon. That's allowed them to modernize so aggressively that in virtually any scenario, an engagement would force us to incur costs we haven't been willing to consider since Vietnam, maybe even since World War Two."

"The Pentagon says Moscow's in a position to launch a ground invasion of the Baltic States in a matter of hours," the president said.

"That's correct, sir. They've tailored their ground forces precisely for that fight. The new T-14 tank, their fifth-generation fighter, the extended life of the Akula-class and Oscar-class subs. They're ready for a fight in the Baltic region."

"And then there's their nuclear arsenal."

"Of course, sir. That goes without saying."

"You tell me anyway, Roth."

Roth sighed. "Over eighty percent modernized. They've phased out the RS-36 ICBMs and replaced them with the Satan 2."

"Aptly named," the president said.

Roth nodded.

"Fair to say they're formidable?"

"They are, sir."

"Ready for battle?"

"They'd bloody us in a fight, sir. There's no doubt about it."

"So, it's fair to say there are valid reasons why a Commander in Chief might want to do everything in his power to avoid a hot war with Russia?"

"A hot war with them would be up close and personal, sir. We'd win. I have no doubt about that—"

"But at what cost, Roth?"

Roth looked at him. He was looking into the eyes of the most powerful man on the planet, and he could tell he didn't have it in him to fight this fight. "If we don't fight them now, sir, they'll only grow more powerful," he said. They'll grow more aggressive. They'll grow ever bolder. They'll invest in ever more destructive technologies."

The president raised a hand. "Now, tell me how we'd fare against China."

Roth shook his head. "For one thing, China doesn't have a Cold War nuclear arsenal," he said. "For another, they lack the war-fighting experience we've gained in Iraq and Afghanistan. Their forces are green, untested."

"So China's not a threat?"

"I wouldn't say that, sir."

"Then spell it out for me, Roth. Tell it to me like it's my first day on the job. What have I got to fear from the People's Liberation Army?"

"Well, sir, first off, there's the sheer numbers. As things stand, they have a fully modernized force of a million troops."

"And they've got a new tank, don't they?"

"The Type 15, sir."

"And their navy? They've been investing heavily there too, haven't they?"

"Correct, sir. Their navy is now the largest in the world in terms of vessel number. They're commissioning twenty new ships per year. Formidable, modern craft. Aircraft carriers, next-generation nuclear submarines, underwater drones."

"And in the air?"

"They've bought or stolen all the technology they need to make active operations in their air space extremely dangerous."

"If we were to attempt airstrikes?"

"We'd lose planes and pilots, sir."

"A lot of planes and pilots?"

"Correct, sir."

"Keep going."

"They've got a new airborne warning system with advanced drones and integrated artificial intelligence."

"And ballistic missiles?"

"Three hundred warheads and growing at a fast clip. At current levels, they have the industrial base to out-construct us, meaning that in an attritional fight, they could replace damaged equipment faster than we could. If a fight went on long enough, we'd run out of blood, treasure, and equipment before they did. They already have more medium-range missiles than us and the Russians combined, thanks to their refusal to join Cold War nonproliferation pacts. They've also developed a hypersonic capability that's potentially on par with our own, as well as formidable new anti-ship missiles."

"Carrier killers."

"That's what they're calling them, sir."

"Could they kill our carriers, Roth?"

"No one knows, sir. They've never tried."

"They've never tried."

"No, sir."

The president let out a quick laugh. "And do we want them to start trying, Roth?"

Roth shook his head.

"They've got a sting in their tail," the president said. "Don't they?"

"They do, sir."

"So keep that in mind when I say what I have to say next."

Roth nodded. There was nothing more he could do. He could see the president's mind was made up. He was too scared to fight.

"As Commander in Chief of this country," he said, "I cannot in good conscience take us into two simultaneous wars that could, even by conservative estimates, cost millions of American lives."

"I don't see—" Roth said before the president cut him off.

"It's not a question of politics, Roth. I know the people would unite around the flag if we went to war."

"Is it a question of preparedness, because—"

"It's a question of faith, Roth."

"Faith, sir?"

The president nodded. He looked very closely at Roth, almost to the point of making him uncomfortable, and said, "Do you *believe*, Roth?"

"I'm sorry, sir. I'm not sure what you're asking."

"Do you pray, Roth? To God? To a Creator?"

Roth looked uncomfortable. He was not an atheist, not by any measure, but it had been a very long time since he'd given himself to thoughts of anything but the most worldly of concerns. He certainly didn't kneel down next to his bed at night and pray.

"Never mind," the president said. "You don't have to answer."

"It's not that, sir."

"The point is," the president continued, "war on the scale you're suggesting, it would be apocalyptic in scale."

Roth didn't know what to say. Of course war was apocalyptic. Every war, since the dawn of time, had been apocalyptic to those fighting it. But fight it, they did. If they had to.

"So you want to let them get away with it?" he said.

"No," the president said. "The man behind this is dead, is he not?"

"Killed against your orders," Roth said, then regretted it.

"Yes," the president said. "Against my orders. You're right on that point. Which leads me to the crux of this conversation."

Roth knew what he was going to say but didn't dare interrupt.

"We've got footage of Spector breaking into the Moscow embassy. We've got havoc outside the front gate while he escaped. For the good of the nation, I've got to pin these attacks on someone."

"Sir—" Roth said, but the president stopped him.

"It's a choice between one man, one life," the president said, "and the lives of millions. I choose the one."

"I don't think you can measure lives like that, sir."

The president shook his head. "I'm sure you're right, Roth, but I don't have the luxury of philosophizing. Our nuclear forces are at their highest alert level since President Kennedy squared off against Khrushchev."

"Who was it that said the ends don't justify the means?" Roth said. "Machiavelli?"

"Ovid," the president said.

Roth nodded. "Ovid."

The president shook his head. "I'm sorry we can't see eye to eye on this, Levi, but the decision's been made. A team at the NSA is already falsifying evidence. The official position will be that Spector was behind the bombings in both Moscow and Beijing."

"I see, sir."

"I need your assurance that the CIA won't pull any more tricks where Spector's concerned. Once that plane lands, you let me take him into custody."

Roth nodded.

"I mean it, Roth. No tricks."

"Of course, sir. You have my word. No tricks."

87

W hen Laurel heard what the president had ordered, it was all she could do not to fling her glass across the room. She was sitting in the living room of the house in Georgetown with Tatyana and Roth. The fire was burning. It was the middle of the night, and Roth had just returned from his private meeting at the White House.

"Lance is the last person who should be taking the fall," she said.

Roth nodded. It was clear he wasn't happy either, but that didn't make it any easier for her to swallow.

"He's the only one who tried to stop this," she said.

"I know, Laurel."

"Sandra Shrader's the one who fucked us."

"They had her daughter," Roth said.

"Who we rescued."

"I know, Laurel. I know."

Laurel realized she was losing her temper. She took a deep breath and tried to release some of the tension.

"What about the Russians?" Tatyana said. "Larissa and Svetlana?"

"They're on Lance's flight," Roth said. "The president didn't mention them, so as far as we're concerned, they're still entering the country under our protection."

"Well," Laurel said, "with all the skullduggery afoot, one of us better be there to make sure that happens. Right now, I trust the president about as far as I could throw him."

Roth looked at her. He seemed to be reading her mind. She kept her face blank, giving away nothing. "I think that's a good idea," he said at last.

Laurel was surprised. She hadn't expected him to agree with anything she said.

"Tatyana," he said. "You should be there too. Larissa's your sister, after all."

"Thank you," Tatyana said. "I would like to."

"I want you both on the tarmac the moment that plane lands. Whatever they've got planned for Lance, there's no reason Larissa and Svetlana should get caught up in it."

"Understood, sir," Tatyana said.

"Sandra's going to have the entire place on lockdown," Roth continued. "The president seems to think it should be the NSA's job to arrest Lance."

"They're the last people he should be trusting," Laurel said, on the verge of losing her cool again. "They're the source of the breach that got us into this mess in the first place."

"Do they know what they've signed up for?" Tatyana said.

Roth shrugged. "I'm sure they have some idea, but it wouldn't have been my first choice to send an agency of computer nerds to apprehend a CIA operative."

"Will they even let us into the airport?" Laurel said. "If they're controlling the scene?"

"Not likely," Roth said.

"You can pull us a clearance, can't you?"

"After all that's happened, I don't think the NSA's going to be in any mood to do me a favor."

"So, how will we get in?" Tatyana said.

Roth looked at each of them, and from the way he did it, Laurel could tell he was about to tell them something off the record. "The best way," he said, his voice taking on a conspiratorial tone, "is the airport eastern service entrance. It will take you directly onto the runway."

Laurel and Tatyana looked at each other, then at Roth. "Are you saying what I think you're saying?" Laurel said.

"I'm just explaining the layout of the airport."

"And they won't know we're coming?"

"In order for the CIA to maximize the safety of our defectors, we're entitled to a presence on the tarmac when the plane touches down. As far as I'm aware, no one's issued any orders to the contrary."

Laurel and Tatyana looked at each other again, uncertain whether Roth was saying what they thought he was saying.

"Go now," Roth said, looking at his watch. "There are two vehicles waiting outside."

"Two?" Laurel said.

The expression on Roth's face left no room for doubt. "In case you don't come back together."

When Laurel and Tatyana got outside, two black Mercedes Benz AMG G-Class SUVs were waiting for them. In terms of acceleration and raw power, it was clear what Roth had in mind for the vehicles. "Nice rides," Laurel said.

Tatyana nodded. "Look in the back."

Laurel looked in the back seat and saw it had been loaded with body armor, infrared goggles, tear gas canisters and launchers, tasers, and an array of firearms. "Fuck," she said.

"He wasn't kidding."

"He wants us to get Lance out."

"It will mean trouble."

Laurel nodded. "Yes, it will."

They drove to the airport with Laurel in the lead, Tatyana

following, and when they got to the service entrance, they found the gate unguarded.

Laurel pulled up to it and got out. Tatyana stepped up next to her. They'd already seen signs of the airport's heightened security state. The military had been called in, and troop transports were lined up along the sides of some of the access roads. The transports were empty, which meant the troops had already been deployed throughout the grounds of the facility.

On the tarmac in front of the terminal, a row of six modified H-60 Black Hawk helicopters sat at the ready, engines running. They couldn't take off without interfering with the airport's commercial traffic, but they were ready to go nonetheless.

"Looks like they're expecting trouble," Tatyana said.

Laurel nodded.

Tatyana pulled a silenced pistol from her coat and, with a single shot, broke the lock on the gate. They then drove out onto the concrete that stretched ahead of them like an expanse of salt flats. In the distance, they could see the force that had been assembled to take Lance into custody, including a dozen MRAP vehicles armed with .50 caliber machine guns.

Laurel drove right toward them, and as she got closer, she saw that Sandra Shrader was there in person with the commanding officers. In her mind, she was probably there to redeem herself, Laurel thought. Some of the soldiers put their hands on their weapons, but when Sandra saw that it was Laurel and Tatyana in the vehicles, she told her men to stand down.

"Why are you here, Laurel?" Sandra said, a hint of nervousness in her voice. "This is an NSA operation. President's orders."

"Relax," Laurel said. "We're just here to see that our two defectors are taken into custody safely."

"We can see to that for you," Sandra said.

"They're still under our jurisdiction," Tatyana said.

Sandra said nothing. The MRAP guns swung slowly in

Laurel and Tatyana's direction. For a second, Laurel thought they might open fire. Their orders were to allow no one to interfere with Lance's apprehension. The military commanders looked to Sandra for an indication of what to do.

Sandra looked at Laurel. Very subtly, Laurel moved her head ever so slightly to the side and raised the hint of an eyebrow.

She waited.

Sandra hesitated.

And then, finally, Sandra raised her hand and said, "She's right. We're here for Lance Spector. The Russians weren't mentioned in the president's order. They still belong to the CIA."

88

President Ingram Montgomery stood at the podium in front of the White House press room, looking down at an audience of dozens of journalists. Next to him was his Chief of Staff and the Chairman of the Joint Chiefs. He didn't want there to be any doubt that the entire administration was united behind the announcement he was about to make.

As he looked down at the crowd, the cameras flashed and clicked like so many machine guns. It was more reporters than he'd seen gathered for any other statement of his presidency. Every national and international outlet had shown up for the event, and his press secretary struggled to keep the crowd calm while they waited.

Sandra had drafted the speech. She hadn't wanted to do it, she was opposed to every word it contained, but he'd given her no choice. Even the president had to admit he felt a pang of remorse as he glanced over it.

It was wrong.

It was a lie.

But it was a necessary lie.

Giving this speech was crossing a red line Ingram Montgomery had drawn for himself many years ago. He was about to do one of the things he'd always sworn not to. He was about to lie to the nation and to the world. He was going to flinch, to stand down in the face of evil. And he was going to throw a good man, a loyal man who'd done nothing but risk his own life in the protection of the nation, to the wolves.

He knew he had no choice.

Leading meant making difficult decisions. Distasteful decisions. Even abhorrent ones.

And the stakes couldn't have been higher.

Despite his earlier attempts to tone down the rhetoric and focus the attention on Lance Spector, the national media was in an utter frenzy, with the coverage focusing squarely on the threat of war. Some were calling the embassy attacks the opening salvo of World War Three. Others were calling them the dawn of a second Cold War. In either case, what they referred to was a war that threatened the very existence of human life on the planet. And the president knew that it had never been so close as it was right now.

Relations between America, China, and Russia were falling precipitously, and President Montgomery was not about to allow the three largest military forces ever created to go at each other. He couldn't allow it. It wasn't a strategy. It wasn't a posture. It wasn't a tactic. To his mind, it was just a cold, hard fact. He couldn't lead the world into war.

"It's time, sir," the press secretary said. "They're ready for you."

He nodded and took a step toward the podium. The camera strobes flashed as if warning him not to say the words he was about to utter.

He cleared his throat. "My fellow Americans," he began. It was an opening he reserved for the most important of announcements. He looked at the assemblage, then at the prompter. "I address you at a time of grave national peril."

The cameras flickered like hornets.

"Everywhere, there is talk of war," he said, looking up to see the effect of his words. "The threat of war can be heard everywhere, on the streets, in the cities, in the heartland of our great nation. Every media outlet, every newspaper and magazine, every op-ed and cable news program is obsessed with what's on the horizon. Even in the most hallowed halls of power, our house of congress, and yes, even in the Oval Office, the murmur of war is on everyone's lips."

The audience grew very quiet.

"There are those who believe the recent attacks on our two embassies in Moscow and Beijing represent the greatest assault on our global position in modern times. They say that not since Pearl Harbor have we witnessed such an egregious affront to our nation's security and prosperity."

Heads were nodding.

"They call it a slap in the face. A surprise attack. An out-and-out military assault."

Every reporter in the room watched with bated breath. Would there be war? That was all they cared about. It would be the biggest news of their lifetimes, and it was the story they were all ready to break.

"They say America has been attacked by our two greatest adversaries—Russia and China—simultaneously." Another pause. The tension in the room was oppressive, a physical presence that bore down visibly on every person present. "Well, I'm here today to tell you that it's all a hoax."

There were gasps from the crowd.

"Perhaps the greatest lie anyone has ever tried to pull on our country."

The cameras flashed like lightning.

"These dastardly attacks, this wanton carnage, were not the acts of our adversaries. They were not a provocation by our great rivals on the world stage. They were the crazed, maniacal, demented actions of a single man."

The journalists whispered among themselves.

"Our investigation reveals no challenge from Russia or China, but rather, that these attacks were planned and carried out by a deranged CIA operative intent on pulling the world's three greatest militaries into a state of war."

The murmur in the crowd grew louder.

"This is not the first volley in a new Cold War. This is not a Pearl Harbor or a 9/11." He cleared his throat. He was about to tell the greatest lie of his presidency, and the words didn't come easy. "This was an attack from the inside. A cowardly act of treason. A pitiable betrayal. And dare I say it, an act of evil that will go down in the annals of our nation's great history as a new low. This was the day one of our own sons tried to tear us apart from within."

The journalists were raising their hands, trying to ask questions. Their murmurs had grown to a babble of shouts and cries.

"This rogue agent," the president continued, ignoring their questions, "this evil traitor has a history of violence, a lengthy record of mental health issues, and a tendency to cruelty and perversion that he hid skillfully from the military and the CIA for years."

"Mr President," the reporter from *The Times* called out. "What evidence is there that this agent acted alone?"

"Let there be no mistake," the president said. "This man is the root of the evil we see before us."

"Sir," the reporter from *The Post* called out, "how could one man pull off both attacks?"

"This man is an elite agent, trained in all aspects of paramilitary warfare," the president said.

The questions began to come in an avalanche.

"Who is he?"

"What's his name?"

"What unit did he work for?"

The president looked down at the crowd. "I can't divulge specific information right now."

"What evidence is there that the Russians and Chinese weren't helping him?"

"Sir, what do you say to claims we're not ready for a second Cold War?"

The president held up his hand to indicate the conference was coming to an end. He turned to his press secretary and was about to leave the podium when someone said, "Sir, is America scared to go to war with Russia and China?"

He turned sharply. "Who said that?"

No one owned up to the question.

The president waited until the room was quiet again, then said, "Let me make one thing abundantly clear to everyone watching these events." He let his voice grow louder as he spoke. "The United States is not now, nor has it ever been, afraid to go to war with anyone who threatens our democracy, our sovereignty, our military, our territory, or most importantly of all, our lives."

The cameras flickered, but the reporters remained silent.

"If we find even a single shred of evidence that a foreign government was behind these attacks, we stand ready to mobilize. We stand ready to go to war. We stand ready to bring our enormous power to bear on any aggressor."

There was silence in the room. Ingram wanted the conference to end. He needed to get out of the spotlight. One final sentence was all that was required.

"If we've been attacked, we will declare war on our enemies, and we will crush them."

89

The Russian President watched the press conference with a wry smile on his face. He'd always enjoyed seeing his opponents squirm, and what he was looking at now was undoubtedly the greatest setback to American prestige in a generation. His American counterpart was on stage, bending over backward, trying to falsely convince his own media that Moscow was not behind an attack. And the reason was that he was afraid to man up and fight them.

It was an enormous achievement, but it hadn't come easy. Decades of diligent preparation by Moscow and Beijing had been required to make this outcome possible. It had cost him Medvedev, but he'd been beginning to suspect Medvedev was getting too big for his boots anyway. The albino had broken the cardinal rule of Russian politics—he'd set his sights on the president's job. That was what had really cost him his life.

The president had known Spector was still loose in Moscow and had fully expected him to find and kill the man behind the bombings, regardless of his orders. He hadn't quite expected it to happen in his own palace, but, apart from that detail, he was glad it happened. It solved a problem for him that would have been difficult to solve otherwise. Medvedev had amassed a great deal of power and support. Many in the Kremlin feared him, and even within the Dead Hand, his power had been growing.

Now he was gone. That was convenient.

The ordinary people had never heard of him, of course, but that didn't stop the president from ordering the largest state funeral Moscow had seen since the fall of the Berlin Wall. It would include a full military parade and draw millions of people to the streets of the capital. It would be televised across the nation, and the president himself would make a speech.

He'd speak of the bravery of a patriot who never once lost sight of the true enemy of the Russian people, and he would make explicit reference to the recent events that had shocked the world and put fear into the hearts of lions. He was looking forward to it.

It wasn't out of affection for Medvedev that he would make the speech. His statement would be directed squarely at the American President. He would be rubbing salt in his wounds, luxuriating in his humiliation, and putting those who could read between the lines on notice that it had been Russia who was responsible for the embassy bombing. The people who mattered, those within the American security apparatus at the Pentagon and Langley, would know all too well that their own president had backed down from a fight.

He leaned back and lit a cigar, inhaling from it deeply.

He'd be lying if he said Medvedev's assassination hadn't rattled him. Spector had proven he could act in Moscow over an extended period with virtual impunity. If he wanted to kill someone, he could do it. He'd done it in the Kremlin. He'd done it at Novo-Ogaryovo. It seemed nowhere was out of reach.

The president had ordered security at the estate to be

dramatically increased. All systems were to be upgraded. He knew, though, that no matter what he did, if Spector decided to come back, there was little that could be done to stop it. Those systems were designed to keep back an army. Against one man, there would always be too many gaps in the net, too many holes to plug. Nothing could be made completely airtight.

He picked up his phone and asked to be connected with his Consulate General in New York. A moment later, Jacob Kirov's granite voice came on the line. "Mr President," he said.

"Jacob, are you watching?"

"Of course I'm watching, sir."

The president laughed. "It doesn't look good for them. The press is already skeptical."

"No one's going to believe the two most important US embassies in the world were reduced to ashes by the actions of a lone rogue agent."

"Well, they certainly won't when we start planting the conspiracy theories."

"And I'll keep you updated on that front, sir. Three separate troll farms are already planting the seeds."

"Very good," the president said.

"A month from now, the whole world will know the Americans backed down from a fight."

"And then we can launch the next phase of our plan."

"Exactly, sir. But we'll need some more assurances from our Chinese friends. I can meet with the ambassador in Washington if that's what you would like."

The president nodded. "Maybe that would be the best way to broach it," he said. "What we'll be looking for is the slightest sign of increased American troop levels in Europe."

"I have no doubt the Chinese will support us in the case of American hostility, sir. They're already increasing their strength level in the Taiwan Strait."

"As long as we coordinate our actions with them perfectly," the president said.

"And they don't stab us in the back," Jacob added.

"And they don't stab us in the back," the president reiterated, "we should be able to each pursue our own expansionist moves without fear of American interference."

"I think Montgomery's speech confirms that, sir."

"Yes," the president said, sucking deeply on his cigar. "I think it does."

He put down the phone and looked up at the enormous map on his wall. The Russian enclave of Kaliningrad, separated from the rest of the country by the three Baltic states, was colored in bright red. He had enough forces in the region to crush the tiny states a hundred times over, but he couldn't move while they were under the umbrella of NATO protection.

But if he could be confident the Americans wouldn't respond to his actions, there was nothing the rest of the alliance could do to stop him. Without the Americans, NATO was nothing but an empty word. The European allies would blow away like a house of straw. The European Union would bitch, it would moan, it would object on humanitarian grounds, but ultimately, if America held back, they would shut up.

Molotov practically salivated as he looked at the map. The Baltics had been part of Soviet territory until 1991, and it was his urgent wish to pull them back to the Motherland. Historically, they were tied to Russia, not the West, and their NATO membership was an aberration.

He'd shown his generals that the Americans wouldn't fight back against provocation, and if the Chinese continued to hold up their part of the bargain, his next steps would be to put in motion events that would lead, ultimately, to a Russian invasion of the Baltics that no one could stop.

False flag operations had worked in Ukraine. He'd been

able to stir up enough ethnic and political trouble that he could justify a ground invasion in the name of Russian national security. He now had confidence that a similar strategy along the Baltic borders, combined with Chinese actions against Taiwan, would force the Americans to accept a similar settlement in the Baltics.

90

L ance had an uneasy feeling in the pit of his stomach. The plane had been circling Dulles for over an hour, and, to his mind, that could only mean one thing. Maybe he was being paranoid, maybe the reason was the bad weather, as the pilot claimed, but his instinct told him otherwise.

"I thought you'd be happier to be getting home," Larissa said as she poured him some more coffee from a pot.

The journey out of Moscow, across western Russia, over the Ukrainian border, and through the disputed Donbas region had been arduous. It was no small accomplishment that all three of them had made it unharmed.

When Lance got back to them at the hotel after killing Medvedev, his clothes frozen to his body from the river water, he'd thought he might die of hypothermia. For her part, Svetlana had been positively traumatized by what had happened to her in the palace. It had fallen to Larissa to get them out of the city and onto separate trains without losing track of each other.

Now that they were in a plane above US territory, they

should have finally been able to breathe an enormous sigh of relief. But Lance didn't feel it. "Something's not right," he said.

Larissa nodded. They were all beginning to suspect it. They'd been circling for too long.

"I thought everything in America would be rosy," Larissa said. "All Cadillacs and hamburgers and movie stars."

"And a few other things," Lance said. He sipped his coffee and looked out the window. A low fog hung over Washington, obscuring the airport and everything else below them.

He'd watched the president's press conference from a hotel room in Kyiv and knew he wasn't coming home to a welcoming committee. The CIA agents who'd met them in Poland, and escorted them to their jet, had confirmed as much. They'd been professional, cordial even, but they'd known Lance was the rogue agent the president had been referring to in his speech.

And Lance understood it. No president could allow the provocations of a man like Mikhail Medvedev to pull him into a global war. Especially if a scapegoat could be found. Lance knew that when the plane landed, he was going to be taken into custody. He was the perfect candidate. The rogue agent. The lone gunman. He'd broken into the embassy just before the attack. His face was already all over the news. The president couldn't have asked for a better fall guy.

He winced as he rose to his feet.

"What are you doing?" Larissa said. She'd been concerned for his wellbeing since his return from Novo-Ogaryovo. He was still weak, but at least they knew he'd live.

"Go tell the pilot to land," he said.

She got up, and when she returned, the pilot was with her.

"Take us down, Captain," Lance said.

"Sir, they keep telling us to wait."

"They're just jittery. What am I going to do? Run? Take us down and hand me over."

"I don't recommend it," the pilot said skeptically. He obviously had an idea of the military preparations that were being made for their arrival.

"They'd shoot us down if we tried anything else," Lance said. "It would save them the hassle of a trial."

"They're still preparing for you down there," the pilot said. "There are more military vehicles than at Bagram Airfield."

"They think I'm going to try to escape. They're trying to guarantee a clean job."

"Will you go willingly?" the pilot said.

Lance said nothing for a moment. He drained his coffee and then said, "Take us down. I won't do anything to put you or your crew at risk. I got on this plane, didn't I?"

The pilot went back to the cockpit and, a few minutes later, announced the final approach.

From the window, Lance saw a wintery afternoon at Dulles. It had been raining, and the tarmac was slick with water. Ice-removal vehicles lined the runway. At the end of it, next to a small terminal building used exclusively by the federal government, was a fleet of military, FBI, and Federal Aviation Authority vehicles. On the roof, he could make out an FBI SWAT team, still getting into position. "They really brought out the welcome wagon," he said. "I suppose I should be proud."

Across the aisle, Svetlana was just waking up. She'd had a few drinks during the flight and still looked a little worse for wear.

Lance knew that whatever else happened, he wasn't going to allow his arrest to put her or Larissa at risk. He'd wait on the plane while they disembarked. Whatever followed, it wouldn't begin until they were well in the clear.

The way he saw it, he had two options now. He could let them take him without a fight. He would take the fall for what had happened, he'd be tried in a FISA court, and he'd go down in history as the biggest traitor the nation had seen since the days of the Rosenbergs.

There were worse things, he supposed. The people who mattered would know what he'd done. They'd know he was innocent. He'd know he was innocent.

And war would be averted.

He'd be able to sleep in his supermax cell at night, knowing that his incarceration had helped prevent a war.

That was one option.

The other was to run.

Either way, the president would have his fall guy. The world would still remember Lance Spector as the man behind the two embassy bombings. War would still be averted. If anything, his running would only make him appear more guilty.

He knew he might not make it out of the airport. It was an enclosed space, a perfect trap, and the authorities certainly seemed ready for a fight. But dying on a runway felt more his style than living out his years in a concrete box. Everyone died sooner or later. At least he'd be going out at a time of his own choosing, in a manner of his own choosing. And he knew he'd done his best to prevent the carnage at the embassy. He'd warned the staff at the embassy. He'd tried to stop the bombing. And when the worst happened, he'd found and killed the man responsible. If that was what brought him down, he could accept that.

There'd been other things in his life that he was ashamed of, things he'd never be able to atone for. He knew better than anyone that there were things a man could be asked to do for his country that he would never be able to square away with his God. There were things he'd done that were incompatible with his very idea of God.

But at least this wasn't one of them.

As near as he could tell, he'd done right in Moscow. If it had ended in tragedy, and if it had included his disobeying direct orders from the very top of the chain of command, he still knew he'd done right. And maybe that was the most a man like him could hope for. To die at the end of a mission he at least believed in.

As the plane taxied in front of the arrayed military force, he realized something.

They wanted him to flee. It would be cleaner that way. A tidier case. A cleaner headline.

Rogue Agent Behind Embassy Attacks Killed while Trying to Flee.

91

L aurel stood by the back of her SUV as the plane came in for landing. She'd parked in a way that ensured Sandra and her soldiers didn't have a clear view into the trunk, and she looked now at the array of weaponry Roth had provided. It was clear from his choices that he didn't want a bloodbath, but he also wasn't messing around. There was an M-32 grenade launcher pre-loaded with six CS gas grenades, and she unpacked it from its case carefully and set it aside.

By the looks of things, Sandra was expecting trouble. The soldiers stood at the ready, fully prepared for a fight, but as Laurel surveyed their heavy caliber guns, all fully loaded with live ammo, she realized that they weren't there to apprehend Lance. They were there to kill him. And not just Lance. Judging from their positions, they were prepared to take out everyone on the plane if it came to that.

Judging the situation through the president's lens, it all made perfect sense. Lance's arrest would go wrong, and he would be killed trying to escape. There would be no trial. He would never have a chance to protest his innocence. And anyone else on the plane who felt compelled to speak out for him would have also been killed in the process. It significantly reduced the chance of the truth ever getting out, and if the goal was to avoid a war with Russia and China, that was critical.

Laurel also realized that Roth hadn't been let in on this plan. Roth had been lied to. He'd been expecting an arrest. That was what he'd said was going to happen. The CIA, it seemed, had been completely cut out from this little deal between the president and the NSA. Looking at Sandra now, standing with her assembled military units, Laurel couldn't help feeling angry. They'd gone out on a limb for her, brought her daughter back to safety, and kept the proof of her wrongdoing secret from everyone. And this was how she repaid them.

This was a clear break from the past, Laurel thought. Roth and the president had always been like brothers. They'd been as thick as thieves, sipping port in the Oval Office at all hours of the night, hatching their plans and plots and strategies. Perhaps she shouldn't read too much into this, given that Lance had just assassinated Medvedev in direct contradiction to the president's orders, but this definitely felt like a power shift, a new dynamic, as if the old days of Roth and the president ruling the roost together were over.

As the plane taxied toward them, Laurel knew the stakes were life and death. For Lance, and possibly for Larissa and Svetlana too. If she didn't act fast, these soldiers were going to open fire, and the president would simply claim Lance had fired first.

She glanced up at the roof of the terminal building. She couldn't see them, but she knew it was bristling with Sandra's sharpshooters. The moment Lance stepped out of the plane, a dozen triggers would be pulled.

And those guys didn't miss.

Tatyana was standing next to her own vehicle, watching the scene unfold with the same sense of growing dread that Laurel felt.

"This is an ambush," Laurel said under her breath.

Tatyana nodded. "They're going to kill him."

"We need to get your sister and Svetlana out of the way before the shit hits the fan."

"Lance will send them out first," Tatyana said. "I'm sure of it."

"If he sees this coming."

"He'll see it coming," Tatyana said. "And he'll give us enough time to get them out of the way."

Laurel nodded. "I hope you're right."

"Me too," Tatyana said grimly.

"Okay, here's the plan," Laurel said, painfully aware that it was hardly deserving of the name. "You get Svetlana and your sister into your vehicle as soon as they get off the aircraft. Then you step on it, and get the hell out of here before anyone thinks of stopping you."

"What about you and Lance?"

"I'll create as big of a diversion as I can. Hopefully, that buys him the time he needs to get off the plane."

"The snipers are the biggest threat," Tatyana said.

"I've got smoke grenades."

Tatyana took a deep breath. "Whichever way you slice it, he's in a tight spot."

Laurel nodded. She went to the door of the vehicle and looked back at Tatyana. "See you soon," she said.

Tatyana nodded. "I hope so."

Laurel got into the driver's seat of her vehicle. The windows were tinted, and she could climb into the back and prepare for the assault without anyone outside seeing what she was doing. From the back seat, she reached into the trunk and grabbed the M-32 grenade launcher. She placed it on the seat next to her, ready for use.

As the plane came to a halt, she opened her window and watched with bated breath. She knew every sniper in the vicinity had his eye to his scope, his finger on the trigger of his gun. The instant Lance emerged from the plane, it was game over. That many snipers wouldn't miss, and there wasn't a thing she could do about it. Her only hope was if he saw this coming.

She waited while the plane's engines powered down, her heart thumping so hard it was difficult to catch her breath. Finally, after what felt like a lifetime, the front door of the aircraft hissed open with a release of air pressure. At the same time, a small set of stairs extended automatically from the vessel, ready for the passengers to disembark.

She reached for the grenade launcher, feeling its icy steel in her hand.

An eternity seemed to pass before there was any movement from the plane. The first person to appear was an extremely attractive Russian woman with bleached blonde hair and an elegantly tailored coat. There was no denying the resemblance. It was Tatyana's sister.

Behind her was another woman, shorter, with dark hair and a certain timidity in her step. This was the second defector, Medvedev's personal secretary, who Tatyana had somehow managed to hone in on from a single red scarf.

Laurel lifted the grenade launcher into her lap, ready to swing it up and fire.

She prayed Lance didn't come out yet.

The two women looked around the windswept runway, shielding their eyes from the low winter sun, and when they saw Tatyana, Larissa led the way directly toward her.

Laurel took one final look at Sandra, trying to read her intentions. Sandra looked right back at her, and the look on her face told Laurel that she wasn't there entirely by choice. She was obeying orders. Nothing more. Laurel shook her head ever so slightly, and Sandra spoke into her radio, telling the snipers to hold off.

Seconds ticked by. Tatyana swept up the two women and got

them into the back of her vehicle. No one challenged them. They were under CIA jurisdiction. The soldiers were interested only in Lance.

But Lance didn't emerge from the plane.

Nothing happened.

It wasn't until Tatyana's SUV pulled off across the runway, back toward the gate it had entered by, that there was any movement at all.

Next to appear at the doorway of the plane was the pilot. He was CIA-trained with a security clearance and knew how to minimize the chance of his accidentally being shot. He first waved his captain's hat at the door, then appeared in full uniform, with his face visible and his hands in the air.

As the pilot made his way to safety, it became clear to everyone that Lance had foreseen what was in store. He'd read the situation, calculated the permutations, and realized that there was no way he was going to be leaving that plane without shots being fired.

The pilot was quickly followed by two hostesses in their prim uniforms, their hands in the air as they descended the steps in high heels and oversized sunglasses.

That left only Lance on the plane.

Laurel knew she had the briefest of windows. Any moment, the heavy .50 caliber guns were going to tear the plane's fuselage to shreds.

She drew the grenade launcher to her open window and fired all six gas canisters, aiming directly at the plane's entrance.

There was confusion as the soldiers struggled to comprehend what was happening.

Laurel prayed Lance had seen from the plane. She'd been sitting with her window open in full view, but she didn't know if he'd looked out at her.

Sandra must have issued a belated order to open fire because a few of the gunners sprayed the plane with bullets.

They fired in short bursts, although many didn't fire at all. They'd been trained to hold back until they could see their target.

Thick smoke wafted around the plane, and Laurel pulled her vehicle slowly closer. She'd thought Lance would come to her, that he'd somehow make his way from the aircraft to her car in the smoke, but she saw now that wasn't going to happen. He hadn't seen her, or maybe he didn't want to risk her life. But as the seconds passed and the smoke began to clear, she realized he wasn't coming.

And then the sound of jet engines running through their initialization cycle filled the air.

He was going to run for it. In the plane!

Acting purely on instinct, she put her foot on the gas. The SUV lurched forward, and she opened her door and leaped out, hitting the tarmac hard. She rolled through the thick smoke until she reached the foot of the staircase as it retracted automatically back into the plane. Then, she grabbed onto it and scrambled up the steps as the gunners obliterated her vehicle with their heavy-caliber fire.

She managed to scramble aboard the plane just as it began rolling forward. It moved very slowly at first, taking devastating fire as the soldiers realized what was happening, but very quickly, it picked up speed. "Lance!" she cried as soon as she was inside. There was no answer. Even if there had been, she never would have heard it over the gunfire.

She lay on the ground, clinging to the base of a seat as the plane gained speed, and bullets clanged everywhere, shooting holes into the walls that spilled light into the cabin like beams from a flashlight.

As the bullets subsided, she saw that the door of the plane had been blown off, and outside on the wing, an engine had burst into flames, casting a billowing plume of black smoke into the sky.

She got to her feet and ran to the cockpit. Lance spun around with a gun, but when he saw her face, the shock of the surprise made him drop it.

"Laurel!" he gasped.

"Watch the road," Laurel said as the plane hurtled toward the rapidly approaching end of the runway. Frigidly cold air blasted in through bullet holes in the windshield. "If you take off," she said, "they'll shoot us down." She could still feel the acceleration as Lance pushed the throttle forward.

They were approaching two hundred miles an hour, and the flat stretch of concrete was going to run out very soon.

Laurel didn't know if the entire airport had been shut down to commercial traffic, but she got her answer when a dark object blocked the sun above them.

"What the hell is that?" she yelled as an enormous jetliner descended onto the tarmac behind them.

"We're in his lane," Lance said, pushing the throttle further forward, picking up ever more speed.

She realized he was driving the plane like a car, with no intention of leaving the ground. A few more seconds passed, and then they hit the end of the runway. It felt like crashing into water.

Laurel was jolted forward, and Lance caught her before she flew into the cockpit controls. They were on the unpaved portion of land at the end of the runway, and the plane bumped and jolted around so violently that Laurel was sure it would fall apart. Only when a high fence appeared in the distance did Lance hit the brakes. There was a line of trees on the opposite side of the fence, and the plane burst through the chainlink, coming to a halt mere feet from the treeline.

The moment the plane stopped, it began to fill with smoke.

They ran to the door, choking and coughing, and leaped out of the burning aircraft and onto hard-packed snow.

Already, a line of vehicles could be seen on the runway

behind them, speeding in their direction in a wide V-formation. Behind the MRAPs and FBI squad cars, an echelon of Black Hawk helicopters fanned out across the sky.

"Come on," Lance said.

They sprinted through the trees. Laurel lost her shoes and ran over the frozen ground barefoot. It felt like running on glass. Behind them, they heard sporadic gunfire, but none of it came close.

They continued through the brush, under the thin tree cover, until they reached a second chainlink fence, twelve feet high, lined at the top with razor wire.

Lance leaped at it, pulling himself upward and over the top in a single motion. He then removed his jacket and threw it over the top of the fence, providing protection for Laurel from the razor wire.

She got over the fence, and they kept running as helicopters circled ever closer overhead. For a second, Laurel wondered why they didn't open fire. Then she slipped, falling down a small slope to the edge of a three-lane highway.

Lance, still ahead of her, didn't hesitate for a moment. He ran right into the frantic afternoon traffic, causing cars to skid and swerve dangerously to avoid him.

He drew his gun and pointed it at the driver of the first car to come to a complete stop. It was a decently powered Dodge, and the driver got out with his hands in the air. Lance and Laurel got in, with Lance in the driver's seat. He put his foot against the metal, the engine gunned, and the car burned rubber as it shot out of its standing position, hitting sixty, then seventy, then eighty in a matter of seconds.

Lance drove recklessly fast, weaving through traffic and using the shoulder to pass other cars as the Black Hawks trailed behind, close on their tail.

"We need to lose them," Lance said to her as he pulled the car onto a steeply pitched off-ramp. The car hit the ramp and bottomed out, sending a spray of sparks behind them as he ran a red light, screeched around a ninety-degree corner, and sped across an overpass.

Laurel had no idea what his plan was, and when he got back onto the highway, headed in the opposite direction, she thought they were going to die. "What the hell are you doing?" she cried.

He didn't answer but kept accelerating through the lighter northbound traffic. They reentered the airport zone, speeding past overflow parking lots, warehouses, and hangars. When they got to the first public entry point to the airport, Lance jammed on the brakes and crashed over a concrete curb into the airport proper.

He turned for the departure terminal and drove into one of the enormous multistory lots reserved for long-term parking. The Black Hawks still circled overhead, Laurel could hear them, but she could no longer see them.

Lance stopped the car as a gush of steam burst out of the hood. They abandoned it, running along the line of parked cars, and stopped at the first older vehicle they reached, an eighties Ford pickup truck. Lance smashed the driver's side window and unlocked the door. They scrambled in, and he reached behind the steering column and found the wires for the starter. It took all of thirty seconds to get the engine fired up.

"Here we go," he said, and then very slowly, like the world's most relaxed driver, he made for the exit at the far end of the parking lot.

They pulled out of the lot, driving as calmly as if on a Sunday cruise. The Black Hawks were overhead, scanning the lot. They must have seen the pickup, but none paid it any special attention. A few moments later, Laurel and Lance were joining a stream of rush hour traffic in the direction of the city, the helicopters still swarming over the airport behind them.

92

Tatyana drove without speaking, without looking behind her, without slowing down. It was not the time for emotional reunions. She was in the driver's seat, and Larissa and Svetlana were behind her in the back.

She glanced over her shoulder once, as they were leaving the grounds of the airport, and saw the thick, black plume of smoke rising from the airplane. For all she knew, Lance and Laurel were already dead.

She didn't know what to do or where to turn. Larissa and Svetlana were eyewitnesses to the fact that the president's official narrative of what had happened in Moscow was a complete lie. That meant their lives were in grave danger, and there were certainly no official channels that they could turn to for help.

She made her way for the highway and didn't speak until they were well clear of the airport. "I thought I'd never see you again," she said then to Larissa.

Larissa seemed to be holding back tears. She reached forward and touched Tatyana's shoulder. "Me neither," she said.

They got onto the interstate at Legato and pulled into the westbound traffic.

"Where are we going?" Larissa said.

Tatyana shook her head. "I don't know yet."

"Lance said you'd take us to the CIA."

"I'm not sure that's such a good idea," Tatyana said, "given what just happened at the airport."

They passed a large sign bearing the iconic badge of Route 66, and Svetlana said, "America, here we come!"

Tatyana nodded grimly. "I'm afraid you might not find it as welcoming as you'd hoped," she said. They drove on for a while in silence, and Tatyana said to Svetlana, "You were his secretary, weren't you?"

Svetlana looked at her in the mirror. "Among other things."

Tatyana nodded. She knew what that meant. She'd known it the first time she saw Svetlana on the satellite feed. "The scarf," she said. "The Young Pioneers. That's what made you stand out."

"Medvedev made me wear it," Svetlana said. "Ironic, if you think about it."

They drove on another few miles, and Larissa said, "Do you really not know where we're going?"

Tatyana shrugged. "The CIA is after us. The Kremlin is after us. What do you think we should do?"

"I thought the CIA was going to offer us protection," Svetlana said.

"The CIA is going to do whatever the president orders," Tatyana said, "and right now, the president doesn't want anyone on earth knowing that a man named Mikhail Medvedev was behind the embassy bombings."

"Do we have any money?" Larissa said.

Tatyana nodded.

"How long until they know we're on the run?"

"Lance is their main priority. I don't think they'll even think about us until they have him in custody."

"And this vehicle?"

"If I know Roth, this vehicle is clean. Completely clean."

"A little makeup then?" Larissa said. "Some sunglasses?"

"That's what I was thinking," Tatyana said.

She waited until they'd made some more distance from the DC area before picking up her phone and dialing Roth's number. His voice filled the vehicle. "Tatyana, did you get them?"

"I got them, Roth."

"They tried to kill Lance."

"Did they get away?"

"Looks like it."

"Thank God."

"What about you?"

"We're on the road."

Roth was quiet for a moment, then said, "I think that's a good idea. Don't say where you're headed. Don't tell anyone."

"We're thinking, keep our heads down a few days, wait for the dust to settle."

"Like Thelma and Louise," Larissa added. "Only there's three of us."

"All right," Roth said. "I'll clear all tracers on you. They won't know where to begin. They won't even have facial recognition."

"We have papers and money," Tatyana said.

"Where will you go?"

Tatyana looked in the rearview mirror at Larissa and Svetlana.

"Somewhere warm," Larissa said.

"All right," Roth said. "Stay low, and stay safe."

He hung up, and they drove on. Larissa climbed up to the passenger seat in front and said, "How about some music?"

"All right," Tatyana said. She was tense, watching the rearview mirror, expecting to see flashing police lights at any moment.

She knew her sister was still in shock after the events she'd just been through. The same would be true for Svetlana. A little time off the grid would do them all good.

"So, where are we going to go?" Svetlana said.

Tatyana was about to answer when Larissa said, "Miami." She looked at Tatyana.

Tatyana had been thinking somewhere a little more low-key. "Do you think you two could tone down the accents? Make yourselves sound less...."

"Russian?" Larissa said.

Tatyana nodded. "Exactly."

93

L aurel looked at Lance. She'd fallen asleep in the passenger seat while he drove, and she didn't think he knew she was awake.

She didn't know where they were. All she knew was that they'd been heading south. It was dark and had been for hours. They were on a straight road with dry grassland on either side. She opened the window, and it was a lot warmer than it had been when she fell asleep.

They were alone. For the first time since they'd met, there would be no one around but the two of them. They would be off the grid, hiding out for what could turn out to be quite a long time.

They'd been listening to the radio before she fell asleep, and there wasn't one word about their escape. The whole incident at the airport was being played off as a crash. Laurel had been afraid they'd turn the whole thing into the largest manhunt in history, but it seemed the president preferred to keep the incident quiet. She wondered why that was. It had been the same way when he'd accused Lance of being behind the attacks in the first place. None of the footage had shown Lance's face. It was as if the president was keeping his options open in case he needed to use Lance again in the future.

That was what Laurel told herself, at least. That the door was being kept open for their return to service. She hoped that was the case. She certainly didn't want to be on the run forever. Before too long, she reasoned, Roth would have them both back on the books. They just needed to give him some time, let the dust settle, and wait for the president to realize he needed them.

She watched Lance drive and wondered how much time they had. "Where are we going?" she said.

He glanced at her, surprised she was awake. "A little place I passed through once," he said. "South of the border. Somewhere no one else knows about."

"Not even Roth?"

"Especially not Roth."

"You seem to know your way pretty well."

He shook his head, and she thought she saw a hint of pain flash across his face as if from a bad memory. "I've spent a lot of time in this part of Texas," he said.

"Doing what?" she said, sensing she was pushing her luck by prying.

"What is it I do?" he said. "I was looking for a man."

There was a tension in his voice that she'd never heard before. She thought for a moment, then said, "A bad man?"

Lance nodded.

"Did you find him?"

He shook his head. "Not yet," he said. "But I will. One day." Behind them, the sun was just beginning to rise, and a ray of light hit the mirror and reflected onto his face. It was a handsome face, she thought, chiseled like someone had carved it from wood and polished it to a fine sheen. "We'll be at the border soon," he said.

He turned toward her again, and there was an inquisitive look in his eye.

"What is it?" she said.

"You sure you want to do this?" he said. "It's not too late to cut you loose. You could say I forced you to do what you did."

She shook her head. "I don't think anyone would buy that."

"Roth would figure out an explanation."

Laurel shook her head. "No," she said.

"You don't think Roth would take you back?"

"Take me back?"

"After what you just did?"

"What I just did was Roth's idea. Who do you think put a grenade launcher in the back of my car?"

"That was Roth's idea?"

"Yes."

"He's really pushing his luck these days. There's only so much the president will put up with."

Laurel nodded. She'd already sensed the turning of the tide against Roth, but she didn't want to think about that now. "Anyway," she said, "even if Roth could protect me, I don't want to go back."

Lance caught her eye. "The border crossing's about thirty miles up ahead," he said. "We should prepare."

A neon sign by the side of the road glowed up ahead. It was the shape of a cactus, with the words 'El Paso Flamingo' blinking in pink.

"Looks like a motel," Laurel said.

As they got closer, she saw that it was a motel, and there was a diner and gas station attached to it. Lance pulled into the lot and up to one of the gas pumps. They had money and false passports for crossing the border, but they each had a little tidying up to do.

Lance filled up on gas while Laurel went to the dingy

restroom next to the store. She locked the door and looked around. The floor was raw concrete, too rough to mop but porous enough to absorb the odor of every spill. Flies hovered around the window, and the stench of urine almost made her gag.

She opened her purse and pulled out a package of dark hair dye and a bottle of water. The ingredients for the dye were in separate containers and had to be mixed. She put them in the bottle and shook them, then put the dye in her hair. While she waited for the process to take effect, she took off her shirt and bra and washed at the sink.

When she was done, she went back to the car and found Lance leaning on the hood, drinking from a pop can.

"All yours," she said, nodding toward the restroom.

"Wow," he said. "You look..."

"*What*?"

"Different."

"That's the idea, isn't it?"

He walked past her to the restroom, and she went into the store to stock up. The pickings were slim. She ended up with chips, some jerky, and a granola bar. She also bought a carton of milk and drank directly from it.

"Got any coffee?" she said to the old man at the counter.

"You dyed your hair," he said.

She nodded, trying to gauge if his noticing was something she needed to worry about. The bell above the door chimed, and Lance entered.

"Coffee's in the back," the old man said, nodding to the far end of the store.

She asked Lance if he wanted any, and he nodded. "Sure," he said. "Black."

She went and poured two cups, and when she got back, Lance was leaning on the counter, close to the old man. "I know what you're thinking," he said to the man.

"I ain't thinking nothing," the old man said.

"You're thinking we're on the run, her and me."

"I'm thinking nothing of the sort."

There was a pause, and then Lance said, "You're a veteran, aren't you?"

The man nodded. "How can you tell?"

"I can tell."

"What's it got to do with anything," the man said.

"Well," Lance said. "It means you know."

"Know what?"

"Know that not everything the government says is true."

Laurel put the two cups of coffee on the counter. Lance and the old man both looked at her.

"We're not bad people," she said. "At least give us time to get across the border."

The man looked from her to Lance. She could tell by the way he was standing that he had a gun beneath the counter. She prayed he didn't reach for it.

Lance broke the silence. "How much do we owe you?"

The man rang everything up, and Lance paid in cash. The man handed him the change, and then they walked out of the store. Laurel looked back from the door. The man nodded.

When they got to the car, Lance started the engine, and they pulled out of the place.

"What if he calls someone?" Laurel said.

"He's not calling anyone."

"How can you be sure?"

"I'm sure," Lance said.

They drove on toward the border, and when they got there, nothing unusual happened. The man hadn't called ahead.

Once they'd crossed, Laurel said, "You look good clean-shaven."

AUTHOR'S NOTE

First off, I want to thank you for reading my book. As a reader, you might not realize how important a person like you is to a person like me.

I've been a writer for fifty years, and despite the upheavals life brings, the ups and downs, the highs and lows, one thing remains constant.

You. The reader.

And I'd like to take a moment to acknowledge that fact and to thank you. Not just on my own behalf but on behalf of all fiction writers. Because without you, these books simply would not exist. You're the reason they're written, your support is what makes them possible, and your reviews and recommendations are what spread the word.

So, thank you. I really do mean it.

Writing about politics is not easy, and I hope none of my personal thoughts and opinions managed to find their way into this story. I never intend to make political arguments in my writing, and I never intend to take a stand. I'm one of those guys who stays out of political arguments, and I would hate to think

544 *Author's Note*

that any political ideas raised in the book hampered your ability to enjoy the story or relate to the characters.

I write about people who work for the federal government. The nature of their work brings them up against issues of national security and politics, but apart from that, I truly do try to keep any views I might have to myself.

Because really, this is your story. These characters are your characters. When you read the book, no one knows what the characters look like, what they sound like, or what they truly think and feel, but you. The experience is created in your mind as you flip the pages. It belongs to you, not me.

So please, don't let any of my words offend you, and if you spot anything in my writing that you feel is unfair or biased, or off-color in any way, feel free to let me know. I do make edits based on reader suggestions.

My email address is below, and if you send a message, while I might not get back to you immediately, I will receive it, and I will read it.

saulherzog@authorcontact.com

Likewise, if you spot simpler errors, like typos and misspellings, let me know about those too. We writers have a saying: To err is human. To edit, divine. And we live by it.

I'm going to talk a little about some of the true facts that this book is based on, but before I do, I'd like to ask for a favor.

I know you're a busy person, I know you just finished this book and are eager to get on to whatever is next, but if you could find it in your heart to leave me a review, I would be truly humbled.

There's really nothing I can offer you in return for the kindness—but a kindness it is, and I rely on it.

If you leave me a review, it will help my career. It will help my series to flourish and find new readers. It will make a difference to one guy, one stranger you've never met and likely never will. That's got to count for something.

Okay, now that those formalities are out of the way, let's talk about US embassy security in Moscow. Because, believe it or not, that part of the book is based on real events. In 2017, the Russian president ordered US diplomatic missions to reduce their staffing level by over seven hundred people. One of the ways the US complied with the order was by axing its own security guards and hiring a private security firm owned by a former KGB officer. The officer maintains close ties with the Russian president and worked for years as a spy against Western interests. While marines still protect the embassy, many security tasks, such as screening visitors, are now performed by employees of the private security firm. The incident has been well-documented, and you can read about it online.

The other part of the story that stems from real life is the depiction of the orphanage Medvedev grew up in. A number of Western governments, as well as international aid agencies, have documented the cases of severe neglect that were often experienced in such institutions. A 1998 Human Rights Watch report outlined 252 Baby Houses, or *Dom Rebyonka*, which housed children up to four years old. When Western observers first arrived, the staff at the orphanages were open about telling mothers of disabled children not to bother visiting, as the children understood nothing anyway. Strong sedatives and tranquilizers were often used routinely to keep children quiet. Despite the risk of liver damage, the use of the tranquilizer aminazine was widespread.

You can read more about these institutions and the harrowing details of how children were housed and cared for by conducting an online search. One report entitled "The Gilded Cage of the Dom Rebyonka" was used extensively when researching the chapters on Medvedev's childhood.

Finally, I'd be remiss if I didn't tell you that Book Three in the Lance Spector series, *The Target,* is available now.

So grab your copy. I promise, if you enjoyed the first two,

you're only going to be drawn into these characters more deeply!

God bless and happy reading,

Saul Herzog